THE SCROLLS OF DEBORAH

THE SCROLLS OF DEBORAH

ESTHER GOLDENBERG

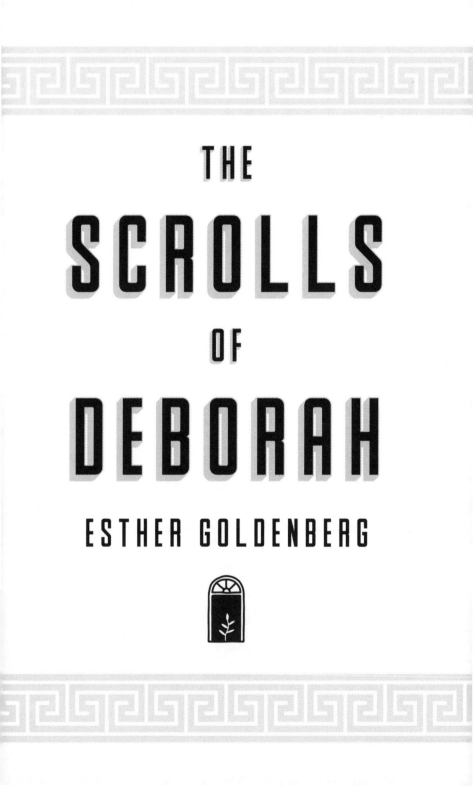

Because we at 100 Block by Row House and Row House Publishing believe that the best stories are born in the margins, we proudly spotlight, amplify, and celebrate the voices of diverse, innovative creators. Through independent publishing, we strive to break free from the control of Big Publishing and oppressive systems, ensuring a more liberated future for us all.

Send all press or review inquiries to us at
100 Block by Row House, PO Box 210, New Egypt, NJ 08533,
or email publicity@rowhousepublishing.com.

Library of Congress Cataloging-in-Publication Data
Available Upon Request

ISBN 978-1-955905-41-1 (TP)
ISBN 978-1-9559054-8-0 (eBook)

Printed in the United States
Distributed by Simon & Schuster

Book design by Aubrey Khan, Neuwirth & Associates, Inc.

First edition
10 9 8 7 6 5 4 3 2 1

To all sisters, mothers, daughters, and friends,
and those who celebrate them and support them.

"Deborah, Rebekah's nursemaid, died and was buried near Beit El, beneath a tree, and that tree was called the Crying Tree."

GENESIS 35:8

CONTENTS

THE FIRST SCROLL

THE SECOND SCROLL

THE THIRD SCROLL

THE FOURTH SCROLL

THE FIFTH SCROLL

THE SIXTH SCROLL

THE SEVENTH SCROLL

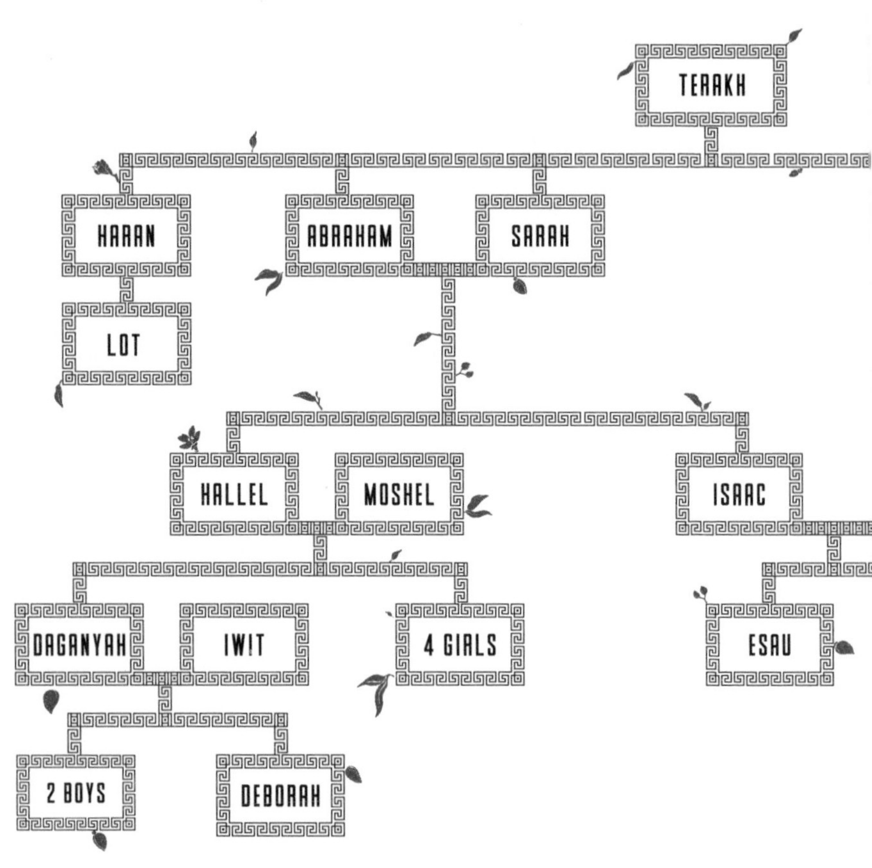
TERAKH
HARAN
ABRAHAM
SARAH
LOT
HALLEL
MOSHEL
ISAAC
DAGANYAH
IWIT
4 GIRLS
ESAU
2 BOYS
DEBORAH

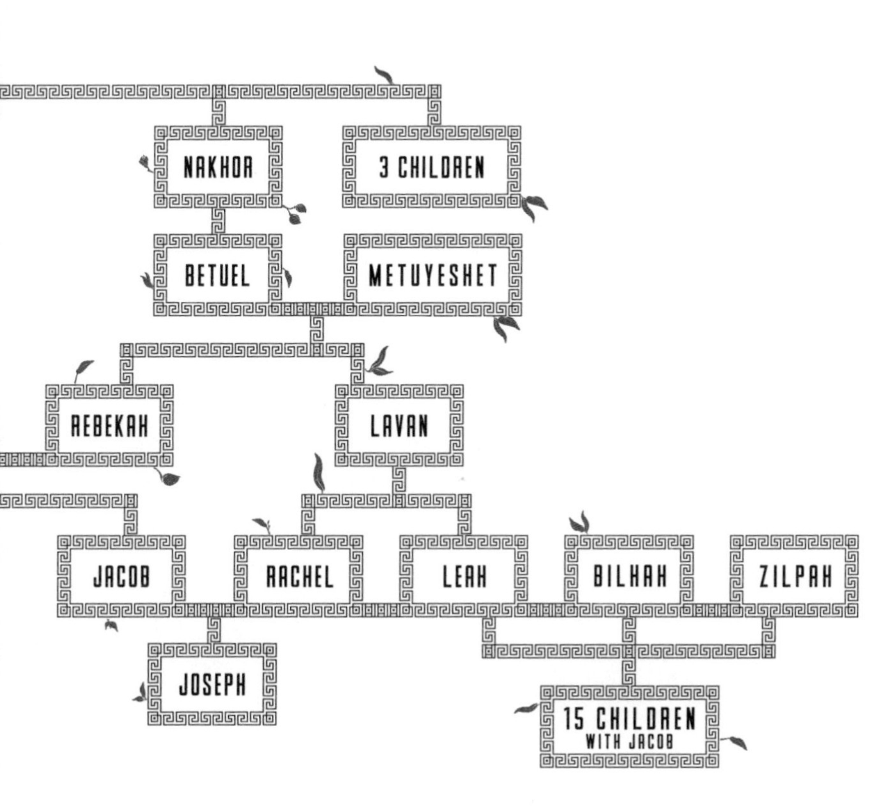
NAKHOR
3 CHILDREN
BETUEL
METUYESHET
REBEKAH
LAVAN
JACOB
RACHEL
LEAH
BILHAH
ZILPAH
JOSEPH
15 CHILDREN
WITH JACOB

THE FIRST SCROLL

THE FIRST PARCHMENT

I am Deborah.
Daughter of Daganyah.
Daughter of Hallel.
Daughter of Sarah.

Yes, *that* Sarah, the wife of Abraham, to answer your eyebrow's question. Yes, Joseph, I am speaking of the same Sarah and Abraham who were the parents of your honored grandfather Isaac. Sarah and Abraham were also the parents of my beloved grandmother Hallel. You know my place in this tribe as your grandmother Rebekah's nursemaid. I have been her companion for more years than we know. And I am more than that. There is much you do not know about me. So, so much. Keep writing. Even these words. That is your job as the scribe. These scrolls will be your education—and my legacy.

I was born in Egypt, the third and final child of my mother, Daganyah, and her husband, Iwit. As I was the only girl to help my mother, we spent our days together like grapes on a vine.

Before I could talk or even understand all her words, she told me stories all day long while my father and brothers worked the wheat fields and at night when she lay beside me on my cushion as I drifted to sleep. I do not remember a time when I did not know of the people in her stories. Far away though they were, they were always present in my ears and in my heart.

Behind my eyelids, I still see the women of these stories: My mother, Daganyah, a young woman, flowing with linens and jewels and smiles. My grandmother, Hallel, tall and beautiful and as noble as a queen, yet still weaving her own belts—the most beautiful in all of Egypt. Sarah the matriarch, glowing with love and beauty, even in old age.

What a blessing it would have been to meet Sarah, but I arrived too late for that privilege. My mother and grandmother are gone now, too. I am older than either one of them ever became. Yet they live within me, for these were the women of the stories my mother told me day and night. Now their stories will be inscribed in these scrolls, along with mine.

When the sun rose on the twelfth anniversary of my birth, my mother shared a brand-new story with me: I was to have a sister in eight months' time. Mother had had pregnancies after me, but none had turned into babies. Only blood that was put into the soil to help grow the olive tree, not a child.

But the night before she shared the news with me, she had had such a vivid dream of birthing a living girl, that she told me about it. "She will be strong and wise and beautiful, just like you, Deborah. We shall have someone new to share the stories with and another pair of hands to help with the cooking and the water and the weaving."

"What will you name her?" I asked.

"I shall name her Matanyah, for she is a gift from Yah."

Mother and I spoke of YhWh as the all-powerful god, Creator of All, only when we were alone. Even then, we used the shortened version of the name—Yah—saving the full name for prayer and ceremony. Father and the other men of the community would not tolerate any mention of gods other than Horus and the king, who was Horus embodied. But Matanyah was not an Egyptian name. Father would not know the meaning, or care. It was the mother who had the privilege of naming daughters.

Matanyah *was* truly a gift from Yah, but it took me a lifetime to understand and accept that. Her entrance into this world was what changed everything. The color and shape of the blood that stained the floor and the pitch and length of the screams that still echo in my ears are details that I shall spare you. What is important to know is that Matanyah refused to exit her warm womb and was removed by the midwife's knife through my mother's belly. Before the cut, we all knew what would happen. Either the baby would come out alive or dead, but if she stayed in, both my sister and my mother would certainly die.

It was unheard of for a man to enter the birthing room, but my mother insisted that before the cut was made, my father must come.

"Iwit," she said. "I shall die soon. Deborah is skilled and can find a wet nurse should the baby survive." She had not told Father it would be a girl or that she already had a name, and she concealed that at the end as well. I knew the name. That was enough. "If we both die, you must swear to me that you will send Deborah to my mother's uncle in Haran. You must pay for her journey and necessities so that she is not here alone. You will take another wife."

In that moment, my father looked at me in a way I had never seen. All these years, he had paid me little attention. He was busy in the fields with his sons or at gatherings with the other men. He came home to eat the meals prepared for him and little more. We had not exchanged a hundred words in my lifetime. Now that my mother mentioned his taking another wife, he asked me my age.

"Twelve," I answered. Though I would soon be thirteen.

He stared at my chest, where one day my breasts would grow and fill with milk to nourish babies, but on that day my flatness was apparent even under my clothing. Father reached his hand out, just to check if I would soon be old enough to bring him a child, and Mother snapped at him.

"Iwit! You will send her to my uncle in Haran, with good provisions, or I shall send Set to you when I meet him. Swear to me on your life and the lives of your sons."

Father's fear was plain. The Egyptians, of which my father was one, believed that the god Set had chopped his own brother Osiris to pieces. What would he do with a little farmer if Mother sent him from the next world?

"I swear," he said, loudly enough for her to hear, even though he was already exiting.

She stopped him before he left the room. "And you will pay the midwife now."

"She will leave here, and I shall have a dead wife and dead child. Why throw my money at such incompetence?"

"Because it is your safest option if you wish to remain alive in this house with your sons," she hissed. Her voice was raspy and weak from screaming during so many labor pains, but she was composed when she made her threat. "The fee is twenty pieces of silver. I shall watch you place them on the table while I still breathe, as a witness who will report to Set."

I knew the price to be half what she claimed, but my father paid the midwife before stomping out.

"Deborah," she addressed me now. Her voice was softer. She was clearly in pain, though she had hidden it from Father to deliver her commands. I went to hold her hand and put my ear closer to her mouth. The stench of her sweat from her efforts at pushing nearly sent me away, but I wanted to be close. "You are my precious daughter. My one and only. Matanyah has stopped moving. She will go under the olive tree with the others. Yet another baby of mine has died." A long time passed while we both cried.

I could see that it was more than the sobs that kept Mother from saying more. She was also struggling to breathe deeply. As soon as she could, she continued, "You will find someone else to share our stories with. The best I can give you is passage to Haran, so that your father does not take you to wife. You are too young." I grabbed Mother's hand and held tight. I wanted to comfort her while she gasped, but I too was gasping. "I bless you with strength, courage, determination, and love," she said. "These are all the things that Yah has already blessed you with. You are my heart. As long as you are in this world, so am I."

My tears flowed in rivers down my face, my arms, my lap. I was covered in a little Nile that I had not known had been in my body.

As Mother and I held hands, she addressed the midwife. "I know I shall require much of your drink supply so as not to feel too much pain. I trust you will do your best. I know it is the rare woman who"—Mother screamed in pain and clutched her side before continuing—"who lives when the life inside her has already died. I hope to be one of those women. But if I am not, please do not spare any amount of strong drink that you have. The extra coins should be more than enough to replenish your supply. Once you have done so, I ask that you give the remaining coins to Deborah for her journey."

Tanqo, the midwife, nodded her consent. She had been deep in prayer the whole time; even while she listened she was whispering prayers. She kissed my mother on the forehead and brought the clay cup to her lips. Mother drank and smiled at me once more before she closed her eyes. Slowly, deeply, she breathed Yah into her body. *Yhhhh*. Slowly, deliberately, she exhaled herself into Yah. *Whhhh*. She squeezed my hand, and I breathed with her in the way we had done so many times. Inhale: *Yhhhh*. Exhale: *Whhhh*. *Yhhhh*. *Whhhh*. In a short while, my mother's jaw became slack and her breaths became shallow.

Tanqo raised her voice in prayer. I opened my eyes to look at her, but Mother did not. She lay peacefully, unaware. It was then that Tanqo took the knife to her.

I screamed until I had no breath left myself, then fell to the floor. When I awoke, Tanqo had already cleaned the blood and placed the baby—my sister, Matanyah—in a shallow grave under the olive tree. My mother had a blanket draped over her. I could not even see her face. My brothers came and carried her body away. Their strong arms carried her with ease, but I saw them shaking from the sobs they held back. As soon as they were beyond my sight, Tanqo put her arm around me and guided me to her house. I slept there on a pallet for two days and two nights before I had enough strength to drink a cup of broth and cry myself back to sleep.

THE SECOND PARCHMENT

Every morning, Tanqo placed a cup of warm broth just inside the door of my room. I had a room. And a door. Neither of which had been in the house of my parents. There my father had a room with a door, but my brothers had pallets to put on the floor in one corner of the main room, and my mother and I shared a pallet by the hearth. When she went to my father's room, I slept alone briefly, but even still, my brothers were in the room.

In Tanqo's home, there was a main room like ours, with a table to eat upon and stools to sit beside it and a few cushions on the floor. Beyond that, she had two bedrooms. One that she shared with her husband, and one that I now woke in each morning to find my broth. There was a comfortable, if lonely, pallet on the floor, covered in a soft linen sheet the color of the night sky. When I was well enough to remain awake without crying, I noticed my mother's satchel beside the pallet. It was open, and I looked inside.

I immediately recognized the red and gold pattern of my mother's finest cloak. I brought it to my nose and breathed it in. The smell of my mother made my tears begin once again, and this time I wiped them with her fabric. I was a little afraid of what else I might find and how I might feel about it, but I searched through the satchel anyway. My mother's brown clay cup was in there. The one from which she had taken her final sips. Tanqo must have put it in the satchel along with the dress, which was usually folded beside our sleeping mat. Already in there was my mother's kohl stick. And I discovered a small area of the satchel with extra fabric that concealed one silver coin. I replaced everything and hugged it—my mother's satchel—close to my chest, then put it beside the mat that had been mine to sleep upon in Tanqo's house.

I spent three months with Tanqo and her husband. They seemed old enough to have grandchildren underfoot, yet it was just the three of us. And most of the time, I was there alone. Tanqo was called to assist with births almost daily, and her husband worked at making sandals. I helped in the house as much as I could, drawing and carrying water for cooking and making the evening meals. Most of my thoughts were that Mother was not by my side, and I tried to do the things Mother and I would have done together.

One morning when Tanqo had no birth to attend, she requested my help in making drums. I could not refuse her this assistance. I would not have refused her any request, for her generosity in taking me in was great. Tanqo showed me a barrel where skins had been soaking. I had thought they were for the sandals, but on this day, we would be the ones to use it. We hung it to dry in the sun and sat beside it in the shade of the date trees. Tanqo took out a few scraps of leather that were already dry and used them for teaching me. That morning I learned how to punch holes in the leather and to cut strips the right size for laces.

When my mother and I worked together side by side, I always heard her stories. Tanqo was quiet other than her instruction, but I had little time to miss my mother as I focused on pleasing Tanqo by doing my tasks correctly. The work was slow and careful and new, and it kept my thoughts on the leather, not on my mother.

I practiced making the holes, lining them, and spacing them as Tanqo taught me. I made many strips for laces. She nodded her approval of my work. The large hanging leather was dry by evening, and Tanqo taught me how to cut it into circles. She took a wooden ring and placed it on one side of the hide; then she cut a circle three finger widths wider than the ring.

Tanqo had several rings of different sizes, and after she had demonstrated how to cut the leather into circles, she watched me cut one. Content that I was doing it correctly, she left me with the materials, and the hide became six circles of varying sizes, from three larger than my head to one smaller than my hand, before the sun went down. Tanqo was pleased, and I was, too. Only after I finished did I realize that while working on the drums, I had smiled for the first time since my mother's death.

For the next few days, I punched sixteen sets of holes in each of the circles, measuring them so they would fold across to each other. Because the circles were of different sizes, the holes needed to be different distances. I worked slowly, deliberately, carefully, to make sure the work was done well. I completed my task while Tanqo was at a birth, and I took some time to admire my handiwork. I believed she would be impressed. I hoped so.

She was, indeed, and so my lessons continued. She taught me to lace the leather over the wooden rings. "Thread down through the hole on the right, up through the hole on the left," she said. I heard these instructions repeated over and over in my ears as I did exactly that. *Down through the right, up through the left. Down through the right, up through the left.* We sat across from each other, and I watched her as she went down through the right hole, and up through the left, crossed the back of the drum with the lace, and did the same thing again. *Down through the right, up through the left. Down through the right, up through the left.* I followed her lead. The lace then went under what had already crossed and over to the next set of holes until we completed them all. *Down through the right, up through the left. Down through the right, up through the left.*

In this way, the plain wooden circle and the plain hide joined together to make something new. I soon learned that though it now looked like a drum, it did not yet sound like one. The laces, Tanqo explained, would need to be tightened. She showed me how to group them in bunches of four, wrapping the lace around each section, and pulling the hide tighter and tighter around the base. I saw that this gathering of laces also made a comfortable place to hold the back of the drum.

I worked at the speed of completing one drum each day. With five drums completed, I was able to work with care and precision to thread the leather strips on the smallest and most difficult drum, *down through the right, up through the left, down through the right, up through the left,* wrapping and tightening until it was finished. I lined the drums along the side of the house so I could look at each one. Though the sun was high in the sky, the drums reminded me of the moon on the nights when it is full and round and glowing above.

I picked up each one of the drum-moons that I had created. In turn, from smallest to largest, I held each drum in my left hand and tapped it with my right hand. The little drum sounded almost as soft as birds running across the roof, while the biggest boomed like thunder. Each one was magnificent, and I looked forward to showing Tanqo when she returned.

Tanqo was often out helping with a birth. Sometimes she returned with a gift from the family, sometimes with coins, and sometimes with only the names of the new babies. When she came home quiet, I knew she was sparing me from hearing a story so similar to my own. On the day she returned to see the drums leaning against the wall, she shared many words of praise. "You are determined, Deborah," she said. "And these beautiful drums show that your eyes looked closely at the details of your work. You did not know how to make drums, did you?"

"No," I told her. I had heard drums many times. I knew, of course, that they did not grow from the ground. But I had never examined how they were made, let alone made one myself.

"So you have learned something new?" she asked.

"Yes, Tanqo," I said. "I am grateful."

"In learning to make these drums," she continued, "I believe you have shown that you can learn many new things. Do you agree?"

I had never considered such a question, but I thought that she must be right. For I had not expected to learn to make drums, and then I did. Could I not learn the next unexpected lesson? I agreed that this was correct. And then she had some news to share: My father had sent word that he had found a guide, Mavheel, to escort me to my uncle in Haran. We were to leave in a week. I knew I would leave one day, but I was not ready. Grief and fear crept through my body and showed on my face.

"You have done a fine job," Tanqo said, bringing our conversation back to the drums. As she lifted each one and played it, I relaxed. She was pleased. "This little one," she said, "was the most difficult. They always are. And they do not make a big sound, but a more private one. One must listen closely to hear the beauty in the quiet beat." She was tapping it lightly with two fingers as she spoke. "You will take this one with you," she said.

I was surprised. "Thank you, Tanqo," I said. "You have been so kind to me. I cannot accept your drum. I have caused you expense already. And," I paused, my frown returning, "I am going into the desert and to a new land to a new life. I have no use for a drum."

"Perhaps you are right, my girl," she said. "Perhaps you are right only for now. You feel you have no need for a drum, but one day, you will experience joy again. And when you do, you will have a drum at the ready. Take it, please, this little heartbeat for your new life. One day, replace it with a bigger one."

The night before my departure, Tanqo helped me sew my mother's silver pieces into my clothes. While we sat together by the flickering light of the oil lamp, she offered me prayers for safe travel and advice in case of unsafe travel. She brought me my mother's satchel to take with me and gifted me with two small bags of silphium seeds that she placed inside. It was difficult to imagine that I might, one day, have a life of joy, but I placed the small hand drum in the satchel under Tanqo's approving gaze. In the morning she added a folded cloth with dried figs to my load, and she whispered a wish for a long, blessed life, though her eyes revealed her fear that it would not be so.

THE THIRD PARCHMENT

I must consider whether I shall tell of my journey north. Although there were many wonders, there were also things that a boy of ten summers perhaps should not yet hear. For now, Joseph, I shall explain how it was that I, a descendant of Sarah and Abraham, who began their lives on the other side of the Euphrates River, began my life beside the Nile in Egypt.

Long ago, our ancestors left the great city of Ur to go to the land of Canaan. Abraham, whose name at the time was Abram, and Sarah, then known as Sarai, and their small tribe traveled as far as Aram. There they settled for many years. In fact, some of the tribe still live there to this day. You probably do not recognize the name Aram, yet you know the land well, for that was the former name of Haran, your birthplace. Of course, Haran got its name from the man Haran, one of Abraham's brothers. My mother knew all this, which is why when the pharaoh had died—and so many in the palace with him—and my mother was dying, she made my father promise to send me to kin in Haran.

The tribe of Abraham and Haran and their third brother, Nakhor, was a small tribe, but growing as children were born. One of those children was Nakhor's son Betuel, who later became Rebekah's father. One was Lot, a son of Haran, and one was my beloved grandmother Hallel, the daughter of Sarah and Abraham. When the tribe grew so big that those around became jealous of their size and wealth, Yah told Abraham to go to a new place.

Sarah and Abraham left Haran, with all the possessions they had acquired while there: sheep and goats, dogs and camels, manservants and maidservants, and the great wealth they accumulated by selling to Abraham's brother Haran the vineyards they had planted and grown. They also took Haran's son, Lot, with them, for he was betrothed to their daughter, Hallel. They arrived here, in this land where you and I sit, Joseph, and Yah promised it would become Abraham's. But the land was overcome by famine, and so our ancestors went temporarily to Egypt. While there, Lot, unbeknownst to Sarah and Abraham, sold Hallel to become a part of the pharaoh's harem, and she was left behind when the others came back here.

My grandmother was not kept long in the harem and never became one of the king's wives. Instead she was married to an important man of the palace. Moshel. She bore five daughters, the youngest of whom was my mother, Daganyah. Daganyah grew up with the songs and stories of her mother, as well as the fancy clothing and delicacies that her father's important position could provide. Her clothes were chosen from the market or made by the servants, and the same was so of her food. She bathed in water poured for her and listened to music played in the streets of the palace with her sisters.

Daganyah watched as one by one her sisters were married to wealthy men. There was a poor farmer, Iwit, my father, who had sold Moshel grain for years. He always asked to wed one of Moshel's daughters but could not afford the bride price. One daughter after the next, Moshel refused Iwit's offers. But by the time Daganyah, the youngest sister, was old enough to be married, Iwit had saved enough money for a substantial bride price. And so, my mother left the palace court, left her parents and her sisters, and became a farmer's wife.

In the village, my mother had to learn to cook and draw water and sew and weave, things she had never had to do when she was the daughter of a wealthy governor. She watched the other village women and learned quickly. Some of those women offered help, but none ever befriended her. She was too different. So my mother was alone as she took care of her husband and her home and the two sons who came along. It was when I was born that she finally had a friend again, a helper, and someone to whom to tell the stories of her life.

I was by my mother's side morning and night. When she cooked a meal, I stirred it. When she drew water, I carried it. When she picked fruit, I put it in the baskets. When she baked bread, we ate it together. She always baked two loaves, one for us and one that my father and brothers shared when they returned from the fields in the evenings. And all the while, she told me stories. They were stories of her life in the palace or stories of her mother's life. Sometimes they were stories of women who came even before my grandmother. Even before Sarah. The oldest story she told me was one that happened even before any people at all had ever lived. That was the story of Yah separating the waters.

"Long, long ago," she said, "Yah separated all the waters into the waters above and the waters below. The waters above were called sky. Sometimes that water rains down on us. The waters below were called sea. They were gathered together, such that there became a place for land. And on that land, all the grains and grasses, all the fruits and vegetables could grow. And the people and animals could live. Except for the fish, which lived in the waters below." It was a short story, for I think even she did not fully grasp that one. But we knew the blessing of the Nile's flows and floods, and we appreciated Yah's majesty.

I loved listening to Mother's voice. Even her spoken words were like song to my ears. And she used many of those words to tell me of things I could not even imagine without her. For her life had been one of riches, while mine was one of simplicity. Until one day, much to my surprise and delight, my mother brought these two worlds together.

I remember every moment of my first visit to Grandmother. When I was six years old and my first milk tooth had fallen from my mouth, my mother woke me in the darkness of the new moon and hushed me. When Mother and I set out on our journey, I did not yet even know where we were going. As soon as we were away from the house, she told me I was a big strong girl now and I could walk all the way to the gates of the palace. She promised that when I showed her that I could do that, then she would show me something even greater than I had ever dreamt.

We both held our parts of the deal. I was tired but encouraged by my mother's soft humming and her joyful step. My curiosity nearly lifted me off my feet, even though I had woken without a full night of rest. Only when we got within steps of the palace gates did she stop long enough to whisper the reason she had woken me in the night and had led me there in silence and mystery.

"My beloved daughter," she said, "tonight I shall present you to your grandmother."

I gasped!

My grandmother was the subject of so many of my mother's stories. My mother spoke of growing up within the walls of the palace. Even at the young age of six, I had heard many times of my mother's visits to the market with her own mother. They often bought spices or new clothing or trinkets to decorate their home. She did her best to describe the fineries she had known as a girl. And she had no trouble telling of the servants who had done the work for her and her family that she and I now did for us and for her husband and sons.

But to me, these were just stories. I was small and had never been much farther than our own garden, other than yearly ceremonial trips to the river—two of which I was too young to remember. So, to arrive at the walls of the palace—walls so white that they somehow gleamed even in a night with no moon—and then to be told that I shall go beyond those walls, and then to be told that within them I shall meet my grandmother . . . My mother was correct. This was far more wonderful than anything I had ever dreamt!

"Now you be quiet," she told me as we approached the gate. "Hold my hand and do not do or say anything, unless I give you instructions. If so, then you follow them immediately. Do you understand?" I was not sure if I was allowed to say yes, so I nodded my head and put my hand in hers. Together we walked up to the gate and the guard standing beside it.

"The girl got lost," she said to the guard. Then she reached into a satchel hanging from her belt and pulled out a silver coin. She continued speaking while she handed the guard the coin.

"You think I would accept a bribe?" the guard asked.

"I thought you would prefer it," Mother told him. "No matter, I shall simply tell Moshel, my father, that you would not allow his daughter to enter." The guard accepted the coin and began opening what he called the eye of the needle. This was a small gate that was within the larger one. It was built just for this purpose, I later learned: so that they would not need to open the large gates at night, and make the palace vulnerable, but could still let in travelers and stragglers coming alone.

"My father and I apologize for the inconvenience of the late entry. I will tell Moshel of your generosity in allowing us to return."

I kept my agreement with my mother. I did not say a word. Did not tell the man I had not been lost. Did not tell Mother that I had forgotten her father was named Moshel, and then remembered when she said it. I only kept holding her hand and walked through the gate when she did. As soon as the guard closed the gate and stepped back to his post, my mother lifted me off the ground and twirled me round and round until she was so dizzy that she needed to set me back down and steady herself with a hand on my head.

"Oh, how it's good to be home!" she exclaimed.

Home? To me, this was not home. This was the palace! Home was the small mud-brick house in the busy streets of the city. Home was where my mother and I tended to our garden, cooked meals, and slept side by side on our pallet in the main room. Home was my brothers chasing after each other and my father telling them the secrets of successful grain crops over and over. Only after I had lived many more years did I have the wisdom to recognize that my mother had known a home before the one we shared. I got only a glimpse of it that day.

"Oh, I have not been here since I weaned your brother," she said. I laughed. I had never thought of my brothers weaning, or suckling. They were so big and always with Father. But, of course, they had once been little. They had once shared a mat with Mother, first Yalad and, five years later, Akho, each one weaning when he was old enough. And apparently, each coming to the palace at that time. But I did not let this news dampen my spirit. Just because they had come here before me did not make this visit any less wonderful.

When Mother was steady, she took my hand again and led me through the narrow pathways, turning here and there, her feet knowing the way. My own feet were tingling with surprise, for they were not walking on dirt pathways, as they had their whole life, but instead walking on smooth stone. The surface was so flat and gentle that I nearly slid on my toes with every step. If I had drifted along those walkways all night, I do not think I would have tired of the fun, but there was more excitement in store for me.

Mother stopped us in front of a red door. It was one of many openings within the palace walls. Here, everything was the same white as the exterior. No mud-brick houses anywhere. Just white. Well, in the morning, I would discover that they were not all white. In the light of the sun, I would see not just red doors but paintings and carvings along many of the entranceways. But with nothing but the starry sky to light our way, I saw mostly white.

"Now, my love," Mother said. "Now is when you will meet your grandmother." In all the excitement, I had forgotten the purpose of this adventure! "When you do, you may call her Grandmother. And you will do anything she asks of you. Only right before you do so, you say the words, 'Yes, Grandmother.' Do you understand?"

I was sure I did understand, for I had just successfully completed a similar task with the guard. But who was a guard, anyway? Nobody to me. This was my grandmother. This was Hallel! The same Hallel of the stories that Mother told me. My mother's own mother! My head nearly swayed with the wonder of it all. Then I felt my mother's firm hands on my head and her thumbs on my eyebrows, smoothing them down. She unplaited the braid that hung on the right side of my head, the one part of my head not shaved, and she separated my thick, black hair into three sections, and braided it again. It was the same as it had been only moments before, but I think doing it again calmed Mother.

Two days earlier she had shaved my head, even though it had been only ten days since the last shaving. A small stubble had already grown. Mother usually said she could not keep up with how quickly my hair grew; we did not have time to shave it more than once each month. But that time, she did. And so the top of my head was as hairless as the bottom of my feet. She rubbed her hand on my head and smiled. "I love to look at your dark skin," she said. "It is the color of the soil beside the Nile when it is rich and fertile and ready to feed us." This was what she always said. One time I had complimented her skin as well, calling it just the same as mine, but as if someone had spilled a bit of goat milk on it. She laughed, and I was never brave enough to say it again. I would simply tell her that her skin was beautiful, too, every time that she said mine was.

Standing beside the door of Grandmother's home, I understood why Mother had scrubbed my skin and my hair and my clothes so long the day before. There was not a speck of filth on either of us. Soon my grandmother would see my beautiful skin, my well-plaited hair, my clean frock.

Mother took my hand again, this time squeezing it harder than before, and quietly opened the red door. Inside it was bright as day! For many moments I could see nothing but light as my eyes opened and shut, opened and shut, trying to get over the surprise. Finally, I was able to discern that there was a shelf that wrapped the room at about the height of my head. And all along that shelf were oil lamps, burning brightly in their abundance. Of course, I had seen an oil lamp before. *An* oil lamp. Father sometimes carried it when he went to relieve himself in the night. Mother once used it when Akho woke, screaming from pain, to see if a scorpion had bitten him—it turned out Yalad had bitten him. But one lamp was all we needed, and even that we used only rarely, for when darkness came, we slept.

Now as my eyes got used to the light, I saw Hallel. Even though she was seated, I could tell that she was tall and important. Her back was straight, her expression serious but pleasant. My grandmother's skin looked as if even more goat's milk had been poured on it than Mother's, but I did not say that. And her eyes . . . at first glance, they looked brown, like mine, like Mother's, like all the eyes I had ever seen. But when I looked longer, the impossible seemed true: There were little flecks of green and gold in them. She was sitting on a wooden chair that had a cushion upon it. Both a chair and a cushion! Other than the multitude of lamps, this was my first glimpse of real riches.

My thoughts removed me from the room for a moment, wondering how I would ever return to our little house with the dirt floors and the backless benches. I had little time to lament my situation as I realized I was expected to speak. My grandmother had said something to me, and my eyes had been so busy that my ears had forgotten to hear.

Mother prompted me. "What do you say to your grandmother?" she asked.

Having not heard what my grandmother had said to me and having completely forgotten that I was to say "Yes, Grandmother" to anything, I said what my mouth longed to say: "You are the most beautiful grandmother in all of Egypt!"

Thankfully, both my mother and grandmother laughed with delight at that. Then my mother sat in a cushioned chair beside her mother, and a servant brought in a tray of sweet treats and wine. Grandmother took a treat from the tray and then Mother did. I stood as still as a statue, hardly breathing, waiting to know if I would get to taste this delicacy. With the nod of Mother's head, I reached my hand out, too, and, as carefully as I could, took a treat. Watching the women, I took bites when they did.

Oh, the sweetness! Even in my short life I had tasted dates many times. But these treats were somehow even more delicious than dates. They were dates, of course, but not only dates. The pits had been removed, and they had been shaped into long treats, each one longer than my finger and twice as wide. They were soft, without the peel, and mashed together with walnuts that were perfectly toasted. The whole thing was then coated in honey. Every bite brought its own bliss, and I enjoyed it so much that I did not notice it was gone until I put the last bit in my mouth and began to frown.

"You may have another, my little granddaughter," Grandmother said. Nobody but Mother had ever told me what I could and could not do, so I looked to her for confirmation. She gave me permission with a nod of her head, and I enjoyed the second treat as much as the first. Whether the two women merely watched me, or continued to talk while I ate, I have no idea. My tongue was so busy my ears once again forgot to listen. But when I finished my second sweet, I was able to hear Grandmother offer me a drink from her wine goblet.

I wanted to keep the taste of the treat in my mouth forever, but I remembered my promise to say, "Yes, Grandmother," and I took the wine she offered and drank it and enjoyed it. She then invited me to sit on her lap. I put my head on her bosom, felt the softness of the finely spun linen she wore, and put my finger in my mouth. What I really wanted to do was reach my hand up and touch her wig. Mother had told me of wigs, but this was my first time seeing one, for I had never seen anyone with wealth before. I sensed that I should not touch it, so I fell back to the new habit of putting my finger in my mouth to feel my bottom teeth move back and forth and to suck my finger, which comforted me. But Grandmother removed it from my mouth and held my hand in hers so that I could not return to sucking it. I did not miss it, though, as I was soon asleep.

In my slumber, I did not notice what my mother and grandmother said to each other. But I remember the awe I felt as I drifted to sleep hearing them talk. That visit was the first time I had heard my mother speak with someone else in what I thought was our private language. I had not realized at that young age that she had been speaking to me in the language of her childhood, just as her mother had done with her. It was the language of the north, not our special language. As I slept on my grandmother's lap, I dreamt that I had two tongues—one that spoke Egyptian like the women and girls at the well and the ovens, and one that spoke the love language of my mother and hers.

When I awoke, the sunrise was starting to enter the window. The lamps had been extinguished, but my mother and grandmother were still talking. I had slept through their conversation but awoke just in time to hear my grandmother request more visits and my mother comply. Then Mother kissed the top of my head and said, "Come, we must go back home now."

We all embraced, and my grandmother gave me one more treat to eat on the return home. To my mother she gave two coins, saying that one would be for exiting the palace, should she need it, and the other for our next return. We did not need to pay the guard to open the gate, for it was already open by the time we arrived there. When we left the palace and my feet once again stepped on the dirt path they had been so accustomed to, they stopped in protest. They longed for the smooth floor. But Mother pulled me along.

"A woman needs time with other women," she said, "with her mother. Too long has passed since we were together. But your father will not be happy to wake and find us missing. There is no time for us to stop now; we must hurry. Do you know the way home from here?" she asked me. With the morning light and the palace behind us, and the memory of the night before sewn into my thoughts forever, I was not sure I could retrace the path we had taken to get there. I told my mother as much. She nodded for me to try. My first step was luckily in the right direction. The other steps brought us closer to home thanks to my mother's guidance. She instructed me to pay close attention as we walked, so that I could know the way myself soon.

When our house came into view, the sun was just getting higher than the rooftop. My father was, indeed, outside searching for us and looking angry. Mother instructed me to wait there for her, out of reach and out of sight. In only a moment, I saw why. When she approached the house, Father hit her across one cheek, then across the other. He shoved her to the ground and kicked her while she was down. I had seen him hit her before, but three times? When she got up to walk away, he pushed her down again.

"Where were you, woman?" He asked her this many times yet never allowed her to answer, either because he was repeating himself again or because he was striking her. Finally, when he was tired of not receiving an answer, he paused long enough for her to speak. I overheard only a few of her words, about the palace, about introducing a grandchild, about her mother. But I heard his response fully, for he was loud.

"Foolish woman! We have no need for you to take a girl to the palace! When you wanted to take my sons for a blessing from their grandfather, I consented. Your father is a respected man. But I shall not be looked down upon by the palace people. I am an honest farmer. Without me, they would not eat. Your father is not better than I, just because he and his jewels reside within the gate!" He ended his lecture with another slap across my mother's face. "He gave you gifts for the boys, what did he give you for the girl?"

I saw my mother give her satchel to my father. He shook it to dump the contents, though only one thing fell out. He bent to pick it up. "One silver coin?" he yelled. "Even your father knows the girl is worthless," he said. My eyes stung so severely I nearly forgot to wonder where the second coin was. Joseph, I see from your excitement that you remember what I told you before. I learned when I received that same satchel from Tanqo that there was a hidden pocket, and the second coin was in there. My father took the one coin he had found and dropped the satchel on the ground, spit on it, and walked away. I waited until I could no longer see him, and then I waited some more. Mother was waiting, too. When I saw her getting up, I ran to help her.

"Mother, Mother," I said, "we shall not go again to Grandmother; she will understand. She will not want her daughter hurt like this." I cried even as I said it. To have such a world open up and then close so quickly was a pain I had never known. But it was still less painful than seeing my mother beaten.

"Do not fret, sweet girl," she said. We were in the house, and she was using a cloth to clean the blood from her lip and nose while droplets of red gathered on her knees and palms. "I knew he would hit me . . . not so much as all that," she confessed, "but it was worth it. We shall do it differently next time, you will see."

After Father left for the fields, our day was uneventful. We made loaves and brought them to the ovens. Mother covered her swollen face with her scarf, but I am sure the other women knew, just as we knew when they arrived with cuts and bruises. We spoke little; Mother was tired, and I was still afraid. When the sun began to set, Mother put food on the table for the men to eat when they returned, and we went to our pallet, exhausted from the long night and day. But I could not sleep, for I was still upset. I cried quietly, not wanting to wake Mother, but she felt it.

"I am feeling much better already," she said. "Do not worry about me; I shall be all healed soon."

"Why does Father have to hit you? Why must I have a father who hits?"

Mother let out a soft laugh. "He is the only father you have."

"Then I wish for no father," I said, quietly but adamantly, even though he had not yet returned.

"I know you are sad," she said. "But you must have a father. Everybody has a song to sing. Even him. He grows the wheat and harvests it. He trades it in the market for other foods and clothes and pots. He built this house. And most important, without him, I would not have you." Many years passed before I understood what she meant. Often when I waited quietly, Mother would tell me more. But that night she just asked if I had had a wonderful visit with Grandmother, and, of course, I had. So she suggested that I go to sleep and dream of the palace and that we would talk more in the morning.

Truly the memory of that day is mostly filled with the wonder and delight of meeting Grandmother. Mother and I talked of our adventure for months, going over every detail. She often asked me to tell her the way to the palace, mentioning things that we had passed to remember when to turn and when to continue straight. She liked hearing what I had noticed—three trees, one taller than the next, that came just before a right turn, for example. Walking the longest straight stretch without taking any turns for the amount of time it took to sing the nighttime song forty times through, and then to the carved pillar just before the last turn to the palace.

Mother was amused by my way of remembering and impressed with my ability to do so. But for me, it was easy. I often heard the words of the song inside my ears, even when they were not coming from Mother's mouth. For unless I fell asleep while Mother was still whispering a story in my ear, then this music was the last thing I heard each night.

Yah, lie us down in peace
And spread over us your blanket of peace
Amen, amen
In the morning, bring us back to life
In the meantime, we will not fear, because you are with us
Amen, amen

And the carving? Who would not remember such a wonder? The rock, as heavy, hard, and immovable as it was, was not merely lying on the ground, but erect and taller than Father and as wide as our house. It was painted, which itself was lovely, though not a marvel. I had seen painted pottery before, and though the colors on the rock were more vibrant because they had white stone beneath them, not brown clay, what was beyond my imagination was how the picture of three men could be cut directly into the stone. I had only a moment to reach my hand out to feel this carving, to feel the groove where one man's leg was a dip in the rock, but the memory stayed with me.

THE FOURTH PARCHMENT

Almost a whole year passed after that first trip to Grandmother before Mother spoke of returning. During that time, Mother often asked me to recount the directions to the palace, and sometimes she even told my words back to me. Then finally one day, when the harvest moon was full and the men would be gone for three nights, Mother asked me to lead her to the palace. We worked quickly that morning and left our house when the sun was still high in the sky. We walked the way we had walked that very first night and rehearsed so many times after. With only a few nudges from Mother, I was able to lead the way almost entirely myself.

When we arrived at the gate, it was open and crowded. The sun was still bright, and I saw carts filled with baskets of grain and jars of beer and mounds of figs. Most carts were pulled by donkeys, one by a horse, many by men. Some were going into the walls, some leaving. The carts that were leaving were empty, or nearly so. Men were going in and out of the gate, some talking loudly with others, and some quietly thoughtful as they walked. There was a guard, but there was no need to talk to or pay him, for the gate was open.

Once inside, we saw more of these men moving jugs of olive oil and barrels of olives. One man had a table with all kinds of scarab beetles—wooden, stone, clay, even one that looked golden in the evening sunlight. One man had a table on which there were many wooden animals. There were cats, birds, bees, and a fish, all carved from wood. Some were painted, but most were not, yet it was easy to see what they were meant to be. My eyes were so full of these sights that my feet nearly forgot to rejoice at their return to the stone. It was my hands that remembered to move. Even though I had not told them to do so, they reached out for a wooden cat.

"Do you like it?" the merchant asked.

Instead of speaking to the man, I spoke to the little cat. "Meeeyah," I said. "Meeeyah, little kitten." I hugged it, and the man addressed my mother.

"Your daughter has good taste," he said. "She chose well. This little cat will keep the mice away and earn its keep. And when the girl pets it, the wood gets smoother and smoother. It is three coins, but I see that the girl loves it; she may have it for two."

I had no coins at all and no experience with such things. I had only seen a beautiful wooden cat and wanted to touch it. I quickly returned it to the table and hid my face in my mother's skirt. Only then did I realize he was expecting coins not from me but from her. I dared to come out and hold her hand.

"The girl was just amazed," my mother said. "We have no coins to buy such beautiful handiwork, even with your generous price."

The man turned to address me again. "This is your first time in the palace?"

"Certainly not," I said. "I have been here once before."

"Have you seen finer carvings than mine?" the man asked.

"I have seen no carvings other than yours," I answered, thinking that the stone pillars were certainly something different. I dared to reach back to the cat and pet it one last time. Its back was already smooth, its tail curled around its body and touching its chin, its whiskers so fine. The whole thing fit in the palm of my hand, much smaller than a real kitten but no less beautiful.

"Then I shall give you one as a gift," the carver said.

"That is not necessary," my mother responded quickly, much to my disappointment.

"Not a cat," the man said. "Something even better." He looked over the animals on his table. I held my breath in anticipation to see what he would give me. I was to have a gift! A carving! If Mother would allow me. Perhaps she would not argue with the man. I held this hope as I waited to see where his hand would land. I was worried the sun would set before he would make a choice and my chance would be lost. But finally, he did choose.

"This is a very special bee," he said. "Like a real bee, it is very light. It is a good size for a little girl like you. And look here." Making sure I was watching closely, the man took a string and pushed it through a hole in the bee's belly. Then he tied the ends of the string together and placed the whole thing over my head until it rested on my neck and the bee bounced gently on my chest.

I heard Mother's voice. "We have nothing to trade for the bee."

"The girl has something," he said. "If she sees another girl who comes to the palace who would appreciate my carvings as much as she does, then she will send the girl here. Will you not?" he asked me.

"I shall!" I nearly shouted. I had not thought of it, but surely if I saw another girl in the palace, I would tell her of these wondrous carvings. Little did I know that I would get the opportunity to do so that very day. For when we arrived at Grandmother's house, I was greeted by a sight more surprising than the oil lamps that had lit the room on my first visit. This time, I saw a girl, only slightly older and taller than myself, and I learned that she was my kin. The daughter of my mother's sister Priyah.

That is to say, my mother and her mother share a mother. Oh, the wonder of it! My mother with a sister, and me getting to meet the daughter of that sister! My head nearly spun from it! I later learned that the children of my mother's sisters often saw each other—the boys chasing each other along the pathways of the palace, the girls often meeting with my grandmother—that is, our grandmother—for sweets and stories. But at that moment, I knew none of that. I knew only that a girl stood before me, in a lovely green dress with her hair in plaits and her kohl perfectly applied, and that this girl, called Yafayah, in some way, belonged to me.

I rushed toward her and hugged her! She stepped back and pushed me away. "Ouch!" she said. "You are poking me." I would do no such thing! But when we pulled apart, I saw that my new wooden bee had been pressed against her chest in the embrace. I had not felt its pressure in my exuberance.

"Come," Grandmother said to me, "I would be happy to have one of your hugs." She took me in her arms while Mother looked from us to the little girl and back again.

"You can have a beautiful bee like this, too," I offered. For I had told the man that I would talk of his carvings, and because I knew that Yafayah, and any child, would be glad to have something so wonderful. I hoped she would smile and offer me another embrace, perhaps with my lovely bee moved aside. But I was disappointed.

"And her clothes are itchy!" Yafayah added, in case she had not yet insulted me enough. She wore a tunic of linen as soft as Grandmother's.

Grandmother ignored Yafayah and put her fingers to my new bee. "This is lovely," she said. "A bee is a powerful animal: a messenger, a traveler of lands, and a creator of sweetness." She paused, looking me directly in my eyes and then moving her gaze to Mother. Mother nodded her head slightly, and Grandmother turned back to me and added, "Just like you."

"Like me?" The thought was so fresh and surprising to me that the question jumped right out of my mouth.

"Yes," Grandmother confirmed. "Like you." I noticed Yafayah frown as the compliment was repeated. "Your mother has brought you here, or rather, you brought her here today, because you will soon come on your own. We discussed it while you slept when you were here last. From now on, each month, when the moon is full, you will make the journey and spend the night with me, in this home, in the palace. You will travel the land, sweetly bringing me news of my daughter, and return to her with messages from me. Do you understand, Deborah?"

Deborah. That was the first time I was called by the name that means bee, but it would become my name from that day forward. When I was born, my mother gave me a name like hers—Daganyah, and those of her sisters—Eliyah, Miyah, Priyah, and Rayah—and their daughters. A name that honored Yah. I was known as Batyah, daughter of Yah. And though I always was and always shall be a daughter of Yah, on that day I was given a name that was more specific to me, that suited me in my new role. Deborah.

I told my grandmother that I did understand, though in truth, I could not yet grasp what was to come. As she said, I would make the journey each month. I was given coins and instructions on getting into the palace, what to say, when to arrive. The coins were to be used only if I needed to bribe a guard. And though my grandfather was always so busy with his duties that I did not meet him even once, I was to mention his name if asked who I was going to see. Grandmother gave me a new, soft linen cloak, as blue as the Nile and with a white belt she wove herself. She kept it for me at her house, and when I arrived, I put it on and wore it while in the palace, looking as fine as—if not finer than!—Yafayah.

With each full moon, I left my mother in the morning, spent the day and the night with Grandmother, and returned by the moon's light to be back on my pallet before my father awoke. My time in the palace was filled with sweets and songs and stories with Grandmother. As was my duty, I told her of news from my mother, of which there was very little, and brought back news of my grandmother, and sometimes of my aunts when there was some. I also listened to and learned the story of my grandmother's life.

She told me the same story on each visit and had me repeat it back to her, to hear that I was learning it and remembering it correctly. She gave me this gift, the gift of knowing her, not only as a treasure for myself, but also in the hopes that I would one day repeat her words, delivering her story exactly as she spoke it. I would not do so for many years, but it would become one of the greatest honors of my life.

I cherished these visits with Hallel, when I had no work to do and wore my palace clothes and feasted on all kinds of foods. I often saw Yafayah, and though we sometimes squabbled, we mostly enjoyed sliding our feet across the smooth pathways in the palace and watching performers sing and dance in the squares. When the sun beat down on us, we retreated into Grandmother's house to play twenty blocks. Yafayah had her own set of dice to play with. I did not, so I used Grandmother's. They were nicer than Yafayah's anyway.

Grandmother had many nice things. She allowed me to explore her fineries, and I ran my fingers over her smooth, red glass beads and felt the weight of her stone scarab beetles in my hand. She also took me to see the gardens inside the palace walls, where flowers grew in rows according to their colors and pillars were painted as brightly as the petals. She took me to smell and taste the exotic sweets at the market, and every time I outgrew a lovely garment she had given me, she presented me with a new one, just as wonderful.

It would be nice to believe that she did all that for me because I was special. In truth, she did it for all of her grandchildren; I was the only one who experienced it only one day each month. After each visit, I returned to carrying water, kneading dough, pulling roots, to plain foods and nights without lights . . . and to Mother. She said she loved to see the joy on my face when I told her of my adventures in luxury. And I loved telling her. But the best times were on the harvest moons, when my father and brothers would be gone for three days, and so two nights each year, my mother and I visited Grandmother together.

My mother and I both changed into our palace garb after bathing in Grandmother's bathing room. Her sisters and their daughters then joined us, also dressed finely, and we ate all manner of foods—sweet and salty, fruits and meats, some of which I knew names for, some I did not. Sitting there in a circle, I watched my mother and her sisters when they talked and laughed with each other. Some of the older girls tried to join the conversations but also wound up listening and watching instead.

On our first of these celebrations, after I was so full that I could not eat another morsel, I noticed Rayah's neck. The sun was high in the sky, but we were shaded and cool inside the stone walls of Grandmother's house. Rayah had been quieter than most; perhaps that was why I did not see earlier. I was looking at each sister when she spoke, and so I had not looked much at her. But now I saw that she had black markings that crossed from one side of her throat to the other. They were two divine eyes with a nefer symbol in between them. When I moved my head slowly to the right, the eyes on her neck followed me. When I moved to the left, they followed me as well, even though the eyes on her head were focused on her mother.

I pulled at my mother's dress and whispered my question. "Why does Rayah have more eyes than everyone else?"

"That is called a tattoo," my mother explained. "Rayah is a priestess in the temple. There it is her duty to embody the goddess to enhance the power of the pharaoh. The pictures you see on her skin, her tattoo, they are the words 'To do good, to do good.' In the temple of Hathor, Rayah's voice does good in service of the goddess and of the pharaoh."

That was the first time that I understood that words could be written and that written words had power. Just as the written words in these scrolls have power. They will carry the stories of my life long after I am gone. That day, when I first met this surprise, I no longer listened to the women talking, as I was deep in wonder until long after the food was cleared away and we all moved to Grandmother's garden. There her maidservants sat at the edges of the garden, each holding a drum and sitting, waiting, quietly.

I sat beside my mother on a cushion on the ground. The moon was bright above, and we were with the other daughters and granddaughters of Hallel. Grandmother herself held a tray of ornate silver cups and allowed each one of us to take one from her. My small cup was smooth silver that reflected the light of the moon. Mother's had small raised circles on it, like bunches of grapes. When we each held a cup, Grandmother broke the top off a plain earthen jug and poured the liquid into a second jug, painted with yellow acacia flowers.

Grandmother came to each one of her daughters and granddaughters and, holding the flowered jug, asked the question: "Do you know of YhWh?" When she heard the *yes* from her descendant's mouth, she answered, "Now you will know YhWh," and she poured the liquid until it reached the lip of the cup, just before it spilled over. Then she sat on her cushion and poured a cup for herself, which she set beside her. She slowly looked at each of us in the gathering, and when she finished she said, "Each breath, the whole breath, will praise Yah!"

Grandmother took a deep breath in. *Yhhhh*. We all did the same. She exhaled. *Whhhh*. We all did the same. Each inhale brought our god, YhWh, the Creator of All, into us, and each exhale helped us become part of our god, YhWh, the Creator of All. *Yhhhh*, we inhaled. *Whhhh*, we exhaled. This was what Mother had taught me before. Ever since I was a child on her knee, when I was sad or hurt, we breathed like this two or three times. But on this night, on all the nights of the harvest moon, we kept doing it, breathing in deeply and exhaling out quickly, getting light-headed.

I kept my eyes on Grandmother and put my hand in Mother's. I was afraid I might fall over, embarrassing her and myself. Mother looked at me and smiled, still breathing in, *Yhhhh*, and quickly out, *Whhhh*. After only a few more breaths, I no longer needed to work so hard to do it right. It was as if my body knew what to do, how to turn itself inside out, so that what was once *Yhhhh* inside of me would now be *Whhhh* on the outside, and the reverse.

I do not know how long we breathed like that, but it was wonderful. The short sessions with Mother always made me feel better, no longer hurt or sad. But this was different. This felt better than not sad, better than being in the palace, better than being with Mother and Grandmother. And just at the point of feeling what I thought was the best, we stopped.

Grandmother brought her goblet to her lips. When she drank, we all drank.

"Hallelu Yah!" Grandmother shouted, and we all echoed her, "Hallelu Yah!" With that, the women on the edges of the gardens began to drum. We lay down on our cushions. "Know YhWh," my mother whispered to me. Turning her head toward me, she showed me she was going back to the breathing. *Yhhhh. Whhhh.*

We breathed *Yhhhh, Whhhh* all night long, accompanied by the drums. With my eyes open, I saw the stars filling the sky above me. And when I closed my eyes, I was brought up to the stars, while they were brought down to me. I was carried in the wind, though it was still. I was hugged by colors and sung to by light. My body was everything, and everything was my body. There are not words enough in this world to tell the details of those nights. Although each one was different, they shared the gifts of wonder, awe, and most of all: love. It was just as Grandmother had said. We not only knew *of* YhWh, we knew YhWh. And to know once was to know always.

We were blessed to have five of those trips together, knowing YhWh and my aunts and their daughters before the king died, and my palace life along with him. We had not yet heard of the pharaoh's death, and so I began my monthly walk to the palace as planned. The morning air was pleasant, the sky already lit by the rising sun. Mother and I always worked extra the day before these visits so that I could leave in the morning, right after

Father and my brothers went to the fields, for they would not notice me missing in the evening if the work was done.

It was not unusual to see people leaving the palace as I approached. Merchants returning with their wares or, if it had been a prosperous day, their empty carts. Priests and priestesses traveling on errands from the palace to the temples all day long. Whoever had business in the palace came and went as long as the sun shone. We passed each other on the road with little notice or consequence. But that day, many people were fleeing the walls. Some had bundles with them, some were empty-handed. All were harried, and none would stop when I asked them what was going on. I considered continuing on my path to Grandmother, but the closer I got to the gate, the easier it was for me to tell that the loudest part of the din was people screaming. I turned around and put myself among those who had the palace at their back.

Occasional glances over my shoulder gave me no more information as to why people were leaving the palace, but I did see a young boy, old enough to walk, but not to run, being pulled along by his mother. Her finery was more beautiful than I had ever seen—even more beautiful than Grandmother's. Her dress was purple and gold, with gold beads along the bottom. She also had beads in her hair, gold and silver and blue. But, of course, a moment later I was reminded that it was not her hair, but a wig. She removed it along with the bangles that were around her wrists because the boy kept pulling them, and that was slowing them both.

"Hurry," she begged him. "Hurry!" Sometimes she lifted the boy for a few paces, but she had an infant in her arms and could not manage them both for very long. "Do you want to go in the grave with the other boys?" she asked him. He smiled at the mention of other boys, too young to understand.

I lifted the boy on my back and bounced him up and down as I had seen other children do with their younger brothers and sisters. I kept step with his mother, who thanked me with her eyes.

"What is happening?" I asked her.

"The king is dead," she said. "I fled the harem as soon as I heard. The mother of the chosen son shall reign until the boy is old enough. The other women and sons go into the grave." She began to hiccup and shake. "I know I should have stayed," she said. "It is an honor to be buried with the king and the rest of his harem, his advisors, and his servants, but I just ran. I grabbed my babies and ran. Perhaps I should return."

I kept walking with the boy on my back, and she stayed alongside me. There were others who had the same thoughts as this woman. Those who fled and kept running, and those who turned back.

"It has been told that drinking the poison brings a painless death. Some are buried without it; they can light the way to the next life. I should not have run, but I just grabbed my babies in my arms, and that was what happened." We stopped to rest. Others kept passing us. The sun had still not set and was hot on our faces. The mother sat at the side of the path and nursed her children, but the bigger one wanted to eat more after, and she had nothing to give him.

"Please, please," she begged me, eying my satchel. "Have you any food for my boy?" She gave me one of her bangles, but then quickly took it back. "I will need that to trade for more food.

Please, take a bead and give me food for the boy. Not even for me." I did not have much, for I was on the way to the palace, not from, but I gave her the piece of bread and fig I had left and did not take her bead.

I ran all the way home. Mother was surprised to see me but hid it from Father, who was eating his evening bread and a fish he brought home. We walked a few steps away from the house. She did not need to ask me why I had returned, for I could not keep the words in my mouth. I told her of the king's death and the woman I had met and that she spoke of poison and graves. I told her of the screams I heard and of the chaos that had caused me to turn around.

"You did well, Deborah," she said. "You chose wisely." Sobs caught in her throat. Tears were sliding down her face. She followed their example and slid down to the ground. Her body shook, and she put her head in her hands. I wished to comfort her, but I needed too much myself. I sat beside her with my arm through hers, and we both cried until we were empty.

After a while, I gathered enough courage to ask what would become of Grandmother and my aunts and cousins.

"They will be with Yah," Mother answered.

"Yes, of course," I said. And together we breathed *Yhhhh* in and *Whhhh* out. I was sadder than I had ever been, but we were now both calmer. I asked her again. "What will become of Grandmother? And the others?" Mother reminded me that they would be with Yah, but I already remembered that, so I asked once more.

I wanted desperately for her to tell me that they were well and we would see them again at the next full moon. I hoped if I only asked the question once more, Mother would share this reassuring news. But her silence gave me the real answer. She could not bring her mouth to say the words that we both knew. If they were not already dead, they would be soon. My life at the palace was over, and their lives were over. My mother and I cried until we fell asleep, not having the energy to stand and walk into the house.

This happened when my mother's belly was round with Matanyah. I looked forward to the birth of my sister, but I thought the ending of my visits to the palace were the end of my life as a messenger, a traveler, and a maker of sweetness. Nonetheless, I kept my name; and as it turned out, my role was not ending but growing. Soon I would leave my home and, with no grandmother or aunts to go to, leave Egypt.

And for now, we shall leave these scrolls. I enjoy that we are coming neatly to the end of this piece of parchment. In the morning, you will read aloud what you have written thus far, and we shall continue with the next story at a later time.

THE FIFTH PARCHMENT

I was thirteen years old when I left my old life. Just about the same age you are now, Joseph. You are not yet a man, but no longer a child. If I was old enough to survive the passage from Egypt to Haran, you are now old enough to write of it. You will hear me tell of great awe and wonder. I hope you experience those someday. And you will hear me tell of great pain and fear. I hope you will not cause those to anyone, or experience those yourself. At the end of my telling of my travels, you will hear of my meeting with Rebekah. May all your journeys lead to such blessed destinations.

The journey north was as dangerous as Tanqo warned me it would be. And I encountered more hardships than she imagined—or perhaps than she dared warn me of for fear I would lose my courage. I had no protection but my own ideas and no comfort other than my own arms and a thin blanket at night when I was allowed. I tried to be brave and strong, as my mother had charged me, but I did not always succeed.

My father and brothers did not come to bid me goodbye when Mavheel collected me for the journey. I did not expect to see them that morning, but I was surprised by my disappointment, for I was sure I would never see them again, nor they me. I was leaving behind everything I knew. Almost everything. I took with me my mother's small bag of possessions, which Tanqo had retrieved and added herbs to, and the grief from the loss of my mother and sister was not something I could leave behind, especially so close to the loss of my mother's entire family, and so all that accompanied me as well.

Tanqo hugged me as I parted. She was a woman I did not know well, but she had shown me kindness multiple times in my life. She had been the midwife at my birth and had cared for me when my mother died. She would be the last person I saw whom I had known as a girl, and I shed a tear, though only one, as I tried to look ahead to what would come.

I followed Mavheel, and we soon joined the caravan of men and goods that he was taking to the north. We walked all day in silence. Not true silence. The wheels of the donkey carts were loud as they rolled over rocks, and the animals themselves made a steady clop-clopping with their feet. The men sometimes ate sunflower seeds, spitting the shells into the dirt with a loud pop out of their mouths. I wondered if my father had sent food for me. I heard the songs of birds in trees, and as we approached the Nile, I could hear its flow. But the silence was louder than all that, for the silence was the absence of my mother's voice in story, and that was unbearable.

Just as the river came into view, the silence broke. It was not only the ability to hear the river's flow better from closer up, but it was my mother's voice in my ears. *Deborah, I remember the first time you saw the river. Do you?* I smiled. I did not remember the first time, yet that was how she always began that story of my first River Festival. I continued to hear her words in my ears, even though she was not there.

You were not yet a year old, and not yet walking, yet you could crawl faster than a salamander in the sun! And that is just what you wanted to do. We came to the river, and hundreds of people were standing along the bank, awaiting the arrival of the king's boat. I had you wrapped on my back, and you wiggled and jiggled and would have fallen right out of there if I had not agreed to free you. And so I did. As soon as your body was out of the sling, you slid right down to the ground and made your way through the feet of the crowd, all the way to the water's edge. Oh, what a fright you gave me! I could not get by as quickly as you, as I was not crawling between legs. I pushed and shoved and kept my eyes on your little body and could see you approaching the water, but I could not reach you!

I imagine that my mother felt great fear in that moment, and I imagine that I did not. To see water, to be near water, to hear water, and to be in water have always been a great joy and comfort to me. The river is strong and powerful, but to me, that is just more reason to go in it, not one more reason to move away. But my mother did not share my feelings, and so she spoke the ending of the story with relief.

Just then, the barque came into view. A large floating platform of cedar wood coated in gold and led by the large statue of the ram's head on its front. While everyone cheered loudly and turned their attention to its arrival, I swooped to the river, where you sat and splashed as happily as a girl who had become a god in that moment. Not a worry in the world, but wet through and through. I scooped you into my arms and lifted you back into the crowd. I rushed you back home, not staying for the festival. The king would have to continue his ritual without me.

Here she would laugh at the thought of the king noticing the absence of one villager, and I heard that little laugh in my ears.

I had been to many festivals and would go again the next year, and the next, and the next, but that time, my biggest reason for celebrating was that you had escaped the water whole and unharmed. We danced, just the two of us, in our quiet courtyard, while everyone else was down at the river.

It was a comfort to hear my mother's story, even if she was not there to tell it. And as full of sorrow as I was, seeing the river on that day still flooded me with the same emotions I always felt at the festival, possibly even that first time: joy, excitement, adventure, and wonder. This time I did not get to touch the beautiful water, but I followed Mavheel and the other men onto a boat. Not as fancy as the king's, of course. Plain Egyptian acacia wood without gold, no carvings, and a lot of stink from crowded people and animals, but on the river!

We rode north for twelve days. The stink did not diminish over that voyage—quite the opposite. But neither did my glee or awe for the water diminish. I found a place to stand by the edge of the deck and stayed there. The familiarity of the acacia wood was a comfort, and the water and sky were soothing. Several times I saw a hippopotamus or crocodile and smiled at the safety that my distance from them allowed. Each day, every passenger was given broth—men, women, and servants alike—and that sustained me for the voyage. I did allow myself the pleasure of eating one fig from my satchel under the full moon. I felt hopeful that night, for I remembered that I was on my way to the land from which my grandmother had come.

I was still unknowing of the journey ahead of me. Would it all be by boat? For how long? I had not known how long the river ride would be until I was told to walk the wooden plank back to dry land on the twelfth day. My legs wobbled, having forgotten what it was like to walk on dry ground. I saw that I was not the only one with this trouble. The scene was as amusing as it was chaotic while our legs struggled to remember their purpose. It was midmorning when we were steady and ready, and we turned our backs from the river and toward the sun, and I followed Mavheel into the desert. I did not know it that day, but we would be in the desert for as many months as we were days on the Nile.

It was a blessing that I did not know that, or I might have jumped into the Nile and let myself end the journey there beneath the boat or in the jaws of a large beast. I would have thought it to be painful to be torn apart by a crocodile, but at least it would have been only once, whereas Mavheel tore me apart many times. The first time was that very first night on land.

On the boat, many had slept lying down, but I did not lie down at night, for fear of being stepped on. I sat with my back against the wood and closed my eyes under the stars and slept peacefully. But in the desert, there was no lack of empty space and plenty of room for me to lie down on a mat that Mavheel directed me to. I relaxed into a comfortable position on my back, appreciating the view of the stars above.

Then suddenly my view was blocked. I could see only the ugly face of Mavheel above mine. I felt his hands with all his weight pinning my thighs open until he moved one of those hands to cover my mouth to silence my scream as my flesh tore. I tried to move, but his body on top of mine was too heavy and the pain was too great. I could do nothing. When he got off, I still could not see the stars, for my view was blocked by my tears.

When the morning's first light came, I discovered my first blood. I thought I would lie in the hot sun of the desert and bake and bleed to death, but it was not to be. I was expected to rise with the sun and walk behind the men. I did so as best as I could, but my movement was slow, every step a painful one. Finally Mavheel got so frustrated that he put me on the back of one of the donkeys. Every movement was still filled with pain, but it did not slow me down.

That night, Mavheel left me alone. I still did not sleep. I had heard of the dangers of the desert my whole life. Everyone in Egypt knew that the Nile was the source of life. Its fertility brought the food. The desert was where water was scarce and there was no shelter from the burning sun. Everything in the desert was scarce, except the thieves and the beasts. And now I knew that I was traveling with someone who was both.

Throughout the months that followed, Mavheel came to me more times than I would ever count or know. Ten times I kept him away with one of my mother's coins. Once the idea had come to me, I had one loosened from my tunic at all times. Then I feigned finding it in the brambles and used it to buy a quiet night for myself. And when the coins ran out, there was a time when my mother's words saved me, by rushing out of my mouth in the form of a curse on Mavheel. After that, I had the silphium seeds from Tanqo. On the darkest nights, when the moon was completely hidden, I meticulously counted fourteen seeds, and chewed them silently, just as she had instructed me. And so, at least, I conceived no children.

Still, the misery was immense. I tried to run once. It was after my coins were gone. Mavheel had come to expect both money and flesh from me, and when I could not deliver the first anymore, he took vengeance on the second. After a few days, my legs were not too sore to carry me between the brambles in the rocks. When everyone slept, I crept away. I knew with one false step I could fall and tumble down the hill or open my head on a rock. But I went slowly, feeling my way. I did not fall or injure myself, nor did I gain enough distance to escape Mavheel. He found me before the sun was high and kept me closer to him until he decided to whip my back as a reminder to never run off again; he needed me to be alive to collect his money.

Ironically it was the whip that reminded me of who I was. A daughter of Hallel, of Sarah, of Daganyah. I knew Yah! I had been taught; I had learned what to do when I had pain. *Yhhhh. Whhhh. Yhhhh. Whhhh.* I practiced bringing my god into my body and then letting myself become one with my god. *Yhhhh. Whhhh.* Quickly, right away, in again. *Yhhhh.* And out, all the way. *Whhhh.* I floated above the girl who was being whipped. My back still hurt, but I was not there. I was watching.

I saw a girl in a linen tunic. The tunic was covered in dust, but underneath the dust were thin orange threads. The onions used to dye the threads had been grown by my mother. The skins were used for the dye, and their layers kept going, and going, and going. The threads had been spun from flax fibers that had grown in the fertile soil of the Nile, picked by people I did not know. Now their work was walking through the desert, lifetimes away from where it had begun.

As my back bled, parts of me became parts of the fibers. We were one, my tunic and I, the farmers and I, my mother and I, the onions and I, the desert and I. Even the whip was made of a branch grown in this desert, held by a man who had walked the hills for days. The whip would return to the dust one day, so would the man, so would I, so would my tunic. The same dust that held the onions, that holds my mother. The beauty and awe of it all filled my eyes with tears at least as much as the pain did, if not more so.

From then on, whenever the pain came, I breathed. *Yhhhh. Whhhh. Yhhhh. Whhhh.* Yah was with me. I was connected. I was in awe. I was peaceful.

That could not stop the pain, but in addition to it, my flesh tingled with the touch of Yah's love. No whipping could cover that. I learned to focus on that feeling when the times were the hardest and I concentrated on it even when I was not suffering. I began to feel Yah in joy. And then we were always One, and I began to understand the quiet messages.

Traveling out of the ease and familiarity of Egypt, to the unknown and with the unknown, was perhaps the most challenging struggle of my life. I shall not deny the horrors that happened, nor do I allow them to be the only part I remember. For in fact, while the pain was sometimes unbearable and the fear gripping, the journey brought beauty like I had never imagined.

Mavheel seemed in no rush to arrive in Haran. He had brought many goods from Egypt to sell and trade and had a route he intended to follow to make his trip the most profitable. He was familiar with the locations of distant cities and their markets, and though none was as beautiful as the one my grandmother had taken me to, each one had its own mix of familiar and exotic sights and smells. Whenever Mavheel was at a market, he was in a good mood. He loved to talk with the merchants, to drink and play games, and, of course, to make a profit on his wares.

He kept me close to him, and that gave me the advantage of seeing people from far-off places with musical-sounding names and even more melodious voices. The language I heard in the markets was familiar to me, even though the words often sounded slightly different. At each market, Mavheel bought dried chickpeas and dried lentils. Those were always the same. But he also had an affinity for trying new things, and so in each city, he bought a different spice to flavor the stews he charged me with making. It was a wonder to smell and taste different herbs from different parts of the desert.

The desert was, indeed, a harsh place, but also a beautiful one. The mountains towered taller than any obelisk of Egypt, and a landscape that at first view looked only brown was actually much more. The hills looked like lumps covered in one large blanket of the softest brown linen. Looking closely, one could see that there were small plants and bushes. Many bushes produced thorns. Those thorns reminded me of the story of Eve and Adam that my mother had told me many times.

> *Eve and Adam had lived in a garden more lovely than any found in Egypt, and they had everything they needed, and life was easy. And when it came time for them to leave the garden and take care of their own needs, Yah told them right away, "Thorns and thistles will grow for you." Mother always paused the story there and added her own words. You see, Deborah,* she would say, *when you meet with a thorn or thistle, this does not mean something is wrong. This is just one of the things Yah created. If you want to find something else, keep looking.*

I do not think my mother anticipated that I would need or use such advice in the wilderness, but it was still true and helpful. For when I did not allow the thorns and thistles to turn me away, I found some bushes also had some small green leaves. Some had red berries, and I even came across small fig trees. The fig trees were a welcome familiarity.

I found hyssop in many places and picked it in bunches, letting it dry and carrying it in my satchel. Another familiarity.

Much of what I saw on the journey was new, though. I was always looking out for something safe to eat, but for some time, I did not know how to distinguish between what would harm and what would help. I watched what the birds ate, what the caterpillars ate, and I picked whatever I could. I looked for things that resembled what I saw in the markets.

While no one was looking, I would hold the unfamiliar greens or berries I found and pray, asking Yah to guide me and feed me. In my stillness, I discovered that if I held the leaf or berry between my thumb and last finger, Yah would make my fingers stronger, making them hold the food tighter, to say yes, it is safe to eat. If it was not safe for me to eat, my fingers would open and drop it, as if trying to get away. After many months of this praying, I discovered that Yah would answer me even if I just pretended to hold something between my fingers. If the answer to my question was yes, my fingers pressed tightly to each other. If no, they were weak. So Yah and the plants kept me alive and sustained and learning.

The land and the plants, the weather and the animals became my teachers and my guides along with Yah. I learned of their unique gifts by listening to their whispers, easy for me when I was One with them. I continued to suffer at the hands of Mavheel, but it was not my only story. I also had the story of travel, adventure, knowing Yah, meeting other travelers, chewing hyssop leaves every day, and learning always. In fact, I choose to remember the day that I walked to the edge of the world as my biggest story of the whole journey.

Oh, Joseph. You make me laugh! To see your face when I said I walked to the edge of the world was a treat for my old eyes. Perhaps almost as wonderful as the edge of the world itself.

On a day that began like any other, we arose at first light and walked until the heat was too heavy. As often happened, there was no shade when it was most needed, and the men erected a small tent to create some. We let our bodies enjoy this escape from the beating sun and we rested. When the light was still good, but the sun was lower, they put the tent away, and we continued walking until dark.

The hills were beautiful, the sky big. A few goats were nibbling on grasses not far away. If there is anything more amusing than a goat wiggling its ears, I have yet to see it. And though it was not an uncommon sight on our journey, it was always entertaining. That was our day. Hills, sky, goats, grass, walking. A day like so many others. Until we came to the top of that hill. And then, instead of seeing hills to the right and left, ahead and behind, I saw them in only three directions. For to the left, there was nothing!

I gasped. Nothing! My body turned to the left, my feet stopped, my jaw dropped, my eyes stared into the distance. Nothing. The men continued walking straight, but I could not. When they looked back and saw me, stiff as a statue, they all began to laugh. Mavheel came back and stood next to me.

"I have traveled here many times," he said. Then he paused and stared with me for a long time. "Perhaps too many, for I have forgotten the wondrous experience of seeing it for the first time. Stand here, girl, and know the power of the goddess Tefnut." I did not think of Tefnut. I did not think. I merely stared. The edge of the world! I had not fathomed that there would be nothing beyond. It seemed silly. Of course, an edge would have nothing beyond it. Of course. But to see it. And then Mavheel said, "We shall go there."

These words brought my eyes away from the nothingness and to face Mavheel. I did not know what to make of his statement. "You will be amazed, girl. We shall go to the edge of the world, and you will step off, and on again. From here, it looks like there is nothing at the edge. That is a trick of the eye. We see only the sky. Soon you will see that where the land ends, it kisses the sea."

I had never heard Mavheel speak like that. Even in the markets. But I had heard of the sea. I had heard it was like a never-ending river. Yet the Nile was a river, a never-ending river, so I tried to imagine this. I had little time to do so, as around the next turn where I followed Mavheel, I saw it for the first time. A never-ending river, indeed! Water and more water and more water and more water! I ran ahead of the men, my feet carrying me down the path, somehow knowing they would take me to the sea. They knew what they were doing.

It was not a short distance, but as I got closer with every step, my excitement carried me forward even faster. The bottom of that hill brought flatness and sand that sank so softly with each step that it begged me to remove my shoes. My feet nearly burned from the heat, yet my toes delighted at the scratchiness beneath them.

Oh, the sea! It was like the whole world, only if the whole world were made of water. Perhaps I had not arrived at the edge of the world, but at the edge of the sea. Did the fish not think the land I stood on was where the world ended? I looked down into the water and asked them. Their silence did not diminish my delight. I danced in the water as it came closer and licked my knees in greeting, then went back to where it came from.

The waves were large and loud. The wind blew off my head covering, and I ran into the water to retrieve it, not caring that all my clothes got wet. I splashed in the sea and submerged myself as I had once done in Grandmother's grand bath, which was like one drop of this sea. But while Grandmother's bath had left a taste of lavender on my lips, the sea washed them with salt, stinging my eyes at the same time. Salt! I had tasted it before and forgotten it had come from the sea!

I laughed in my good fortune and began to cry with joy. My tears washed the salt from my eyes, but I put my hand to my lips to taste more of it. I shuddered. Without food, the salt was not as pleasant, but it was still decadent. I felt like the richest person in the world. The richest person at the edge of the world. The sea roared, and I roared back: "I am here!" I said. "I am here!"

I do not know when the men arrived. I did not see them until the sun was setting, going down at the far edge of the sea. Yet another edge! Oh, how beautiful it was! But before its last light disappeared, Mavheel called me to exit the water. "Come along, girl," he said. "You must not stay in there in the night. You will have another bath in the morning, if you like, before we depart."

Depart? Oh, how I wished to stay in this place forever. But I heeded Mavheel's calling and walked toward the men and the fire they had built. I could smell fish cooking. I had not had fish since we left Egypt. How long ago was that? I added it up quickly. It had been more than nine moons ago. My nose beckoned me to follow the smell, but looking down, which I had not done upon arrival, I saw the most magnificent objects lying in multitude in the sand. When Mavheel saw me sit to examine them, he told me they were shells. "Each one used to be the home of a small sea creature," he told me. I held a shell in my hand and knew him to be speaking the truth.

While the men cooked the fish, I picked up shells in the sinking sunlight. Each one was more beautiful than the next. Pinks and purples, blues and greens, whites and yellows. The shells were painted more beautifully than the pillars at the palace. To have these shells would be to have more riches than my grandparents, more than the pharaoh himself. But I could not keep these shells. Even the sand of the beach was not large enough to hold them all. How could my little satchel? Not able to choose a favorite, I selected the first seven I saw, rinsed the sand off in the sea, and placed them in my bag. Then I continued to gather others, admiring each one.

In the light of the fire and the rising half-moon, I made a circle of shells in the sand. I readily ate the fish when it was cooked. The men had caught enough for a feast. A salty, fishy feast. And then I returned to my shell circle. I lay on my back on the sand that stuck to me as if it could not get enough of me, just as I could not get enough of it. Above me the dark sky sparkled with stars.

I breathed in my god. *Yhhhh*. I breathed myself into this beauty. *Whhhh*. The waves drummed, and I breathed. Woosh! *Yhhhh*. *Whhhh*. Woosh! *Yhhhh*. *Whhhh*. Woosh! *Yhhhh*. *Whhhh*. Woosh! I was the sound of the water. *Yhhhh*. The stars came into me, became me. *Whhhh*. I became the sand. Woosh! Water. *Yhhhh*. Stars. *Whhhh*. Sand. I knew my body to be lying on the ground, yet I felt it to be at once sinking into it and floating above it to the stars. The stars were fire. Little fires in the sky, I could see that now. They were not burning me, burning only the sky. I was the stars. I was the water. I was the sand. I was the air as I breathed the name of my god. I was Yah. And I spoke to Yah, to myself.

"Yah, thank you for bringing me to this day, to this place, to this edge of all. Now, here I am! I am open, Yah. Open to receive your gifts, your creation. I am open to being One with you. I am open to doing my part, just as the fish do theirs and the shells do theirs. For we are all united. We are unified. We are you. The edge has revealed this to me and about me. I vow to integrate this and carry it with me for always. I know that whatever will come, you sustain me with your love and support me with your creation. Now I know that I am holy, for you are holy, and we are One."

My body was filled with all the love and glory that met at the edge of the land, the edge of the sea, the edge of the sky, and the edge of me. Hallelu Yah! Hallelu Yah!

THE SECOND SCROLL

THE SIXTH PARCHMENT

Upon my arrival in Haran, I was filled with relief to finally have reached my mother's family. But I was not greeted with the same feeling. I had not considered that Hallel's uncles, Nakhor and Haran, would both be dead, but when Mavheel inquired about them, we learned that they were. We were met by Betuel, a son of Nakhor, and he questioned my lineage. "Messengers were sent to my uncle Abram announcing the births of many sons to his brother Nakhor. But no word was returned. This was a generation ago. Now you say this filthy girl is a descendant of his and you bring her from Egypt? How do I know this to be true? And what do you wish me to do with her?"

Before Mavheel could speak, I had enough time to fill with worry. Would I be sent back? Or put out in the desert? Or become the property of Mavheel? Each fear was worse than the last. The question of my fate would not be answered by these men, though, but by a girl who ran up to Betuel and declared loudly, yet respectfully, "Father, I am in need of a new nursemaid. Do you recall? Yankah died many moons ago, and I have been alone since that time."

Mavheel saw this as a great opportunity. "Only two pieces of silver for the girl," he said. "Not because she is lame, no, no. She is not. I always offer good prices. She is strong and a good worker. She cooks well and eats little. She will be no trouble, I am certain." Mavheel opened his hand. The thief would be able to report back to my father that he had done the errand, and Betuel would not need to believe that I was kin but would have me there just in case. As Betuel slowly placed two pieces of silver in Mavheel's hand, the girl grabbed mine and pulled me behind her, running to the well.

I soon learned that this girl was called Rebekah. That is right, Joseph. Your grandmother was once a girl who ran quickly. And she thought quickly then, as she does now. She offered me a wonderful life while saving me from a terrible fate. Now she is missing three teeth from old age, but when I first saw her smile, four of her teeth had not yet grown in. She was twelve years old when I arrived, or as she told it, she had twelve summers.

In Egypt we marked the time with the three seasons of the Nile River: the flooding, the growing, and the harvesting. A year was the passing of all three. In the north they marked two seasons: summer and rain. At twelve summers, she ran as free as the wind, and her dark brown hair flew behind her, when it did not get caught in brambles. My hair never fell down my back as hers did, no matter how long the comb went through it. When allowed to grow, my black curls reach for the sky, not the ground. We now both keep our hair short under our scarves, but at that time, she had not been taught how to properly comb or plait or cover it. Her scarf was always falling off.

Her mother, Metuyeshet, did nothing but eat and sleep all day long, and she had no older sister. No sister at all. Her mother had borne Rebekah and then a year later, a boy, Lavan. Then she declared she would not be carrying any more babies. She insisted that Rebekah and Lavan leave her tent and go to one with a nursemaid. When the nursemaid died, Lavan said he would not stay in a tent with a girl and made himself a sleeping mat in the corner of Betuel's tent.

I learned all this on the way to the well. "Sit," Rebekah said when we got there. "Would you like to drink?" I nodded that I would, and I rose to draw the water, but she pointed me to sit again and drew it for me. It was refreshing and cold, a sweet comfort to my lips and insides. "More?" she asked when I had swallowed the last drops from the ladle. Her kindness was as refreshing and nourishing as the water itself, and I accepted. As soon as I finished my second drink, Rebekah took my hand, and we were running again.

We left the camp behind, and she led me to a hill thick with cedar trees. Oh, how Pharaoh would have loved this hill! How many boats he could have made! But instead of planks floating on the Nile River, these trees were here in all their beauty.

"You should know," Rebekah said, "that this is my favorite place to be. That is why I brought you here straight away." She continued talking as she lay down under one of the trees, motioning for me to follow her.

"Do you see how the leaves create a tent over our heads?" she asked. "The green is the most beautiful color I have ever seen.

Except for the yellow of the forsythia flowers, that is also beautiful. And the blue of the sky. That is lovely. And the purple of the hollyhocks! Oh, how I love them! I do also love the brown of the barley when it is dry and the white clouds when they gather like sheep above. But the green leaves are my favorite color of green for a tent over my head," she said. "And sitting under the branch I can feel the breeze and the shade of these leaves. I can sit here as long as I like!" She said that especially loudly. But then she added, "As long as I have already gotten the water for the sheep and I do not tarry when called for weaving or spinning."

Rebekah's excitement kept her talking while we lay in the shade of the leaves, which really did act as a tent above our heads. "Do you know how to weave and spin?" she asked. "I can teach you, if you like. Or if you would rather, I am sure Auntie would teach you. She taught me. She says I weave the finest baskets, so tight there is not even one hole large enough for a flea to get in or a grain to get out."

Although I knew how to weave baskets and spin flax, I did not have a chance to tell her this before she went on. I had not yet said a word, but that would soon change.

"When the sheep finish their shearing, we have much spinning to do. My father trades our wool when he goes to the market. He has never allowed me to go to the market with him, but one time, he traded for a large clay wine jug. My brother, Lavan, liked it so much that he took it and hid it in the crevice of a rock and kept it to himself. Lavan did not think I saw, but I did. Only two days later, the jug fell and broke and he threw it into the trash heap. Later, I went and retrieved two large pieces. Would you like to see them?"

Without waiting for a response, Rebekah began to crawl out from under the tree. I knew I was to follow her, and so I did. We went to her tent, which would that day become our tent, and she showed me the clay. She kept it hidden behind cushions in the corner, so they would not be discovered and removed, she said. It was, indeed, pretty. It could not compare to what I had seen in Grandmother's house, but the dark reds and browns were nice to look upon, even on the broken shards. Rebekah placed one of the shards in my hand.

"Lovely," I said, for it seemed she sought my approval.

It was lovely, but when I held those shards, I thought more of my mother's clay cup than Rebekah's broken jug. The cup that had touched my mother's lips had arrived in Haran unbroken, even after the long journey. Yet I knew that someday, it, too, would be shards, and I would need to accept that. And perhaps by then I would be ready to accept it, but I was not yet. And so I decided that I would keep it wrapped in my mother's clothes, inside the satchel, and behind the cushions, safe from being stepped upon.

While I was lamenting the cup that would someday break, Rebekah laughed at herself. Such a joyful laugh. "I am so glad to have someone to speak to!" she said. "I forgot that you, too, could speak to me. What is your name?"

"My name is Deborah," I told her.

She repeated my name, letting herself feel her tongue against her teeth with the beginning and her lips join and part in the middle, ending with *rah*. I feared she might not know that my name meant bee. What if she thought me a worshiper of the Egyptian sun god, Ra? But she knew nothing of Ra and spoke of a beehive she had once seen, telling me about the sticky honey she left behind for fear of being stung. I wondered how anyone, even a bee, would want to sting a girl so sweet as Rebekah.

"May I ask you a question, Rebekah?" This time it was my turn to feel her name in my mouth. It started soft and quiet in my throat, then was strong in the middle, twice, then ended with a relaxed little *ah*. I enjoyed saying her name. I had spent twelve moons traveling with Mavheel, trying not to be noticed by him, and before that, I had been by my mother's side always. I did not know the rules of being a nursemaid. I did not know if I was allowed to ask questions. I was glad when she nearly yelled her "Yes!" because she was so excited to receive a question.

"Why did you choose me for your nursemaid?" I asked. I could have been sold or sent back; the men would negotiate without a girl speaking up.

"Oh!" she said. "It is because you are filthy! Absolutely filthy! Your hair covering is itself covered in dirt, and the few hairs that have escaped the covering have not escaped the dirt. Your tunic does not have a clean spot on it. It is dusty and stained, yet I can see it is of a different style than we wear, and perhaps a different kind of wool." In fact, my tunic was linen, but I did not have a chance to tell her that as she continued.

"One look at your hands and I can see that the dirt under your nails looks as if it has been there since your birth. Even your face, with markings from where you have tried to wipe it clean, is not. And when I saw you, I thought, 'Here is a woman who has come a long distance. She has seen the other side of the hills, and perhaps the hills beyond those, and the hills beyond those!' And though I had never longed to meet a person who had been on such adventures, I knew in that moment that I could not live another day without doing so. I rushed to Father before it was too late, for I would be heartbroken if I did not even try to keep you here."

My whole body swelled with joy. I had felt ashamed when she called me filthy. She was not wrong. I had tried to keep myself clean. In Egypt, Mother and I had used well water to wash our hands and faces and feet daily, and Grandmother indulged me with a bath in scented water in a tub in her bathing room each month. But I had had no wells nor baths since leaving Egypt, and, indeed, I was covered in dirt that I could not wash off in a rushed moment in the occasional stream. Now I was grateful for that dirt.

"I do not know how to be a nursemaid," I admitted. "What did your old nursemaid do?"

Rebekah frowned and scrunched her face into a stern expression. "She told me not to climb the trees," she said. "And not to run to the well. Not to run at all. She told me not to drink so quickly and not to take big bites of my meals. She told me not to sing before the sun was up in the sky and not to speak to the birds and lizards and sheep and dogs."

"I think I understand," I said. And not knowing what Rebekah would do, I risked teasing her a bit. "I believe I can perform those tasks." Would she know I was speaking in jest? Disappointment was on her face but quickly changed to a sly smile, and I saw she understood. I smiled, too.

"Ooooh," she said, "but I have told you only what Yankah *told* me, not what she *did* for me. Every night before sleep, she rubbed my feet with fragrant oils and told me I was the most precious person she had ever known." Our eyes were locked on each other, and we quickly both failed at our attempts to have the other believe our deception as we fell into laughter.

"I shall not rub your feet every night," I said. "But I shall do so tonight, in celebration. Have you a jar of fragrant oil?"

Rebekah jumped up and hugged me, wrapping her arms around me tightly. "Thank you, Deborah!" My body filled with joy as I heard her say my name again. She did not have any fragrant oil, but she brought the olive oil from two lamps in her tent, lighting a third one so that we could see, for we had not even noticed when the sun had set and the darkness had entered the tent.

That night I rubbed her feet while she lay on the mat. I could see her smile in the dim light of the one lamp, but I could feel her happiness with my hands. "Your feet are long," I said, "Soon your body will grow taller to match them." This was something my mother had always said to me when she noticed my feet growing closer and closer in length to hers. If she were here now, would our feet be the same size? I had not thought of Mother all day. I knew she would love to hear of this adventure, just as she heard the news of the palace. On the journey, missing her was painful, wishing for her protection. Here, missing her was easier.

"My mother always said that to me," I told Rebekah.

"Oh, to have a mother who speaks to you," she said. "That must be lovely."

"It was," I told her.

Rebekah sat up. "Now, I shall rub your feet," she said.

"My feet are filthy," I reminded her.

"Yes," she said gleefully. "I shall rub your filthy feet, and my hands will touch the dirt of distant lands, and you will tell me of them."

And that is what we did that night. She removed my sandals, which had not been off my feet, other than the one day in sand and sea, since leaving Tanqo's home. My toes immediately relaxed at her touch.

"That piece of dirt thanks you," I said, "as does the skin beneath it. So does that piece, and that one," I said as her hands moved along my heels and arches and toes. And as she rubbed, I told her that my feet had come all the way from Egypt, traveling on a boat and on donkeys, on wide paths and narrow ones, over hills and to the end of the world and back again. It was just the first few words of stories that would go on and on for months and years. But that night, tired and safe enough to succumb to a peaceful sleep for the first time since my mother died, the only other words I could manage before falling asleep on Rebekah's mat were "Hallelu Yah."

THE SEVENTH PARCHMENT

In the morning, I woke to the sound of Rebekah singing before the sunrise, and I did not chastise her. Quite the opposite, I could not keep the smile from my face. I was in the land of my grandmother's birth, and though not accepted as a part of the tribe, I was a nursemaid among them. And thus far, that seemed to mean joy and adventure and talking that stopped only for sleep and song.

"Oh, good, you are awake!" Rebekah threw herself at me the moment I stirred. She took my hand, as she had the day before, and brought me all the places she wanted me to go. We began that morning with her showing me the food, the cooking area, and the area for relieving myself. From there we went back to the well and she again drew water for both of us. Then she drew water for the trough so the sheep and goats would be able to drink. She was content to let me watch her do the work, but I pulled the bucket up several times. She appreciated my help and told me so.

She also told me of her dreams the night before and how soft her feet felt from the rub I had given them. She gave me a gentle laugh when she said I had fallen asleep still talking, and she was very curious to know the meaning of *Hallelu Yah*. "Who is this Yah that you praised when going to sleep last night?"

"Do you not know Yah?" I asked, surprised. She did not. I thought, perhaps, the problem was that I was saying Yah, the shortened version of the name. Perhaps we used that only in Egypt. Perhaps here in the north, they said YhWh even when not in prayer. But when I explained this, she still did not know. "This is the god that Abram and Sarai came to know," I explained. Rebekah looked at me, wanting more explanation. "Do you not know Abram and Sarai?" I asked. She did not know them either. "But surely, you must," I said, fearful that Betuel was right: Perhaps we were not kin at all.

"Tell me," I pleaded, "Do you know of Haran? For whom this land is named?"

Now Rebekah relaxed. "Of course," she said. "Haran was the brother of my grandfather Nakhor."

I clapped my hands. "Yes!" I said with relief. "Haran was the brother of Nakhor and also of Abram. Abram and his wife, Sarai, were dwelling in this land when they first understood that Yah—that is, YhWh—is the god who is the Creator of All." Joseph, you must remember that Abraham and Sarah were once called Abram and Sarai, and neither Rebekah nor I knew of them by any other names.

"Oh," Rebekah responded. "Perhaps we have a sculpture of this god and I did not realize. What does it look like?"

"We cannot see Yah," I said. "But we can see what Yah has created, be what Yah has created, be with Yah." She was listening attentively. "Would you like to try?" I asked, and she shouted her yes before the words had fully left my mouth. "I shall show you," I said. But then I hesitated for a moment. "Rebekah?" I said her name tentatively, still enjoying the new sounds in my mouth and uncertain whether what I was about to request was acceptable.

"Yes?" she responded.

"May I ask something of you?"

"Certainly!" she said. Her enthusiasm showed no trace of anger at me for wanting to make a request.

"I have traveled for nearly a year," I said. "As you saw from my filth." We both giggled. "It has been months since I have been clean." I thought of bathing in the palace before meeting Yah with Grandmother and Mother. In the gathering of my filth, I learned that Yah was with me whether I was clean or not. Now, whether there would be a little ceremony or not, it did seem that I had arrived at a place where I could remove some of the dust of my travels. Before I could finish my request, Rebekah stood, grabbed an old tunic that Yankah had worn, and beckoned me to follow her.

She took me to the well, where we each filled a bucket and carried it down a small hill. There was a large dip in a smooth rock. Next to the rock there was a jar of olive oil. "I put that there," she said. "I have come to bathe here twice before, when my nasty brother, Lavan, pushed me into the latrine. Nobody knows about it—except you, now." I could see that it would be easy and comfortable to sit in the dip and pour water over myself from the bucket. I took off the tunic I had worn every moment since leaving Egypt. Even before that. The last time I had changed had been months before Mother died—on my last visit to Grandmother. I raised the tunic over my head and threw it down the hill. "Goodbye!" I yelled.

I sat in the rock and dumped a bucket right over my head. The water was cool and refreshing and so clean! I was not, but I laughed at the shock of the water and at the tiny river of mud trickling down the rock. With my wet hands, I pushed water and dirt from my body into that little river. While I was doing so, Rebekah dumped the second bucket over my head and laughed so hard at my squeak of surprise that she fell to the ground with her hands on her knees. When she finally stopped laughing, she announced that she would bring more water from the well.

When she returned, she handed me a small square of frayed wool to scrub my skin. That little piece of wool did not stay clean long, but it was enough to wipe away much of the caked-on blood and dirt that I had been carrying since we left the sea. Rebekah dumped the fresh well water on me and had so much fun doing so that, although I was ready to dress, she insisted on refilling the bucket and doing it again. Whether I allowed her to do so, or complied because I was her new servant, was unclear to me, but the water felt good.

Once clean, I used the olive oil to freshen my skin, then put on Yankah's old tunic that Rebekah had brought for me. I wanted only to tame my hair, but even with the help of a strong wooden comb, I could not. I asked Rebekah if she would shear it like that of a sheep, and she bounced with glee and eagerness. We sat in the shade of her favorite tree, and she pulled and sawed at my hair. When she had managed to get most of my hair off without removing any skin, we put the hair under the tree and walked back up to the tents together.

Rebekah showed me where I might make some flatbread for us. I did so, and we ate together beside the tent. When we finished, I said, "I have not forgotten to show you Yah. I thank you for this day. My body feels fresh and ready for that now, and for all the things that I shall do in Haran."

"With me," Rebekah said with a smile.

"Yes." I returned her smile just as warmly. "For all the things I shall do in Haran with you."

Rebekah followed me into the tent where I retrieved my satchel and the small drum I had made in Egypt. Oh, Tanqo, what a wise woman! I did not see any drums in the tent. I assumed Rebekah had one, or many, but I wished to use mine. My little drum would play the beat for a lot of joy!

"You wish to know YhWh?" I asked her, and she confirmed.

"First"—I said, suddenly very aware that I had learned this from my mother and grandmother, practiced it on my own, and never taught anyone—"you must watch me, and do as I do." I took a deep breath in, saying the first part of Yah's name as I did. *Yhhhh*. Rebekah did just as I did. Then I pushed what was inside me out, to be taken up by Yah. *Whhhh*. Rebekah again copied my breath exactly. "When you breathe in," I said, "you bring all that is Yah into you. It is not important your size; you bring in what fits, what you need; it is all from Yah. Then," I continued, "when you breathe out, you take all that is yours and give it to Yah. It is with this taking and giving, taking and giving, that we become one with Yah. It is like this all the time, but we do not feel it all the time. I have done this for many years, and I know how to feel it often. I see you will learn quickly."

I had Rebekah lie down on the rug where we sat. I remained sitting so she could watch my breaths, the full, receiving *Yhhhh*, quickly followed by the free, giving *Whhhh*, then immediately, without pause, repeating the cycle. I began to play my drum for her. I held it in my left hand, and it was so small that it took only my first two fingers of my right hand to beat it, but it made a lovely little sound. It brought me joy, pride, and gratitude. I saw Rebekah begin to feel sickened by the breathing. I knew that would pass soon if she continued and told her so. She did as I instructed. I suggested she close her eyes.

I remained sitting, so the drumming would be comfortable, but I chose to close my eyes, too. So we were, in our new tent, the two of us, and Yah. The drumbeats filled my head with sound and color. I tasted honey. It filled my mouth with stickiness, such that I could not move my tongue, but I did not need it for speaking, for I could speak with color. And I did not need it for eating, for I was sustained by the honey. My hand kept moving, kept beating the rhythm on the drum, or was the drum beating on my hand? When I woke, it was beside me, and I did not know when I had released it.

When Rebekah woke, she was full of bliss. She described her experience as a dream. "I dreamt that I became the wind," she said. "I was blowing, to and fro, to and fro, and in my blowing, I gathered up your hair from beneath the tree. Only *gathered* is not the right word, for it was not together, but in many, many separate pieces, all going different ways, and I was going with them all those ways—taking them all those ways. I did not see myself, yet I knew it was me.

"I took your hair to the hills and the valleys, to birds' nests in trees and snakes' holes in the ground. And I even took some of it to Egypt. I cannot tell you how I knew it was Egypt, for I have seen nothing farther than the second hill," she said. "And all I saw in the dream was dirt, but I knew it was Egyptian dirt, and I knew your mother was in there," she said. "And she was happy, she was very happy because your hair had blown there, and little lice had crawled out of it and into the dirt, and your mother said, 'Hello, little lice, I remember you,' and she kissed them, so happy was she to see something from your head. And I felt that happiness; it was a happiness of love. Not just your mother loving you, but her loving the bugs and the bugs loving her, and loving your hair, and me, I was loving your hair and your mother and the birds, and I loved myself, for I was all those things."

She paused. "Deborah, is it real?"

"It is Yah," I answered her.

IN SOME WAYS, life in Haran was difficult for me to get used to. In other ways, the familiarity was easy and welcome. The best part was being with Rebekah. I admired and envied Rebekah's free spirit. I was only a few years her elder, yet the struggles and trials of my journey had caused me to forget the curiosity of youth already. But Rebekah's wild smile and easy laugh reminded me.

Even though I was in Haran as a nursemaid, I was glad to share a tent with Rebekah and tend only to her needs. I taught her to dress and bathe and take care of her body—and I had the opportunity to care for mine. She will tell you that I taught her much more than that, and I am sure it is true. But I was in such awe and ecstasy from what she was teaching me that I hardly noticed.

Rebekah taught me to be free again. She reminded me that I could experience safety and delight. And though I could not become a child again, I could become joyful again. We explored the hills, climbed trees, watered the sheep, and told stories. I thought I would teach her to play twenty blocks, but she already knew! There were many times that we played after our meals, sharing her set of dice.

Rebekah took me to look for a beehive she had once seen, and though we did not find it, we had great fun following the goat paths and finding nooks and crannies to hide from view in, yet watch the world. For three days we secretly listened to Ro'ee, one of the shepherds, complain to a sheep about his wife.

He never said hello or asked how the sheep was doing that day or if she wanted to speak in the conversation, too. Rebekah and I laughed at that thought. The only thing funnier than a man talking to a sheep would be a sheep talking to a man.

It was not always the same sheep. Ro'ee was a responsible shepherd and tended to the whole flock, not just one ewe. But we were lucky enough to find a hiding place far enough not to be noticed, yet close enough to hear a man not too embarrassed to talk to a sheep in a loud voice. It was nearly the same words every time.

"She is always complaining. 'You smell like the field,' she says. 'Why are Betuel's feet clean and yours are not?' she asks. 'When will you move the water trough closer to the well?' Does she think I am the master? Does she think that she is? That she can one morning wake up and decide she wants water in a different place, and so it is?"

He pondered these questions aloud several times in the days that we heard him. Perhaps because the sheep never did provide him with a response. But he seemed to like the quiet that the sheep offered. "My wife," he would say, "she is not like you. You are quiet. I always know where you are; you can never sneak up on me. My stink does not offend you and you do not make unreasonable requests. And you are soft to the touch."

At this he would reach out and affectionately pat the sheep's wool in a not so muddy spot. Then he broke into laughter. "You are soft to the touch, and so is my wife," he said. "I am a blessed man that I can spend the days in the sunshine with your quiet softness and the nights in the tent with her softness. Then I do not mind if she is loud." Ro'ee laughed. He seemed unconcerned that anyone would hear him. He did not know we were listening, and the other shepherds were too far away to notice. Perhaps they spoke to the sheep also, though we never heard them do so.

"And I will tell you another difference," he continued. "If I were to bring you to her, she would spin your wool into a yarn to dye and weave and place as a rug between our feet and the cracked dirt floor of the tent. Then she would cook your flesh into a delicious stew that would satisfy me for days."

Ro'ee rubbed his belly, and then the sheep's. "If I brought her to you, you would do nothing of the sort. You would just stand there, as you do, slowly, quietly grazing. Yah has blessed you greatly, giving you a shepherd who would never steal from his master. Because you are so blessed, when we have the next celebration, I shall make sure that you are not brought to the feast." Ro'ee laughed at his own cleverness. He had this same talk with the sheep every day—more than once—for three days. And perhaps even after that, but at the end of three days, we had heard it often enough that we moved on to a different adventure.

"Today I shall show you something special," Rebekah told me one morning. When I asked her what she would show me, she first refused to say, wanting to make it a surprise. But then she could not contain her own excitement, so she told me to take a water jug and come with her. "We shall not be getting water from the well today," she said. "I shall take you to the river."

The river! I had not thought to ask if there was a river nearby. I had not seen one when I arrived and had forgotten to imagine it could be in the other direction. But the night before, I had told Rebekah about the flooding of the Nile River and how my father and brothers—and so many other men—could grow their crops in the fertile soil that remained when the river shrunk back down again. And I mentioned that I missed seeing the river, and even more so, I missed hearing it.

The whole walk to the river I could not contain my excitement. But once we arrived, I could easily contain it—and all the water I saw, as well. "This is not a river," I said. When I saw Rebekah's proud smile turn to confusion and frustration, I felt bad about my choice of words. "This does not look like a river," I said next. "Is this the river?" I knew she would say yes, because she had just announced our arrival at the river. But what I saw was a shallow valley with hardly enough water—*still* water—to wash our feet. It was little more than a few leftover raindrops that could not escape the trap of the lower land.

"There is more," she said. "This is only the beginning. Follow me." I followed her through shrubs and some wet ground. Soon I heard the soft trickle of water. Behind some trees was a small pool at the bottom of a few rocks. We went around the water to the top of the rocks. "Watch me!" Rebekah said. She removed her tunic and sat in the shallow water at the top of the rocks. Then she raised her hands and shouted "Wheeee!" as she slid down a smooth dip in one of the rocks and landed in the pool of water that reached just above her waist. "Your turn!" she shouted.

I followed her lead, and we did have a grand time sliding and splashing. The water was cool and refreshing. It was a lovely place to be. It just was not a river. As we dressed, I told her about the great river I knew.

"Rebekah," I said, "a river is flowing water, yes, but this is as if someone spilled their jug and the water dried ever so slowly. The river is so wide that a hundred men could lie down head to toe and not reach the other side. And it is so deep that if you stood a tent pole in the middle, you would not be able to see it for the water that rose high above it. A river makes a whooshing sound as the water goes by, and it is big enough to be the home of fish and crocodiles and the great hippopotamus."

"Hippotamatus?" she asked, trying to say the new word. "What is that?"

I told her about the great hippopotamus of the Nile. And I told her about crocodiles and the catfish. I told her about the bolti fish that my father would bring home for supper when the river began to recede, and he could catch them with his hands. I told her about the cats of Egypt and the red radishes and green lettuce and the sweet, juicy melons we bought at the market.

In our time together, I told Rebekah every story my mother had told me and every story I could think of about my life. Rebekah had an unlimited capacity for listening. She enjoyed hearing the stories over and over as much as I had from my mother. And though it was new for me to be the one telling the stories, I heard my mother's voice when I spoke, and that was a comfort.

Rebekah wanted to hear everything from the mundane details for fetching water at my old home to descriptions of the palace. And she loved hearing stories of Hallel and Daganyah and, of course, Sarah. Rebekah had not known, for example, that it had been Sarah's idea to plant the vineyards that her own father, Betuel, now tended. Nor had she even heard that the reason Abraham and Sarah departed from Haran was to follow Yah to a land that they would inherit.

She took in these stories, asked questions, and added her own details about what life in Haran had been like in her twelve years of life before my arrival. In my first months in Haran, one of her favorite stories was that of Addah and her son Yuval. Rebekah reveled at hearing Addah's love of song. "Do you suppose she really sang as beautifully as the morning birds?" she asked me. I told her I was sure of it, because that's what my mother had told me, and certainly her mother before, and her mother before, all the way back to Addah's own daughters.

Joseph, here you shall write the story of Addah. This way, her name can live on with mine, even though we never met. I shall like that very much. When I tell you how she was so special to me and Rebekah, I think you will understand the pride I feel in having her name written down for everyone to know.

Addah was blessed with a voice that could make the trees sway with happiness and the flower buds open so that they could hear more. She sang as beautifully as the morning birds. She sang to every one of her babies, of course, and to her children as they grew older. Addah bore two daughters and two sons who lived into adulthood. Shara had her mother's gift for song, and Shiri had a gift for storytelling. The two sisters often combined their loves and created stories in song. Her son Yaval was the first to gather sheep into herds and tend them and have them nearby so their milk and wool could be easily used. And her son Yuval, he was the mischievous one. Addah was most surprised that he had lived to sire eight grandchildren for her."

A mischievous child is not an easy one to care for. Joseph, I have met your brothers, and I know that some can be mischievous. This worries their poor mothers. Just think of all the babies who are buried in the ground before they even learn to walk on it. No mother wants to bury her child, Joseph. Yet this is more likely to happen to one who is ill-behaved or disregards rules, who believes he can do whatever he pleases and need not listen to his parents. Yet it is also this kind of child who clears pathways to new places.

Yuval was always getting hurt. He fell from trees, had bloody knees, and had been bitten by more creatures than Addah could count. He also was a child who brought her stones that sparkled in the sunlight and herbs she had never smelled to spice her stews. Yuval collected animal bones and long sticks, birds' feathers and nests, all kinds of fruits and grasses—anything he could find. He once brought a rock that looked as if it had a small lizard's footprint on the surface. Yuval used his collections to create new things. Two of the things he made were the lyre and the flute.

Think of it! Before Yuval, people had no musical instruments. And then thanks to Yuval, their entire tribe got to hear a new sound that had never been heard before. This was the part in the story that Rebekah always *did* stop and think of it. As did I. What a wonder to be the first people to ever hear a musical instrument!

Before that, they had enjoyed their singing and dancing very much. They were not lacking in expression or fulfillment. Addah's children would gather around her and fall asleep smiling if she sang a lullaby, or get up and dance if her song was filled with joy and glory. They stamped their feet and clapped their hands, and their awe and appreciation rose to the tops of the mountains. Their delight was daily, but it was most heightened when the moon was full and the women gathered and sang and danced in the light.

At Addah's request, Yuval made instruments for his mother and sisters, and for his father's other wife, Zillah, and Zillah's daughter Naama, who both joined them under the moon. As the sons married, their wives were brought into the circle of dancing beneath the full moon, and as the daughters married, they took the practice with them to their new tribes.

It was when I first told Rebekah this story that she had the idea that we should sing and dance under the moon like them, but it was not until I had repeated the story many times over months that she revealed that she was nervous to ask me. What if I said no? But she finally did ask. She asked me to create something new with her. She had both excitement and nervousness in her voice. She might not make new instruments, she said, but she would bring the new tradition to her tribe. Of course, I agreed to help her.

Rebekah did not ask her mother to join. She had long ago stopped expecting her mother's attention, but she invited Milkah, her grandmother. And she eagerly invited Auntie. Auntie was her father's second wife. If she had a name besides that, I never heard it. She was always called by her role: Wife, Mother, Auntie. Auntie seemed to be heavy with child most of the time but still made an effort to smile at Rebekah or share kind words with her. Rebekah confided in me that she wished Auntie were her mother but felt guilty for doing so. "But would it not be nice to have a mother who smiles? A mother who gives you warm bread and teaches you about healing herbs? Who combs your hair, or just sits beside you during the weaving?"

I agreed that such a mother was a wonderful blessing, and I ached for my own mother, who had done all these things with me. But we created many joyous occasions when the women gathered each month to sing and dance under the full moon. I brought my little drum and Milkah brought a drum that she said she had carried all the way from Ur. We wove baskets and put almond shells in them and shook them as we danced. Auntie's nursemaid, Metapelet, joined us, and as Auntie bore daughters, we grew to a small band of seven celebrants. It was during one of those nights of music under the moon that I formed the words to the song that we still sing to this day:

Sister, Mother, Daughter, and Friend
You shine with love from beginning to end
We give you our hopes, our dreams, and our pain
You keep them safe, until we meet again

That was how the years passed in Haran—from month to month. Of course, there were many things that happened when the moon was not full. We shared stories and grew gardens, drew water for our tribe and the sheep, spun wool, wove rugs and baskets, wandered in the sunshine, and prayed for rain in the season. But it was the celebrations under the full moon that we always looked forward to and reminisced about.

THE EIGHTH PARCHMENT

On the morning of the third new moon of Rebekah's fifteenth year, she woke with blood on her thighs. She said she had felt tight little pulls in her belly the last couple of days, but as this was her first blood, she did not realize the two went together. Rebekah had seen me taking care of my monthly blood for years already. She saw me shave, so that the blood would not get stuck in my hair. Saw me place wool between my legs and straw upon my mat each night, which I then took out in the morning. She did not mind taking on this extra work; she was eager to be called a woman, to have the body and experiences of a woman. I remembered feeling the same way when I watched my mother do these things each month.

To celebrate Rebekah becoming a woman, I brought out the little sack that I had carried with me from Egypt and had kept in the corner with the cushions all the while since then. When I had first arrived in Haran, there had been many nights when I had woken in tears and felt my way to the sack, just to touch and smell something that had belonged to my mother. But as the years washed away my sadness, I replaced those restless nights with comfortable ones, and visits to the sack were few.

I took out my mother's fine linen tunic, the one she had worn during our yearly trips to Hallel at the palace. Rebekah ran her fingers across the softness. "This has been gently folded in a sack for years," I said. "Today, it will begin a new life, just as you do, Rebekah. We shall sit together and make this tunic into two cases that can cover the small pillows that cradle our heads at night, so that we may sleep with the softness against our cheeks." Rebekah held the fabric to her face. It was a dark red, darker than her woman's blood, but a reminder of this special time.

"And," I continued, "today we shall put kohl around your eyes."

Rebekah nearly squealed with joy. She had long admired my mother's kohl stick. She knew of the care my mother used when putting it on her eyes and my own. Rebekah had nearly begged me to use it when she first saw it, but kohl was not the custom in Haran, and I did not wish to diminish anything that remained from my mother. Sharing the kohl with her on this day would certainly be meaningful and memorable for her.

I took out my mother's kohl. The last time I had held this stick in my hand was when I had applied the darkness to Mother's eyes just before she delivered Matanyah. Every person I had seen in Egypt had kohl around their eyes. It kept away sun and insects and was a constant reminder of Horus's healing powers, as well as a request that he heal us. It had been shocking to me when I left Egypt and saw for the first time a person without kohl around their eyes. How funny they looked! How strange! It was as unexpected as seeing a person with three arms or no nose.

Now I held the stick in my hand, smelled the familiar powdery, metallic scent of the kohl, and began tenderly applying it around Rebekah's eyes. I had become so accustomed to the naked eye that it was now the Egyptian style that looked almost funny to me. Except that with it, Rebekah's eyes reminded me of my mother's and my grandmother's and certainly of how my own eyes must have looked in that lifetime.

Rebekah sat tall as I applied the kohl as effortlessly as if I had not stopped doing it daily. Her eyes moved slightly, following my movement as I adorned her. I could feel her love in those looks and knew that she felt mine. In our lives, we laughed together as often as possible, consoled each other when necessary, helping each other always. And probably the best of all was knowing that her love for me was the same as mine for her. Painting her eyes was one of the many times I felt that. After I finished with her eyes, I put kohl on mine for the first time since leaving Egypt. In that way, I felt that I was not only giving Rebekah a celebration but that we were having one together.

The day of my first blood was not a day of celebration or joy. Nor was it a connection to the moon. But it was a connection to countless women before me and after me. My first blood came in the desert, before my time, and as a result of Mavheel's forced entrance into my body. There was nobody there to celebrate with me or console me. And when my blood did begin to flow regularly, even then it was not marked by anyone but myself and my fear of pregnancy. Rebekah's day was not marked by violence, which was already a blessing. But I wished to do whatever I could to make it a time of joy. I could see that I was succeeding.

Rebekah was still filled with excitement and wonder from seeing me with kohl and feeling her own when I confessed to her, "There is a story I have been withholding from you." Her surprise was plain to see.

"Why?" she asked. "I love to hear you tell stories! Why would you withhold one from me? What is it?"

"I withheld it because it is possibly the most special of all, and I knew that one day you would become a woman, and I would want to celebrate you with something special. I have been saving this story for this day. Would you like to hear it?" I asked her, already knowing the answer.

Rebekah nearly jumped with excitement and wrapped her arms around my neck. I fell over and we laughed. Though Rebekah remarked that the movement caused the blood to gush between her legs again, she was able to quickly compose herself to receive her gift without being distracted by the new feeling.

"You know, of course, that when I was a child, I visited my grandmother Hallel." Rebekah nodded. She loved to hear the stories of the palace and my time with my grandmother. "And you know," I continued, "that while I was there, Hallel told me stories of her life." Rebekah nodded. "What I shall tell you today," I said, "are the very words my grandmother spoke to me. That is, I shall not just tell you about her life, but the story of her life in her own words. For what I did not tell you was that on each of my visits to her, she not only told me her story but told it the exact same way each time and had me repeat it back to her, so that she could hear that I was telling it correctly.

"Everybody has a story to tell, a song to sing, a life that makes a difference in some way, large or small. Now, for the first time, Hallel's story will be told in Haran, the land where she was born to Sarai and Abram."

I got caught up in the wonder of being in Hallel's birthland, but Rebekah did not let me get distracted for long.

"Yes," Rebekah shouted. "Tell me!"

On that day, I composed myself and then began to recite the very words that went from my grandmother's mouth to my ears so many wonderful times. It was the first time I said the story aloud—except for when I repeated it to Hallel. Telling that story was a gift to Rebekah, yes. But it was also a gift to my grandmother, and even a gift to me. Just as now, Joseph, when I say her words to you, and you will write them in ink in the promised land, that is a gift to you, to me, to her, and to descendants we may never meet. Let us start a new scroll for this. Hallel will have her own scroll for her words! Hallelu Yah!

THE THIRD SCROLL

HALLEL'S STORY

THE NINTH PARCHMENT

I am Hallel. Daughter of Sarai. Daughter of Emkol. I was born in the land of Haran, a land named for my uncle Haran, brother of my father, Abram. Abram, Haran, and Nakhor were the sons of Terakh. Abram was the youngest. Terakh was also the father of Sarai. The mother of Abram was Mishni. Emkol's sons were Poel and Oved. Her daughters were Sarai and Yisca. Sarai was the youngest.

My mother, Sarai, was born in the city of Ur, across the great river of the north. There she lived in a mud-brick house but spent her days in the square, where she and her sister helped their mother sell the clay figurines that her father sculpted and baked each day in the large oven behind their home. My mother described these days as happy and easy. She remembered the feelings more than the details, for before she lost her first tooth, there was a fire that ended the life that she knew.

Sarai and Yisca were in the square when it happened. Emkol had been in the house with Poel and Oved when the flames swept into the house and scorched everything, even the roof, which fell onto the floor. All those nearby rushed to the sound. Mishni did not allow Yisca or Sarai to see their mother burnt and broken on the ground, even to say goodbye.

Terakh took his family to begin a new life. They took bread given to them by others and a donkey from a man who had been a frequent buyer of figurines, on the promise to bring back the donkey, or replace its value with new figurines upon their return to Ur. But they never did return. Terakh had heard of the trade route in Canaan and hoped he would find clay and an oven and buyers and make himself a rich man in a new land. But he got only as far as Aram, later called Haran, before he could travel no more.

Terakh and his family nearly starved on that long journey. They had only what they found to eat and nothing to trade. Mishni and my mother and Mother's sister collected fruits and barley that hardly sustained them. Sometimes they were able to catch a bird or hare. When they reached Haran, the king saw Yisca's beauty and wished to marry her. He gave Terakh a fine bride price, which included land, flocks, manservants, and maidservants, and a large marriage feast.

From that day, my mother never saw her sister again. But she ate. They all did. And they were grateful for the food, but they needed more. Tents and mats, pots and jugs, a wagon, blankets . . . they needed everything. It was my father, Abram, who got those things, for Terakh spent his time chasing down clay and ovens. He was gone many days and even months at a time and never came back with tools for his trade. Finally, he just never came back.

A lot happened in Terakh's absence. Not only did my father arrange for their needs to be met, so did Mishni. She missed Yisca terribly and did not want to lose my mother Sarai. As soon as my mother reached womanhood, Mishni saw to it that she married my father so that they all might stay together. They continued to prosper in Haran. My mother and father and grandmother, my uncles and their wives, learned shepherding. Their flocks grew; their wealth grew. And Sarai instructed Abram on growing a vineyard.

"Here there is good soil for growth," Sarai said. "The barley grows in fields as wide as the river, and the people use it for bread and beer. They will pay a higher price for wine. In three years' time, we shall have grapes enough to eat and to drink."

"How do you know such things?" my father asked her. "From the women," my mother stated. "Yisca and Mishni and I, wherever we went, whomever we passed on this journey, we spoke with the women. We shared our wisdom." And so, my father, Abram, planted a vineyard, and their little tribe tended to that along with the sheep.

Life in Haran was different from the city. There was always work to be done, but in the city, my father had been training as a sculptor, always with his hands in clay, his father's instructions in his ears. In Haran, his hands were in the soil and the wool, his ears unclogged by his father's voice, and he began to hear a different voice. Abram came to know that voice as Yah, the Great Creator. Just as he and his father and brothers had created figurines from clay, Yah had created him. Well, not him, but the very first people, who then made more people, and eventually Abram. This Great Creator sculpted the hills, the valleys, the rivers . . .

everything. And so my father and mother, and their whole little tribe, took Yah as their god.

Yah brought the rain and the sun, and, indeed, in three years' time, the first crop of grapes was ready for eating and drinking. More workers were hired to help with the harvest. The wine that flowed was a blessing to our whole camp. And the wine was not even the biggest blessing. The biggest blessing was me. My mother had buried her blood from lost pregnancies many times. Finally, a baby grew and grew for nine moons, and when I emerged from her womb, she proclaimed: "Hallelu Yah!"

I heard Yah praised in that way many times. When the grapes ripened, when lambs were born, when new wells were dug. On and on we praised Yah, for Yah was the Creator of all our abundance, of everything. Even the night that Mishni died, I heard my mother and father whisper the words *Hallelu Yah*. For whether we are joyful or whether we are sad, Yah is still good.

One month after my grandmother's death, my mother told my father it was time to leave Haran.

"How do you know this?" he asked. "Has Yah spoken to you?"

"The women have spoken to me," she said. "They have told me of the jealousy here. Our tribe and our abundance have gotten attention. Others want it and will come after it. We have more than we need. We can stay here with Haran and Nakhor and continue to fuel the jealousy with our combined wealth, or we can go on another great journey. Was it not a blessing to travel from Ur to here? Will Yah not continue to bless us if we move on?"

Thus, my father went to ask Yah these very questions. His ears, which were now accustomed to the messages in the silence, brought him this: *Go, go from your land, your birthplace, your father's house, to a place that I shall show you. I shall make of you a great nation, and I shall bless you.* And so we did go.

My father Abram took his wife, Sarai, his brother's son Lot, all the wealth he had acquired, and, of course, the soul my parents had made in Haran: their living daughter. Me. This came as no surprise to me, for Yah had spoken with me all my short life. Not in my ears, but in my dreams. I had always dreamt of Egypt, though I did not know its name at the time.

I had dreamt of smooth palace paths, large, painted walls, colorful gardens, people everywhere, and all of them with big, black eyes. Many were wearing jewels that I was surprised I could even imagine, for I had never seen such things other than in my dreams. Sometimes I woke from these dreams and immediately pressed my fingers to my nose, for inside my nostrils, it smelled as if there were a field of flowers, yet when I touched my face, nothing was there.

When my mother and Yah spoke to my father, I knew my journey to this place of wonder would begin. We traveled south. We camped often and moved when the flocks were ready. I enjoyed meeting other travelers and seeing new places, but none of them matched my dreams. And when we arrived in Shechem and Yah blessed my father and assigned that land to his seed, I felt sorrow even as an altar was built. This was not the land I expected. But from there, it only got worse. We moved farther into the desert and into famine.

I had not known hunger in my lifetime, but my parents, Abram and Sarai, had and did not wish to do so again. We continued south, toward Egypt, which was rumored to have more food than could be eaten by all the people in the land. Before we arrived, my father remarked on my mother's beauty and pleaded with her to proclaim herself only his sister, not also his wife, so that should the king wish to wed her, my father's life would be spared. She agreed to this plan, and together they made one for me: I was to travel with Lot from then on. Even though we had not yet married, we would soon, as my womanhood was approaching. Until then, he would care for me.

My mother was, indeed, desired for the king's harem, and my father received a large bride price for her. He and his men were kept busy managing the wealth. My father saw this as his wealth, exclusively, and separated his flocks from those he shared with Lot, putting my betrothed in charge of what they shared. When Lot saw my father's abundance, he approached the palace with me in hand and received a bounty of his own.

I was glad to be sold to the king, for I not only knew this was the fulfillment of my dreams, I also expected to be reunited with my mother. Alas, that did not happen. As I was bathed and perfumed, oiled and painted, I was separate from the other women of the harem, as she must have been, as well. I later learned that it was only the women who had already lain with the king who mingled, but the new women spent months in isolated preparation.

When I reached my first blood, the women who had been softening and adorning me came to prepare me for my first visit to the king. They told me what would be physically required of me in order to conceive a child, hopefully a boy . . . a prince. I was afraid. Afraid I would be hurt. Afraid I would disappoint the king and be punished. But I held my head tall as I nearly flowed into the king's chamber as I had been taught. My very presence there was responsible for Lot's riches. I had reason to be proud, and I would not forget that, despite a fear that was so strong that it prevented me from noticing the beauty of the king's private section of the palace.

To everyone's great surprise, the king screamed when he saw me. I put my hand to my mouth, thinking the sound had issued from me, but it had not. I felt my hair, my face, my clothing, my jewels. They were all in place, and I knew, from the flattened copper mirror that had allowed me to see my reflection when I was fully prepared, that I looked beautiful. His courtiers rushed to him, attempting to remedy the problem they could also not detect. But the king did not speak to them, he spoke directly to me.

"Your face, your skin, your shape is not that of an Egyptian," he said. "What is your birthplace? Who are your people?"

I was not instructed on speaking to a king, but I could not remain silent when he asked me these questions. "My father was a wandering Aramean. I am the daughter of Abram and Sarai, who come from the other side of the great river in the north, and my birthplace is Haran." I answered.

"'Out!" he yelled. "Out!"

I was shuffled immediately back to my room. I did not know why. I was both disappointed and relieved at once. It was not long before I learned the reason for the pharaoh's outburst, and my feelings turned to fear and gratitude. Since being separated from my parents, I had neither seen nor heard of them. But that night, I learned that some time ago, the pharaoh's own house had been struck with plagues due to my mother's pleas with Yah that he not take her to wife. I looked so similar to my mother,

Sarai, that the king wanted me out of his chamber immediately, never to return. Never to bring plagues upon him.

I learned that the pharaoh had banished my father and mother from Egypt. I, alone, was not to receive the same fate but instead was to be removed from the harem and married to a governor. I never did see my mother in the harem, and thus . . . the ending of her story is one I do not and shall not know.

But my story will not be such, and at least her beginnings will live on through me. For I have told my story to all of my daughters and all of my granddaughters. I bore two sons and five daughters to my husband, Moshel. The sons both died before I was able to hear their first words, but all my daughters lived on. I gave each one a name that honored Yah. Eliyah, Miyah, Priyah, Rayah, and Daganyah. The oldest three were married with fine dowries to men of the palace, and they bore children who visit me often.

The fourth, Rayah, became a priestess in the temple of Hathor. And the youngest, Daganyah, became the wife of a grain farmer outside the walls. It is her I miss the most, for we see each other the least.

In Haran and Canaan, my duties had been to the flocks, the food, the weaving, and the water. In the harem, my duty had been beauty. And as the wife of a governor, my only duty was his pleasure—which sometimes was also mine.

And so I spent my days exploring the pathways of the palace, admiring the paintings, buying anything I chose from the markets, and listening to the laughter of my children. It was the life I dreamt. Yah had shown me I would live in Egypt. It was a life of abundance. Endless food and sweets and the great river with its bounty and beauty. My feet are cradled in soft shoes, and my body draped in the finest linen. I thank Yah at the arrival of every new grandchild, new year, new moon, and new morning for reaching another day to live this life.

Now, I am an old woman, and Yah shows me dreams of the desert. Shall I return there? I think not. But I believe my seed will, for this was a promise that Yah made to my father—that the land would belong to him and his seed. I know he has likely fathered other children by now, yet Yah shows me these dreams. This is how I know that I shall return to the desert, even if only in the form of my name on a tongue. So, remember this story well, this story of your grandmother Hallel, and her mother, Sarai, and her mother, Emkol, in case you are the one to bring these names to the promised land.

THE FOURTH SCROLL

THE TENTH PARCHMENT

That was the story that my grandmother recited to me and had me recite back to her month after month on our visits. It is the story I told my dear Rebekah on the occasion of her first blood. Although it was just the two of us in the tent, it felt, to both of us, as if we were embraced by all the women who had come before us. Most of all, my beloved grandmother Hallel.

After sharing Hallel's story with Rebekah, I, too, began to dream of the desert. I wondered aloud that it must be because we repeated that story to each other over and over after the first telling. Rebekah insisted that my own dreams must be as prophetic as Hallel's. She began to talk of leaving Haran and going to the land promised to Abram. We began to amuse ourselves by imagining taking a journey like that of Sarai and Abram's. I believed it was all in jest, but Rebekah argued that my dreams held a message from Yah.

You are a dreamer, too, Joseph. Yah speaks to us through our dreams, but we do not always understand right away. I did not immediately understand the meaning of my dreams, but Rebekah did.

We learned that it was Rebekah who was right on the day that Eliezer came to our compound. Rebekah had been the first to see him. She had been drawing water for the sheep when a tall man trailed by ten camels and two young men came into view. She watched them for most of the morning as they got closer. She thought of how thirsty they must be, having traveled the dry, dusty hills for so long, and she offered to bring them all water.

As soon as the camels and servants finished drinking and the man himself had quenched his thirst from Rebekah's ladle, Eliezer unpacked a satchel from one of the camels. Inside was a small, golden nose ring and two heavy gold armbands. He offered them to Rebekah, and she accepted.

"Tell me," he said. "Whose daughter are you? And is there room in your father's home for us to spend the night?"

Rebekah answered his question plainly. "I am the daughter of Betuel, the son of Milkah, whom she bore to Nakhor. There is plenty of straw and feed and also room to spend the night." While it was rare to have traders or caravans pass by, it did happen sometimes, and it was the custom of the household to invite them to wash their hands and feet and have a meal and stay the night. Rebekah was extending that same hospitality and was surprised by Eliezer's strong reaction, for as soon as she finished answering him, he bowed and thanked Yah.

"Blessed is Yah, the god of my master, Abraham, who did not give up on His faithfulness to my master, for this god has guided me to the house of my master's brother."

Upon hearing this, Rebekah ran home. She immediately found me in the garden where I had been picking the ripe cucumbers. "Deborah, Deborah!" She was panting from her run, but it was her new jewelry that caught my attention more than her labored breathing. "Deborah, a man has come, he was sent here by a man he called Abraham and said was kin! It must be the same Abram, Hallel's father!" I could not believe my ears. Could this be real?

"Rebekah, do not jest," I said when I could finally regain myself.

"I do not!" she exclaimed. "Just look at me. Look at these ornaments." She showed off her jewelry while telling me of the encounter. "Clearly he comes searching for a wife," she said. Yes, it was clear. And he did not come a moment too soon. It had been three years since Rebekah had entered womanhood. We had celebrated, yet her transformation had gone unnoticed by Metuyeshet and Betuel, and no wedding arrangements had been made. Rebekah and I were secretly glad, for we both harbored a deep fear that her marriage would mean our separation. We made no attempts to bring that upon ourselves.

Though Rebekah's womanhood was unknown to her parents, Lavan, merely one year younger than his sister, had taken quite an interest. More than once he had surprised her by grabbing her from behind and rubbing himself against her until his desire was fulfilled and he slept in the sun while she ran back to the tent. We knew it would not be long before he wanted to take more liberties than that. We were happily surprised when Eliezer brought this other possibility. Even our fear of being separated faded with the appearance of this miracle.

It was plain on Lavan's face when he saw his sister decked in gold that he understood that he could either have her to release his urges, or he could release her to another man and have great wealth. He ran out to greet Eliezer. "Come in, come in, praise your god! Why do you stand outside when I have made room for you in my home and have a place for your camels?"

After washing, Eliezer was invited to sit for a meal with Betuel and Lavan. Food was brought and drinks were served. Rebekah, Milkah, and I stood just outside the tent, listening to the men. Before any food was eaten, Eliezer insisted that he state his purpose, and so I got to hear the words directly from his mouth.

"I am Abraham's servant," he began. Of course, I had believed Rebekah when she promised she spoke the truth, but to hear them directly from this man's mouth—that he had just days ago been with Abraham—I could only praise Yah. Quietly I whispered, "Hallelu Yah." And though nobody else could hear my words, I could hardly hear their speech due to my concentrated praise. But I heard and saw enough. Eliezer had asked Yah to deliver a sign when he came upon the right woman. Yah had answered his prayer, and now he wished to bring Rebekah back with him, to marry Isaac, the son of Haran's brother Abraham. He would not even eat of the specially prepared meal until he heard an answer.

Betuel responded, but without answer. "This matter was decreed by Yah. We cannot tell you whether it's bad or good." Lavan repeated his father's words, sitting tall as if he, too, were the head of the clan. There was a long silence. Betuel began to eat from the feast, and Lavan followed his father's movements. Eliezer still did not eat.

Lavan rose from his seat and walked out of the tent to where Rebekah and I were standing, toes on the rug, watching and waiting. Lavan took her by the elbow and brought her to the center of the tent. "Here is Rebekah before you," he said. "Take her and go and let her be a wife to your master's son as Yah has spoken." When Abraham's servant heard those words, he bowed low to the ground before Yah. Lavan was indifferent to this show of commitment, but he was pleased by the show of wealth that came next.

Eliezer opened his sack and put more gold bracelets on Rebekah's arms, such that when she moved she sounded like walking music. I thought of Yuval and Addah and of how Rebekah had now created a new instrument—herself. I would tell her of that thought later, and she would smile with delight. In that moment, we were not free to talk, as she was still receiving gifts. Gold bands for her ankles and a cloak of fine linen cloth that I had not seen the likes of since leaving Egypt. Even before I touched it, I could tell that the weave was close, and the dye was expertly done. The blue was the color of the sky on the brightest of days. Surely this would be the garment she was to wear at the wedding.

Eliezer excused himself from the tent to gather gifts from large woven baskets that were waiting with the camels. "Those are for the bride," he said, "but was it not this family that created such a bride for my master's son? Thus, he has sent gifts for you, as well." Eliezer made a great show of presenting jars of beer and wine to Betuel and Lavan. He took out hard cheeses wrapped in cloths that themselves were beautiful to behold.

Colorful rugs and soft pillows were brought out. Each gift that emerged from the baskets was met with an approving eye and nod from Betuel, followed by Lavan imitating his father. Finally, a small but heavy sack was removed from the bottom of the basket. Even without opening it, I could plainly see that it was filled with coins. Betuel reached out his arm and accepted the sack from Eliezer.

"Congratulations!" he said. "Your master has found a wife for his son. We shall eat of this feast in celebration." And so they did. We were given plates of the stew that had been prepared and cheeses that had come from Abraham. We ate them outside our tent while the men ate and drank and eventually fell asleep with full bellies.

Rebekah and I could hardly sleep with the anticipation of all that needed to be done. In the morning we would begin to pack baskets of dried meats and cheeses and fruits and barley cakes for the journey. Our rugs would need to be beaten clean and rolled for the journey, the tent would need to come down; that would be last, of course. Another basket would be packed with garments, now including the light blue one that would be for the wedding day.

Between discussion of our preparations and fantasies of what it might be like to meet Abraham and his son, we fell asleep long after the moon began to set in the sky, probably while still talking with one another. It was a short sleep, for at the first hint of sunlight, I sat straight up and shouted, "Sarai!" Rebekah startled awake.

"What?" she asked, having not heard my word but only my sound.

"Sarai," I repeated. "Eliezer kept speaking of his master, Abraham, and the son, Isaac, and so that is who we thought about. And we have forgotten to think about Sarai. Rebekah! What a miracle that we shall meet Sarai! I shall tell her of Hallel, tell her of her daughter, tell her she was not made one of the king's wives, after all. Tell her she grew to be a regal woman of stature and many descendants. Oh, Rebekah!"

We were so filled with joy that we had no room for any tiredness that might have been left from the night before. We jumped to action, merrily dancing through the tent, gathering our goods to the sound of Rebekah's new gold bands twinkling as they touched each other. This was how Metuyeshet and Lavan found us when the sun was shining through the peaks of the hills. Metuyeshet was wearing gold bands and a belt of fine purple linen. As usual, she had not left her tent last night, but clearly Eliezer had found her and bestowed these gifts.

"Eliezer wishes to leave now," Lavan said.

"I asked for him to allow you ten days to prepare," Metuyeshet said. These were the most words I had ever heard from Rebekah's mother. She added even more. "But he wishes to leave now, to return to Abraham and complete his errand. He says there is no need to prepare. His wife, called Sarah, has died and her tent will become yours. You need not bring anything. He has food and drink for the journey. Will you return with him?"

I saw Rebekah's face fall at the news of Sarah. Mine did, as well. We had thought of her only last night, and now, so quickly, she was gone. But that news was not the reason for her mother's appearance. There was a question at hand, and she repeated it. "Will you return with him now?" To which Rebekah answered that she would.

Rebekah did not ask me if I was ready, or even look to me. She was ready. Her parents and brother, grandmother and auntie blessed her to be the mother of myriads of sons who would seize the gates of their foes. And as they did so, I was reminded that I was there because I had been bought. I was Rebekah's nursemaid, but I belonged to Betuel. I was not asked if I was ready to go. I would not be asked. As I carried Rebekah's satchel that contained her gown for the wedding, I did not even know if I would be allowed to go. My love for Rebekah—and hers for me—and my excitement about meeting Abraham had distracted me from this.

I stood beside a camel, holding Rebekah's belongings. I would be ready to either hand them to her or carry them for her. While I waited to learn which it would be, I gazed at the compound. This land had been my home. I had learned to talk as they did, wandered the hills, drank the grapes, breathed the stink and the sweetness. Mostly I had grown from an orphaned child into a happy woman. All of it with Rebekah, in Rebekah's love. And now what? Would I hold my love for her here while she went to her betrothed? Or was I parting from this home and accompanying her as her nursemaid?

I said a silent goodbye to Milkah and Auntie, with whom I had danced under the moon so many times. I imagined them giving me a blessing, too. *May Yah always guide you and protect you, Deborah*, they said in my thoughts. I said a silent goodbye to the goats who had given us milk, and to the garden that still held slightly more flavor than weeds. *May Yah always sustain and nourish you, Deborah*, I imagined they said. I swelled with the kindness of these words but became cold when my gaze fell on Rebekah and I could not gather the words for a silent goodbye. I could do nothing more than stand as still as a stone next to the camel.

Rebekah came and, with Eliezer's help, sat atop the beast. She reached her hand down toward me. She would carry her satchel, she would not need me. I tried to speak, to say a real goodbye, not a silent one, but no words could part my lips. But Rebekah's mouth opened, and her words were, "Will you ride with me, Deborah? Or do you prefer to walk?"

"What?" I asked.

"Will you ride with me?" she asked again. "Or would you rather walk? I do not mind walking. Eliezer says the journey is a few days, but my legs are not tired—we are just beginning!" She was overflowing with excitement. And she was speaking as if my coming along was obvious. For a moment I remembered the night before, when it had been obvious to me, too. I was not able to match her joy, but I was able to manage a few words.

"I shall walk," I said.

"Very well," she said, "we shall walk. Eliezer, I would like to walk."

"No, no," I quickly shouted, before he could help her down. Then in a more proper voice I said, "You stay there. I will walk beside you and the camel."

Thus, we began, and thus we continued for the entire first day of the journey. There were large, sheep-like clouds, soft and white, providing shade so that the sun did not blaze on us. My feet began to hurt toward the evening, but I did not notice often. My attention was, and had been the whole day, on fear. Fear of losing Rebekah. Fear of what might be to come on this journey. Fear of the reminder of my status. Fear of what that might mean when we got to Abraham. If we got to Abraham. I tried to imagine how Rebekah might bless me if we had needed to part, for surely it would have been a beautiful blessing. But my thoughts kept turning to the fear. By the time our sleeping mats were laid out beside the road, I was as covered in fear as I was in darkness.

"What is wrong? You look like a child under the gaze of a scorpion. What is it, Deborah? You are scaring me. Speak to me," Rebekah insisted. We were close enough to the men's sleeping mats to see them but far enough for them not to hear us. But I could not speak. I could only cry. I wished to wail, but for fear that we would be heard, I covered my mouth with my hands. My body shook, and I could not stop it. My tears covered first my face and then Rebekah's hands as she tried to wipe them away with no success. She took my whole head in her arms, and I sobbed into her chest until I had no strength left for anything but lying still and staring at the stars.

Finally, I turned to Rebekah, who was now looking as scared as I felt, though not knowing why, and I said, "We should not have come." I do not think she could have been more surprised if the moon had fallen out of the sky. In her quiet, I let more words spill out of my mouth.

"We should not have come," I repeated. "We do not have enough food. We should have put dried meats and dried fruits in our sacks. They are the smallest and easiest to carry and the quietest to eat. Barley cakes create too much noise when bitten. We would not be able to carry enough for months, but we could eat a little as we went along and still have enough to keep our strength. Perhaps we should have brought Lavan. For as much as he took his pleasure from you, he would make sure you were still whole when we arrived; he would not forfeit his new riches.

"But Eliezer will not allow anything to happen to you, either," I continued, not even knowing from word to word what I would say next. "For then he will not be serving his master. But I can be defiled. He will come for me in the night, he or one of his men will."

I had not told Rebekah the details of the forced nights with Mavheel. I had done my best to forget them, and I had done well most of the time until this new journey began. "Listen to me, Rebekah. I could not always keep the man away, but there was a time when I opened my mouth and heard my mother's voice come from my throat. She said, 'May you be covered in the itch and have no hands to scratch,' and that night he walked away from me without touching me. It worked only one time, but you must remember that, Rebekah. Do you remember those words?"

"Yes, Deborah, yes," she said to me. By then, she was crying, even though my tears had stopped, having been replaced by urgent whispers. "But I will not need to say that," she reminded me, "for they will not wish to bring a defiled bride to Isaac. And Deborah, I am so sorry that happened to you. It will not happen now. This man is not Mavheel; he comes from Abraham. He is on an errand from Yah, and he is devoted."

I shook my head no. My dear, sweet Rebekah, always filled with excitement for life, open to the world and adventure. She did not know the danger. While I was shaking my head, she kissed my wet eyes. She dried my face with her sleeve, and I heard the music of her new gold bangles.

"I had the coins from my mother," I said, "that Tanqo sewed into my clothes. Mavheel never discovered where I kept them hidden. With that silver, I was able to buy some peaceful nights. No, they were not peaceful, but they were without pain. Until the silver ran out. Now we have your bracelets, and surely they will buy us some nights . . . that is . . . buy me some nights if you will allow me the bracelets to trade. We have no seeds, another reason we should not have left so soon. The silphium seeds from Tanqo at least gave me the miracle of not carrying the child of that monster."

"Deborah?" Rebekah asked me, her voice soft and calm. "Let us be with Yah. Breathe Yah in, just as you taught me; we shall do it together. *Yhhhh*. Now, breathe yourself into Yah. *Whhhh*. Again, *Yhhhh. Whhhh*." We kept doing that until I was able to settle enough to hear her words. "Do you believe that I am safe?" she asked. I answered that I did. I did believe she was safe, for she was the bride. "Then I shall protect your body with my own," she said. And she laid her body on top of mine. "Now you are safe," she whispered into my ear. "We are safe. We shall sleep and be safe. And you may have every one of my bangles if you need them, but you will not need them."

I did not fall asleep right away, but when Rebekah's breaths slowed and she became heavier on me, yet soft and still, I allowed my eyes to close and my fists to open, and I slept. And she was right. We both passed what was left of the night safely. Our journey continued without event. Except seeing the river. It was not the Nile, but it was a real river, and I was so comforted to see one again. Of course, Rebekah was overjoyed when she saw the amount of water. We camped by the river the night before crossing, which allowed us to sleep with the sounds of its flow in our ears.

Once the morning light came, we were quickly on our way again. During the days of travel, Eliezer made clear that he wished to travel as far as we could as fast as we could to arrive as soon as we could. We stopped only briefly each day when the sun was the highest and hottest. The men raised a small shade, and we ate a small meal—small but sufficient—and then Eliezer directed us to return to the path.

For six days we traveled like this, without any trouble, and for six nights, we slept just as safely. With Rebekah's help, I was able to trust that Yah would allow us to be unharmed, and I could dream of meeting Abraham. I was sad that Sarah would not know of Hallel's story, but I would tell Abraham, and that would be a blessing.

THE ELEVENTH PARCHMENT

When we awoke on our seventh day of travel, Eliezer informed us that if we encountered no obstacles, we would arrive at his master's camp before nightfall. My excitement was uncontainable. I leapt into action, packing our pallets from the night and exiting the tent to load the carts.

When I stepped into the daylight, I saw what I could not perceive in the dusk of our arrival the night before. The valley was jumping with color that would make a rainbow embarrassed to appear for fear of looking dull by comparison. The yellows, purples, and greens of the flowers and plants around us took my breath away. Certainly, I was standing in a land where none other than Yah had planted the seeds of this beauty. The delight made me dizzy, and I lay on the ground for a moment to soak up the fragrance and fertility of the land.

But I could not stay there for long. My heart beat with the anticipation of meeting Isaac—and his father, my dear grandmother's father. Abraham. What would he look like? Sound like? Would he grant me an audience? I was just Rebekah's nursemaid as far as he would know. The questions would not stop swirling in my ears unless my body was in motion. I helped prepare the breakfast, load the carts, and water the animals. Anything to get us closer to leaving. When we finally did leave, I was so jittery that I wished to ride with Rebekah on one camel. Holding on to her would hopefully steady me.

Rebekah agreed, and we climbed the sturdy camel that walked alongside Eliezer. We sat on a well-woven brown blanket on the camel's furry back, Rebekah in front and me holding her waist, and rode that way all morning.

"What do you think he will think of me?" I asked her.

"Isaac?" she asked.

"No, Abraham," I said, "but I suppose Isaac as well." In all the stories from my mother and grandmother, I had never heard the name Isaac. Of course, he had been born after the last time Hallel saw her mother, so she would not have known about him. I had been so focused on meeting the father Hallel had spoken of that I had nearly forgotten that the whole reason for this journey and destination was Rebekah's betrothal to Isaac.

"I think he will think you are beautiful and wise, kind and loving," she said. "I think it would be nothing but impossible for him to think otherwise."

I laughed. "That is what *you* think of me," I said, though I still found comfort in her words.

"Yes," she responded. "I think of you that way because you *are* that way. Shall I go on? I think Abraham will think you are a great storyteller. I think he will think you know Yah, because the spirit of Yah is always shining through you. If he is as wise as you have said he is, then I think he will rejoice in your very existence and love you like his own granddaughter—which you are."

Rebekah paused. I knew her thoughts. I was not his granddaughter, but his daughter's granddaughter. And now she, who was younger than I, was to marry Abraham's son. Not his great-grandson, or even his grandson, but his son.

"Will he be so old?" she asked. "Shall I be Isaac's second or third wife? Have I come merely to give him more children and make him feel like a young man once again?"

"He is not old." I reminded her of what Eliezer had told us. "You are to be Isaac's first wife, brought from his family so that he would not have an idol worshipper in his tent, but someone who knows Yah. My beloved grandmother was your betrothed's older sister by so many years that she herself could have been his mother . . . or perhaps grandmother. It is Abraham who is old, not Isaac." We rode in silence for a long while after that, each of us imagining the men we would meet upon our arrival later that day.

We smelled Father Abraham's wealth before we heard it, heard it before we saw it. As the wind drifted in our direction, Eliezer stopped our little caravan and addressed us. "That is the multitude of my master's flocks," he said, referring to the aroma and bleating of what was surely hundreds of sheep. He was not boasting, merely freely showing his pride in his master's possessions, which he surely helped care for and increase.

And indeed, not long after, when the sight of the flocks followed the sound, we saw the abundance. The sheep covered the hillsides and grazed peacefully under watchful eyes of men and dogs. We had thought Betuel's flock to be large, but what we saw before us was like seeing his animals four times over in the same place. The men wore long tunics like Eliezer's, with a skin of water and a slingshot hanging around their waists. The dogs were hard workers and also brushed sleek and clean.

It was the dogs that greeted us first. Eliezer bent and laughed and petted each in turn, addressing it by name and thanking it for the welcome. The strong shepherds followed the dogs and welcomed Eliezer just as warmly—though without licking him. One shepherd stepped forward.

"All has been well in your absence," he said. Then he looked at Rebekah. His eyes grew wide, then he averted them. "Is this the maiden for Isaac?"

"Yes," Eliezer responded. "Run ahead and tell the master of our arrival. He will want to prepare a feast." Eliezer paused for just a moment, then gave the shepherd a longer answer to his question. "She is from Abraham's brother's family. She is kind, wise, and generous. Yah brought me to her. And as you can see, her beauty needs no announcing." The shepherd blushed and ran off, and we continued on our way. I tightened my grip around Rebekah's waist, nervous with anticipation. Surely, we would see tents soon.

In fact, as we topped the next hill, we looked down the other side at a lush vineyard followed by a compound with more than ten tents. The cooking area was easy to identify, with smoke from a small fire rising and women bustling around it and in and out of the tent beside it. There was a well with a small fence around it and a trough of water not far. Naked babies were playing in the sunshine while older ones were making themselves useful carrying things that could not be identified from our distance.

The sun was already on its way down the sky, but it was plain to see that we would arrive long before it hid behind the hills. We were nearly there. I thought, perhaps, Eliezer would say a few words, but he looked as excited to return as we were to arrive, and we continued onward.

As our camel stepped off the path at the bottom of the hill and onto the trail that crossed through the field, I spotted a man sitting quietly. His back was to us, but I could see that he was communing with Yah. Do not ask me how, but it is not difficult to identify a man in prayer. "Surely this must be Isaac," I thought. For not only was he free to excuse himself from any work, but his tunic was cleaner and fancier than those of Eliezer and the shepherds. I put my finger against my thumb and asked Yah if it was Isaac. I quickly got an answer: Yes. A warmth filled me as a smile crept through my body. I had not prayed like that since the last time I had journeyed.

I squeezed Rebekah. She turned to look at me and then followed my gaze. Together we observed this man who was to be her husband. There was not much to see, as he sat there a long while, not moving. His back was to us, but we could see that he was wide. Eventually he rose, and we could see that he was wide and short. He lifted his face and hands to the sky, and we were close enough to hear his voice, though not distinguish his words. Finally, he turned around and faced us. I gasped with surprise, then quickly covered my mouth with my hands. In so doing, I released Rebekah from the grasp I had held around her waist the whole ride, and she fell off the camel.

Oh, it was a sight! Rebekah crumpled, shocked and dusty on the ground beside the camel who, relieved of a load, flexed its muscles and quivered with freedom. Eliezer's face was covered with horror. What had just happened to the bride he had brought back? He helped her up and began to brush the dust off her with his hands.

"Isaac did not see you," he said, whether to Rebekah or himself was unclear. "He will not notice any dust on your clothing when you approach. It will be fine. You are a daughter of his father's tribe. This is what is important. And you are kind and generous. You will be kind and generous to Isaac, I am certain. Now, you wait here. I shall greet Isaac and go on to my master's tent and tell him we are here."

Eliezer rushed toward the largest tent, and Rebekah and I looked at each other. Oh, how I love the joy in her! She was able to stifle her laugh only long enough for Eliezer to be far enough away not to hear. Then we fell into each other's arms and laughed about her fall from the camel until our breath left us and our sides hurt. Only then did she ask me what happened.

"I saw Isaac," I said, for not only was I already certain that it was Isaac, but Eliezer had confirmed it. "I was so surprised that I covered my mouth and forgot to hold you on the camel. Rebekah, I have seen a face like his only one time. I was young. Three or four years old, perhaps. Mother and I were walking to the well when a woman we had never seen asked for our help. She had come from inside the palace walls, but she did not look refined or robust. She had a baby in her arms. The baby was silent and still, yet there was breath in him that he worked to continue.

"The woman said that her baby was three days old but had not suckled once. It was plain to see why. His tongue would not fit in his mouth; he could not have had room for a breast to suckle. In addition, his eyes, which he had no strength to open, were almond shaped, tilted up, and wide apart. I must tell you, he was the most beautiful baby I had ever seen. His face was flat and smooth, and even like this it was plain to see that his soul was as sweet as honey. But he would not live through the night. My mother told me, after she directed the woman to the home of the midwife, that sometimes babies were born like this, but they always died shortly after.

"Rebekah," I continued, "that Isaac has lived to be a man, and a man who speaks with Yah, it is clear to me that Yah has favored your betrothed. Isaac purely beams with the light of Yah. He is blessed. You are blessed."

After living with Isaac for a short while, we learned many things that you already know about your grandfather, Joseph. He is kind, loving, and talks to Yah. When he speaks, his words can be difficult for us to understand, and he has to work harder than we do to move his mouth and his voice, but he does well. His eyes have always turned in, and this makes it difficult for him to see what is around him, but he looks closely and sees what he needs to see, and feels what he cannot. His arms and legs seem a bit too short for his body, and, indeed, it took him longer than most to learn to use them, but he has.

But we did not know all that yet. In that moment, we just knew how blessed Isaac was by Yah. Rebekah embraced me. "Thank you, Deborah," she whispered in my ear. And then she released my body and took my hand, raising it above her head and mine and shouted, "Thank you, Yah! Hallelu Yah!"

Eliezer returned and gathered us and the camels. We chose to walk the rest of the way, even though I was not sure if my feet would remain steady on the approach to Abraham. I need not have worried, as we were directed to a tent that would be Rebekah's. "Everything you need is here," Eliezer said as he left us. "The wedding will take place at sundown and the feast will follow."

That is the story of how your grandmother and I came to this land. I shall tell you of the wedding when we next meet. We shall begin a new piece of parchment. It is fitting, for I was, once again, beginning a new life. But do not put this one away yet. I shall admire it a bit more. Your writing is neat and careful and has improved greatly. You are a skilled scribe, Joseph. I am pleased.

THE TWELFTH PARCHMENT

We were taken to a large tent, Sarah's tent, that would become ours. It was true that we did not need to bring anything from Haran. The floor of the tent was already covered in beautifully woven rugs of red and orange. There were large purple cushions placed on one side for sitting and eating, and a large, soft sleeping mat with blankets adjacent to it on another side. There were several woven baskets with Sarah's worldly goods.

She had three day-cloaks to choose from and a fancy tunic that I am sure came from her time in the harem. It was bright pink with golden threads woven into it. She had a water jug and a wool spindle, clay bowls and cups, and even two golden scarabs. There was more, but we did not have time to look with leisure through these inherited treasures. There would be a wedding shortly.

The preparations were fast and efficient. A pot of herbed water was boiling alongside the larger pail of well water that had been carried to our new tent. The smell of myrrh and lavender permeated the air. A bottle of olive oil with frankincense had been left on the cushions, and I used it to anoint Rebekah, rubbing it deeply into her skin. Before I could take the bottle to her hair, she stopped me and insisted on using the other half of the oil on me.

"I am not marrying," I protested.

"But you are here," she said. "And the oil is lovely, and I love you. I want you to have things as wonderful as I do." And so she rubbed the oil into my skin, and I felt anointed. For her hair I used the scented water and combed it until it was dry and glistening down her back in the setting sun. I helped Rebekah step into the blue gown that we brought from Haran and fastened the veil to the top of her head so that it draped down the front, as her hair draped down the back.

"What do I look like?" she asked.

"You look like royalty," I said. For she did. Her confident stature and beautiful garb reminded me of my grandmother and the other women I had seen around the palace. The veil that covered Rebekah's face was a dark purple that my grandmother favored, and it had small gems woven into it that made it even more gorgeous. I told Rebekah these details, and though I could not see her smile through the veil, I was confident that it was there.

When she was ready, we were uncertain what to do next. I used the moment to take her hands in mine. "Rebekah," I said, "you are a beautiful bride, because you are a beautiful woman. You know you are a blessing from Yah, and this makes the light and joy flow through you. You are strong and kind, and you will make Isaac a very happy husband. And the promise that Yah made to Abraham will come to fruition through you. You will be the mother of multitudes, more than the stars in the sky, and shining just as brightly, I am sure." I remembered the promise that Eliezer had told us, saw the proof in her veil, and felt it in my whole body.

She embraced me. "Hallelu Yah!" she exclaimed.

"Hallelu Yah!" I echoed.

Back and forth, and then together, we praised Yah for all our blessings. Just as we were becoming ecstatic, a young girl entered the tent. "I am here to show you the way," she said.

Rebekah squeezed my hand, and we lowered her veil again. I followed the girl and led Rebekah to a clearing that was outside of what I would soon learn was Abraham's tent. Lanterns had been placed in the shape of a large circle surrounding Isaac in the middle, such that it looked almost as if he were glowing in the middle of the moon. And he was glowing—both from the light of the flames and from his light within. The smile on his face could not have been extinguished with all the water of the Nile.

"He is ready," I whispered in Rebekah's ear. "And he is perfect. He will be kind to you." Gone were any concerns I had earlier about Rebekah's wedding night. My fear of her being hurt as I had been on the way to Haran disappeared when I saw Isaac there. Worries were unnecessary and inappropriate. I walked her until she was standing face-to-face with her betrothed. They were almost the same height; she was a finger or two taller. I took the hand I was holding and guided it to Isaac's, giving it one last squeeze before I stepped back.

When I left the circle, someone else entered. A much older man, walking in with the help of his shepherd's staff, yet commanding the respect of all gathered. I gasped, realizing this man could only be Abraham. My suspicion was confirmed when he spoke.

"My son," he said. "I charged Eliezer, my trusted helper, to find a suitable wife for you. In his wisdom, he requested the guidance of Yah. And now here you stand, with a cousin from Haran, chosen by Yah and brought to you by Eliezer. Do you accept her as your wife?"

Abraham's voice was strong and steady. Not the voice of an old man past his years, but the voice of a leader. The voice of someone who knew Yah and knew the world. The voice of my great grandfather. I was transfixed as he spoke and almost agitated by the pause he gave for Isaac's response, for I wanted to hear him talk more. Once Isaac had given his yes, Father Abraham went on: "Blessed are You, Yah, our god, and god of all the world, who created joy and happiness, groom and bride, gladness, jubilation, good cheer, love, friendship, peace, and delight." Those were the final words. Isaac then led Rebekah to his tent to complete the wedding.

Music erupted and plates and plates and plates of food were brought out. The feast included cured olives and fresh dates, three kinds of stews and two kinds of breads; cheeses and honey and figs flowed before my eyes. I could eat none of it, though. For I could not stop staring at Abraham. There he was. Oh, if only Sarah had been there! If only she had lived just a little longer so that we could meet! But she had not, and here I was, a woman, a maidservant, at a feast. I could not approach Abraham. Nor could I keep myself away.

I stood from the cushion where I had been reclining and observing him. My feet carried me forward as if they were in a cart hooked to a donkey that I could not control. One step and another found me closer and closer, until I fell on my face before him, praying that he would allow me an audience, even if brief. With tears caught in my throat and my forehead on the carpet at his feet, I allowed words out of my mouth that I had not knowingly put there.

"Father Abraham," I said, "I bring word of Hallel."

Abraham jerked to attention. "What did you say, woman? Arise so that I may hear you clearly."

I rose to my knees, for he was sitting on a cushion, and I could not have him lift his chin to look up at me. We were eye to eye, and I dared to look into his brown, wise, and still clear eyes, as I spoke. "Father Abraham," I said again, "I bring word of Hallel."

"Hallel?" he asked, hardly even whispering. "You know of Hallel? But how?"

And so I began to tell him. "Father Abraham, my name is Deborah. When I was a young girl, I knew your daughter, Hallel."

"My daughter, Hallel," he said. And then he repeated it several times quietly, cautiously, until finally he took my face in his hands and looked into my eyes. He squeezed my head. His fingers were gnarled but stronger than they looked. The pressure came from disbelief, however, not cruelty. "My daughter, Hallel," he nearly yelled. And then he released my head and fell on my neck, crying like a baby, heavy sobs that shook his whole body while I held him.

As soon as he caught his breath, he held my face in his hands again and pleaded, "Tell me of Hallel. How do you know my daughter? Is she living? Is she well?"

I then had the burden and honor of telling my grandfather of the death of his daughter, but also of her life. "Father Abraham," I started, "I am sorry to tell you that Hallel is no longer living." He did not seem surprised. Perhaps because he had thought her dead for many years already. "But I hope you will find joy in what I tell you next." Then I got to tell Abraham what became of his first child, his only daughter. Of her release from the harem, her marriage to the governor, her five daughters and eighteen grandchildren. "I know this because I, Deborah, am the daughter of Daganyah, Hallel's youngest daughter."

At those words, Abraham reached his hands out to touch my face yet again. This time it was with the gentleness I imagine he used to touch his babies' faces when they were first born. This time I felt just the tips of his fingers glide down my cheeks. "Hallel," he said. "Hallel." And then, "Hallelu Yah! Oh, praise Yah for bringing me to this day! My son has a wife, and my daughter has grandchildren!" Together we broke into the laughter of the joy of being united. Father Abraham jumped to his feet and began to dance. His old legs were slow, but every move was a joyful one. Men with instruments quickly surrounded him with music, and I clapped as his feet stomped on the ground. I was bold and exclaimed "Hallelu Yah!" and Father Abraham returned my call with a deep and joyful "Hallelu Yah!" of his own.

When he had exhausted himself, Abraham sat back on his cushion and wiped his eyes and nose. "My daughter, Hallel," he said again. "Nobody has spoken of her for generations. Oh, Hallel. She was such a beauty! Like her mother. And she was filled with spirit and courage! She would explore anything. One morning, when she was little . . . we still lived in Haran . . . she came to me with blood on both arms, yet a smile across her face. 'Look, Father! Look!' she squealed.

"I had both concern and curiosity. Her delight was evident, yet she was covered in blood. 'What is it, Hallel?' I asked her. 'What is this blood?' And she told me it was the blood of birth. She and her mother, my beloved Sarah, had been walking when they came across a deer near death, for her baby was trying to exit the womb bottom first. Hallel had lived only three or four summers. Her hands were small, and with her mother's directions, she reached in and turned the baby until Sarah was able to pull her out by her front legs. Mother and daughter then walked away and hid, watching from afar, to see what would happen. The deer mother started licking her baby, and after some time, they were both able to rise.

"That day I said to her, 'Oh, my little Hallel, you are a big helper! You even helped Yah create a deer. There is nothing you cannot do!'" Abraham paused for a long time but did not invite me to speak. I waited, and he continued. "That is why I helped that no-good-murdering-lying-cheating thief of a nephew of mine, Lot. Not because he was once Hallel's betrothed, certainly not. And not even because he was the son of my brother. No, it was because Hallel took such pride in being a helper after I said that to her."

I did not interrupt Father Abraham to tell him that Hallel remained a helper even when she was a grown woman. I would remember to tell him later.

"She helped her mother with the spinning, the maidservants with fetching water, sometimes even the donkeys with their burdens—adjusting the items on their backs or requesting carts for them. She came to me in the fields and asked if I needed help with the flocks. She took the insects off the grape leaves and set them in the soil. She helped the snails and worms after the rains. And so, when Lot was kidnapped by King Chedorlaomer, I took my men and went after him and brought him to safety so that I could be a father Hallel would be proud of—if only she knew.

"Little that helped, though." Abraham shook his head sadly. Then he took a deep breath, closed his eyes, and mouthed some words I could not hear. "My anger has overcome me again. I do not wish to talk about the one who caused me to lose my daughter. I wish to talk about my beloved daughter. Hallel. Hallel! Do you know how she got that name?" He did not wait for a response. "Her mother and I had traveled from the other side of the great river, all the way to Aram, now called Haran, after my brother. Sarah had noticed that the men there were either shepherds or grain farmers. 'Grow a vineyard,' she said. 'The people need wine.' And I did."

I knew this story from Hallel's telling, and from my mother's. I reveled in the unexpected blessing of hearing it come from Father Abraham's mouth.

"What started as one vineyard grew into many. I continued to work as a shepherd, of course, and it is a good thing I did. For we could not take the grapes with us when we left, unlike the flocks. We grew prosperous and wealthy. We had many manservants and maidservants. We had land, vineyards, and flocks. We had everything but a child. Sarah had been pregnant many times. Many. But no children. Until Hallel. We were so grateful to Yah for the gift of this living, breathing soul to hold in our arms. Upon seeing her for the first time, Sarah uttered the words 'Hallelu Yah.' And when my wife and daughter exited the birthing tent, my first act was also to shout praise: 'Hallelu Yah.' When Sarah heard that, she decided our daughter's name should be Hallel."

"That name has not been spoken since we left Egypt," Abraham said. Of course, it *had* been spoken many times *in* Egypt after he left, but he never got to hear it before my arrival. "I could not bear to see my wife's sorrow, and she could not bear the sound of our daughter's name. If she was finally able to remember the joy and gladness, she still did not utter Hallel's name. What could I do but respect her decision? Am I a mother who has lost her daughter? Do I know such a pain? I have endured the suffering of a father whose daughter was stolen from him, and that is difficult enough."

I THOUGHT I WOULD MISS Rebekah terribly during her seven days in Isaac's tent. We had not been apart since the day I had arrived in Haran. But I had little time to long for her company. Each night I recited Hallel's story in her own words for her father, and each night I went into our tent so full of new stories that I had heard from, and told to, Abraham, that I fell asleep satisfied and fulfilled.

As a child in Egypt, I had always known who I was: Deborah, daughter of Daganyah, daughter of Hallel, daughter of Sarah. Knowing that and feeling that had been one and the same when I was a child. When I arrived in Haran, I received the biggest blessing of my life: Rebekah. I became a maidservant and also a beloved friend. And at the same time, I unknowingly let go of who I had been. The seven days of not caring for Rebekah, which were also days of getting to know my great grandfather, brought me back to the feeling of being a child of Sarah.

Perhaps it was that knowing and feeling that helped me have the courage to ask Father Abraham what had happened to his wife, Hallel's mother, my great-grandmother. On the final morning of Rebekah's wedding week, I watched Father Abraham as he stood in the light of the rising sun and thanked Yah. Sometimes he was quiet, and I could not hear. Sometimes his gratitude brought out a great voice, and I heard him thank his god for his life and his bounty. I greeted him as he returned to the camp.

"Father Abraham, please, allow me to bring you drink and sweets and let us sit in the shade of the date tree."

He readily agreed. It had quickly become our habit to sit in the shade and admire the hills, the sheep, the flowers, the sky . . . all of it and more. When we were not telling each other stories, we wondered quietly at the beauty. I had enjoyed our time greatly and was also eagerly looking forward to Rebekah's return. I brought the food and drink and met Abraham in the shade. "Soon I shall return to Rebekah," I reminded him. "She will be a wonderful wife for Isaac, and I shall support her in that. Before we part, Father Abraham, may I ask for one more story from you?"

He beamed with delight. In his old age, he told me, he was glad to have someone new with whom to share his life. He enjoyed telling me of his journeys as much as he enjoyed hearing of Hallel. "Please, Father Abraham," I said, "Hallel did not know the end of her mother's story. You have blessed me with hearing more of it. Please, grant me the blessing of knowing how Sarah's life ended."

He frowned and sat quietly for a long time. I did not know what to do with myself, so I did not move. Finally, he took several deep breaths, then agreed. "I shall tell you how her life ended. These words have never left my mouth, for I would not wish for Isaac to feel that his mother's death was his fault. It was mine, and mine alone."

I tried not to show my surprise. I did not wish to interrupt him or distract him from telling me what I wanted to hear.

"Yah never spoke to Sarah in the way He spoke to me. Sarah never heard the Voice and spoke to it only a few times at my insistence. Yet somehow, she always knew Yah and always knew what Yah wanted. It was often her voice that guided me before Yah's, and they were always in the same direction.

"When we lived in this land, Yah blessed me and said I would have many descendants. And Yah blessed Sarah. It would be through her that the land would pass to my children—our children. When we went to Egypt, she was given all the treatment of a woman being prepared to lie with the pharaoh. But she spoke to Yah, and Yah brought plagues upon the pharaoh because of her words, and the pharaoh banished us from Egypt. It was she who kept our marriage undefiled and got us reunited. I was grateful to be together.

"Though we were together and had great wealth, we mourned for an entire year, for in leaving Egypt, we learned that we were leaving our beloved daughter, Hallel. We were going to live side by side with her and Lot, growing our tribe. But without her, we could not do that. The sorrow was insufferable, and Lot's dismissal of the devastation of his act incited us even more. Our shepherds began fighting against each other as well, with his defending his treacherous act and mine in anger, in solidarity with me. Finally I could stand it no more and instructed him to choose which direction he wished to settle, agreeing to take the other just to be away from him. And so we parted ways."

I wished my grandmother could know this. I wished she could know that her parents were not pleased with Lot's choice. Even though—and this is funny—I think she was glad to live in Egypt. I know she mourned the loss of her parents, but Yah had shown her that she was to live there, and so she felt at peace being in the right place.

"For many years after leaving Egypt," Abraham said, "we lived with the promise that this land would someday be mine and my descendants'. Yet, I had no descendants, for Hallel, our only child, was gone. Sarah gave me her Egyptian maidservant, Hajar, to bear an heir. And thus, my son Ishmael was born. Oh, to have a baby again! He was full of smiles and curiosity, just like the sister he never knew. His hair grew high in dark curls, like Hajar's, and his eyes shone with wonder, and he learned about Yah and came to know Yah, just as Hallel had.

"But Hajar held on to her Egyptian gods, and that bothered Sarah greatly. She tried not to hold Hajar's faults against Ishmael, but nonetheless it happened. As did jealousy. And I think the most difficult was the anger that Sarah felt that Ishmael was there and Hallel was not. All the days of her life, she pined for her daughter. She did not say so, but I saw her loneliness."

I could easily imagine Sarah's loneliness, even while others were around her. If my mother and I had ever been separated, I know she would have longed for me like that. As I did for her. And Hallel had four daughters within the palace walls but still longed for her fifth, Daganyah. I hoped that Sarah was able to love Ishmael, but I knew he would never replace Hallel for her.

"And then, when Ishmael was just getting a shadow above his upper lip, we received three guests. Once we offered them food and lodging, we learned that they were messengers. They had come to tell us that Sarah would deliver a child. We had longed for this for our whole lives, yet we finally accepted it would not happen. Sarah no longer had the monthly blood. How would she carry a child? We both laughed.

"Yet the messengers were correct, and Isaac was born one year later. When Sarah saw him, she laughed again. She felt she had been the object of a cruel joke—to carry the weight and discomfort of a pregnancy at her age, only to deliver a baby boy who would die in her arms. But Isaac did not die. Oh, there were many days we thought he would. He had such trouble drinking, sometimes trouble breathing. And even when he was able to suckle, and then later eat food, he struggled with walking, with talking, with hearing, and with seeing.

As I listened to Father Abraham tell of these difficult times, I put my hand on his. I knew that Isaac did not die as an infant. But still, it seemed that I should offer the little comfort I could. At least I could attempt to show that I heard the sorrow and the struggle.

He continued the story. "Sarah took care of all his needs—and there were many. She did not leave the boy's side for a moment of his entire life. She helped him prepare his food to a comfortable size for biting, she helped him walk the hills without tripping, she helped him speak his words more clearly so others could understand him better. She helped him with everything. Finally, when he had had fifteen summers, he told his mother there were some things he could do on his own. He began to spend time alone in the close fields in the afternoon, talking to Yah. Then he began to come with me to care for the sheep. I promised Sarah that he would sleep on his mat each night, so I never took him far.

"He has grown into a man who can do many things. That is thanks to his mother, who taught him so much, and who helped him stay alive so that he would inherit Yah's blessing, for Yah had promised that the blessing would pass through him. It is Sarah's seed that will inherit this land. As is fitting, for it is thanks to her that we even have it."

Here Abraham paused and choked back some sobs. His body shook, and he covered his eyes with his hands. Oh, my dear grandfather, how he missed his Sarah; how I wished I might have met her. For a while we sat in silence, sad together. I waited for him to be ready to talk more, and when he lifted his head, I was listening attentively.

"The last time we spoke before she died, the only words between us were exchanged in anger. We had only one fight that we fought for many years. It was about the land. We had said the same words so many times, we could keep the fight brief. 'Yah said this land will belong to you,' she would say, 'yet you do nothing to own land. We are merely sojourners here.' To which I would respond the same as always, 'Yah has blessed me with this land, and so I know it will someday become mine.' We were so used to that argument that it became boring, even though it never went away.

"But that day, we yelled at each other from sunup to sundown. Yah had instructed me to take Isaac to the land of Moriah and present him as an offering to the Creator of All. And so I prepared for the journey, for it would be three days. Sarah scorned me. 'When Yah was going to destroy the cities of Sodom and Gomorrah, you argued, you negotiated, you said, 'Far be it from you to bring death upon the righteous as upon the wicked, such that the innocent and guilty fare alike,' and yet when it is time to kill our son, our innocent son, our righteous son, you are silent?'

"I told her I would follow the word of Yah, that I would always trust Yah. 'But you questioned Yah at Sodom and Gomorrah,' she said. 'Will you not do at least as much for your own son? Our only son? Through whom the blessing is to pass? From the day he was born, I spent every moment trying to keep him alive. When he could not suckle, when he stumbled on rocks, when we did not know if he would ever speak. I helped him, sustained him. Now you will sacrifice him? He has no heir; who will inherit the blessing? Do you think I shall carry another baby?'

"The truth is, I do not know what more she said. I was packing the carts with wood for the burnt offering. The other gods required sacrifices, and Yah is the most powerful of all. The Creator and Sustainer of Everything. Would I deny such a god my greatest gift? And Yah had already shown me He is fair and just, for He said He would not destroy Sodom and Gomorrah if even ten righteous men were found there. There were not, so the cities were destroyed, but Lot was spared. My son is righteous, far more so than Lot. Yah made a promise that Isaac would inherit the land. I reminded Sarah of this—our son would not become a sacrifice."

This time he cried for much longer than the last. His body shook. Should I offer him a drink? How could I console him? I did not know, so I waited. When he was finally able to let the words leave his lips, he said, "It was Sarah who was to become the sacrifice."

"I woke early the next morning, to begin the journey before Sarah rose. I did not wish to argue with her once again. I would take Isaac for the three day's journey, and she would object over the distance if she did not return again to her worry about the sacrifice. The night before, she had even declared that if I did not stay, then she, too, would go. The animals were packed, and the young servants who would carry the rest of the supplies were ready. I would show my son the glory of Yah without another argument.

"When we arrived at the mountain, Isaac asked about the sacrifice. He saw there was no animal, but I assured him that Yah would provide one. Even as I bound him to the stone altar, I trusted in Yah. All I knew was what I needed to do, what I was guided to do, so I did that. When I raised my arm with the knife, I heard a voice. *Abraham, Abraham*, the voice said. It was a sweet and soft voice like Sarah's, but a part of the wind. The voice continued. It said, *Do not lay a hand on the boy, do not do a thing to him. For now I know that you are a god-fearing man, for you have not withheld your son, your only son, from me.*

"I looked in the direction that the voice had come from, and there was a beautiful black ram. Somehow, it had gotten stuck in the thicket. I wondered why it had entered the brambles, when it could have walked around. Nevertheless, it was halfway through, and I took it by the horns and pulled it closer to me. I unbound my son, and he and I placed the ram on the rock and offered it as a burnt offering to the One who had saved his life. We ate of it and slept. We would return in the morning, but when the first light arrived, I went to erect an altar to Yah in the place where I found the ram, in gratitude."

Father Abraham seemed as if he would stop the story again, but he continued talking, even as he sobbed. "Sarah was there. Oh, my beloved Sarah. She was there, on the other side of the thicket. She was lying peacefully and beautifully on the ground. My first thought was surprise that she had followed us, my second was pride, to show her that I was right that our son would not be sacrificed. My next thought was what a loving mother she was, that she had come to watch over her son. And then I saw a clump of the ram's black hair in her hand."

The next part was difficult to hear. Father Abraham continued the story, but with his head bent low, his face in his hands, muffling the grief and shame that came from his lips. "Long ago, Sarah had told me that Yah had shown her death. 'I am to die staring at the stars that are numerous like my descendants,' she said. She was pleased. And then she laughed. Oh, what a laugh my Sarah had! As beautiful as birdsong and quick to escape her lips, even at the least expected moments. Like when telling of her own death. She laughed because she said she would die with a handful of black hair. When she told me this, so many years before, before our son was even born, already all her hair had turned white. She laughed at the thought of having dark hair once again.

"It was only when I saw her clutching a handful of the ram's black hair that I looked for her breath and did not see it. I dropped into the brambles myself and took her white head into my lap." The telling of this story was shaking Abraham's body, but he did not stop. "I cried in silence then. Sarah would not want Isaac to hear me or see me. She would not want him to see her. I kissed her hand, the one that held the ram's black hair, and laid it on her chest. It was clear to me how the ram got stuck. It had not walked there but had been pushed there by a mother who had come to save her son's life."

Oh, Sarah!

When Abraham's confession was over, he was calmer. But there was more to the story. "I wiped my face and took many calming breaths. I could not face my son," he said. "I could not let him see me or see her. I walked ahead of him and called behind me that we must go. When I got to the bottom, where the servants were waiting with the supplies, I saw two more boys, who I learned had left the camp with Sarah right after we had, keeping a distance so as not to be seen. I told them of Sarah's body and instructed them to get her, carefully, gently, and bring her back to the camp. I told them to rush, so they would be ahead of us, and not to let Isaac see.

I thought of these boys, and all the others in the camp, who must have lived all along knowing of Isaac's uniqueness. He wore his difference on his round face and almond eyes. He wore it in his short stature and muffled speech. Later I would learn that it was also apparent in his kindness and in the love and joy that radiated from him. But those who had already lived in his camp knew this. They knew that anyone who had been born as he had, and yet lived past infancy, past childhood, and become an adult, was certainly blessed by Yah. And so, it was not only Sarah who nurtured and protected him but the whole camp. When Abraham asked the lads to protect Isaac from what had happened, they would certainly do so.

Joseph, now I shall get the same agreement from you. You have just learned that Sarah died when protecting Isaac. It was Abraham's wish for Isaac to never know that. Isaac is old now. I know that you honor your grandfather when you see him. I expect you to continue to do so and not reveal this secret.

Now you will write the rest of what Abraham said, the part that Isaac knows of.

"When we returned, I found Sarah in her tent, covered with a lovely green blanket that had gold threading. I cried again. That time, I did not hold back, for I would need to show my son that his mother was dead. We mourned her all day and all night. We sang her praises and shared our memories and eventually succumbed to a short sleep next to her body. When the sun rose, I went to Efron, the leader of the Hittites, and paid four hundred pieces of silver to bury my beloved in the Cave of Makhpelah. We had wandered this land for years, waiting for the fulfillment of Yah's blessing to own it. Sarah's burial plot was the first parcel."

Now tears were flowing down my face as well. Having the ending to Sarah's story was a great honor and gift. I kissed Father Abraham's hand and thanked him. My grandmother would not know, my mother would not know, but I would know for them. Of all the stories I had heard from him during the past seven days, this story of bravery and determination, of guiding destiny and of how Sarah ensured the fulfillment of Yah's blessing, was the one I most looked forward to sharing with Rebekah.

THE THIRTEENTH PARCHMENT

Rebekah and Isaac's wedding was not the only one during our first year in our new camp. One month later, Father Abraham called me to his tent.

"Deborah," he said, "you are as beautiful as your grandmother and her mother. Listening to your stories has lifted my spirits, and I feel happier and younger having shared the tragedy of Sarah's death. You showed me more compassion than I showed myself, and I am grateful. My son now has a wife to bring him comfort. I am an old man, but I still wish to have comfort and more children. It is not right for you to be a servant in my tribe, for you are of my tribe. I wish to marry you, Deborah."

Father Abraham brought out a folded cloth from beside him. He opened it and displayed an array of golden bangles as beautiful, if not more so, than the ones Eliezer had brought to Rebekah. "There is no one for me to pay the bride price," he said, "for I would pay only myself." He chuckled softly but kept his eyes serious and looking into mine. "Therefore, I pledge to you that I shall bestow upon you the lavish gifts that befit a queen and a matriarch."

He lifted one of the bangles, a beautiful gold bracelet, as wide as my thumb and hammered with dips and crevices that I am certain my fingers would have enjoyed feeling throughout the day. But as he brought it near, I jerked my hand backward. I did it without even thinking, and then I needed to think quickly.

"Father Abraham," I said, and then I repeated myself while bowing my head to the ground before him, hoping to have enough time and courage to find words to follow. "Father Abraham, your generosity knows no limitations. You are a man of Yah's boundless creative spirit. It is an honor to be in your camp. I plead with you, compassionate one, I pledged an oath to Rebekah to be by her side and care for her. I was free to be with you when she was with Isaac, but now that she has returned, my duties are to her. Soon she will have children, Isaac's children, and she will need me even more. Would you not, perhaps, prefer me to be by her side? Tending to the heirs of Yah's blessing to Isaac?"

I never would have imagined speaking with such disrespect and dishonor. It was only my love for Rebekah and my desire to stay by her side that allowed these words to grow on my tongue and escape my mouth. For so many years I had known joy with her. I could not imagine my life without her. And what of hers without me? We had feared this moment and thought it behind us.

Abraham was quiet and continued to offer me the bangle. "You are not a slave girl, Deborah. You are a daughter of Hallel.

Of Sarah. If only I had known my dear Hallel lived! I would not have sent Eliezer north, but south, to retrieve a wife for Isaac from the descendants of Hallel. Perhaps you would have been that very wife," he said.

My breath caught in my throat. I could not allow in what might have been. Here I was, both a daughter of Sarah and a servant. Sarah was no longer, but Rebekah was. Elevating my status would put an end to our lives together. This was unbearable to me.

Before I could think of words to say, Abraham found new ones. "But my son has a wife now. Someone to care for him and comfort him. I do not. When we wed, I shall have not only that but more children. These children, our children, they will be the children of mine and Sarah's, and they will inherit the blessing. Hallelu Yah!"

"Father Abraham," I said, more quietly and slowly than before, but still insolent. "Did you not say that the blessing is to pass through Isaac?"

"You are correct, Deborah. It would not be right for you to become my wife. You are as wise as your grandmother Hallel. As holy as her mother, Sarah. I shall find a different wife, for you will wed Isaac. Yah's blessing will pass through him to his children, not through any other children of mine. And who better to be the mother of those children? So, I give you to my son. You will be the favored wife, the continuer of the blessing."

"I am not pure!" I told him loudly. I did not know I was going to say it, I knew only that I could not take Rebekah's honored position as first wife. She had saved my life. She *was* my life. Abraham was right, I was closer kin and would be the favored wife. I could not take that from my dear Rebekah. "Isaac is a man of Yah. It is beneath him to be with a woman who has already been defiled." My body shook as I said these words. I knew they were a poor excuse, disrespectful, and a last hope. And that was how they were received. I had been so hurt by Mavheel, and so scared. I grasped at whatever words might keep me safe. Abraham put a hand on my arm to lift me from the ground, then waved his hand for me to leave his tent. We did not speak again for many years.

I was already sobbing when I returned to our tent to bury my head in my mother's cloth that covered my pillow. Rebekah followed me and rubbed my head while she waited impatiently for me to tell her what was wrong. When I did, she chastised me. "Why did you not marry Isaac?" she asked.

"I am your nursemaid," I replied, "and gladly so. You would have become the lesser wife."

"And we would have remained together!" Rebekah responded.

"But I could not do that to you, Rebekah," I said. "The blessing will go through you. Yah has determined this. Abraham did not send Eliezer to fetch me. You were the one he found for Isaac. You will be the matriarch of a nation who knows Yah."

"You could have been that matriarch!" Rebekah responded. "It could have been you, and we would still have the assurance of remaining together." I could hear the anger in her voice. The fear. This was the most certain way for us to stay together. "Deborah! You had the chance to leave your service without leaving me! And now? Abraham is reminded that you are his property and that he is spurned by you. What if he sells you? We might never be together again!"

Rebekah was right, and she named many of the reasons for my tears. "I was afraid," I said, and covered my face in shame. Rebekah put her arms around me as I cried. I might have had everything. Instead, I left Father Abraham angry and myself at risk. But Father Abraham did not sell me. Hallelu Yah!

He found another woman to wed and bring him more children. Keturah became a part of our tribe and a part of our women's circle. She was a short woman with long brown hair that she could sit on when it was not wrapped above her head. She did not tell us of her past but shared freely of her thoughts in the present. Keturah came with a nursemaid, Ozeret, and so, for a while, we became four women under the moon. Keturah gave compliments easily and received them frequently from Abraham, for she quickly bore him six more sons.

Zimran was the first of them. On the morning that he was born, after nine full moons of Keturah's belly growing and her steps slowing, only on the morning of the birth did I realize this was the first baby I would witness entering the world since Matanyah. My body reflexively filled with worry, but then I was able to find gratitude: I thanked and praised Yah that I had not realized this earlier and so those months had not been filled with my fear. Even my morning of fear was unwarranted. Keturah's laboring pains were unremarkable, and the boy was born breathing and wailing.

It was exciting to have a baby in the compound. Surely, we heard the cries and laughter of the children of the servants, but it was not the same as having a little boy to play with. Zimran was the happy recipient of cookies from his mother and Ozeret and Rebekah and me. Abraham could not lift the boy once he started walking—he was too heavy and too wiggly for Abraham's old arms—but he tickled Zimran's toes, tousled his hair, and taught him every morning.

Each morning when the sun rose, Zimran would run from his mother's tent, a barley cake in each hand, and go sit in his father's lap in the shade where he liked to watch the sunrise. Together they would break the fast and praise Yah.

"Do you see that beautiful sun?" Abraham asked.

"Yes," Zimran answered.

"Who created that sun?" Abraham asked.

"Yah! Yah created the sun!"

"Do you see those beautiful hills?" Abraham asked.

"Yes," Zimran answered.

"Who created those glorious, brown hills?" Abraham asked.

"Yah! Yah created the hills!"

"Do you see the never-ending sky?" Abraham asked.

"Yes," Zimran answered.

"Who created that sky?" Abraham asked.

"Yah! Yah created the sky!"

Thus, they would sit and pray together. Zimran did not know yet how to speak in a quiet voice, and Abraham met his loud one with praise. The whole camp heard them every morning. They went on and on just like that, with Abraham encouraging Zimran to add his own as well.

"Who created that blade of grass?" Zimran asked.

"Yah!" Abraham's enthusiasm matched his young son's. "Yah created that blade of grass!"

"And who created *that* blade of grass?" Zimran asked.

"Yah!" Abraham shouted again. "Yah created *that* blade of grass."

One morning I counted their questions out of curiosity. Together they pointed out one hundred things that Yah had created. And then they rose from their position and closed their eyes and said, "Hallelu Yah," over and over again. I could not help but close *my* eyes and add *my* praise. "Hallelu Yah," I said with them, even though from afar. "Hallelu Yah."

That was the only time I inserted myself into Abraham's morning prayers, but it was a ritual he continued with Zimran, and then Jokshan, who arrived at the end of his brother's third winter. Zimran was not excited to have another child in the camp, but when he saw that his brother could not take his sweets or run as fast as he could—or even walk—he felt no jealousy. By the time Jokshan was old enough to do these things, Zimran could not remember a time without him and was glad to have a playmate.

The two of them kept Keturah busy, and she was glad for the time she had each morning when they prayed with their father. One day when Keturah's belly was large with the child who would be Midan, Jokshan burst into the garden, stepping on sesame plants and poppy flowers, and got all of our attention when he nearly knocked his mother to the ground with his speed.

"Mother, Mother!" he called. "Soon you will have a new child, and soon I shall become a sheep. But I do not wish to be a sheep! Please let me stay in the tent with you, not go to the fields. Or if I must be an animal, I wish to be a lion! Or a hawk!

Please, Mother, please." He was crying now. "Please, I do not wish to be a sheep! They only eat grass all day and they stand in the sun. They are so far away. A pack of jackals can take them and bite them and eat their flesh and blood, even if there is a shepherd who is good with the sling. I do not wish to be a sheep, Mother, please!"

Keturah took her crying child into her arms. His hair was long; one day it would be cut for him to look like a big boy, not a baby, but not yet. We had all been startled by the change it had made in Zimran when he had been weaned and had his hair cut. He was still playful but more serious and responsible also. Now he had lost his first milk tooth and was walking, tall and purposefully, into the garden, stepping carefully around the growth.

"Zimran," Keturah said, "what is Jokshan going on about? Have you been teasing him?"

"No, Mother," he said. "It was Father's words that upset Jokshan, not mine."

"What did he say?" Keturah asked.

"We were praying by his tent." Zimran spoke clearly and paused to show the importance of the story, and the messenger. "We were thanking Yah for all of His creations. The sun and the sky, the rain and the goats and the big rocks and the little rocks. For each one, Father said, 'Who created the sky . . . or the rain . . . or the goats . . .' like he does when we are in prayer together, and each time, we said it was Yah. And I got excited when Father talked about the big rocks and the little rocks and I said, 'Who created Jokshan?' and Father and Jokshan answered, 'Yah! Yah created Jokshan.'

"And then Father giggled a little, and he said, 'Well, your mother and I helped.' And this was when we paused our prayers. Yah created everything, and so I thought the answer would be Yah. And when Father said that he and you helped, I was curious about such a thing. Can you help Yah create? Can it be that Yah cannot create alone? How do you help Yah create a son? Shall I one day help Yah create? And I asked Father these questions, only to have him ask me one.

"'Zimran,' he said, 'have you ever seen the sheep when one is on top of the other?' I said that I had, of course, and Jokshan said that he had, too, even though Father was asking *me* and not him. 'The sheep help Yah create more sheep, and people are the same way,' Father said. And then Jokshan ran away yelling, 'No, no, Father, no, no, Mother, do not get on top of the other and make me into a sheep!'"

We could not help but laugh at the ending of the story. Poor little Jokshan buried his head into his mother's large bosom. Through his sobs she promised him over and over that she would not make him be a sheep. She ran his long hair between her fingers, stroking his head until he fell asleep. Zimran stayed to see that his brother was cared for and tended to. When he was satisfied, he turned on his heel to go but then paused and hesitatingly asked his mother a question.

"Mother, it was silly, was it not, that Jokshan thought you and Father and Yah would make him become a sheep? Yah can create anything and do anything, but not that, right, Mother? Even the new baby that you will birth will not become a sheep, is that right, Mother?"

Keturah smiled at her firstborn. "You are a very wise boy, Zimran. You are right. Nobody will be becoming a sheep or will be born a sheep, other than the sheep."

Satisfied, Zimran left the garden, and we women had a nice giggle. At the end of it, I saw Rebekah staring longingly at Jokshan, sleeping in his mother's lap. She had wed Isaac at nearly the same time that Abraham and Keturah wed, yet Keturah was going to have her third child, and Rebekah had none, though she longed for one deeply.

That night, alone in our tent, Rebekah cried over the children she did not have. I stroked her hair and suggested maybe she try creating sheep, and I was able to make her laugh a little. I felt her pain, though. And it was not lessened when Keturah gave birth to a blue baby boy the next month. Little Midan had the cord wrapped around his neck and no breath.

It was a difficult delivery. The baby was upside down and the midwife was doing everything she could to turn him right. She prodded poor Keturah until she could stand it no more and then had us hold Keturah with her hands and feet on the ground and her rear in the air, so the baby could come right side up. But it did not turn. I began to shake with the memories of my mother and the day that I lost her and my sister all at once. I ran out of the tent in search of the littlest servant girl I could find.

Promptly I brought her into the birthing tent and looked her in the eyes. "What is your name, girl?"

"My name is Amitza, daughter of Menakah and Gozez."

"Amitza, you are a strong girl," I said. "Someday you will be a strong woman, carrying a strong baby inside you. Now, you are bigger than a baby and smaller than a woman." I guessed she had been born four or five summers ago. "Now listen, I will tell you exactly what you will do. And you might not like it, but you will be Yah's own helper and you will save a life, maybe two."

The girl nodded. She would not have disobeyed me no matter her fear, but I wanted her to be calm if possible. The midwife instructed her on putting her hand in to turn the baby. She was able to grab the baby's leg, and with the midwife's help from the outside, the two of them turned the baby while Keturah screamed loudly enough to wake the dead. With every bellow, I was glad she was not among the dead herself. Sadly, Midan was. We all wept, except for Keturah, for she had fainted, whether from pain or from the strong drink just beginning to help her sleep, we would not know.

"I shall bring word to Abraham," I said. I was eager to leave the tent. We all were. Ozeret stayed with Keturah. She would be the one to clean little Midan and prepare him for burial. I took Amitza out of the tent. She had seen enough.

"You did a fine job," I commended her as I guided her to the well. The little girl was shaking. I understood. I spoke to her calmly as I washed the blood from her arms, her hands, her fingers. "Did you know that Abraham had a daughter who was a little girl once?" This caught her attention. "Her name was Hallel," I continued. "And one time, Hallel saw a deer giving birth, but the baby was stuck, and could not come out. Little Hallel put her arms inside, just as you did, and helped the baby deer come out. You are as brave as Abraham's daughter, Hallel," I said.

Amitza smiled. The blood was gone from her body but still on her garment. Her mother would have to take care of that. For now, I needed to tell Abraham of the death of his son and the survival of his wife. I had an idea to take Amitza with me. She led me to her parents, so that I could bring them, too. As we approached them, they were surprised to see me with her and even more shocked by all the blood on her frock.

"Please," I said, "come with me, and I will explain everything to Abraham. Your daughter has done well."

They both relaxed their shoulders. Amitza put her hand in her mother's and could not help but smile with pride.

Abraham was sitting outside his tent, writing on a scroll that accounted for his flocks. "Father Abraham," I said, bowing low before him. It had been many years since I had approached him, but I rose and stood tall, as if I belonged there. He did not dismiss me. "I bring news of your son. Keturah birthed another boy, and he did not breathe," I said. "I know this brings her great sorrow, and you, too. May Yah comfort you among the mourners."

Abraham nodded, crying. "And Keturah?" he asked when he caught his breath.

I put my hand on Amitza's shoulder. "Father Abraham, this girl, Amitza, daughter of Menakah and Gozez, has saved the life of your wife. It was her bravery and small arms that turned the boy so that he could receive his proper burial and his mother would not need one. Your wife lives because of Amitza."

He cried again, his whole body shaking. Then he walked to Gozez. "Your daughter is a helper of Yah. In her honor, I give you twelve ewes and three rams to start a flock. You may take your wife and children, your tent and the pots and clothing you use, a manservant and maidservant. You are free to choose whether you stay with my camp or depart. The gifts belong to you either way. May Yah bless you and make your flock abundant and your bravery even more so."

I had not anticipated that Abraham would make a gift of gratitude, though I should not have found it surprising. His generosity was expressed in many ways. I was pleased for the reward that came to Amitza. Pleased and exhausted. Though the sun was only beginning to set, it felt as if months had passed since it had risen. I returned to our tent to lie down. Rebekah was already there, for the day had been long for her, too.

"Tell me a story," she pleaded, her face and sleeve still wet from tears. I did not mind, for I could lie down and tell her. My voice would console her, as hers did for me. There were many nights when one or the other of us fell asleep during stories. It was a compliment to the comfort we found, and nothing was ever missed, as the stories were so familiar. But this night, I told her a new story.

"A new story?" she asked. "You have withheld a story from me?"

"Maybe one or two," I admitted. "We have seen each other nearly every day since I arrived in your tent in Haran. There are not many surprises left to reveal, but I hope I can do so sometimes." All this was true, Joseph, for I would not tell a lie to Rebekah. Also true was that then, as now, I did not always remember a story until it was just the right time to tell it. Even these scrolls cannot contain every story of my life. But it will have most of them. Just like Rebekah does.

After the difficult day, we let our mat cradle us. Rebekah's body was relaxed and her interest piqued. "This is a birth story," I told her. "Mine."

"The day I was born was nearly the day I died," I began. "The midwife caught me as I slid from my mother's body but then nearly dropped me." Rebekah gasped. "She was so startled by the sight of me." Rebekah, who had been lying on her back with her eyes closed, turned to look at me. We had seen each other every day except her wedding week for more years than I could count. We shared a sleeping mat all those nights, other than the ones she went to Isaac. She knew my face and my body as well as she knew her own, yet now she turned to face me, to look for what she had missed all these years.

"You cannot see it now," I said. "When I was born, I did not come out as a screaming baby. In fact, my silence first scared my mother. But you see, when I was born, I did not yet know I had been born, for I came out inside a sack, filled with water . . . and me." Rebekah looked at me, blankly, and I continued my story. "The midwife had caught hundreds of babies, but I was the first to enter the world with a part of my old world still with me.

"She had heard of this, she told Mother later, in her training to become a midwife. Her mentor had never seen such a birth, nor her mentor before her. But from generation to generation, they passed on the stories about such births, just as they did with teachings about herbs and prayers. A midwife needed to be prepared for anything. So my midwife, Tanqo, for as I mentioned, she was the one who delivered me as well, she was startled for a moment when she saw me but quickly recovered.

"Instead of letting me fall to the ground, she gently placed me on my mother's bosom. The two women admired my body, folded knees to chest, fingers on my cheeks. They watched my mouth open and close. They saw my peacefulness and beauty. Then Tanqo took a knife, and, telling my mother of the plan so as not to scare her, slid the blade into the sack. In that moment, my mother's belly was covered in the water that had been my home inside the home of her body. It was only then that I went from warm wetness to warm dryness and screamed my protest while my mother laughed with joy and relief.

"Tanqo took the emptied sack with her and dried it in the sun. She brought it back to my mother at the next full moon and told her that her daughter would have a life as full as her birth had been. Along with the dried sack, she brought the coins my father had paid for her services. 'You and the child have been my teachers,' she said to my mother. 'What I have learned from this birth is worth more than the coins I give you, but I am grateful.' My mother accepted the coins and put them in the satchel she hid under our mat."

After some silence, Rebekah asked me, "Is that all?"

I laughed. "All? No. That is the beginning. Everything else has come after that. And now here I am, still, and in darkness, and in gratitude to be able to share stories—and life—with you." I was overwhelmed by my blessings, but in that moment, my story had been only a temporary distraction for Rebekah.

"Keturah was a mother to that baby," Rebekah said, "even if she got to hold him only once. I have not done even that." Those were the final words of the night, and we both fell asleep with them in our ears.

Rebekah had several pregnancies, but only one that lasted more than two moons. Even that one had not been long enough. And while she longed for a baby, Keturah had another, another, and another. Midian, Ishbak, and Shuah were cute little boys. They laughed often and were always willing to have a hug. Mostly they ran after Zimran and Jokshan, trying to keep up as well as their little legs would allow. Every time one went by, Rebekah smiled, feeling the joy of their freedom and wonder, and then frowned, feeling her own loss.

This began to change when Abraham decided it was time to move his little sons far from Isaac. It was Keturah who shared the news with us. She was saddened to be leaving. Who would she celebrate the full moon with? Who would run after her boys when they all went in different directions? These were her worries about what her new life would be. But it was also clear that she held some resentment.

"Abraham has promised me that he will give my sons gifts," she said, "but Isaac will have everything. This land, the fields, the flocks. He will have the blessing of Yah, and my sons will have trinkets." She paused. "I am grateful to have a husband who gives my sons gifts, who provides us with food and shelter, and who, most of all, is kind. He has never raised a hand to me, even though I always have known that Sarah was his beloved, and I was . . . am . . . merely his concubine. But can a woman not be disappointed? Not be jealous?"

"A woman can be jealous," Rebekah confirmed. "Yes, she can." But Rebekah herself was less jealous when Abraham and Keturah, Ozeret, and the five boys went eastward. Abraham took their tents, four manservants and four maidservants, two shepherds, one small flock, and one dog and, as he had promised, left everything else to Isaac. One could not see the difference in the camp when they left, but we could feel the difference right away. The sadness about the separation departed along with them, for they were hardly over the next hill when Isaac began leading the tribe.

THE FOURTEENTH PARCHMENT

In all the years of her marriage to Isaac, Rebekah had been pregnant four times, and had no babies. The first pregnancy was celebrated with quiet joy and excitement.

"A little life is growing inside me," she whispered one night. We were huddled under the warm blanket that we had woven together before leaving Haran. It was as black as the night sky when the moon softens the darkness with its glow. That night there was no moon, and I was bleeding. I had not noticed she was not bleeding.

"Really?" I asked, more surprised by my lack of noticing than by her news. It had been more than a year since she and Isaac had wed. She placed my hand on her belly. There was nothing to feel, but we fell asleep that way. We did not share the news with Keturah or Ozeret, nor did they wonder. It was a time for resting from the work and from the men, not for paying attention to the blood of others. They would learn soon enough.

But the next new moon, Rebekah was bleeding again. Something had happened though. She had told Isaac and his usual big smile turned enormous. “Let me see your round belly!” he shouted with excitement. Rebekah laughed. “It is not round yet,” she said. “Then let me see your flat belly,” he said, and she obliged. The two of them then disappeared into Isaac’s tent for the rest of the day and night. She awoke with blood on her thighs, and her dreams of a baby drifted into sorrow.

After that, she told Isaac only once. It was after three months without blood. She and I had guarded her secret with hope and extra prayers. She finally let herself believe that she would bring a baby into her arms. Isaac was thrilled. He had said he would be just as happy without a baby in his arms, as long as he had Rebekah to hold. But he still talked with Yah every afternoon, and surely some of the discussion was around how Yah would fulfill the promise of Isaac’s children living in the land if he had no living children.

Of course, I was not a part of those conversations. But I never saw Isaac worried. Sometimes he was curious, but never worried. After being moments from his own death on the top of the mountain, and then being saved, Isaac had complete faith that all would be well and even the most trying moments would pass like the rest of them.

He did mourn when Rebekah began having cramps and expelled blood with lumps thick enough to be buried under a tree. We chose a date palm near the camp, and Rebekah always petted the trunk when she walked by it after that. I took to doing the same. That had been the hardest of the losses for her. She retreated into her thoughts for many days. Isaac let her be but after a month called her to his tent. She complied, and I could hear the distant sounds of their love. But instead of sleeping there, she made her way back to our tent where she cried until the sun rose.

"What if Yah allows another baby to grow inside me," she asked, "and then my body expels it before the time? I do not wish to go through that again. But," she continued, "what if Yah never allows another baby to grow in my womb? What will this womb be for?" She neither expected nor wanted responses to these questions. There were no answers. She just needed to voice her thoughts, over and over. Even on the nights that we danced under the moon and she was filled with joy and ecstasy, we barely regained our breath before she expressed her worry again.

It was on one of those nights that I had a new thought. Still panting from our drumming and dancing, I asked, "What if I go to Isaac for you?" As soon as the words parted from my lips, fear enveloped me and I wished I could stuff them back in. But I could not.

"Deborah," she said, "would you go to Isaac? You would carry a baby for me in your womb? It is such a warm place, I can tell." She put her hand on my belly, already imagining it rounding in pregnancy. "And the baby would grow wisdom like yours, just from being inside you. We could be mothers together, if only there were a baby. I cannot grow one. Will you do it for me?"

Rebekah knew I would do anything for her, and yet she could feel my hesitation. For many days and nights we discussed this. Who would really be the child's mother? What kind of inheritance would he get? How would we feel sharing a husband? Would we be different with each other? To every question I raised, Rebekah offered the same answer, "Deborah, we will find the answers to these questions together. We will have only the life that we agree to, for we will do it together."

"Isaac might not wish this," was the only excuse I gave that brought a different response. Rebekah laughed. "You know better than I that it is in a woman's hands to make the decisions and that the man will go along with them. Have you not told me that hundreds of times?" Indeed, I had. I had told her enough times—and she had listened well—and now was her turn to tell me. And so she did.

Rebekah told me the story of Eve and Adam. Not the whole thing, but enough to remind me that it was the woman who would be Yah's hand for making new ways and the man who awaited her wisdom to follow. Isaac would follow Rebekah's lead. She would not force me. What would I do?

Isaac was as gentle as Rebekah promised. I could have thought for a moment that she had spoken to him, requested extra tenderness on my behalf. But I knew that had not happened. Such talk was common in our tent, not in his. He just was a gentle person. When he touched my skin, I could feel his awe at my beauty. I could feel him wondering at the curves and lines that were the same yet different from the ones he was used to. Just as when he saw a ewe with markings that reminded him of the hills, or a plant that reached toward the sun, he praised Yah; that night with me in the tent, he praised Yah, and so did I.

I had agreed to Rebekah's request to lie with Isaac once, but when he called me the next night and the next, and she was eager for me to conceive a baby, I went willingly. Isaac continued to be gentle, and I expected his kindness and was free to enjoy it. Again, we praised Yah, and each other. Isaac prayed on behalf of Rebekah because she was childless and asked Yah to deliver her a child, whether through her own womb or through mine. Then he told me that his father had sent his oldest son Ishmael out, because he was the son of a concubine, but that he would never do that to any child of mine, and I believed him and was grateful, and we came together a second time that night.

On the fourth night, I told Rebekah that I wished to decline Isaac's invitation. It seemed that Yah had already had enough opportunity to help me conceive a baby, and I had too much opportunity to complicate my feelings. I was correct about both things. When the new moon came, my blood did not. Though we were alone in our tent when I told her, I whispered the news to Rebekah quietly

I could see her face rise with excitement and just as suddenly fall with sorrow. But the joy returned quickly, and she stayed by my side in the tent while she alone bled, asking me to describe every feeling and every thought until I could stand it no more.

"Rebekah, you have been pregnant before. And perhaps you will be pregnant again. You do not need me to tell you of this part. And when my belly grows rounder, you may spend every moment of the day and night with your hand on it so that you feel your baby from the very beginning."

Her baby.

My voice caught on that phrase, and I knew she heard it. It was not intentional. I already had many complicated feelings.

"Your baby too," she said. "For you are the warm womb in which it grows, and we already spoke of what a joy and help it would be to be mothers together. Yes, this baby will be mine, born on my knees as if from my body. But I shall still be me, and you will still be you, and we shall still be us, and Isaac will finally have an heir, and we shall all love the baby."

It was all a beautiful dream. Who knew what would happen during my pregnancy? The thing that surprised us the most happened just a month later. Rebekah became pregnant again. And this time, she stayed pregnant.

By the time she entered her third moon, her belly was rounder than mine in the fourth. Two moons later I was round, and my breasts were beginning to fill with milk, but her belly and breasts were fuller. I felt the occasional kick and tickle from inside that brought a smile to my face and my hand to my skin, but Rebekah could barely stand for the movement that was going on inside her.

In her seventh month, Rebekah could hardly eat anything, and the pokes and prods she was receiving from the inside could be seen on the outside. I walked beside her at all times, to help her keep her balance when a leg or an arm thrust forth inside her and threatened to knock her off her feet. She spent most of her time lying down. I continued with my duties but also spent time lying next to her, belly to belly. In this way, the babies got to know each other, and we both became mothers of the whole bundle.

Rebekah's physical endurance was tested at every moment, and her emotional tolerance was also tried. While she suffered blows and hunger and dizziness, I grew a soft glow and an elegance to my walk. She told me this herself, and not without jealousy. Her heart had always been kind, and she was happy for me but not for herself. She was finally having a pregnancy without blood and loss, and yet it was such a difficult one that she could hardly survive it.

And it was not just difficult for her compared to my bliss. She asked all the maidservants in the compound—each and every one who had ever been pregnant—to come to her so that she might ask them if they had struggled like this, and none had. My sweet Rebekah who was always strong and knew her worthiness fell into despair and self-pity. Several times a day she could be heard asking, "Why me?" and "What did I do to deserve this?" And I am sure she asked herself even more than she wondered aloud.

"Pray for me, Deborah," she pleaded one day. "Pray for me the way you do, with your fingers. Ask Yah why this is happening."

"When I close my fingers, Yah helps open them or helps tighten them to tell me if the answer to my prayer is yes or no. That is all. Perhaps you should pray, Rebekah," I said. "You are as much a daughter of Yah as I. You need not pray the same way I do."

Finally, after nearly falling on her face tripping over a rock she could not see because her view was blocked by the growing life inside her, she cried out to Yah, asking why. That very night, as she dreamt fitfully, she received her explanation and comfort. She woke before the sun and told me every word.

"Deborah," she said. "Deborah," she called me again, as it was hard to wake me from my peaceful slumber. As soon as I stirred, she began. "Deborah, Yah came to me in my dream last night. I dreamt I was on the birthing blocks, though it was not my time. I had the pain of motherhood, but not the worry, for Yah was with me. But the pain was great, even more severe than now. And Yah explained, 'Two nations are in your womb; two nations that are within you will become separate as they issue from your body. One will be mightier than the other; and the older will serve the younger.'"

We both put our hands on her belly. Two . . . there were two babies inside! She would soon deliver two babies, and I only one. I had not realized, but during all these many moons of pregnancy that had passed, I had come to accept that I would be the first wife after all. Accept and expect. For it was true that I was a direct descendant of Sarah and Abraham, while Rebekah was only a descendant of their brother Nakhor. I had resisted it but could not change the fact that I was going to bring Isaac's first child and, with that, a rise in status for myself. Now I learned that Rebekah's children would be the heirs, and mine the extra. The extra of the extra. If her older was to serve the younger, certainly my older was to serve them both.

"Deborah," she said, interrupting my thoughts, "we shall have three babies. Three. Oh, I hope yours is a daughter since mine are boys. Then we shall have heirs and a little girl to love!" I knew I was not carrying a little girl. The boy in my belly had been whispering to me the same way that the hills and the herbs did. I had not shared those whispers with Rebekah. In all our years together, it was only the details of my times with Isaac and the details of my whisperings with our child that I did not talk about with her. I would have shared had she asked, but it felt as if those were stories to keep to myself—even if I did sometimes feel sorrow from not sharing them.

Well, soon we would share three babies! And her saying so lifted my mood from that of jealousy and fear back to excitement and joy. A month later I felt a joy that surpassed all others: the birth of my baby boy. Every pain, every push, every scream that parted my lips also had joy with it. For I was joining the ranks of women. I, too, would have a baby. When I held him in my arms a flood of tears released from my eyes.

My mother had been allowed to name me because I was a girl, while my father named my brothers. But here, the mother was the one who gave all the names, and so I named my son Zacharyah—Yah remembered—because Yah remembered that I am a part of this tribe, a child of Sarah and Abraham, not just a nursemaid. Yah remembered and reminded me that I am a descendant deserving of birthing a son to Isaac. But I did not tell anyone this was his name. It amuses me. It was an Egyptian tradition to give a person a second name, one that everyone calls him so his first name is a secret, and the gods cannot bring harm to him. When in Egypt, my mother helped me hold on to the traditions of her mothers from generations and lands past. Then here, in the land promised to my ancestors and descendants, I somehow was drawn to the tradition from my birthplace. It did not help, though.

On Zacharyah's eighth day of life, Isaac circumcised him and welcomed him into the covenant with Yah. It pained me to watch a slice of his skin be removed from his perfect little body, yet I was ecstatic that Isaac was welcoming him into the tribe. Besides, with the wine on his lips, Zacharyah had no complaints. That day, we had a great feast, and Rebekah gave me the honor of dancing with me, even though she could barely rock her tremendous weight from one foot to the other. "We shall dance in the joy of this son!" she exclaimed. And then she held him to her chest and named him Rananyah—a joyful song of Yah. I was pleased.

I, too, would have been happy to have a girl, someone to share the stories of my life with. I did not get a girl, but I have gotten to share my stories. In Rananyah's first days and nights of life, I whispered to him about his grandmother Daganyah and how pleased she would have been to know him. I told him of the great river in Egypt. I told him how beautiful he was and how kind he would grow to be. He suckled peacefully, and I saw his eyes moving behind their lids as he heard my voice. He held my finger in his soft little hand as he drifted into sleep.

Sometimes when I nursed him, Rebekah stroked his thick dark hair, or his smooth little feet. She lay on the mat next to us, sometimes staring at him in wonder, sometimes at me with the same awe. She loved Rananyah as she said she would. And Isaac honored him with a visit every day. Once he even took Rananyah with him to meditate in the fields in the afternoon, even though it was brief so he could come back and suckle.

Those are the stories of Rananyah, of Zacharyah. He was a reminder and a joy, but only briefly. On his tenth day of life, his little body filled with heat. I do not know where it came from, but every little part I touched was burning. I could feel fire coming from his insides, cooking him, burning him. He would not take my milk, would not even open his mouth or his eyes. We prayed for him, sang to him, pleaded with him and Yah. We bathed him in cool water, and I put herbs in the water that I would have fed to him if I could have. I got only slight comfort that Yah prevented him from suffering. He slept peacefully during every moment of my agony. When his body finally cooled, it was only because he had died.

I would not allow him to be buried under the tree that was nourished by the blood of unfinished pregnancies. This boy had lived, and he had died, and he would be buried accordingly. Rebekah took a blanket she had been weaving and laced it with golden thread. She sat and wove through her tears. Rananyah was placed in a shroud of her handiwork and carried by his father to the top of a hill that overlooked the valley to the north. This land belonged to Isaac, and Rananyah would stay there permanently. When his little body was in the ground, I clutched the dirt in my hands and vomited into the cruel soil that would separate me from him. Rebekah stayed by my side until my eyes began to close from exhaustion. Then she beckoned Isaac's most trusted servant Elioded. He brought us back to the camp in a cart and Isaac walked beside us.

Rebekah deeply grieved the loss of our baby boy. Yet, as sad as she was, she still had two kicking sons inside her belly. My womb was as empty as my arms and would remain that way. I felt alone in the depths of my loss. In addition to the pain of the grief in my heart, I had the pain above it. My breasts were swollen with undrunk milk and as hard and heavy as rocks pressing me into the ground. And so I laid down on the dirt beneath the carob tree and wept. Many times I reminded myself to breathe

Yah's comfort into me there. *Yhhhh*. And to breathe my sorrow—some of it anyhow—out, for Yah to hold it with me. *Whhhh*. I reminded myself that the sons that would soon be born to Rebekah were a part of my family. If I could not overcome my grief, I would need to at least overcome my envy and summon my love for them, so Rebekah and I could be mothers together.

I do not know how long I would have stayed in despair beneath the carob tree had I not been interrupted. Usually, Rebekah and I helped each other through difficult moments, but we were both deeply saddened by this one. While I took to the tree, she took to the tent. Not for long, though. Only two days after we had buried Rananyah, birth water gushed through Rebekah's legs, and we could stay still no longer. The midwife was called, the bricks were laid, and after a full day and night of pain and pushing, poultices and impatience, two boys emerged from her womb, just as Yah had said.

The first baby was plump and hairy, just as my Rananyah had been, though this new baby's hair was red. Never had I seen such a sight, and I reacted with an unexpected squeal of delight in seeing something new and wondrous. Holding on to the ankle of this firstborn was a smaller baby, sliding out of the womb with the momentum that his brother had begun. When they both started wailing with the force of a pair of bulbul birds, Rebekah's tears flowed with relief, and my milk began to pour down my front and release the pressure that had been building in my breasts.

Instinctively I took the first baby and brought him to my breast. He was big and hungry and sucked me dry, one side after the other. As I satisfied his appetite, he relieved my pain. I smiled at his sweet, sleeping face. I had been so busy nursing him that I had forgotten my surroundings. When I looked to Rebekah, I saw that she was nursing the little one. I worried—maybe I should not have taken the first baby. He, too, could suckle from the woman whose womb had carried him. She looked at me, and our eyes locked. I saw gratitude. Indeed, later she told me that she had been worried about nursing two babies and was grateful that there were four teats to do the job.

I had told Rebekah about the Egyptian tradition of private names. After what happened to Rananyah, she was reluctant but did not tell me one way or the other what she chose to do. I suppose this was her little private place, like I had mine. The names she chose for these boys to be called were Esau, for the first one, and Jacob, for the second. Yes, Joseph, the very Jacob who is your father. Rebekah named him thus because he held on to his brother's heel as they exited the womb. Isaac announced their names when they were circumcised and entered into the covenant with Yah on their eighth day of life. Once again Rebekah and I danced with babies in arms. These boys could not replace Rananyah or the pain of losing him, but they did keep us busy.

THE FIFTH SCROLL

THE FIFTEENTH PARCHMENT

My milk was a miracle for Esau. Rebekah often said that. She nursed him sometimes but was concerned that Jacob would not have enough milk if she fed Esau first. Sometimes, when Jacob finished his leisurely drinking and was sleeping dreamily on the pallet next to Rebekah, she would let Esau finish the milk his brother had left. This was not enough for even the smallest of kittens, merely a chance for Rebekah to hold her first baby in her arms. When it was clear that the milk was gone, he quickly wriggled away.

And so it was that Jacob drank from Rebekah and Esau drank from me, and there was enough for everyone. We spent the first months of their lives relaxing on rugs in the sun during the mornings before the heat, nursing, singing, telling stories, and just wondering at the little babies. When the stars came out, we retreated to our tent, the four of us huddled under blankets like snails sharing one shell. There was plenty of room for us to spread out in the tent, just no reason to. And so, though we got little sleep from our day and night nursings, we were as relaxed as royalty.

Esau was the first to roll over, the first to sit up, the first to crawl, and the first to run. At every new accomplishment, I clapped and praised him and paraded him before Isaac, who also was generous with praise for his son. Rebekah was happy to see Esau's progress but worried about Jacob each time. Whenever Jacob seemed behind his brother, Rebekah reminded herself of what she had learned directly from Yah. Her sons would grow into two nations, and the older would serve the younger. Instead of succumbing to the worry, she worked extra hard to help him keep up with his brother. Jacob's time would come; she would help make sure of it.

I tried to help Rebekah see that it was always Jacob's time, just as it was always Esau's. They were the most different boys anyone could imagine, and it was hard not to see one ahead and one behind—each of them taking his turn. Jacob sucked on his fingers quietly when his teeth were coming in, while Esau burst into screams that scared the birds away. Esau was quick to crawl out of the tent, while Jacob could only sit still. But Jacob was able to sit still and entertain us by pointing to every body part when we named it, while Esau crawled too far away to even hear us say those words.

And when Esau was chasing butterflies, Jacob was beginning to say words. He began to call Rebekah Kah Kah and me Ba Ba. We realized that he was trying to say Rebekah and Deborah and did not even have a word for *mother*, because we never used one. How to change that became a point of worry for me and

Rebekah. She had always said we would be mothers together, that the babies would be mine as well as hers. And with all the months of nursing and singing, feeding and teaching, laughing and sleeping, I did feel like a mother. And yet, was I?

We knew we needed to do something but did not know what. Rebekah spoke first. "The boys will be confused if they call us both Mother. And we shall be also," she said. She was right, of course. "Rananyah was your son," she said.

"Rananyah is gone!" I yelled. "I nurse and nurture these babies, yet I am just their maid." I quieted my voice. Then I said what was really hurting me. "You said Rananyah was your son, too."

"Yes," Rebekah said quietly. "You interrupted me. For I was going to say it again now. When Rananyah was born, and I held his little body in my arms . . . When I looked into his dark eyes and saw you in there . . . When I sang to him, and even when I heard you sing to him . . . When he succumbed to fever . . . I loved him. I felt that even though you grew him in your womb, I was his mother. I was his mother also. And," she hesitated, "I never told you this, Deborah, but I was jealous of you."

I looked at her, more curious than angry now. Listening.

"Not because you had borne the first child. Not because you would have been the higher wife than I. I told you, that did not bother me. What saddened me is that little love of a boy would one day call you Mother. And that seemed like the most wonderful gift. That one day, Rananyah would open his mouth and cry, 'Mother,' and mean you, not me."

I cried at the loss of having never heard this word from his mouth. Never having heard any word. Rebekah cried with me.

"And then," she said, "when Rananyah died and these babies were born . . . it was all so much. So much at once. We were busy with them night and day. And I missed Rananyah. I still do. I know you do; please know that I do. But gone was the worry of the name *Mother*. Who had time for such thoughts?" We laughed, for we knew that certainly we did not. "We have time now," she said. "Let us think about it, pray about it." This was another time when Rebekah's eyes said: *I love you as much as you love me.*

We did think about it and pray about it and talk about it. Rebekah was first to have an idea, and one idea was enough. "You remember my mother," she said. Of course I remembered Metuyeshet. I did not spend much time with her or know her well. Nobody did. But, of course, I remembered her. "And you remember my father's other wife, Auntie," she said. Of course I did. We had woven together, danced together, drummed together.

"I always wished to have a mother like Auntie," Rebekah said. "A woman who was kind and smiled easily and stroked my hair and wiped away my tears and also encouraged me and celebrated me and cheered for me. That is you, Deborah. You do that for these little boys. *Auntie* is a name said with love. Perhaps they could call you Auntie."

I would have done anything for Rebekah, but this took no effort. I felt grateful, for I knew she meant every word she said. I tried to give her the same kindness. "And they will call you Mother," I said. "For your body was the first home they knew, and you held them in there even when they tried to get out. And now that they have, you provide for them and marvel at them and *be* with them. You give *Mother* a new meaning."

And so, I started calling Rebekah *Mother*, and she started calling me *Auntie*. Soon the babies were calling us Mama and Titi until both of their little mouths could say big words, and we became Mother and Auntie. What felt like only moments later, they were running and jumping everywhere and yelling behind them, "Auntie, look what I can do!" and "Mother, watch me!" This was around the time of their weaning and first haircut. Oh, what a day that was!

Abraham and Keturah had already traveled to the east. With Father Abraham gone, the rest of the tribe had time to adjust to Isaac being the new head. Word was sent that our boys were thriving, and Abraham and Keturah and their boys came back for the celebration of the twins' weaning. It was wonderful to see them again and to introduce them to the twins. It was the first time that someone from outside the camp had seen Esau. We were all so used to his wild red curls that we hardly noticed them anymore. But for Abraham and Keturah, their sons and servants, it was a sight never before seen. They pointed and oohed and aahed until Esau took cover behind our skirts to avoid all the gawking.

By the second day, Esau was walking around covering his head with his arms. When this did not provide him the privacy he was seeking, he fell to the ground and began pounding it and wailing so loud that even Isaac came to learn the cause of the yells. Esau told his father how angry he was that he had red hair and that everyone could stare at him and talk about him.

"You are helping Yah," Isaac said. "A person does not often see a rainbow or a hiding lizard, or a star falling from the sky, or a child with red curls. When we do, it is special, and we are reminded of how special Yah is and we point at that thing to share it with others."

I do not know whether Sarah once said similar words to Isaac when he was a young boy, wearing his distinctions so plainly on his face, his height, his eyes, his speech, but I imagined it so. And Esau stopped covering his hair and walked tall and proud after that and joined Jacob in running around after Keturah's sons, trying to do what the bigger boys did. For many days they had great fun together, even though Esau yelled a lot, expressing his frustration that he could not keep up with the older boys. He was used to mastering everything he tried, but these older boys could do things he had not yet thought to try—nor was immediately able to do.

One morning he was throwing rocks at a tree and stomping his feet. His brow was wrinkled with concentration and anger. "What is wrong, Little Esau?" I asked him.

"I am not little!" he yelled back at me.

I would not accept him lashing out at me with anger, and the look in my eye made that clear.

"I am not little, Auntie," he said. "Midian, Ishbak, and Shuah say I am little all day long. But just because I am smaller than them does not mean I am little. I have had four summers and five winters. I am to have my hair cut in a few days! Is that a boy who is little?"

I sat on the ground, and Esau let me take him into my arms. He liked to be active but was always willing to let me hold him if I was quick enough to let him go. “Esau,” I said, “you are a big boy. Strong and brave. But little is not a bad thing. A seed is little but has all the power to grow into a tree. A rock is little but can keep a lion away from the sheep. Even the sun is just a little part of the sky, and it brings us much warmth when it shines. But you will be bigger one day, and shall I tell you how to get bigger faster?”

“Yes!” he shouted as he jumped from my lap. “I am ready, Auntie!”

“Are you certain?” I asked him. “There are three things you must do, and they are not easy. They require patience, courage, and a keen eye.”

“I am certain,” he said, standing tall. “I am very patient. Every day I wait for everything. I wait for the breeze to cool my face, and I wait for Jacob to catch up to me. I wait for you or Mother to make my meals, and I wait for Father to watch me jump. I am very patient. And I am filled with courage in my whole body! My feet and legs bravely take me down the ravines and up the hills. My arms help lift the carts to attach to the donkeys. And my eyes, Jacob says that I have *two* green eyes, not just one!”

I could not help but laugh at our little boy. He was, indeed, getting bigger every day, but I still had time to enjoy his littleness. “All right then, you are ready. Listen closely. Close your beautiful green eyes. Feel the sun on your face and the breeze in your hair. Take a long deep breath in like this—*Yhhhh*—and hold it inside you. This is how you bring your god to be a part of you.” I paused to enjoy my little boy in his stillness. “Now, slowly let your breath out, do not rush it, like this—*Whhhh*. This is how you become a part of your god.” He did as I said.

"Next, say these words: *Yah, god of my father, Isaac, god of my father, Abraham, please help me be a bigger boy.*" Esau said it, with deep feeling. I felt him getting bigger already. "Now, another slow breath like the first," I said. "*Yhhhh, Whhhh.* Soon you will open your eyes. Not yet. I shall tell you. Before you open them, I want you to prepare yourself that whatever you see will be a message from Yah, but you might not understand it right away. You might need to sit still, even after you open your eyes, do you understand?"

Esau nodded that he did.

"Then you may open your green eyes," I said. "Now, sweet boy, look around you. What has Yah shown you about becoming bigger?"

Esau opened his eyes. I could see disappointment on his face. "I am not bigger," he said. "Auntie, you have not helped me be bigger."

"Shall I tell you what Yah has shown me? Perhaps these clues will help you become bigger."

Esau stomped his feet but allowed me another moment to speak. "I see a carob tree," I said first. "When you were born, that carob tree was shorter than it is now. You cannot see, because it grows slowly. But I spent many days staring up at it when your older brother died. I even nursed you in its shade when you were a baby. I can see that it has grown taller in the years since then." Esau put his hand on mine. I no longer needed comforting when I mentioned Rananyah, but I always welcomed a tender moment with Esau.

I turned my head to look in the other direction, and Esau followed my gaze. "I see Zimran sitting in the shade of an olive tree. You have been busy running around with Abraham's youngest boys. Zimran is the oldest. I hear that his voice sounds like a man's voice, I see that some whiskers have darkened his upper lip. Maybe you thought he was a man. But he is still a boy—the biggest boy. I see he has a bow and arrow and is doing something with them. What do you think he is doing?"

Esau paused. He strained his eyes and stretched his neck for a better look. "I do not know, Auntie. I am going to go ask the biggest boy what he is doing."

Esau sat under the olive tree with Zimran until the sun began to set. He was quiet and looked up to the older boy, listening to his every word. In their time together, Zimran taught him to be still and watch the animals, to anticipate their moves, and he let Esau sharpen his arrows, even though he was too small to shoot them. Somehow this did not disappoint Esau. He had found the patience to wait to be older, because he had found something to improve upon along the way.

When it came time to celebrate the boys' weaning, Esau asked to sit beside Zimran. Isaac sat on his high cushion with his boys to either side, and Zimran sat next to Esau. We put Jokshan, the next oldest, next to Jacob. Isaac offered Abraham his seat, but Abraham declined. "I have seven sons," he said. "I have done this many times. It is your honor now."

I knew that Abraham and Isaac had already planned the ceremony, and this exchange of honoring words was a part of it. Rebekah and I had made hundreds of sweets for the occasion, and the boys were sitting on their hands to keep from grabbing them.

Isaac opened his mouth to begin. "Blessed are you, Yah, god of my father, Abraham, who has sustained me and brought me to this day, to celebrate the life of not one son, but two." Then Isaac turned to each son and had the boys sit in front of him so he could look at them. "Esau, Jacob, you are blessings to us from Yah, and Yah will bless you many times. Now I shall tell you a story of a time when Yah blessed me."

The boys sat straight and looked right at their father. He had never told them a story before. Sometimes he took them to meditate in the fields in the afternoon, but they could not stand to stay long. Sometimes he shared with them from his plate. And he often rubbed their heads and laughed with them. But a story, this was a special treat. I turned to Rebekah, wondering if she knew in advance, but she shook her head no and shushed me.

"Many years ago, my father was called by Yah to make a sacrifice on Mount Moriah. He allowed me the honor of accompanying him. I was already a man, so I had joined him for many years in tending to the sheep. I had joined him in prayer and had learned from him. But I had never been with him on a journey that Yah had called him for.

"We woke early in the morning and took our supplies and two boys to help carry them. But as we were going to ascend the mountain, my father, your grandfather, instructed the boys to stay below. Only the two of us would participate in this sacrifice."

Joseph, you remember this story, of course. For you have already written it in these scrolls. I heard it first from Father Abraham. Now it was Isaac's turn to tell it. They told of the same day, yet the story was different.

"We climbed together," Isaac said. "It was not a tall mountain or a difficult journey, even though we carried wood for the burnt offering. We followed a goat path but saw no goats. We had brought no sheep with us for the sacrifice. 'Where is the sheep?' I asked, and my father simply told me that Yah would provide it. When we reached the top, there still was no sheep. Even so, my father, your grandfather, found a large rock and laid the wood there for the ceremony.

"'My son,' he called to me. 'I am here,' I responded. 'Yah is our god,' he said. 'Yah is our god,' I repeated, 'that is true.' He went on. 'Yah is reliable.' 'Yah is reliable.' I repeated. 'Yah always exists.' Everything he said, I repeated. My father always told me that even if my speech is slower than others, or sounds different, that Yah understands me always. 'Yah always exists,' I said. This went on and on, with his voice growing louder each time, and mine matching his.

"'Yah is honest!' My father yelled.

"'Yah is honest!' I yelled.

"'Yah is loyal!'

"Yah is loyal!'

"Yah is beloved!'

"Yah is beloved!'

"'Yah is kind!'

"Yah is kind!'

"'Yah is mighty!'

"'Yah is mighty!'

"'Yah is perfect!'

"'Yah is perfect!'

"'Yah is good!'

"'Yah is good!'

"With that, my father, Abraham, your grandfather, began again, and I repeated after him again. This time we stomped our feet and clapped our hands and raised them to the sky. We went around and around the altar and praised Yah and let the sweet sweat pour down our necks as our joy and excitement grew. Finally, when we had exhausted ourselves, my father instructed me to lie down. On the altar."

The boys gasped when they heard this. As did I. As did Rebekah. Lie down on the altar? Isaac had paused the story to look each boy in the eyes. Then he closed his eyes and breathed deeply.

"'My son,' my father whispered. 'Yah is our god, reliable, ever existing, honest, loyal, beloved, kind, mighty, perfect, and good.' I listened to his words, even as he was binding me to the rock. Finally, he said, 'Close your eyes, my son. Yah will provide the sheep.' And so I did. I trusted my father and my god. I felt the sun on my face. I heard the wind weaving between the leaves in the thickets. I smelled my own sweat. I breathed. *Yhhhh. Whhhh. Yhhhh. Whhhh.* I did not open my eyes.

"I do not know how long that lasted. I only remember hearing my father cry out, 'Yah has provided the sheep! Yah has provided the sheep!' while untying the ropes. I stood and saw my father walking to a black ram caught in the thickets. The ram would be sacrificed on the rock!"

Rebekah and I both let out a small squeal of joy and relief. Of course, Isaac was sitting there before us. We knew he was not sacrificed, and yet we had been so caught in the story that our fear had been real.

"Now, my sons," Isaac continued, "I shall tell you two things. One is, when we ate the ram, it was the most delicious food I had ever eaten. Perhaps because it had saved my life, or perhaps because the flesh of a wild beast is tastier than that of those we raise. And more importantly, today we shall give a piece of *you* to Yah, but only the piece you do not need. Today I thank Yah, and you will thank Yah, for allowing you to reach this milestone. I shall cut your hair short like mine, and you will put the hair in the fire yourselves. Who will go first?"

Esau leapt to his feet. "I shall, Father! I shall! I was the first to be born." I believe Isaac knew that Esau would jump to be first. He jumped to be born first and was the fastest at everything. Even if Jacob wanted to be first, he would not have been quick enough to say so.

Isaac took Esau's hand and walked with him to the fire. He took out his knife. Though I knew he would cut only the boy's hair, I imagined Abraham raising his knife to Isaac and was grateful that it was a sight I never saw. Isaac cut Esau's long red hair and gave it to the boy. Isaac instructed Esau to throw the hair in the fire. Once he had done so, Isaac had Esau circle the fire with him, repeating the words that he had said with Abraham on the mountain. Esau did his job perfectly! And oh, what a big boy he did look like!

"Hallelu Yah!" I sang.

"Hallelu Yah!" Rebekah sang back.

Isaac took Esau's hand again and led him back to the cushions, beckoning Jacob to come for his turn. "Little Jacob," he said, "you are not the oldest, but you are no less important to Yah or to me." He took his knife out again and cut Jacob's long black hair. Jacob knew what to do, as he had seen his brother.

He threw his hair in the fire and circled it with his father, repeating the ceremonial words.

"Hallelu Yah!" I sang out again.

"Hallelu Yah!" Rebekah repeated, full of pride and gratitude.

When Isaac and Jacob returned to the cushions, Isaac gave his final words. "Now," he said, "we shall eat. We have no wild ram for the feast, but we have lambs, and we have the delightful sweets made by your mothers, and I think it will be some of the most delicious food you have ever eaten."

The food was, indeed, delicious. The little boys and Abraham's sons swiped up the sweets and ran around under the darkening sky. Torches were lit, and musical instruments were brought out. Abraham invited his son to dance, and Rebekah and I danced together as we had when the babies were born. We tried to persuade them to let us pick them up, but they were officially big now and would hear nothing of it.

When he had enough of chasing Abraham's sons, Jacob did come and join the dance. He spun around and jumped, danced with his father and grandfather, and finally honored us with his presence if we promised not to take him into our arms. Eventually we all danced together in one large circle, clapping and rejoicing on the special day.

When we were all exhausted and ready to fall on our mats, satisfied and happy, Isaac requested that I accompany him to his tent. He had not called for me in years. Rebekah went to him often, but no babies had come of their unions. After the twins were born, Rebekah's body was exhausted. She could not imagine carrying yet another body in hers, and she began chewing the silphium seeds Tanqo had introduced me to. They had worked well. Perhaps so well that Isaac was now ready for more sons.

If we had known of Isaac's desire in advance, Rebekah and I could have made a plan. As it was, I had no choice but to follow him. I reminded myself that I had no reason to fear. Isaac was gentle, loving, and kind before. He was still the same man. I would be safe and, actually, maybe even happy. I could not quite convince myself to be fully excited just yet, but I went with willingness.

"Please, sit," Isaac said, pointing to the cushion next to his own. The tent was mostly the same as it had been all those years before. This time I noticed that the odor of sheep was fainter, masked somewhat by the more pleasant smell of sage. Isaac had four little lamps on the short side of the tent with some sage smoldering, and twenty of the same along the long side. Rebekah had told me years ago that he had accepted this idea she had for making a nicer smelling sleeping area, and now I was experiencing the pleasantness of it myself.

I sat on the cushion, and he sat on his. I could not hold my tongue or curiosity. "Isaac," I asked quietly, "were you not afraid when Abraham bound you on the sacrificing stone?"

"Deborah," he whispered, "my eyes were closed, yet I could see him readying to raise the knife to me. My eyes were full of fear when I saw this. I could hear him raising his arm to strike. My ears were full of fear when I heard this. My whole body was full of fear, even inside, even my feet, even my hair. I would have run if I had not been bound. Yes, I was afraid. And I was also at peace. Both. I trust Yah. As much fear as I had, that was how much peace I had. But not more. I did not have more peace than fear. I was afraid."

I thought of Sarah and of how much fear she must have felt for her son in those same moments. I thought of the sacrifice she made out of love. I wondered if she had also been able to feel peace, even if it was alongside fear. Of course, I said none of that to Isaac.

I was grateful for his answer. In my journey from Egypt, I had often felt peace, even though the fear would not go away. We had that in common. I nodded and thanked him.

Isaac faced me and handed me a small pink rock, about the size of my thumb, and as smooth as the red glass I had once felt in Hallel's home. There was a golden chain attached to the top. I held it in my hands, stroked the sides of it, felt its warmth, and admired its beauty. Where had he gotten such a treasure? When I paused from examining it to ask him this very question, he spoke before I could open my mouth.

"Deborah," he said, "today was a very special day. We celebrated two boys. Three are still in my heart, as I know they are in yours. I celebrate Rananyah today . . . in a different way." Isaac took the chain from my hand and placed it over my head so that the smooth rock dangled between my breasts. It had been many years since I had worn a necklace. The rope of my last one had broken long ago; the bee now rested comfortably in my satchel.

I had no words. No thoughts. No feelings. I could only clutch the rock and cry. And that is what I did. I just cried, with my body shaking, tears and snot running from my face. I rocked and swayed; I am not certain, but I may have howled. I cried until all the grief that had ever been in me left. I cried until I had more peace than fear. When I was finally still, I reached out to Isaac and kissed his hand. Then his cheek. And then we lay together for what would be our last time. No baby came of our night, but so much more did.

THE SIXTEENTH PARCHMENT

With Esau and Jacob officially boys and no longer babies, some changes were made in the camp. Isaac began allowing them to go to the fields with him to look over the sheep. He tried taking them both together, but they would fight, and Isaac became uneasy. So sometimes he took Esau and sometimes Jacob. By the time they had six summers, the boys both demonstrated a skill for knowing the needs of the flocks and tending to them. But neither wanted to do so.

When Esau came back from spending days and nights with his father and the sheep, he would report frustration with the idiocy of watching idle animals. Whenever he could bear it no longer, he would wander off after a baby deer or a rabbit, following it silently, watching it with unbroken focus, and finally mastering it and roasting it. He stood taller every time that he reported his father's appreciation. "Esau, this tastes as good as the wild ram that saved my life." Esau would not turn down his father's requests to join him in shepherding, but he used his time to carve his bows and sharpen his arrows.

Jacob was most at ease when Esau was away. When the boys were together, their playful wrestling usually ended with blood coming from Jacob's nose or knees or lips. Jacob was often the first to instigate an argument when Esau returned, and Esau was the one to end it. Neither seemed to enjoy their time together. And as much as Jacob liked being apart from Esau, he disliked being the one to leave. The time with his father was an honor, he said. The sheep heeded his shepherding, he said. The blue skies and green hills were gifts from Yah, he said. But he preferred to be in the tents at the camp.

What were we to do with a boy who was staying underfoot? We did not know an answer to that other than to treat him as we would a girl who was there. Rebekah and I had considered the possibility of birthing more children. Rebekah was still sleeping in Isaac's tent many nights, though his requests had become fewer over the years. She was still chewing the seeds and praying to have her body remain her own. I was willing to have another pregnancy, even if not eager. With no requests or complaints from Isaac about more children, two it was. Perhaps it was a blessing to have one remain close by some of the time.

So as the children got bigger and our duties changed, so did Jacob's. He began removing insects from the garden plants and drawing water. He spun wool from the sheep and tried his hand at weaving. He did well in his first lessons, but we sent him for other tasks, deciding we preferred to have this time together without him. Jacob built fires for our stews and breads and made many himself.

Eventually a balance was struck with Esau watching over the farthest sheep and Jacob the closest ones. The shepherds who were tending the flocks with them and their father guarded and grew the sheep. The boys learned from them but also had freedom to wander. Esau went out farther and farther, testing and mastering his skill with the bow and arrow. The game he brought back grew larger as he did. Jacob learned to mind and care for the sheep but complained about his time away from the camp and always wanted to be there.

"Why must I tend the flock?" he asked. "My father sees to it that the animals are well cared for, healthy, and strong. There are plenty of shepherds without me. I am not needed. I could stay here and tend the garden instead."

"Jacob," Rebekah said, "one day the sheep will be yours. One day you will be the one who needs to make sure they are healthy and strong. How will you do this if you do not learn from your father and the other shepherds?"

Jacob did not have an answer.

"Jacob," I said, "your honored grandfather Abraham talks to Yah every morning. He thanks Yah for the blessings and abundance. Your honored father, Isaac, talks to Yah every afternoon. You have seen him; you have gone with him. Should the sun set on the day before you, too, thank Yah? Talk with Yah? Listen to Yah?"

Jacob jumped up and hugged me with a huge smile. "You are right, Auntie! That is what I shall do! I shall stay in the camp and pray. In that way, I shall help the sheep *and* the garden, for I shall ask for Yah's help."

"Listen, Jacob," I said, "when you are speaking to Yah, like your fathers do, begin like this: 'Blessed are you, Yah, god of my father, Isaac, and god of my father, Abraham. Thus, each time you speak to Yah and listen for Yah, you will be reminded of your fathers and their respectful ways." Jacob nodded. "You may begin today," I said. "If you just look at the beauty of the hills and the sky, breathe *Yhhhh* into yourself, and *Whhhh* out of yourself, you will be connected."

Jacob knew the breathing, and he hugged me once more before going to find himself a quiet place to appreciate everything around him and pray. He returned to the tents in the last light of the sun. He looked blissful and pleased.

"Well done," I said to him. "I see the benefit of your time with Yah. You will do that every evening after you return from the sheep."

"What?" Jacob asked, startled. "But no, Auntie, I shall talk with Yah *instead* of tending the sheep. Because I shall ask Yah to take care of them."

"You will take care of them," I reminded him, "with Yah's help. And after you take care of them, you will thank Yah for helping you do so. You will begin by invoking the names of your fathers—shepherds who looked after their sheep *and* talked with Yah. And hopefully when you talk with Yah, you will move from your frustration in the field to gratitude for your gifts."

"Mother?" Jacob turned to Rebekah, hoping she would spare him from the sheep.

"Auntie certainly is wise, is she not?" Rebekah said.

"Yes, Mother." Jacob dropped his shoulders in resignation.

Jacob tended the flocks closest to the camps so that every evening he could return to the tent for sleeping. He continued to pray, and he continued to complain. He also continued to learn good shepherding skills. He mastered the slingshot and protected the sheep. He helped deliver the lambs and learned to give commands the dogs would heed. He learned to catch the sheep with his crook and tell their age by their teeth. Isaac reported that he was quite a skilled shepherd, actually, but still not satisfied. While Esau was also unfulfilled by shepherding, he had his hunting in addition—which he enjoyed and excelled at. Jacob merely had disappointment, for he only had the flocks.

It was Isaac's idea that Jacob learn to read and write. He had recently hired Katib, a scribe, and did not have enough work for him to be busy all the time. And so he tasked Katib with teaching Jacob this skill. "He can learn to count and write lists of the blessings that Yah has given us," was Isaac's reasoning. Jacob reported to Katib and studied under his tutelage with great enthusiasm and interest.

Whether out in the fields or at the tents, Jacob frequently practiced his writing. He would use his shepherd's crook to write in the dirt, or a stick he picked up from the ground. Katib challenged him to write seventy words or more every day, and Jacob was pleased to do so and could often be found admiring his creations. When I saw him in such a position, I always said, "Jacob, you have done a fine job writing; now read what you have written," and he proudly read from the words on the ground.

So eager was he to practice his skill that he would jump at any opportunity to do so. When a pot was broken, I brought him the shards. "Jacob," I said, "your writing in the dust is admirable. Now, see if you can write the same thing smaller, on these shards. Do you think you can do it?" His face would turn into a grin so large that it left little room for his eyes and nose. Later he would return to me with the shards, and I would ask him to read me each word, and as he did so, to write it in the dust, so the ground and the shard would match.

Can you imagine it, Joseph? Your father learning the same skill that you now practice in these scrolls? He was much more content once he started. For then he not only had the prayers in the evenings but the writing practice all day long, only sometimes interrupted by the sheep. Even when he did need to tend to them, and tend to them he did, he knew he would soon be writing again.

As for Rebekah and me, we had moved our sleeping cushions to the far end of the tent after the weaning. No longer were the boys nursing. No more nights of warm little breath on our bosoms, and no more nights of restless legs kicking us in their sleep. We made a pallet for them, and they slept together like puppies, even when they spent the days apart, or arguing, even as their second set of teeth grew in, and their voices began to crackle with upcoming manhood. When Esau returned from several nights in the far field, he still cuddled with his brother in sleep. This never failed to bring us smiles. And we were left to pass the nights in comfort.

This was our life in the land that Yah promised to Abraham. Everyone had a purpose and a place in the camp. Rebekah and

I wove, cooked, and tended to Isaac and the children when they needed help or healing. Isaac watched over the flocks and wealth with the help of his sons and his trusted overseer, Elioded. Esau hunted, and Jacob wrote; they both grew taller and stronger with mouths full of large teeth. We appreciated our blessings, the wind, the rain when it came, the land, the sun, and the moon. We praised Yah and knew Yah.

One morning, with the sun just starting to bring the morning light and dry the evening dew, that is, a morning just like all other mornings, I awoke to find a praying mantis lying on its back on the edge of the rug just inside our tent. I had always admired the creature, though I had seen only a handful of them in my lifetime. Each time I did, it inspired me to stop what I was doing and watch it. I always heard Mother's voice in my ears during these special times.

Moshel's father, my grandfather, was buried with two praying mantises. Such was the value he brought to the pharaoh that two were placed with him to guide him to eternity so that someday, he might serve the pharaoh again when the pharaoh passed to the next realm.

The praying mantis on the edge of the tent that morning was on its way to the next realm. It was lying on its back. It was clearly coming to the end of its life. I gently lifted it off the rug and placed it on the dirt just outside our tent. From the dust it had come, to the dust it would return. I crouched on the ground next to it, watching as it gently, slowly, moved its legs, sometimes up, sometimes to the side. Its eyes were closed and its mouth puckered. I at once felt sad that I could not help it feel comfort, and at the same time awed that I was allowed to witness it in its last moments.

As it turned out, its last moments were much of the day. Rebekah sat beside me when she saw me there, and neither of us could look away from its beauty. The green was as bright as grass after a fresh rain. The arms had small yellow stripes. Its face was triangular and perfect. Its legs, as thin as hairs. We sat with it, admired it, appreciated it, and sang to it.

Yah, lie us down in peace
And spread over us your blanket of peace
Amen, amen
In the morning, bring us back to life
In the meantime, we will not fear, because you are with us
Amen, amen

For a flash I felt embarrassed. Why would I forego everything else and sing to this little creature? At the same time, I admired Rebekah for doing so. I felt her love, her appreciation for this animal and for Yah, its creator. And I felt blessed for being beside someone who felt as I did. And so, though we did not understand why, we sat with it for the whole day. In gentle voices we thanked it for coming to us, for allowing us to witness it, for witnessing us. When the heat of the day had passed and the sun was preparing to set, the praying mantis died. Still, we sat there. I recall the last thought I had before we were pulled out of our peace. It was, "We wish to be sad when something is lost, but there is no need, for one thing going makes room for another coming."

I did not have a chance to voice that thought to Rebekah before the next thing came. It was Ben Meshek, standing in the open area between our tents, panting and wiping sweat from his brow. He had run from Abraham's camp in the east. He was a man of strong legs, strong will, and strong loyalty, which was why he was the one chosen to deliver the message he would recite. He arrived in time for the evening meal. Isaac was preparing to eat beside his tent, and when he saw a messenger, he invited him to wash his hands and feet and partake in the meal.

"Thank you," Ben Meshek said. "Before I eat, I must deliver my message." Isaac, with his poor eyesight, did not recognize Ben Meshek as the son of his father's trusted servant Eliezer, but Rebekah and I did at once. Even before he spoke, we knew the words he would deliver. It was in that moment that I realized that the praying mantis had already delivered the message even before Ben Meshek arrived.

"I am Ben Meshek, son of Eliezer. I come from the east to inform you that my master, Abraham, died this morning."

Upon hearing this, Isaac reached for his knife and thrust it into the top of his tunic, tearing it as far as his breastbone. Then he dropped it in the dirt by his side and began to weep. Rebekah went to put her arm around him and add her tears to his. I looked down at the praying mantis, then covered my eyes with my hands. When they became too wet, I lowered them and wiped them on my clothes.

"Where is my father now?" Isaac asked.

"He is being gently carried to Hevron," Ben Meshek informed. "He wished to be buried in the Cave of Makhpelah, beside Sarah."

"Then that is where I shall bury him," Isaac said. "We shall leave now."

We would not get far before the sun slid behind the hills, but nobody objected. Isaac gave instructions for Elioded to pack enough provisions for us for a month and then follow. We left with only three young servants carrying a tent and sleeping mats and the food that we could carry on our backs. And I delicately carried the praying mantis in my hand.

Rebekah walked with Isaac, the two of them behind the young men who carried our supplies and led the way. Esau and Jacob walked behind them and talked of what we might encounter on the journey. I walked with my thoughts, and they kept me very busy. We had not seen Father Abraham in many years, yet I already felt a difference between living with him far away and living without him. My sadness at losing him wished to leave no room for my happiness for having known him. At the same time, my happiness for having known him wished to leave no room for the sadness of his death. All the while, I tried to meet with curiosity what his absence created a space for.

The first thing I noticed was grief. Not for the loss of Abraham, but for my mother, Daganyah. Right away I began shedding tears for her. They were joined by tears for Matanyah and, to my surprise, for my own life that I lost in Egypt. I had no way of knowing what that life might have been had my mother lived. I felt certain that my life in Haran and Canaan held better things for me. Even so, this was the first time I grieved the life I had lost in Egypt.

Then my tears fell for Metuyeshet. Why would I cry for Rebekah's mother? I had not even known her. I believe it was only because her death came when we were so far away, when we did not even hear word for many years. Next my tears fell for Yafayeh. We never said goodbye. I never knew what became of her or her sisters. I would never know. I would never know of Hallel's last days and would never know Sarah. For all these reasons, I cried. And when those tears cleared the way, I cried for Rananyah, for Zacharyah. For the one I wanted to know most but knew least.

With every step, I was alone with my tears, except for the mantis, which I still held carefully in my hand. The little green reminder that even in death, there was beauty, and even in sadness, there was Yah. By the time I had shed the last drop of water from my eyes, I felt as cleanly bathed as I had the day Rebekah dumped water on me in Haran.

That evening we traveled only far enough that the camp behind us was no longer in sight. It was enough, Ben Meshek assured us. A brief sleep in the moonless darkness would allow us to arrive in Hevron the next day while there was still light in the sky. I was grateful for the rest. As soon as there was a hint of morning light, we woke and resumed our walk. Now Isaac walked ahead with Esau and Jacob, and Rebekah and I were together. The sun was unforgiving on our brows but sometimes served as a welcome distraction from our sadness, though talking also helped us create our own.

"I am sad," Rebekah voiced. "I wish it were not so."

"What?" I asked. "You wish that what were not so?"

"That Abraham is dead."

"Me, too," I admitted. "But then what?"

"Then he would be alive!" Rebekah said.

"Yes, but for how long?" I asked.

She was silent.

"I also wish that Father Abraham were still alive," I said, "but that is silly. It would not happen. We all die. We all must die."

Rebekah nodded and took my hand. We walked in silence together for a long while, then began to appreciate the surroundings. A lizard slithering by, flowers miraculously grown up from the cracked soil. Any passing wisp of a cloud. The sounds of the birds. The footsteps of our young men in front of us. A drink of water that quenched our thirst and soothed our throats. As Ben Meshek had assured us, we arrived at the cave while the sun was still out, though it had lowered enough to allow a slight cool breeze on our faces.

We were surprised to see many faces already outside the cave, though perhaps we should not have been. We had rushed to get here, not thinking of what we would find, other than Abraham, lovingly, carefully brought by someone. Indeed, he was lying under a blanket, guarded by boys who would not let even the smallest ant approach his body.

We learned that the boys were the grandchildren of Abraham's first son, Ishmael. Was he, too, here? Certainly if he lived, he came. For all of Abraham's children were there: Isaac and the five sons of Keturah. I recognized them right away, for each one had the face he had as a boy, just covered in hair. Esau saw them at the same moment and went to greet Zimran. They clapped each other on the shoulder and easily began talking and laughing.

Jacob, too, found someone who caught his interest. A girl we later learned was a wife of Abraham's son Ishbak. When she revealed this to us, Jacob walked away and sought solitude. There were not so many people there, but enough that it was difficult to see Keturah right when we arrived. But when we turned our heads to the sound of the wailing, we saw her there, on her knees, banging her fists on the ground as she cried.

Rebekah and I rushed to her. When she saw us, she rose. "Do not rise on our account," Rebekah said. "We come to you; you are in mourning."

"Mourning, yes," she said. "Mourning that I gave this man five sons. I destroyed my altars. I followed him east. I covered his wounds and brought water to his cracked lips, which I then bathed in oil. I was his prize, his showpiece, his proof that he was young, even when he was old. And it was not enough for him. 'Tell me a story,' he would say. 'Tell me of your life.' What was to tell? My life was his life. He looked at me in scorn with the same eyes that asked me to carry his food. And now? Am I to marry again? Am I to be sold? Do I now belong to Isaac, like everything else? To my sons, he gave trinkets. 'I gave them Yah,' he would say. 'Yah will be with them, always.' Can they eat Yah? Can they plant in Yah? Can they pay servants with Yah?"

She went back to her howls and tears, and I wished to join her. Oh, Keturah! Oh, me! Was that what my life would have become? Or would my sons have inherited from Abraham as the children of Sarah? Would he have turned on me, or would he have been a happy old man listening to stories? I could not find words of comfort for Keturah, so I sat in the dirt beside her and wept. Rebekah joined me, though her sideways glance told me to stop bothering myself with thoughts of what might have been, and I tried to obey.

A tall man approached us. He was strong and dark, like an Egyptian. His beard was cut close to his face and his tunic was of a style I had never seen.

"Which of you women is Keturah?" he asked.

We stood, and Keturah stepped forward.

He took her hand and kissed it. "I understand you were the wife of my father. Please, if you need assistance, allow me to provide it."

"Ishmael?" Rebekah asked.

"Yes," he responded.

"I am Rebekah, the wife of Isaac. He is here. Have you seen him?"

"Yes," he said again, adding no other details. He looked to me, the woman unexplained. I was not a wife of his father or his brother. It would not be proper for a nursemaid to introduce herself to the master's brother or son. I could see that he understood that I was one of the servants. Just as he was turning to go, I spoke.

"I am Deborah," I said. "Granddaughter of Hallel."

This stopped him from leaving. "Hallel?" he asked.

"Yes," I said. "You know her?" This could not be right, I thought to myself. Yet I must have had some hope, for why else would I have spoken these words?

"She was my sister," he said, "though I heard her name only once. My mother, Hajar, was an Egyptian woman. When my father went to Egypt, he became a rich man. He left with many gifts from the pharaoh, including maidservants. My mother was one of those maidservants. She became Sarah's maidservant. When Sarah was barren, my mother went to Abraham in Sarah's stead, at Sarah's request. Nine months later, I was born. I was a good boy! A righteous boy! My mother said that Sarah tried to love me, but she could not.

"'Why not?' I asked my own mother. 'Why will she not love me?' And my mother told me, 'Have compassion, my son. Sarah had a child, a daughter named Hallel who was sold in Egypt. She is no longer. A mother cannot be blamed for mourning the loss of her child.' And now," Ishmael continued, "you tell me you are the granddaughter of this child?"

"Yes," I confirmed for him. I briefly told him of Hallel being cast out of the harem and married to a governor. I told Ishmael that his sister had five daughters, including Daganyah, who bore me, then, on her deathbed, sent me to Haran to reunite with her family.

He took my hand and kissed it. "It is a blessing to be reunited," he said.

"Hallelu Yah," I said.

"Hallelu Yah," he said. And then he repeated it once more, with Rebekah and Keturah joining him.

WE DID NOT SPEND a month in Hevron, but seven days. On the first, Isaac and Ishmael took their father into the cave and came out without him. The sight of them carrying the small body, wrapped in linen, to its resting place, and then exiting without it was the most clear reminder that Father Abraham was gone. We all stood quietly for a long while, moved only by the sun's retreat. As lamps were lit, I placed the praying mantis gently at the mouth of the cave, then walked to the tent that the young men had erected for Isaac and us with him.

"What are we to do next?" Rebekah asked him.

"We shall do whatever comes next."

Esau and Jacob seemed to eat at any opportunity ever since their eyebrows had grown bushy, so they suggested food. In fact, we smelled the aromas of something on the fire already and went out to discover that seven young and tender goats had been sacrificed earlier and were now roasting. It would be enough for a feast.

After the feast, at Ishmael's request, we fasted for three days, eating only after the sun went down. In that time, we visited with Keturah, who had calmed down as she planned to go with Ishmael, and Ozeret, who would go with Keturah. Three of Keturah's sons had taken wives, and we got to know them. We shared stories with the wives and daughters of Ishmael's tribe, and every once in a while, we looked at what the men were doing. We watched Esau and Zimran and Keder and Massa, two of Ishmael's sons, make contests with their bows and arrows and see who could hit the farthest mark. Not to be outdone, Jacob and other skilled shepherds in the clan took out their slingshots and hit just as many marks. Abraham's death had given us a chance to celebrate. Although he was gone, newness was already beginning to develop.

On our last night, Isaac and Ishmael called everyone around the bonfire. "My wives are excellent Tipheret mushroom hunters," Ishmael said. "Tonight, in our father's honor and memory, we shall drink their broth and we shall know YhWh. Listen to the drums." Already the servants had made a wide circle around us and were tapping their drums softly. "Feel the drum beats going down into the ground, into the land, our land, and back into your body. When the broth comes to you, look to your left and to your right. Look in front and behind you. Look at the faces in this circle, the tribe that is the living blessing given to our father, and drink of the broth, then pass it to another of Abraham's tribe. It is through us that the world will be blessed. Tonight, we shall bless our father and praise Yah. Hallelu Yah!"

"Hallelu Yah!" we all responded.

I drank my share of the broth and gently lowered myself to the ground. There was hardly a sliver of moon in the sky, but it was the same sky that held the full moon all those years ago with my mother and her sisters, my grandmother and her granddaughters, all of us descendants of Abraham and Sarah. Now, in the desert, the descendants of Abraham's daughter and seven sons were numerous. I breathed this miracle into my body. *Yhhhh*. And breathed myself into the miraculousness of it all. *Whhhh*. Together we were the fulfillment of Yah's blessing. *Yhhhh. Whhhh*. Together we knew Yah. The drums beat on.

THE SEVENTEENTH PARCHMENT

Life was the same after Abraham's funeral, but we were different in ways that could not be easily explained. And so we did not explain. We lived. We prayed, we laughed, we cried, we danced, we worked. We grew. The boys, especially. It seemed every time I looked at them, they were taller, wider, stronger, hairier, stinkier than the last time. They were still sweet in their sleep, but the quarreling between them seemed to go to blows faster than before whenever they were awake together. Thankfully, that was not often, as Jacob was even more focused on the work he continued to receive from Katib, and Esau was often gone hunting for days at a time.

It was after one of Esau's many hunting adventures that serious trouble grew between the two of them. He came back bloody and exhausted after ten days in the field. He had caught a rabbit on one of the days, cooked it, and eaten it. But for the other days, he had only the few dried figs he had brought and the small handfuls of greens he could find. He had never been gone that long, but he had never had to search and wait for an animal that long.

Just before returning to the camp, he saw a lone deer, trying to eat the few leaves that were left on a bush. He studied it and shot it in the flank. As the deer began to run, he ran after it, shooting again, hitting it in the rear. Then he turned just in time to see that a lion was after the same meal. She was thin, ribs showing, but her pace was not slowed; if anything, it was increased by her hunger. She ran toward Esau, and he shot her in the chest. She slowed and lay down and removed the arrow with several swats from her paw. The deer got away, and so did Esau, scrambling over rocks, cutting his arms and legs as he fled for cover in the few moments he had gained by hitting his mark.

When he was certain the lion was far, he began his journey home. When he finally stumbled into the campground, he saw that Jacob had a bowl of stew. "Give me some of that red, red sustenance," Esau said, "for I am so tired."

On this much of the story, the boys were in agreement. When Jacob tells of what happened, he swears that Esau said that he was so tired he would be willing to give his birthright for a bowl of the stew. But when Esau tells the rest, he insists that it was Jacob's idea that there be a trade, stew in exchange for the blessing of the firstborn son. They could come to blows over this, even though they both once again agreed on what happened next. Esau said, "I am at the point of death, of what use is a birthright to me?" And they both also agreed that, indeed, Jacob gave Esau some of the lentil stew, and Esau did eat.

The next day, when Esau had recovered from his hunger and had slept with honey and herbs on his wounds, he was ready to reclaim his birthright. "I would not sell such a thing," he said. "My brother deceived me. He would have me die rather than give me some of his ready food. It was not even good food! A mush of lentils, without even any meat. His punishment for such greediness should be to lose any blessing at all from our father. But the blessing of the firstborn is mine. There is no question."

"You have sold that blessing to me, Red," Jacob responded. He had taken to calling his brother Red at every chance. He said it was because Esau could see only red meat stew, though there was none. He saw what he wished to see. I think what Jacob wished to see was his brother's face turn red with anger. "I told you one hundred times: There was never any meat! Anyway, without my stew, you would have died of hunger, and I would have received the blessing of the firstborn. I took only what was rightfully mine and spared you your life in my getting it. You should thank me!"

"Jacob!" Now it was me yelling. I was loud enough to be heard over the fight. Rebekah never raised her voice at Jacob. She either stayed out of the boys' arguments or took Jacob's side, always influenced by the message that he would be the greater one someday. But I did not hold back when I raised my voice in that moment. I did lower it to a normal tone once I had everyone's attention. "Jacob, each evening you go out and speak to Yah, the god of your father Isaac, the god of your father, Abraham. You are meant to connect with Yah but also be reminded of who has come before you and what tradition they have taught you.

"Neither your father nor your grandfather would *ever* sell a pot of stew. They are known among travelers and kin to be men who open their tents to share their blessings. They offer meals to strangers and respite to travelers. Your own mother offered water to Eliezer *and* his camels after his long journey. It does not matter whose idea it was to barter the blessing for the stew. We do not do that."

Rebekah and the boys continued their silent stares at me, in case I were to continue. But I had said all I had to say. All there was to say. I wished I could tell the boys to embrace in a hug. I wished a reminder of the comfort they had felt from each other's mere presence when they were babies would settle them now. But as soon as it was clear that I had finished speaking, Esau put his hands on his hips and said, "I *told* you," to Jacob, and then Jacob tackled Esau to the ground.

Yes, Joseph. Your father did that. Sometimes we must learn from our elders what *not* to do. This is one of those times. It is best if you make your own mistakes—for you do, and will continue to do so. We all make mistakes. That was one of Jacob's.

Jacob and Esau began to wrestle and would not release each other, even with stern yelling from both me and Rebekah. It was only when Rebekah managed to put her body in such a place that either one of them who struck out would hit her that they released each other. "Enough!" she yelled. "Enough!" But as soon as she stepped aside, they continued their brawl. I retrieved a bucket of water from beside the cooking fire. It had not been boiled; it was waiting to be used. Little did it know how I was about to use it.

I threw the bucket—not just the water, but the whole bucket, with the water—at the boys. It hit Esau in the shoulder and splashed its contents onto them both, surprising them into stopping. Esau looked at me and stomped away. Jacob, not to be outdone, picked up the bucket to throw it at his brother, but a small sound from Rebekah stopped him before it left his hand, and he, too, stomped away. From then, neither one was willing to sleep next to the other again, and neither was willing to be the one left in the tent, so they each took a mat and slept outside the tent, on opposite sides.

This foolishness went on for a month. Being around them was unpleasant. Their voices had gotten deeper, and their hair thicker. Esau was covered in orange hair. Though it was thick, it was so light in color that it was possible to see the redness of his skin beneath it. Jacob, with skin as brown as dried almonds, had dark hair covering it. His hair, too, was coarser and thicker than before. But other than these physical signs, they showed no more closeness to becoming men—especially with this foolishness. Neither would talk to the other or help the other. If one was working on something, the other would avoid him. Jacob spent more time with the flocks, Esau more time hunting. If they sometimes found themselves accidentally near each other, they nearly growled with contempt.

Rebekah and I argued over whether to help them make amends or to ignore their displays of aggression. Depending on our moods, one of us would feel one way on one day and then argue the opposite the next. And to make matters worse, all of us were feeling concern about our food. The rain had not come in the right season. We ate less and less each day. The grass was brown and dry, and so the flock also ate less and less. We sent the buckets lower and lower in the wells to retrieve water. We had our dried fruits and grains, of course, but the supply was dwindling. We relied on the milk from the goats more and more, and with a hundred men, women, and children in our camp to feed, Isaac was having sheep slaughtered every few days.

The famine was heavy upon us. Rebekah and I walked in the hills, finding shade from boulders more than from trees. We saw the shepherds, tired, the flocks, tired, waiting. We were all waiting for the rain. But it would not come in the dry season, and so it looked like everyone was waiting to die. We could not go on like this.

"Rebekah," I said. "Do you remember I told you that we do not have such seasons in Egypt? The Nile floods and makes the soil fertile. The crops are planted, harvested, and eaten. We cannot sit here waiting to die." My voice lifted with excitement at the thought of seeing my birthland again, seeing the river. "We can go to Egypt, as Sarah and Abraham did before us in the time of famine." A little piece of me felt fear. For it had not worked out well for Hallel to go to Egypt—or had it?

"Oh, Deborah!" she exclaimed. "How I would love to see your beautiful river! And see the giant hippopotamatus with my own eyes." She said *hippopotamus* wrong to make me laugh, and it worked. "I would even like to see the palace." This she said a little more quietly. She held some fear along with her excitement. But the journey would be an adventure! And we would eat and be free of the famine!

Joseph, one day you shall see my beautiful homeland. Where the river is wide and giving and the palace glowing golden under the sun. But we did not go at that time. No, when Rebekah brought the idea of going to Egypt to Isaac, he was meditating in the field. He agreed at once, with the caveat that he needed to hear confirmation from Yah. Rebekah left him to talk with Yah in the field, and when he returned, he called us both to his tent, and Esau and Jacob as well. Isaac said we would not travel to Egypt. And so I never returned to my birthplace. We did, however, take a journey and become free of the famine.

"The famine is heavy," Isaac said.

"Yes, Father," the boys responded. I was grateful that even in their storm of anger they remembered to honor their father.

"When my father, Abraham, experienced such a famine, he and his wife went to Egypt. Yah has appeared to me and told me not to do this. In the field, Yah said, *Do not go down to Egypt. Stay in the land that I tell you. Reside in this land, and I shall be with you and bless you. To you and your heirs I give all these lands, fulfilling the oath that I made to your father, Abraham. I shall make your heirs as numerous as the stars in the sky. I give your heirs all these lands, and the nations upon them will be blessed by them. So, too, did Abraham abide by my commandments, my laws, and my teachings.*"

"Will you be taking a son to sacrifice?" Esau asked. "Take Jacob. He is a worthless liar and brings no blessings."

"Take Red," Jacob said. "He is a fool who thinks with his fists."

"Take Jacob," Esau said, "He is—"

"Quiet!" Isaac never raised his voice, and the boys lowered their eyes in shame for having provoked him to do so.

"I shall not take anyone for sacrifice," Isaac said. "Yah does not want this. I shall take everyone to the land of Avimelekh, king of Gerar. My father sojourned there and dug many wells, and the king showed him kindness. We shall move to a place without famine, but it will not be Egypt. And for now, I shall allow both of you to come with me."

They gasped. They had not considered not being allowed to come with.

"When I was a boy," Isaac continued, "I had an older brother. His name was Ishmael. You saw him when we buried my honored father. Ishmael taught me to jump and run; he taught me to use a slingshot. He taught me to sing praises to Yah, and he taught me how to ask nicely for a sweet and receive one. I loved him. We laughed together in the wadis, but often his laughter was at me, not with me. My mother could not tolerate this for long and so had my father send him and his mother away."

"He should send *you* away," Jacob said quietly, directing his speech to his brother.

"He should send *you* away," Esau said, teeth clenched, just as quietly.

"I shall send you both away," Isaac said, "if requested. So make yourselves useful in preparing the camp to move to Gerar, and do not bother your mothers. For if I hear that your mouths are big enough to bother them, then surely your bodies are big enough to take care of yourselves in the wilderness." The boys stared at each other but spoke no more words as they spent the next several days preparing the camp as directed.

I was disappointed not to go to Egypt, as was Rebekah. But we would have traded nearly all our possessions and promises of

Egypt to no longer be around the fighting boys, and so we were relieved to have calm and quiet. We, too, helped prepare for the journey, loading what remained of our food supply into carts, rolling our rugs and packing our jugs, and overseeing the dismantling of the camp. Isaac organized the men into sections for moving the flocks and wisely separated Esau and Jacob to escort them on different ends. We were a large group, traveling slowly, and arrived seven days after leaving.

Every night we set up camp just before the sun went down. We women and children had our mats in the center of the camp, while the men and dogs made a wide circle around us. Esau and Jacob were pleased to be counted among the men, guarding the camp at night, even while they slept. They kept far away from each other, but it was good that they were both a part of the pack of men, and there was a part of them that was sharing that responsibility.

Along the way, we saw many other travelers. Most were fleeing the famine, but some were traders with tales of Egypt! We met a woman named Nabirye who had left Egypt only four months ago. She was traveling with a group that included her husband and twin sons! These boys were not like Esau and Jacob, but like one young man standing next to himself. So similar did they look that I was not able to see a difference between them. Nabirye said she herself knew only because she knew them from birth and they had different likes and dislikes, and different scars from healed wounds in different places.

Nabirye had come from lower Egypt and had never seen the palace and, of course, had no knowledge of Tanqo or my father. I did not really expect her to answer with news of them when I asked, though I could not resist asking. I was so happy to meet another woman with skin as dark as mine and whose tongue spoke with the familiar lilts and pronunciations from my youth. She spoke of her home and her family and her travels thus far, and I heard almost nothing, so mesmerized I was by looking into eyes with kohl once again. She offered me some, and I surprised myself by declining. I was not that woman anymore. Rebekah accepted and asked if her boys might have some, as well.

That is right, Joseph. Not only did your grandmother get kohl upon her eyes once again, but your father and uncle also got to have some. I saw your interest when I first mentioned it. If I had some, I would paint it around your eyes right now. But I do not. It is common in Egypt. So common that when you go there one day—and I do believe you will—you will see it on every eye, and you, too, will have a turn to wear it.

Rebekah gave Nabirye a small pot of olive oil for the kohl. A poor trade, I advised her, as kohl was plentiful in Egypt. "It is not plentiful here," Rebekah said, "and I wish to have some. It reminds me of when you first put it on my eyes. I felt so womanly, wise, and powerful, like you."

"There is nothing special about kohl," I said. "Every man, woman, and child wears it in Egypt."

"Well, I am not in Egypt," she said, "and I may never be. But my eyes can be painted, and I may enjoy it." Nabirye applied the kohl for Rebekah, and for Esau and Jacob, who laughed together for the first time since their fight began, so amused were they by the sight of the other with the kohl. Rebekah looked at me.

How wonderful to hear their laughter! "You are, indeed, a wise and powerful woman," I told her.

Though this was true, always true, just before we arrived in Gerar, Rebekah got her first sight of the sea and seemed more like the child she had been when we first met than a woman with children of her own. She still retained her wonder at the world and the excitement for adventure that she had always had, but the sea brought back her exuberance in a way I had not seen in a long time.

"Deborah!" she shouted as we came to a high point with a long view. "Deborah!"

I quickened my pace to catch up with her. We had been walking separately, each quiet in her own thoughts that morning, but never far apart. I did not need to see her view to know why she called. I could smell the salt in the air. Though I had not known when we set out on this journey that we would come to the edge of the world, I began to suspect it last night when I smelled that salt.

"Deborah!" she squeezed my hand, my arm, my shoulder. So great was her excitement, her body could not stay still. Nor could mine, as while she jumped up and down, she moved me, too. "Deborah!" She did not say more, nor did she need to. Still with my hand in hers, she took off running. It was not as easy as when I had first come to the edge of the world. We were women with aging knees in a large camp with many people and even more animals. But as we weaved past and between the others, I felt as if we were children, running free with joy.

In fact, we passed the children, Jacob, and then Esau, who were so struck by the sight that they were as still as I was upon my first arrival. But when they saw us running, they followed and then quickly passed us. Once down the hill, the path to the water was long, but our feet carried us forward. When we arrived at the sea, they were already splashing, wrestling, floating, running, bobbing, and laughing in it. We took off our shoes and went in with them. Isaac joined us shortly after. He had taken longer to give instructions to some of the shepherds to keep the flocks heading toward our destination, with promises to let them have a turn in the sea the next day.

Soon the five of us were dancing in the waves, laughing and splashing, and in the company of the men, women, and children of our camp, who were also overwhelmed with the joy that resides at the edge of the world. Esau, always the hunter, began grabbing at fish with his hands. They were quick and eluded him at first, but he studied their swimming patterns and caught one. He raised it high above his head with a shout of triumph, and we got to see the little slippery catch before it slid right back into its home.

Soon we were all chasing the fish, trying to grab them and, if we were lucky, keep them in our hands long enough to toss them to the sand where they could await cooking. I caught one in my hands, but only one. Rebekah removed the scarf from her hair and used it to chase after more. "Your hair will become stiff with the salt," I said.

"Let it!" she replied. "I, too, am a traveler! Oh, how I remember my excitement the first time you removed your scarf. I could not tell what was your dark black hair and what was dirt, but I could see little sparkles from the white salt that was stuck in there. And you let me taste it!"

"Yes," I laughed. "That was disgusting."

"Not too disgusting for you to taste it yourself," she said.

This was true. If Rebekah was going to try it, I would, too. It tasted like dirt and hair—and salt. One touch to the tongue was enough for both of us, and we laughed with the memory.

"I needed to cut all your hair off, remember? It was far too tangled to brush. But it grew back more beautiful than ever."

"How do you know it was more beautiful than ever?" I challenged her. "You had never seen it before."

"Sometimes, you just know," she said. "And today, I shall get my hair full of salt, because I have traveled to distant lands, and even to the edge of the world! And I shall celebrate by being filthy. And in the morning, you may cut all my hair off, so that it may come back and be more beautiful than ever."

I agreed to cut her hair. While we were making that plan, Esau had gotten a basket and a blanket from one of the carts. He carefully dumped the figs from the basket and brought it, empty, to the sea. He was able to gather fish easily and then remove them with his hands and toss them into the sand. Many of the boys followed his example. Soon we had a blanket that was covered in figs, dates, and barley cakes, and Jacob took out another blanket and began washing the sand off the fish and laying them on that one to dry. It looked as though we would be having a feast that night!

And indeed, we did. Some of the men began a fire, and the smell of the fish filled the air. The boys kept catching them, the men kept cooking them, and we all kept eating them. We had the fruit and barley cakes, and jugs of beer were opened. We had left our home to escape the famine, and escape it we had! For that night, and the two that followed, it seemed that the food would never end. Nor did the celebrations. For three days, we were all full and free.

At the end of the third night, Isaac called Rebekah and the boys and me to sit beside him by the fire. We were covered in sand and salt and smiles. Even Esau and Jacob had suspended their fighting to splash and catch fish together. Rebekah's hair was shorter than her fingernails, and she had convinced me to let her cut mine, too. During the days we made sure to keep our head coverings on to protect us from the sun, but when it set, we enjoyed the breeze as it kissed the bare skin on the tops of our heads. Sitting by the firelight, the boys looked at us with smiles of embarrassment, but Isaac's smile was clearly one of joy.

"In the morning," he said, "we shall move our camp to Gerar."

We knew we would not stay at the edge of the world forever. Though I, at least, wondered why not.

"We must have a place for the flocks," Isaac continued. "And we shall have land and grow crops. For Yah promised me and my father, Abraham, before me, my descendants will be more numerous than the sands on the seashore, and the stars in the sky, and we shall inhabit this land and be blessed."

More numerous than the sand and the stars! The sand and stars themselves were without number. And we would be even more . . . that is, they would be even more. For I had not borne a child who would receive this inheritance. I did not know it was possible to feel sadness when so close to the sea.

"Rebekah," Isaac continued. "You have birthed two sons of Abraham who would not be here if not for you. You are a part of the fulfillment of Yah's blessing." Rebekah's face glowed in the firelight and the compliment. "Esau, Jacob," Isaac said, "I have inherited this land, and someday you will. And your children after you, and their children, and their children, until you have as many descendants as the stars we see above us, and the sand rubbing our skin and stretching as far as the eye can see." The boys sat taller.

I was proud of them, proud of my part in raising them. Even if Zacharyah was not here, I had helped fulfill the promise by helping these heirs grow from boys to young men, who would soon be old enough to marry and bring more heirs.

"Deborah," Isaac said. I was surprised to hear my name. "You and I are the children of Abraham and Sarah, here, on the land Yah gifted them. We, too, are in this multitude, are the first of the stars, of the sand."

Now it was my turn to sit taller and glow.

Isaac was always a man of few words. He had no more to say. He rose from the fireside and beckoned us to follow him. We walked into the darkness and sat in a circle by the sea. I sat to the left of Isaac, with Jacob on my left. Rebekah was on Isaac's right, and Esau sat between his mother and brother, completing the circle. "*Yhhhh*," said Isaac. "*Whhhh*." We followed his lead, each of us having our own experience at the edge of the world that night, yet together. When we woke, we walked the one-day journey to Gerar.

THE EIGHTEENTH PARCHMENT

We stayed in Gerar for three years. From the very beginning, it was a success, and we thought we would stay there forever. Our barley crop yielded one hundredfold in the first year alone. Esau thought it was because of the extra fish he had brought from the sea but were too stinky to eat once we had arrived. He threw them in the soil that was being tilled for the barley. Jacob thought it was because he had prayed to live near the sea and Yah granted him a life near a sea of green barley grasses.

This was only one of the many ongoing fights that Esau and Jacob had in Gerar. They could fight about anything. And they did. Gone was the peace they had found together at the edge of the world, and back was the anger and incessant arguing. If they so much as walked near each other, they were just as likely to jump into wrestling as they were to hurl insults. Thankfully, Esau often went out hunting, and Jacob was taking more responsibilities with the flocks in addition to increasing his reading and writing practice, so their interactions were fewer and further between.

But then, one day, as I was cooking a stew, things at once got both worse and better. It was evening, and both boys were near the tents. Jacob approached me and made a show of smelling my stew and giving it a loud compliment. "It smells delicious, Auntie," he said. "I can understand why Esau was willing to sell his birthright for something this wonderful."

"I was near death," Esau said. "You took advantage of my hunger. No man would sell his birthright if he were going to live through the night."

"But perhaps you would not live through the night," Jacob retorted. "It is a good thing I had the stew ready, to save my brother's life."

"Auntie," Esau said, speaking just as loudly as Jacob had, but needlessly so, as they were both near the cooking pot now. "Your stew smells wonderful. So much better than the trash that Jacob fed me."

"So, you admit that I fed you!" yelled Jacob.

"Of course!" Esau said. "Who else would make such a horrid stew?"

"If it was so bad, why did you eat it?"

"Because I had not eaten for days! I told you! That is the only reason to eat such a stew. If you were smart enough to know how to track an animal, you would know the challenge of being in the field for days."

"Do you know what, Red? If you were smart enough to track an animal, you would have caught one!" Jacob said. And with that, they were at blows. It was all I could do to keep them away from the fire beneath the pot. If I were not so annoyed by this, I would have laughed. Their large bodies and deep voices sounded like those of men, but their words and actions proved they were not.

Rebekah came to the pot, and they did not even notice. She put a ladle in and scooped herself a taste. Then she made a show of spitting it out—on them. This got their attention.

"This stew is flat," she said. "It needs salt. We are not far from the sea; why should we pay a fortune for salt when we can get it ourselves?" She pointed to four large jugs nearby and looked at the boys, who were already looking at her. "Take these jugs and fill them with salt water so that we may have a tastier stew." Then she turned to me. "I am sorry, Deborah, but it will simply taste better with salt."

I nodded.

Then nothing else happened.

We were all stuck in our spots. I by the stew, Rebekah beside me with the ladle still in her hand, the boys still lying in the dirt, unwilling to give up their fight, unsure about continuing it.

"Well?" Rebekah said. "The stew will not stay fresh forever. We will keep it on the fire until you return. It is but a half day's journey without the animals, I am certain. If you rush, you may return before dark. Or come back tomorrow, if you must." She lifted two of the jugs and handed one to each of the boys, then lifted the other two, and handed a second one to each boy. They stood to receive the jugs but did not otherwise move.

"Goodbye," she said, and because she did not move, it was evident that they should.

"Goodbye, Mother," they said, as if in one voice. "Goodbye, Auntie." They sulked away, toward the sea, carrying a jug in each hand, unable, therefore, to strike the other without risking breaking a vessel.

"Rebekah," I said. "You are brilliant!"

She smiled and served us each a bowl of stew, which we enjoyed in silence.

Thus, our time in Gerar was pocked with their arguments and trips to the sea, followed by a brief respite before they fought again. It was not their fighting that finally drove us from Gerar, but that of the men there. First there was a concern that we would need to leave when the king, Avimelekh, discovered that Rebekah was Isaac's wife—not his sister, as he had said upon arrival. Following Abraham's example, Isaac had made that claim when we arrived. Thankfully, Avimelekh did not take Rebekah into his bed.

It was a lovely time for me and Rebekah, for she did not spend any nights with Isaac. Not that I begrudged her those visits, but it was an enjoyable rhythm to get to talk with each other every night, not just some nights, about the days that we spent together. It felt much like all those years ago in Haran, when we lived our days together, and then relived them at night, sometimes through words, and sometimes it was enough just to share the mat.

Isaac had a large camp to oversee, and with his father gone, he was the one the men turned to with reports and questions. On the nights that he himself returned to his tent to sleep, he was exhausted. Other nights, he did not have time to leave his abundance, but slept under the starry skies in the field. One of those nights, he had sent a servant to bring Rebekah to him. In the morning, she was spotted by one of the men of Gerar and the news was brought to Avimelekh. Realizing that Isaac and Rebekah were not just kin but were husband and wife, Avimelekh was angered.

Thankfully, he instructed his men to keep a wide distance from Rebekah, and they did. But the blessings we were receiving from Yah were more noticeable than Rebekah's beauty, and Avimelekh's disappointment at being deceived left him angry. Our crops grew, our flocks grew, and our wealth grew. Isaac directed his men to re-dig the wells that Abraham had dug in the area many years earlier. His knowledge for where to dig was not admired but envied. We were not looked upon favorably, and it was clear that it was time for us to leave Gerar.

Slowly we moved our camp through Esek, Sitna, and Rehoboth, until finally returning to Be'er Sheva. By that time, not only was the famine over, but our food supply was almost too large for our caravan. What we did not take with us, Isaac sold, and we occasionally supplemented our own food with delicacies from the market. Most times, one of the manservants made the trip to the market, but once we had been settled for a while, Rebekah longed for the excitement of change. She asked Isaac to take her to the market. Isaac took all four of us, and we made an adventure of it.

Rebekah and I put on our finest cloaks. Mine, the clean brown one with the belt dyed red from pomegranate juice, and hers, the pink one with shapes of pomegranates sewn in along the bottom trim. Now that we had left Gerar and were no longer fooling anybody about her being Isaac's wife, she could wear her fancy garb again and her bangles from her betrothal. She went to market as Isaac's wife, and mother of Esau and Jacob, two young men with much to inherit. And I went along, too.

I had not been to a market since my journey from Egypt. The idea was the same here, with many goods and wares from near and far.

"They have no wooden carvings," Rebekah said with disappointment. Although her jewelry was fancier than mine, she always enjoyed the story of my wooden bee.

"Let us look at what they do have," I suggested. We admired everything from the beaded sandals at one end of the market to the metal plates at the other. Rebekah wanted neither of these items but chose, instead, several aloe plants. The blooms looked like orange fingers, reaching out to her, asking to be taken and planted where she might view them every day, she said. And so Isaac purchased six aloe plants and had one of his men load them in a cart.

That day, he also purchased some spiced wine, a large bag of hashish, two beautifully painted oil lamps that soon adorned our tent, and a number of other items. The most permanent acquisitions of that day were Adah and Oho, two Hittite sisters who would become Esau's wives. They did not marry on that day, of course, but Esau could not remove his gaze from these two beautiful women when he saw them, and his desire was clear. He declared to them, their father, and us, that he would return to the market in one month's time with a fine bride price for the women.

Esau had always been strong and a hard worker, but the twenty-eight days that followed our trip to the market showed us the height of his abilities. Nearly every day he presented his father with fresh meat. Along with it was a promise to dry it and a request to trade that meat for items for his future wives. Thus, Esau earned necklaces and bangles, scarves and jugs, and even coins from Isaac while feeding our camp with fresh game and preserving the rest for later.

When the market day came, Esau woke early and dressed in his cloak that he had painstakingly laundered himself. His face was scrubbed clean of all dirt; his curly red beard held no crumbs. He walked tall and proud, carrying a sack of gifts and leading a donkey with more. When the sun began to set, we saw him approach the camp with two beautiful women, adorned in the jewelry he had bought from his father, and a smile of pride so large it seemed it might somehow be longer than the great river itself.

Rebekah and I quickly took the women to the tent that had been prepared for them. We brought them milk and dates and fed them with our own fingers. We brushed and braided their hair; we helped them into their cloaks. All the while, we told them of Esau's strengths.

"He is a good provider," Rebekah said.

"He is patient and observant," I told them.

"He wishes to please," Rebekah said.

"He is strong and powerful, and also gentle," I said.

"He will be an excellent husband, I am certain," Rebekah told them.

"And he knows Yah," I added.

"What is this, Yah?" Adah asked. These were the first words she had spoken since her arrival.

"Yah is the Great Creator," Rebekah explained, "the All of All. Yah has promised my sons that they will inherit this land. You are going to wed a blessed man." Rebekah's joy and pride were great in that moment. So great that she did not notice the frowns that were appearing on the faces of Adah and Oho.

After a long look at her sister, Adah said, "We shall add a statue of Yah to our shrine if it is important to our husband. In a place of honor, next to Astarte."

"There is no statue of Yah," Rebekah explained. The god YhWh is always in us, always around us, we need no statue. *Yhhhh. Whhhh,*" she demonstrated.

With this information, the sisters looked even more uneasy than only moments before.

"Esau is a good man," I said again, wanting to bring the subject back. "And he awaits you eagerly. He said many times over the last month that it was the longest one of his life, but that the work and the wait were worth it for his brides. Let us not make him wait any longer."

Adah was the eldest and would be the first wife, and so she was given the veil. Rebekah and I offered Oho a mat in our tent so that she would not need to sleep alone on her first nights, but she declined. And so, we left their tent, Rebekah escorting Adah along the path lit by lamps to stand beside her new husband. Oho stood a few steps behind.

"Esau," Isaac said, "may you be fruitful and multiply. Your children will adorn this camp more than any possession. May Yah bless you and keep you."

Esau took his new bride by the hand and led her to his new tent. Any sounds being made in the tent went unheard by those of us on the outside. Drums and flutes were played, and songs were sung. Jacob danced the night away, as any time there was music he was the first to start dancing and the last to stop. But on this night of his brother's wedding, he seemed to finally have some joy for Esau, and also some relief. Or perhaps that was my wish playing tricks on me.

The marriage did bring about a cease to their endless fighting. Esau was in the throes of learning to be the head of a new tribe, and the boys, that is, the men, rarely saw each other. Unfortunately, this did not mean peace, for a new anger arose, one between Isaac and Rebekah and Esau's new wives.

Adah and Oho refused to learn of Yah, refused any ceremonies other than the ones they held themselves in service of Astarte. Adah was even so bold as to tell Rebekah that Astarte was such a powerful goddess of fertility that Yah was not needed, for, she said, both she and her sister were pregnant with the help of this goddess.

Rebekah bit her tongue and walked away. On the next full moon, she doubled her efforts in trying to get the women to join our circle of dance and prayer, but they still refused. After that, she did not invite them again. The four of us spent many months walking politely by each other without saying a word. When the two women began their birthing labors on the same day, they had no choice but to accept our help, as they could not help each other.

The midwife came and kept the two women together so they could at least have that comfort. I supported Adah, holding her as she pushed, while Rebekah did the same for Oho. All feuds were momentarily forgotten when each woman pushed a wiggly baby boy into the hands of the midwife—first Adah bore Eliphaz, and merely breaths later, Oho delivered Yeush. Rebekah laughed when he came out as red and hairy as his father. Both new mothers lay down with their sons and nursed them.

Rebekah and I looked at the four of them on the mat. I knew her thoughts were the same as my own. It was as if we were seeing ourselves with Esau and Jacob. Long ago, that was how we looked. She took my hand and squeezed it, then said softly, "Come, let us go make them a tray of food." I looked at the food that was already prepared and awaiting them for when they were ready. "Yes," Rebekah said, "but let us make them some." And so we did.

Together we prepared sweet treats and bowls of barley with sesame paste and cups of fresh goat milk. We brought them beer in the evenings and broth in the mornings and were on hand to hold the babies in the sunshine while their mothers slept. For seven days we lived in this gift of love. On the eighth day, while we were singing to the new babies in the sunshine, Isaac came to us with Esau beside him. Isaac brought a sharp knife, and Esau brought the look of a man trying not to vomit up his last meal.

"Bring me the older one," Isaac said. Rebekah was holding Eliphaz and brought him before Isaac. "I welcome you to the covenant of my father, Abraham," he said to the sleeping baby. He handed the knife to Esau. Then to Rebekah he said, "Hold him well." She did, and the boy did not squirm, for he slept until the moment he felt the pain, and then, it was over. Rebekah pressed him to her chest and sang to him as she walked him back to the tent to find comfort at his mother's breast.

Isaac nodded to me, and I brought Yeush before him. He, too, slept until the pain awoke him. Esau threw up in the dirt as I walked the baby to his mother. Both babies calmed immediately with the milk in their mouths and their bodies pressed against the familiar curves of their mothers. But once they were sleeping and their mothers discovered the source of their cries, they seethed with anger. Neither would yell, for fear of disrupting the babies again, but their disgust and fear were clear, and we were never again allowed to touch those babies, only to see them from afar.

Of course, Adah and Oho's ongoing refusal to speak to us or let us near their sons brought us sadness. But we watched them and enjoyed seeing their pudgy little thighs grow long and strong as their milk teeth loosened and their smiles grew gaps. Their mothers each bore daughters and were kept busy with the babies such that they did not mind our proud gazes, as long as we kept a distance. And so, our lives were peaceful, even if not our desired design. This is how it was until Isaac fell ill.

He was sleeping in his temporary tent in the field, as he often did, when he awoke in the middle of the night. He began screaming, "Yah will provide the sheep, Yah will provide the sheep." Rebekah told me he had done this a few times before, but that was when she was by his side in his tent. That night we heard of it only from Isaac's account the next day.

"I was screaming," he said, "and my own screams woke me. I began to walk back to the camp. I took no lamp. I had not walked for long before I tripped and landed on a rock. I remember bumping my head as I fell. I do not remember going to sleep there, but the next thing that happened was that I was waking in the morning light.

"When I awoke, I thanked Yah. 'I am thankful before You, Yah, for returning my breath to me, in your loving kindness and your belief in me.' I slowly pushed myself off the rock. I saw dried blood. Feeling myself, I discovered it came from my tongue and the front of my head. Every part of my body hurt, most of all my head. I began my slow walk back to the camp. With thanks to Yah, Elioded saw me walking this way and that way and nearly falling again. He came to help. When he saw me from a close distance, he insisted that I sit in the shade and wait for him to bring a cart."

For many days, Rebekah brought him broths and poultices to heal his wounds, but his head continued to hurt too much for him to rise from his mat other than to walk outside and lie down again. The only duty he kept up was his afternoon meditations in the field. With Elioded's help, he walked the shortest distance from his tent to the edge of the closest field, where he stayed as long as he could tolerate the light before being helped back.

Isaac feared his days were numbered, so he charged his most trusted servant, Elioded, with overseeing his wealth. And then he asked Elioded to send him his firstborn son, so that he might bless him.

Rebekah was carrying broth to Isaac's tent when Esau went in. Rebekah waited outside for the two of them to finish speaking. She heard the words they exchanged and soon shared them with me.

"I am old," Isaac said, "and my death could come any day. Please, take your arrows and bow and go out and hunt me some game. Then make me a tasty dish, such as I enjoy. Bring it to me so that I may eat and give you my soul's blessing before I die."

Esau came out of his father's tent with his chest out and his head held high. He saw his mother and kissed her hand. He called to me and met me as I walked toward him and kissed my hand, too. "I am going to the field," he said, "for my father wishes me to bring him his favored meal, so that he may bless me." Oh, he was so proud!

Rebekah did not feel proud, she felt worried. Worried that Isaac would give Esau the blessing that Jacob should have. Rebekah had never forgotten what she had been told by Yah even before the twins were born. *The older would serve the younger.* She thought of it every day. "Deborah?" she asked. But there were no more words in her question.

It was our habit to discuss all the happenings in our lives, and that was even more true of all the decisions. But this time was different. She sent a boy to go and fetch Jacob from where he was watching over the sheep.

"Rebekah?" It was my turn to ask the empty question. We stood in the noise of our unspoken thoughts.

When Jacob arrived, she said, "I heard your father speaking to your brother, Esau. He said, 'Bring me game, and make me tasty food, and I shall bless you in front of Yah before I die.'" Jacob gasped in surprise. Rebekah reached her arm up to his shoulder and placed it there. She looked into his eyes and said, "Listen carefully, my son, to what I am going to instruct you to do. Go to the flock and choose two young goats, and I shall make them into tasty food that your father likes. Then take it to your father to eat, so that he may bless *you* before he dies."

Jacob shifted his weight from one foot to the other. "But my brother Esau is a hairy man, and I am a smooth man," he said. "If my father touches me, he will think me a trickster, and I shall bring upon myself a curse, not a blessing." Rebekah dismissed this idea and told Jacob that it would not happen—but if it did, the curse would be on her, not him. And so, he went to follow Rebekah's orders.

I asked my question once again, this time finding a few more words. "Rebekah? Are you certain this is the thing to do?"

"All I know is what I needed to do, what I was guided to do, so I did that," she said. I tried to hold on to the memory of Esau feeling proud and happy. I felt neither.

When Jacob returned, Rebekah made the stew as promised, and she made bread. Then she dressed Jacob in Esau's finest cloak, which was waiting in the tent while he hunted, and covered Jacob's arms and neck with the skins of the goats she had just cooked so that they would be as hairy as his brother's when he presented the dish. "Rebekah," I said. "Isaac's eyes are weak, but he knows the difference between the hair of a goat and that of his son. What are you doing?"

She turned her back to me. I could not remember another time she had done that in all the years I had known her. Before the sun set, Jacob took the food to his father. Rebekah and I waited outside. The two men spoke softly to each other, and we could not hear. We breathed slowly to calm ourselves. *Yhhhh. Whhhh. Yhhhh. Whhhh.*

After a long while, Jacob came out smiling. "He has blessed me," Jacob said. "My father has blessed me! Oh how I feared that he would not do it. He beseeched me to come close, to feel my hairy arms. 'It is the voice of Jacob,' he said, 'but the hands of Esau.' I began to shake with fear. But then he blessed me! He blessed me! My father has blessed me with the blessing of the firstborn!" He hugged us, and we him, before he ran to the hills to thank and praise Yah. No sooner had he gone than Esau returned from the other direction. He carried a ram over his shoulders. He had caught the ram and bound its legs but not killed it. He would do so in the morning, to prepare it fresh for his father.

Isaac had always shown favor to Esau because of his skilled hunting. Esau shared his meat generously with his father. With all of us. And while Isaac had hired Katib to teach Jacob to read and write, Isaac himself spent little time with his younger son. Rebekah had always loved Jacob. Whether it was because she knew Yah's blessing for him or because he was the smaller one, we will never know. I still hold a fear that it was perhaps because I had taken Esau to nurse. Maybe had I not done that one thing, Rebekah would not have helped Jacob take the blessing from Esau. Whatever the reason, she had convinced herself that she was right about this trickery and would not even talk about it further. That, perhaps, was the thing that shocked me the most. I could not think of another time that she or I would not talk about something further. Even if we did not agree, we could still compassionately understand the other. But not this time.

I could not sleep that night.

The next evening, Esau walked into Isaac's tent with the stride of a king. He held the dish he had caught and prepared with his own two hands. His smile was as broad as his shoulders. But when he left his father's tent, his disappointment was in equal measure to Jacob's joy the day before. He fell to his knees and threw the empty stew pot to the ground. The scream that came from his mouth brought tears to my eyes. I rushed to comfort him, but he would not allow me to do so.

I stood beside him as his tears watered the dirt. When he was ready, he stood. He straightened his clothes and wiped his face. Then he looked at me in a way he never had. Before his mouth uttered any words, his eyes said, *Auntie, you have betrayed me. You have all betrayed me*. He took two long breaths to calm himself, and I breathed with him. *Yhhhh. Whhhh. Yhhhh. Whhhh.*

Then he spoke softly. "My father found a blessing for me as well, granted me a blessing from his heart. Yet he had already given what was mine to Jacob. Jacob. Jacob! He was given that name when he held my heel, trying to move me out of his way so he could exit the womb first. The name still suits him. This time, he has succeeded. He moved me out of the way and took what was mine!"

Esau began to walk away, but then he turned and looked back at me. "My father is an old man, and soon he will die. When I complete the days of mourning for him, I shall kill my brother, Jacob."

I gasped! I wanted to comfort him, plead with him, apologize to him. But I could do nothing of the sort, for he walked away and did not look back this time. So, I sought my own comfort from Rebekah. But, when she heard me tell Esau's words, she had no comfort to give me, only worry.

"How shall I protect Jacob?" she asked.

I had no answer, other than to remind her that Isaac still lived, and so Jacob was not yet in danger. I was not certain that Esau's anger would cool in time, but I hoped that it would.

"But Isaac feels his death is approaching," she said. We both sat quietly with the sadness of that for some time.

Then Rebekah nearly shouted with relief. "I shall send him to Haran! Just as your mother sent you there to get back to your tribe; just as Abraham sent Eliezer there to fetch me as a wife for Isaac. I shall send Jacob back to Haran, to my brother, Lavan, to find a wife from his daughters. He can stay there for a number of days while Esau calms himself. And he can take a wife. It is perfect!" Rebekah said.

But it did not feel perfect. Isaac sent Jacob to Haran to find a wife. Isaac, Rebekah, and I embraced him at once. I do not think we had ever done that before. Isaac then put his hands on Jacob's head and blessed him with Father Abraham's blessing of becoming a father of many and inheriting the land. Jacob left immediately after, even though the night would be moonless and dark. Esau heard that Jacob was told to avoid taking a wife from the local tribes, and so by the time the moon was full, he had taken a daughter of Ishmael as a third wife, then moved his whole clan east to Edom. Our boys were gone, and Isaac was dying. It was the first time that Rebekah and I could not bring ourselves to dance under the full moon.

THE SIXTH SCROLL

THE NINETEENTH PARCHMENT

Joseph, you have been blessed to know your grandfather Isaac, so you know that he did not die when Esau and Jacob left. And you could not have been born had your father Jacob not survived his trip to Haran, so you know that he did survive, he did make it there, he did marry. But, of course, we did not know this would happen when he left. We could only hope.

Rebekah had a difficult time when Jacob left for Haran. From her worries, one would think she had sent a toddler to make the journey alone, not a grown man. "What if he encounters thieves?" she asked. "Or beasts? He will be hungry. I should have sent him with more provisions. He does not know how to hunt like Esau or find plants as you do, Deborah."

Up until the time of Jacob's departure, she knew he was a strong, capable, and wise man. If the question of a journey had arisen, she would have leapt to tell of his ability to thrive in such a situation. But the weight of the trickery and of losing both our sons, at once no less, was heavy on her shoulders and caused all parts of her to be down. Two full moons came and went without her lifting her drum or her feet or her voice in celebration.

One evening, Isaac called me to his tent. He had not called for me in years, but perhaps with Rebekah refusing to leave her tent, he was lonely. I knew to have no fear, but my skin prickled with concern. His request, I learned, was not for me to lie with him. He called me to his tent and sent me back to Rebekah's in only the amount of time it took him to request that I help. He, too, saw that she was suffering.

"My father told me that Yah always instructed him to listen to my mother. He told me there was only one time in which he did not do so, and he regretted it painfully. So when I married, my father instructed me to always listen to my wife. I think I have done that. I do not know why Rebekah went to such lengths to twist my blessings to my sons. But she did. And it is over now. She cannot lie in her tent with her head in her sleeve for the rest of her days. Deborah, please help bring order and peace back to our camp."

He was right. I went back to our tent partially cleansed of my own disappointment and able to see a glimmer of hope. "Rebekah," I said, "I know you worry over Jacob. But has Yah not blessed him? Will you doubt the One who told you this child will receive the blessing of his father? For how long will you ignore your weaving? For how long will you refuse to have the joy of our full moon celebrations? For how long will you leave me to do all the talking between us?" Here I added a small laugh, little more than a smile, but I knew that our conversations were as special to her as they were to me. Yet she did not smile.

"What is your plan, then?" I asked. "Are you to become like your mother and sit in the tent day and night for the rest of your life?"

This caught her attention, and she gasped at the thought.

"Come," I said, "at least walk with me."

To my pleasant surprise, she left the tent for the first time since Jacob's departure and walked with me in silence. When we reached the top of a hill, we sat together in the shade of the trees and looked below us at the camp.

"Rebekah," I said, "tell me what is bothering you."

Rebekah cried again. I had seen her cry daily since Jacob's departure, but this was a different cry. This one was loud, not with a few tears, but many. Her body shook, and she spat and pounded the ground with her fists. When her gasping finally returned to easy breathing, I invited her again.

"I have done terribly wrong," she said. "I have worked for a lifetime to prepare Jacob for receiving his father's blessing. Since the time that Yah spoke to me in my dream, I knew Jacob was the one who was important. 'The older will serve the younger.' I would do everything I was able to make Jacob worthy of that blessing. And now I have ruined all of that. I have turned him into a trickster and a fugitive. Oh, Deborah . . ." She resumed the sobs.

"And do you wish to hear the worst part of it all?" She did not pause, for she knew she had my attention for anything she would say. "The worst part is that I have both failed at preparing him, and I have failed my firstborn son. In all of my efforts to guide Jacob, I did not think enough of Esau. For his whole life! Right up to betraying him in his moment of earned pride and glory! Oh, Deborah, I am the worst mother who ever lived! I have ruined both of my children, and I shall not even have more chances to do a good job with a new baby."

"This sounds terrible," I said. I paused, so that she might have a moment of sympathy before I continued. Then I said, "Yet, it is not true."

Rebekah looked at me.

"Has Jacob not become a skilled shepherd? Has he not learned to read and to scribe?" I asked. "And are those not skills of great importance?"

She nodded.

"Did you not watch Jacob with pride as he strode to his quiet places every evening to talk with Yah? Is that not a great practice that you helped him build?"

She nodded again.

"Does Esau not feed his wives and children? And laugh with them and love them?" I asked.

She had to agree, for he did.

"When Esau returned from a hunt, did you not praise his patience and persistence, as well as the flavors of his food? When he returned with a swollen arm, did you not cook the herbs for the poultice and wrap his bandage every morning and evening?"

"I did," she said.

"And did you not catch his very first son on your knees and insist that he circumcise the child himself? And has that not happened for all of Esau's boys, thanks to you?"

"It has," she said.

"These are just a few examples from a lifetime. Perhaps our sons are not ruined," I said. I was not pleased with her trickery, but I was proud of the skills our young men had acquired. "Do you think you can call yourself the worst mother who has ever lived? Surely there is one mother, or possibly two, who have done worse." I could see that she was still thinking of ways she felt she had failed, but she also laughed, for she heard the absurdity of it. "Perhaps in a distant land?" I added, giving her hand a squeeze.

"Perhaps one, far, far away," she conceded. "Though probably not as many as two." Now she gave me a small smile. I could see her pain was still there, but she was making room for it to leave.

"Beautiful Rebekah," I said, "can you please see yourself with my eyes? I see a mother who has loved her children the best she knew how. She fed and clothed them, licked their wounds and sang them songs, made them with a generous and kind father, who has also taught them—not to mention a generous and kind auntie, who has taught them many things."

Rebekah put her head on my shoulder and let her quiet tears fall there.

"Can you do that?" I asked. "Can you see the mother that I see?"

"I would like to, Deborah. I believe you would not lie to me. But you also see me with soft eyes that often miss my imperfections."

I laughed heartily. I spoke only after catching my breath. "Rebekah, we have shared a tent and a mat for more years than

I care to count. Do you think I have not smelled the wind that escapes your bottom in your sleep, or the odor of your breath before you have chewed hyssop or mint in the morning? Have I not waited on you to return from Isaac with word of where we were to go next while you gathered wildflowers in no haste to inform me? Have I not heard you complain for days when you bump your toe or trip over something that you yourself forgot to return to its place? I have seen your imperfections. And I disagreed with you trying to deceive Isaac, taking away Esau's blessing and turning Jacob into a trickster. But I do not judge your worth on this one act." I paused for her to consider. "Now do you believe that I speak the truth? That you are a loving mother?" I asked.

She looked as if she was considering it. From that day forward, she was less upset about herself, and she was able to experience many joys, even while a piece of her missed the babies she still held in her dreams. I assured her I missed those babies, all three babies, as well. For with one long gone and two grown into men who left the camp, there was much to miss.

Thankfully, three months after Jacob left, we received a message from him.

A message to Isaac of Be'er Sheva, from his son Jacob in Haran.

Honored Father, Beloved Mother, Dear Auntie,

I arrived at Lavan's camp in peace, having made a covenant with Yah—loyalty in exchange for a safe return to you. For now, I am far from such return. I was met in Haran by the most beautiful girl ever to draw water. When I saw her, she was standing by the well, her jugs still empty, waiting for the stone covering it to be removed. She said it took four men to push it off the mouth of the well. But so strong was my love for her, I pushed it alone, in exchange for the pleasure of seeing her happiness.

Yah has certainly blessed me, for that girl is the daughter of my esteemed mother's brother, Lavan. When Lavan heard of my arrival, he made a show of meeting me with food and drink and escorting me to his tent. But he threatened to throw me out after only one month, for he knew that I came with no gifts. He told of the riches that Eliezer brought for his sister Rebekah and wanted the same for his daughter, if not more.

As I have no wealth to offer, I told him of the blessings I have received. He spit seeds in my face but consented to my request to marry Rachel—that is the name of the beautiful girl—if only I would agree to work for him for seven years. I would gladly do that, and more, for Rachel. Thus, I shall remain here until my oath is fulfilled, not concerned about Esau attacking me, yet missing you.

May Yah bless you and keep you well until my return.

Rebekah was able to ease her concerns once she heard from her son. She did not return to her ways but, rather, made new ways. She began creating new weaving patterns, first making small samples, but quickly choosing to make large rugs. Keshet was the maidservant who had done all the dyes, and Rebekah asked her to experiment with new ones. Soon she soaked her wool in these dyes, making colors as vibrant as the flowers in the spring. She then began using thicker dyes to paint on earthen jars as well. These decorations could not rival the ones in Egypt, but they were quite nice to look upon, and she was at ease.

For the first time since Rebekah and I had come together, we began to drift apart. In her determination not to spend her time wasting away like Metuyeshet, Rebekah went to Isaac more nights, walked the hills more mornings, and wove and painted in the shade of the tent when the sun was high. We still enjoyed some meals together, some nights, some stories, and some laughs, but without boys to feed or keep from fighting, without sorrow or adventure, life was different than it had been. We were different.

I was free, possibly for the first time in my life, to look for what it was that I needed. I had spent many wonderful days in the hills. Walking alone was quiet. I loved to walk with Rebekah, and now I was reminded that I also loved to walk alone. I noticed more color, more birdsong and frogsong. I reveled in my own thoughts, and in the quiet that took the place of conversation. It was an unexpected gift.

I recalled the story of Abraham hearing Yah's voice once he was able to be alone. I had heard, seen, and felt Yah with Rebekah. Joseph, in my view, your grandmother Rebekah is one of Yah's finest creations, and her love is a path that brought me deeper to Yah. With her love still there, but our bodies farther apart, I began to discover a new path to Yah. Or perhaps I should say, rediscover. For it was on these quiet walks that I recalled my early travels, the ones that brought me from Egypt to Haran. Then I was with Mavheel and his workers, of course. On some nights he attacked me, but during the days, he left me alone. Now, walking, I was feeling that freedom in the aloneness once again, this time without any accompanying fear.

I think that is why, one day, during our third summer of living in this new way, I kept walking. I walked farther and farther, even though I knew I would not be able to return to the camp before nightfall. I had not made a plan when leaving the camp at sunrise, but because I found myself walking toward Edom, I decided in that moment that I would walk to Esau. Because I had not made this plan early in the morning, it would require spending a night alone on the journey. I felt confident I would be safe. I was less confident that he would receive me. I would understand if he still held anger. Perhaps I could help him, help us, reunite. I would at least try.

I began to open my senses for leaves and fruit, and I found them easily enough. As the evening progressed, I looked for a safe place to sleep. The first cave I came upon, when I asked Yah if it was a safe choice, my fingers fell apart from each other, telling me no, it was not. And so I continued until I found another sheltered place. This, too, would not be safe. I chose not to question my choice to go to Edom, for it was too late to arrive back at the camp before nightfall. Whether I continued or returned, I would spend the night on the path. And so, I checked several caves until I found one when my prayer was answered by my fingers gently squeezing more tightly together. Yes. I slept there, peacefully, until the sun rose again. Before the heat of the day, I walked into Esau's camp with a smile of accomplishment on my face.

"Auntie," Esau chastised me, "you should not have come here alone. Do you know what trouble you might have met along the way?"

I reminded him that, indeed, I did know. I had encountered such trouble before and had survived.

"But think of me, then, Auntie," he said. "Shall I be forced to survive seeing you injured? Or worse? You will be my guest here today. You will have the freshest of the cheeses and fruits, Auntie. And Basemat is making a delicious stew." He saw my eyes squint in disbelief, and he laughed. "Do not worry, Auntie, it is not with lentils, but with barley and mushrooms. My wife is a great hunter, also. She finds all the best mushrooms."

I was happy to hear the joy in Esau's voice as he mentioned his third wife. This was the one we had not met. Now I would meet her. I would see our son's life. I accepted Esau's invitation. In truth, I had not made a plan to return to our camp, for I had not made a plan to wander this far. Esau called for his children to come and entertain me. The youngest, Jinjeet, sat on my lap while her brothers and sisters jumped and danced and tumbled before me, each one shouting, "Look at me, Auntie!" or "Look what I can do!" until the sun began to set on their games, and they were called to eat.

Basemat brought me a cushion, and I sat beside her and Adah and Oho. I was brought a bowl of stew that did smell delicious, and I complimented Basemat on her use of spices. She received my approval with a smile. The food was even tastier than it smelled, and when I was offered a second bowl, I graciously accepted, though everyone else had finished.

"Children," Esau said while I ate, "I must tell you who our special guest is."

"Auntie!" several of them yelled together.

"Yes, Auntie," Esau confirmed. "But that is not all."

Eliphaz, the oldest, jumped to his feet and spoke importantly. "I know, Father, for I have known her since my birth. She is your Auntie, and her name is Deborah, and she comes from far, far away, from the land of Egypt."

"Yes," Esau said, and clapped his son on the back. "And . . . ," he paused to make sure that all the children were looking and listening. "And, she is the bravest woman you have ever met!"

"She is?" Eliphaz asked. "Braver than my mother?"

Esau, perhaps forgetting for a moment that he was in the company of his wives, the mothers of his children, quickly acknowledged that all of those women were brave, very brave, and wise and beautiful and good mothers. "But," he added, "Auntie is still the bravest. Shall I tell you why?"

He need not have asked. All the children were listening so intently that it seemed their ears might jump from their bodies to be closer to him. And his wives were listening, too, not sure how they felt about the compliments he had finally remembered to deliver. Perhaps I myself was the most curious of all, for I did not know he thought of me as such and could not imagine why.

"One time," Esau said, "when I was still a boy, but already taller than Auntie, already a brave and seasoned hunter, Auntie came into our tent and saw me shaking in the corner. 'What is wrong, Esau?' she asked me. I was so scared that my mouth would not even agree to answer her, so I used my finger to point. Auntie looked down and saw the scorpion that was staring at me. She walked over, picked it up by its tail, and threw it over the hill and into the brush!"

His story was met with a collective gasp. Even I was impressed. I had not remembered that moment until he recounted it. Then it came back to me. Esau scared in the corner, me seeing the scorpion, my body moving forward. My fingers closed together in a practice grasp of the scorpion, and I prayed, "May I pick it up?" My fingers grasped more tightly together, as if they already were picking it up. Yes. And then I did. I grabbed the scorpion, its tail between my fingers. "You will be happier out there," I whispered, and threw it as far as I could. I am certain I could not throw it over a whole hill, but it was enough to make an impression on Esau. What else did he remember that I had forgotten?

I asked him. "Esau, tell of more memories."

"Another time, Auntie," he said. "For now, I shall show you to your cushion. Adah has set it up for you, and I am certain it will meet your needs." Once we parted from the group, Esau continued. "I have many memories, Auntie. But I also have three wives who have not found favor in my family's eyes. I must go with them now. They are here, I am here, and you are here for only one day."

"We are alone," I said. "Indulge me in one more story of something you remember from your childhood."

"I remember the first time I brought a hunt to my father," he said. "It was a hare. It had been a fast one. I had tracked it silently and caught it by surprise when it stopped to nibble on a shrub. I skinned it and cooked it in the field, so that the aroma would not alert anyone to the surprise. Oh, the aroma, Auntie! How I wanted to taste it! But I did not. I brought the whole thing to my father and placed it before him. His lips curled into a smile, and his large hand grabbed my shoulder.

"'This was a wild hare,' I said. 'Wonderful, my son,' he said. 'This is very special. Come, let us enjoy it together.' And we did.

We enjoyed many meals together after that. I always brought him my hunt, whether it was a whole rabbit, or later, only part of a deer, or anything in between. My father always said he loved the wild game, said that the meat was tastier. Eating with my father is always an honor, but the first time I brought him the hunt was very special."

We had arrived at the sleeping cushion that Adah had prepared for me. I had an oil lamp and a large blanket whose details I could not see in the dim light, but in the morning, I would discover it was a beautifully woven green one with four little butterflies stitched into each corner. "Perhaps you will consider bringing your father a meal again," I said. "You are missed. And if an old woman can make the journey in only one day, certainly you can, too."

He nodded and let me hug him. When I was going to release him, as not to hold him for too long, his strong arms still held me in his. He kissed my hand and promised to accompany me part of the way in the morning, but I chose to leave before the sun rose and make the journey alone. My eyes took in the bright colors, my ears the desert sounds, and I gave myself to Yah, and took myself back. *Yhhhh. Whhhh. Yhhhh. Whhhh.* Oh, how glorious it was to be me! Hallelu Yah!

Esau did begin making trips to our camp to share a meal with Isaac. He came a few times each year and sometimes brought one or more of his sons. But that day, I walked alone, through the hills, under the open sky, with only the birdsong in my ears. Although I had been gone for only two days, the smell of the flocks excited me as I came closer, reminding me of my first arrival from Haran. Seeing the camp from afar allowed me the opportunity to appreciate just how large it was. Isaac had been successful and blessed. The sheep and goats were abundant. The people looked as many and as busy as I had seen as a child in Egypt. I could see women gathered around the well with jugs and some by the kitchen fires. I saw many others—men, women, and children—walking through the campground with purpose, though I could not distinguish what the purpose was from so far away.

As I approached, I chose to walk through the camp rather than go directly to my tent. Yes, I would tell Rebekah of my visit with Esau, but there would be time for that. Right now, I saw that I had an opportunity to do something new. And so I walked among the manservants and maidservants. Some gave me a wide berth, a few asked what I needed, and I told them I was not in need of anything. Most just kept up with what they were doing. That was when I saw Orry and the goatskins.

He was off the path, under a shade of skins that had been tied between two trees to dry. He was crouched low and not wearing the common long tunic of our area, but a short one, as Egyptians did. His skin was dark, like the soil when it was fresh and fertile from the Nile's flooding. That dark skin was uncovered, the sun shining directly on it, and shining on the beads of sweat that collected at his shoulder blades. He nearly glowed. His hair was not covered but shaved. I stopped my walk and merely stood there. In part, I was admiring the goatskin. In larger part, I was admiring the muscles on Orry's back and arms as he used the wood in his hand to scrape the hair off the hide. And in yet another part, I was lost in confusion. It seemed as if I were in the busy squares of Egypt, but that could not be right.

As I tentatively walked closer, I received yet another surprise. The smell of the hide brought visions of Tanqo to my eyes. Tanqo. She had been so kind and important in my life, so long ago. I had given her little thought in recent years. But now, the odor of the lye crawled up my nose and down through my lips, exiting as a whisper of her name. I had not intended to speak, but the sound caught Orry's attention. He looked up, saw me, and stood. Looking in his eyes, I was fully revealed. It was as if I stood naked before him. Yet I was not embarrassed.

Bowing slightly at the waist, he asked kindly, "What can I do for you, Deborah?"

"You know my name?"

He chuckled. "Of course," he said. "We speak of you often. You and Isaac and Rebekah, Esau and Jacob. It is because of you that we are here, that we have work. Are you in need of new cushions?" he asked. "Or sandals? These skins will be complete soon, but some are already dry and supple. I can make them into whatever you need."

My surprise kept my tongue from moving. It was for the best, as I did not know what to have it say. What tricks were my eyes and ears playing? I saw a man with a bald head and thought he had shaved it in the Egyptian tradition, but now that we stood closer, I saw that the hairs on his dark chest were unshaven, and white. Perhaps those from his head had merely fallen out and he had chosen to have his head uncovered. But why? For the heat during his work? Did that also explain the short tunic?

"You remind me of Egypt," were the words that finally came from my lips.

Orry looked at himself and realized he was dressed for his labor in the sun. Blushing, he put his cloak back on. Thankfully he was not so embarrassed as to walk away—though he told me later that he was tempted.

"I came from Egypt many years ago," he said.

This surprised me even more than his appearance, and once again, I was rendered to stunned silence. Orry felt the opposite effect and filled the quiet air with soft, melodious words.

"I was born by the great river," he said. "Many years ago. I did not have hides to work with then. I was a carver for the king. I did not meet him, of course, but still was proud to do his bidding. The great god Ptah blessed these hands with the ability to carve stories into stone. I watched the words come to life as my chisel carved them, and then the painters painted them."

As Orry spoke, he prepared cups of beer for us and a plate of figs, dates, and almonds. He continued to tell me of his life, while also inviting me to sit with him in the shade of a date tree and enjoy this treat. "When the king died," he said as we ate and drank, "I did not fear for my life, for I was a valued worker, and no threat to the next ruler. I would not be killed. But it was a time of chaos. And life was not easy. My wife had died not long before. Only my son and I remained."

This man beside me was there when the king died! I was there! We were there. I did not tell him, not yet. For my tongue was still slow, and my ears eager for more.

"After discussing it with my son, I decided we would join a caravan and come north. The boy was five years old and had already learned to read and write from me. I thought we would both become carvers. But that is not needed in the north. I served Abraham when we joined this camp, and now I serve Isaac. My son serves as his scribe."

"It was he who taught Jacob," I said, finally able to utter words, curious why those were the first ones. "Katib. Katib is your son."

"Yes," Orry confirmed. "It was easy for Katib to find work here, for he is a skilled scribe. He learned well. But Abraham did not need two scribes. That is what Eliezer told me when we met, for I never did meet Abraham himself. He was going to take only Katib, but I asked him, if not a scribe, what did they need? And so Eliezer told me someone was needed to dry the hides and make use of them. 'The one who does this job will carry the stench of the lye,' he said, but I agreed to the job, for I did not wish to be separated from my son. Now," he continued, "Katib has a wife and children and a place of honor here. I have my own tent, small but worthy."

A tent! I must return to my tent! Of all the thoughts I was having, these were the ones that won my attention. I believe I thanked him for the food and drink as I arose and turned to leave.

"Deborah," he called after me. "I enjoyed this very much. Please come back tomorrow. I wish to give you a token of my gratitude." He said this to my back, as I felt I should have already begun to prepare the evening meal.

I left in such a rush that it was not until the next morning that I learned that his name was Orry. So, when I returned to my tent, I could not tell Rebekah the name of the man I had met. Even if I could have, I am not sure I would have. That night, I did not mention Orry at all. I was not ready. But neither was she.

When I returned to our tent, Rebekah was curled up on the floor, her knees in her hands and her whole body shaking with sobs.

"What is it, Rebekah?" I ran to her as soon as I saw. What could have transpired to lead to this?

"Deborah?" She immediately jumped up and held me first at arm's length, and then so close I thought she would crush my bones in her embrace. When she finally released me, her face was no longer sad, but filled with anger, as was her voice. "Why did you leave? Where did you go? You were gone for so long! I begged Isaac to send Elioded to look for you and feared he would return with only your tunic, covered in your own blood and hairs from the hungry wild boars that devoured you."

I could not help but laugh. "Boars do not eat people," I said. "You know this."

"That is not the important part!" she yelled.

"I know," I said. I hugged her softly and then released her and took her hand. "Come," I said brightly, leading her toward the cushions, "let us sit, and I shall tell you of my visit with Esau." I had almost said "our boy," but I was afraid she would think I had seen Jacob, so I wanted to be clear.

"You have seen Esau?"

I told her of my walk to Edom and how Esau hosted me like a queen. I told her of his talented wife and the scorpion story he told his children. I told her the details of his tents and the gardens, told her of the birds I heard along the way, and the cave where I spent the night.

At some time, during these details, Rebekah drifted to sleep to the sound of my voice. When I stopped talking, in the silence

I imagined Orry's voice telling the story of our meeting, and what it might be like to feel his breath in my ear as he told it.

The next morning, after we ate, Rebekah hummed as she examined the wool she had dyed and contemplated her weaving for the day. I bade her goodbye, promising not to walk to Edom, but to be back by her side by nightfall. And as soon as I left, my feet wished to carry me back to Orry. At first, I would not allow them. I coaxed them around a hill and nearly begged them to keep walking, but they refused. They insisted on turning around, and they brought me right back to the place where I had first seen Orry. When we arrived, and he was there, fully dressed and smiling, I believe my legs whispered, "I told you so."

Orry, far more polite than my feet, greeted me with a smile and gratitude. "I was not certain you would come," he said, "but I am very glad that you did. Please, allow me to bring you some figs and cheese."

"No," I said, "I shall stay only if you promise me that my presence will not keep you from what you would do if I were not here."

"But Deborah," he protested, "you *are* here."

I stood firm, perhaps too firm, because his next words were, "I understand. I shall complete all my tasks. Do not worry." Did he think me to be spying for Isaac? To make sure he was working? Did he think I was only interested in his work? What *was* I interested in?

While these thoughts captured me, they did not seem to bother him, for as he removed soaked skins to hang them to dry he spoke of his life in Egypt. His voice was so smooth and his accent so homelike, that it did not matter much to me what he was saying, and sometimes I did not hear the words, only the beautiful sounds. I happily listened and watched as he went from hanging some skins to brushing the hair off others and sewing others together.

When he assured me that he had done everything possible that day, I allowed him to serve me figs and cheese as the sun began to set. We ate under our tree from the day before and enjoyed the flavors together. While there was still some light in the sky, I rose to walk back to my tent. This time when he asked me to return the next day, I readily agreed.

That night on our sleeping mat, I told Rebekah that I had met someone else who had come from Egypt, a man who works in the camp. I told her of our day together.

"Why do you spend the day with one of the servants?" Rebekah asked.

"You spend every day with one of the servants," I reminded her.

"You know that I do not think of you as one of the maid-servants," Rebekah said. "You are my sister. My friend. My storyteller. My teacher. My love—"

"And your servant," I interrupted her, before she could continue the list. But she only got angry and went on.

"You are a child of Abraham and Sarah," she said. "A granddaughter of Hallel. A mother to Esau and Jacob."

"And your servant," I said again.

"Only because that was how Yah reunited you with your tribe!" Rebekah nearly yelled.

"Reunited me as your servant," I said.

She was angry and turned her back to me. I was surprised by her anger because I felt none. Of course I was a child of Abraham and Sarah. I walked my life feeling the honor of that status. Most of the time. However, there were also countless times that I felt that being Rebekah's servant was less than being a child of Hallel, less than being Abraham's or Isaac's wife—had I accepted that fate—less than being Esau and Jacob's mother. But on that day, when I called myself a servant, I did not feel less than. I felt happy that I shared something in common with Orry. I went to sleep with excited anticipation for seeing him the next day.

Five more mornings I awoke with thoughts of Orry and allowed my feet to take me directly to him. I watched him carve and I listened to his stories as we drank beer in the shade. I told him of my trips to the palace to visit Grandmother, and he told me he had heard the name Moshel. Long ago, my grandfather's name had been in my ears—and in Orry's. That thought made me giddy. It still does. I told Orry my memories of the day the king died and we discovered that there was likely a moment on that day when we were fewer than one hundred steps apart from each other. Perhaps we were even in the same crowd.

On my seventh visit to Orry, he met me with a downtrodden face. He had no figs to offer, and his story that day was not one of reminiscence. That morning he told me that his son Katib had visited him the night before and delivered the news that the camp was chattering about us. They were saying it was not right of Orry to spend time with the master's wife. It did not look good.

"Rebekah was here?" I asked.

"No," Orry said, confusion on his face. "My son said I should not spend time talking and laughing with *you*."

"But . . ." Again my words did not travel to my tongue for some time. Orry used my silence to continue.

"They are right, Deborah." He looked at me then, and I saw sadness, but also something else. "I have enjoyed our talks of Egypt, but I have enjoyed so much more. Too much more. And I would like to spend even more time with you. But you are Isaac's wife, and I allowed myself to forget that. You, though, I will never forget."

He spoke as if we would never meet again. "But, Orry!" I would not let my lips stay silent and simply allow this to happen. "I am not Isaac's wife, I am Rebekah's servant. A servant. Just like you. There has been a misunderstanding. I do not wish to stop our visits."

Orry shook his head and walked away.

I could see that it would do no good to follow him, so instead I walked to Isaac's tent. He was outside in the shade, reviewing his holdings with Elioded. Elioded rose to greet me. I told him they could continue their meeting and I would return. In fact, I was not sure what I would say. But Elioded took his leave, and so I needed to find words.

"Isaac," I started. "Isaac." What was I to say? "Some people in the camp, I know not who, have a misunderstanding about my role in our tribe. We need to make this right. I have been gently talking with your servant Orry. We have found much in common. He was also in Egypt when the king died. And he used to make carvings for the palace where my grandmother—where your sister—Hallel once lived. We have talked of the buildings and the smooth-stoned passageways between them. We have shared memories of the markets and the smell of the river. It is all quite nice, and I would like to continue to speak with him about these things. But there are some in the camp who believe I should not, because they believe I am married to you."

Isaac sat quietly, waiting for me to go on, though I had finished. I repeated myself, hoping the next time he would say something. When he was still quiet, I added, "So if you please, you must address the servants and explain to them that I am not your wife."

At that, he spoke. "But Deborah," he said. "You are my wife."

Joseph, I do not think there was a day on which I was more surprised. My chin dropped. The rest of my body followed. I sat on the ground, neither speaking nor moving. Isaac stood silently beside me, then instructed me to rise and move from the heat of the sun into the cool shade of his tent. I do not know how much more time passed before he spoke.

"Deborah, you bore my first son."

This was true. But Zacharyah had died. Esau and Jacob had lived. Boys who had come from Rebekah's belly, not mine. I had gone to Isaac in order to help Rebekah. I had turned away Abraham's request of marriage for the same reason. I told all this to Isaac in broken phrases, with many gasps and pauses for breath between tears. I thought he had known it all. He had. He told me he had known that. And he reminded me that it did not change the fact that I had born his first son.

"But . . . we had no ceremony." This was a foolish thing to say. He was married to Rebekah. We would not have one.

"Of course that is true," Isaac said. "And you would not have been my wife if you had not brought me a son. But you did. I do not know why Yah did not choose my firstborn to live and carry on my traditions. There were many times when I talked with Yah in the field and asked about this. Next I would often ask why did the line not continue with an heir whose father *and* mother were from the seed of Abraham and Sarah. I have never received a response, and so I stopped asking. No matter the answers, they would not change that you birthed a son for me, and thus became my wife."

I could barely speak. My feelings, Joseph, were muddled. What did this revelation mean among Isaac, Rebekah, and myself? All these years, he had considered me his wife. Even though I had not been the first wife. Even though we had not had a ceremony. Even though he called only Rebekah to his tent. Even though our son lived only for a few days. Even still, in Isaac's eyes, all these years, I had not had the status of Rebekah's servant, but rather as a fellow wife who—especially had our son lived—would have had superior status to hers in the camp.

I turned my eyes up to Isaac's. And while I felt love and gratitude at his honoring me, my biggest feeling was shame. What woman does not *know* she is a wife? How could I have been a wife for all these years and been unaware? I had not been to his tent since the weaning. But I thought about the gift he gave me then, about our tender moments, our respect for each other, our love of the same children, our shared loss of a baby. How had I not known? I cried again while Isaac sat beside me patiently. Finally he asked, "Do you wish to marry Orry?"

Orry. I had almost forgotten the reason I had come to Isaac. Did I wish to marry Orry? "I do not know," I said. "I came here because others say we should not spend our days together talking, laughing, sharing food and memories."

"Deborah," he said. His voice sad and quiet. "Deborah, you are the granddaughter of my sister Hallel. A sister I never met, whose name I never heard until your arrival. You brought her here with you. And you are my wife of many years. But I can see on your face, and hear in your fumbling words, that it is not your wish to be my wife."

I gasped, my shame intensifying. Not only was I ignorant, but now I was offending my husband, the leader of our camp. But Isaac went on.

"My father told me that you were not an ordinary woman, and I have seen over the years that this is truth. I see your devotion to Rebekah. If you have now met a man with whom you wish to spend time, who you care for enough to leave Rebekah's side and keep his company, then I shall release you. You shall no longer be my wife."

I began to weep in relief and gratitude that Isaac cared for me enough that he would do this. Then I quickly wondered what it would mean to not be his wife. Would I need to leave the camp? But Isaac calmed my thoughts without hearing them. "Do not worry, Deborah," he said, with the kindness I had recognized in him my very first day at the camp. "You shall remain as Rebekah's nursemaid. And as my sister," he added. "I will tell Elioded. He will tell the others. You will be free to be with Orry however you wish." Isaac stood and left me in his tent. His head was low, his shoulders bent, and his hands wiped his eyes as he walked away. When my own face was free of tears, I walked to our tent to share my experience with Rebekah.

I spoke between sobs as I told Rebekah of all that had happened. She listened. She stroked my hair and my cheek. She held my hand—and my body when the sobs shook me. She told me I was not a fool and I must stop saying that I was. She told me she agreed that I must have been Isaac's wife, but that she had never thought of me as that, either.

"You did lie with him, Deborah," she said. "And," she admitted, "I had really always thought of Rananyah as *our* son—yours and mine. But he did not fall from the sky. He was yours, mine, and Isaac's." She said no more after that. We were both quiet with our thoughts until we drifted into sleep.

The next morning, I did not go see Orry. I did not go farther than the opening of our tent. I did not weave or collect water or cook. I did not even eat. I could do no more than cry. First, for my misconduct with Orry while married to Isaac. Then for my foolishness for not knowing I was a married woman. And finally, Joseph, I do not know if you will understand this, but I grieved the loss of being married, despite my relief. I had not wanted to be married to Isaac, had not known that I was, and yet somehow, it felt as if I lost something. It was all so very heavy.

Finally on the third day of my sorrow, Rebekah dragged me from our tent. "Walk in the hills," she said. "Do not go as far as Edom, or I shall worry about you." There was a light laugh in her voice as she tried to lighten my mood. When I did not smile, she became serious again. "Deborah," she said, "you have been breathing Yah into yourself and yourself into Yah here in our tent, and it has not been enough. Let the sky that Yah made enter you. Let in the sunshine. Let in the smell of the sheep and the rocks of the hills. And give them your sadness. Would you like me to go with you?"

I told her that I would go alone. And of course, she was right. I did release my sadness and let it become a part of Yah. *Whhhh.* I let Yah enter me and fill those holes with calm and beauty. *Yhhhh.* I breathed as I walked. *Yhhhh. Whhhh.* And when the sun was high in the sky, I found that my feet had taken me back to the servant's area, back to the path that led to the drying hides. Back to Orry.

THE TWENTIETH PARCHMENT

I saw Orry before he saw me. He was busily working on cutting leather into strips. I watched as he moved the knife from one edge of the leather to the other. One swift movement that left a large piece of hide in one hand and a strip on the ground next to his feet. I stood and watched his movements. Watched his shoulder as he raised his arm. Watched his head tilt as he found the right place for the next cut. Watched his back rise and fall subtly with each breath. Perhaps he heard me breathing. Maybe my foot loosened a stone that moved the dust beneath it. Or perhaps he felt me watching him. I do not know what caused him to look up at me. But when he did, his face filled with surprise and joy.

Orry jumped to his feet. He approached me quickly and stopped just before he reached me. His smile somehow wider even than the moment before, he said, "Deborah, I am so glad you returned!" We stood briefly in awkward silence, but then he insisted I sit in the shade where we had sat together before, and he ran to fetch beer and dates. "Katib told me the news," he said quietly, "and I do not know how this news came about, the exact news I wished for, but, Deborah, I did so hope you would return."

I did not share with him the details of my conversation with Isaac or Rebekah. I just sat in the gentle breeze, feeling happy and peaceful that we were together again. We finished our food and drink without words, with just the sounds of our chewing and swallowing and the birds who chirped in song in the trees.

When we had nothing left but to stare at each other to the point of giggles, Orry returned to his cutting. And, as if I had never been another man's wife and granted release from that role, I settled in and our words fell into a natural rhythm again. I told Orry how the strips of leather reminded me of my drum making with Tanqo. He listened with attention and curiosity, even as his hands kept moving. When I finished telling him of all the drums I had made, ending with the smallest one, which I had brought with me, he asked if I would like to make drums again and offered to prepare hide for me to do so.

"Is there enough?" I asked.

Orry laughed, and though I did not know what was funny, I laughed with him, for it was the most natural thing to do. There we were, beside the hides, laughing until we clutched our sides and needed deep breaths to calm ourselves. Finally, he said, "Isaac is a fine shepherd, blessed by the gods with a large flock. There is always more hide." In fact, this was not funny, but I was grateful, for the laughter was joyful. Indeed, our laughter was not about the abundance of hide—which is not amusing. No, our laughter that day was one of joy and relief. The joy we felt to be in each other's presence again. The relief we felt at the reprieve of never being able to speak again. The laughter was at once thunderous and melodious, and Orry and I were both overcome with it.

When we were calm, he said again, "There is always enough hide. Sometimes, I even use some of the extra scraps to practice my carving. Would you like to see?"

"Yes!" I said, and my excitement was clear.

"Will you come with me?" he asked. I gladly followed him along the path. We passed some small tents and small children playing around them. Women were sitting in the shade of the tents, weaving and talking together. Soon we came to a different work area. This had a wooden bench with leather scraps drying on it and metal tools beside it. Orry signaled for me to wait there a moment. He ducked into a tent and quickly returned with a cushion. He placed it on the bench and insisted I sit there.

"I made this cushion," he said. "The leather is older than any of the animals in the flock today. It has had many years to become soft."

"It is very soft," I said.

He smiled. Orry showed me large squares of leather, each with a different design carved into it. One had squares getting smaller and smaller until they reached the middle, and there was no more room. This one played tricks on the eyes, making them think that the leather was moving, when it was not. Another square had the eye of Horus carved on it, reminding me of Egypt. Yet another square had most of the leather carved away, such that it left a raised hollyhock flower across the middle.

"Each one is more wonderful than the last," I said to him. I gave each square of leather a turn in my hands, leaving the others resting on my knees until their turn would come again. Finally, when I had had my fill, I handed them back to Orry.

"I have others," he said. "They are not as large, but I hope they are as beautiful. Would you like to see?"

"Certainly, I would like to see," I said at once.

He took three small pieces out. These were not squares, but each one was the shape of a leaf—a leaf with a small hole in each end. Each leaf could easily fit in my hand. I took the first one and examined it closely. The carving on it, a small turtle, was so well done that it looked equally like it might crawl right out of the Nile or off the leather. I stroked it and admired the smoothness and the detail. The second had hills carved into it. The detail was so well done that it was easy to see and feel where a small goat was wandering along a path.

"You have great skill," I said.

He glowed with pride and handed me the third leaf. This one had a bee. The whole leaf was carved with the stripes and the wings, the head and stinger. I gasped.

"I would like to give this to you," Orry said. "It is not silver or gold. It will not show wealth or high status." As he spoke, Orry pushed thin leather cords through the holes on the carved leaves. If you will accept them, I shall become rich, indeed." His eyes pleaded with me, not in desperation, but filled with hope, joy, and possibility. I met his gaze and emotion and placed my left hand before him.

Orry took my hand and led me into the tent we had been sitting beside. It was nothing like Isaac's. It had room for only two people. It did not need to host guests or celebrations or even meetings with scribes or accountants. It needed only to be big enough to sleep and provide shade from the sun and shelter from the winter rains. It was all that, and beautiful, too. The floor was covered in a soft rug, and the cushions were abundant and all bore his handiwork.

Orry had pushed the leather cords through the holes in each of the leaves to make three bracelets. He tied them around my wrist. They made no sound as I raised and lowered my arm, but the soft, brown leaves silently stroked me and reminded me of placing my hand in water. Orry's eyes looked into mine, silently asking a question. I had not known the answer to this question when Isaac asked it of me, but now, with my entire body, I did. My lips pressed against his, answering. The two of us became one in his tent, though as soon as we did, it seemed as if we had already always been one.

THAT EVENING I went back to my tent with the last rays of light. I was not certain whether I was to return there at all, but I could not imagine doing anything different. And so, when I rose to leave, Orry walked me most of the way, leaving me with the same question as before: Will you return tomorrow? But it was not necessary, for now we both knew that I would. However, it became the question he asked me each night, even though I spent most nights sleeping in his tent, in his arms.

That night I slept in the tent I shared with Rebekah. She was already lying on our mat in the darkness when I came in. I sat beside her, and she said, "This time I did not worry, Deborah. I knew you would be back." And so I was glad that I had returned.

"Rebekah," I said. In the long pause that followed, she sat up to look at me. We did not need sunlight or lamps to see each other. We were familiar with each other's every expression, every line, every hair, even with only the faint light of the moon sliver hardly glowing outside. I looked at Rebekah looking at me, waiting for me to speak.

"Rebekah," I said again, "I . . . I am married!"

"What?" she yelled. Though she had not known what news I brought, this was not something she would have guessed. "What are you saying?" she asked. "Tell me everything!"

I did. This time, I knew I was a wife, and I knew who my husband was. What a joy it was to tell Rebekah all about Orry! I told her of how he welcomed me back with smiles and treats. I told her of watching him work and of the bracelets he gave me. She lit a lamp so she could admire them as much as the flame would allow. I told her of the peace in my heart when I heard him talk and of the joy I felt when he took me to his tent. I told her of my excitement to see him again in the morning.

I hoped Rebekah felt the happiness coming through my words. I was surprised when she yelled at me. "How could you do this?" she asked. "Why do you tell me only after you are a married woman? Do you not remember when I married Isaac? Do you not remember anointing me and dressing me and walking me to my betrothed? Do you not remember the feast and celebration? Was it not wonderful?"

"It was wonderful," I confirmed.

"And your day should be just as wonderful!" she said.

"But mine was just as wonderful," I answered, "only different."

Rebekah paused. "Will you at least permit me to anoint you and dress you?" she asked. "Before you go back to Orry? Will you permit me to lay eyes on the man who must love you as much as I do? For if he does not, I hope you will not go back to him."

Go back to him. This thought at once excited and scared me. I would go back to him in the morning, and I agreed to allow Rebekah to anoint me before I left. But then what? Return to the tent each evening? Rebekah and I spent most of that night talking, trying to guess how things would be different, trying to choose how things would be different. Other than the nights I had recently spent traveling to Edom, she had not slept alone since her first nursemaid, Yankah, died. She had either been in our tent with me or in Isaac's with him.

I had spent many nights alone in the tent while she was with Isaac, but even on the occasions that I had gone to him, all those years ago, I had still returned to our tent after. And what would become of sharing our days? Our stories? Our celebrations?

"Perhaps," Rebekah thought, "perhaps it will all be the same, only some nights you will sleep in Orry's tent, just as I have done with Isaac. But all the rest will be the same."

In fact, Joseph, it was not the same. Orry did not work in the fields like Isaac. He worked beside his tent, and slept there every night, and wanted me to sleep there every night. I wanted to as well. We spent much of our days together, too. I began making drums with the leather he prepared. Sometimes we worked on a drum together, with him carving the leather before I attached it to the rim. In only a few months' time, Rebekah and I had new drums for our full-moon celebrations. And those celebrations did continue.

For three nights each month, we shared our tent again: the night of the full moon, and the one before and after. We sang and we danced, we knew Yah, and we were together all day and all night. We told each other stories and recounted our days apart. Perhaps that was the funniest part because we had very few days apart. Even though she was busy weaving and painting, and I was busy making drums, we saw each other nearly every day. But it was usually for a brief time. So our monthly celebrations became even more special.

One night under the full moon, after we had danced and collapsed with a thrilled exhaustion, I told her of what Orry had said to me only a few days before. "'I have been enjoying planting my seed in you,' he said. 'And I shall continue to do so for as long as you allow me.'" I expected to keep allowing him. "'Soon,' he said, 'that seed will grow.' 'Into what?' I asked him. For I thought he was being poetic or funny and wondered whether he might say a love song or a date tree. 'A baby!' he said, shocked that I would even ask. And then I laughed so hard that I clutched my sides and gasped for breath!"

Rebekah and I had an equally robust laugh under the moon. When she calmed down, she asked if I had said anything to him after. "Yes, I told him I am an old woman, and there would be no more babies in my womb; my blood had stopped long ago. And do you know what he said?" She looked at me, expectantly. "He said he would pray to Yah and ask that my womb be opened, as Sarah's was in her old age."

"I thought you said he does not pray to Yah, that he prays to the Egyptian gods."

"He will pray to whomever he thinks will listen."

"I am surprised this does not bother you," she said.

I was surprised, too. For I was surprised that I could love someone so much who could not understand that Yah was the Creator of All, and the other gods were not worthwhile. I had tried to teach him about Yah, to show him, to help him know YhWh, but the closest he had gotten was to accept that Yah was one of the gods, not the one god. Which was exactly the same as what he thought before we met.

It turned out, this was not a hindrance to our love. I ignored him when he left gifts in his little shrine, though I did request that he keep the shrine outside the tent, and he agreed. I still knew Yah, and when he mentioned something about another god, I tried not to think him a foolish man, even though it was clear. His kindness outweighed his foolishness, though, and our new life together did as well.

Orry and I worked side by side most days. He prepared the hides, carved, sewed, and worked the leather, and I made drums. Orry taught me how to carve a little bee into the leather of each drum. Of course it was not as beautiful as his work, but it showed that it had been made by me. When I had made two new drums for myself and two new ones for Rebekah, I still had ten that were extra. Orry suggested that we take them to the market. And so I learned that the servants went nearly every month to the market; it was not a rare occasion as it was for us, but common. Many things we used came from trades or purchases made at a market.

The next month, Orry and I walked with several of the servants to market. The journey was pleasant with our wares carted behind donkeys and an air of adventure between us.

"You never know what surprises might be at the market," Tavlin told me. She was one of the cooks who had befriended me when I was living with Orry. "Certainly, there are many things we can rely upon," she went on. "The spice man will be there, and he will give me a pinch extra of everything I buy, because I am a good customer. There will be craftsmen, perhaps selling things made of leather, like you and Orry, or perhaps woodworkers or stone masons. And sometimes there is dried fruit of sorts I have never seen, that has traveled long distances to be tasted by my tongue, here in the hills. Those are my favorites."

There were dried fruits at the market that day, and they quickly became my favorite, too. There was melon that had come all the way from the side of the Nile, just like me. I had not tasted melon since my childhood. Then it had been juicy and would drip down my chin and cover my fingers with its sweetness. At the market, because it was dry, eating it was different, though the flavor was the same as I remembered it. I ate my fill at the market and bought some to bring back for myself later and for Rebekah to taste. I knew she would love it.

I do not remember the names of the other fruits, for they were so foreign. But even now I can taste the tartness of some and the sweetness of others. My tongue remembers. And my heart remembers that I bought the fruit with coins that were placed in my hands by people who bought my drums! Very little can compare with the wonder and joy and pride I felt. Even Orry telling me that I could have gotten more silver for them than I had did not dampen my spirit.

Such was life with Orry: going from one kind of joy to another. Rebekah has suggested that perhaps I see only the good things, because our time together was so short. It was short, but it was long enough for fun and healing. I did not anticipate that being with him would lift my sadness about leaving Egypt. In fact, I had not known that I still carried sadness about leaving Egypt. Yet hearing his speech, seeing the sun on his dark skin, dark like mine, being with someone who knew my homeland, was a comfort. One morning under the rising sun, we even realized that though I had never seen one of his carvings, my mother's sister Rayah had likely seen some of his handiwork at the temple where she was a priestess—perhaps even seen him. This thought brought me happiness.

That was Orry. He brought me happiness in so many ways. And I him. He told me this daily and nightly, and I never tired of it. I never did bring him a child, though. As I had told him, my body was too old. And he was even older than I. I was content to have no more children. We had Katib's babies underfoot and enjoyed their youthful smiles and energy. I had Esau and his sons, who accompanied him one at a time, when he came to bring hunt and honor to Isaac. They were already turning into young men, strong, fast, and handsome. Some carried Esau's coloring, beginning to grow wispy orange beards; others had darker skin and hair, looking more like Jacob at their age. All walked with confidence and respected their father, grandfather, grandmother, and me.

We held hope that we would soon get to see Jacob and his wife and his children. Rebekah counted the summers that passed, looking forward to Jacob completing his debt to Lavan so that he might return with his wife and bring grandchildren to the camp. But when the seven years passed, instead of receiving Jacob, we received a message from him.

A message to Isaac of Be'er Sheva, from his son Jacob in Haran.

Honored Father, Beloved Mother, Dear Auntie,

This is a message of both sorrow and joy. I completed my obligation to my mother's brother, Lavan, and I was wed to his daughter. She is kind, beautiful, strong, and an exceptionally talented weaver. I write this message after only one month of marriage, and I can already tell you that she is a fine wife. Hallelu Yah. Her name is Leah. That is right, not my beloved Rachel, but her older sister Leah.

I have now also wed my beloved, Rachel, and am obligated to Lavan for another seven years in exchange. I pray that when those years are complete, I shall have a safe return, free of fear of my brother's revenge, and with sons who will bring you honor and pleasure. May Yah bless you and keep you well, may Yah sustain us and watch over us until our reunion.

Rebekah cried for three days when we received this message. She begged Isaac to travel to Haran, if not to persuade her brother to let Jacob go, then perhaps to pay Jacob's debt, or at the very least see her son. Isaac did all he could to comfort her, but she found none in his answer that Yah wished him to stay in the promised land and not leave it as his father had. I stayed in Rebekah's tent, by her side day and night, knowing I could not comfort her in the way she wished, but at least I could be with her in her sorrow. I, too, wished I could see Jacob. And his wives.

A few days later when I returned to Orry, he suggested just that. "I shall take you, if you like," he said. This had not occurred to me. I did not know it was even possible. Orry laughed. "I have traveled far and wide," he said. "I came to work for Abraham many years ago; I have stayed to work for Isaac. I have been sustained and blessed in his camp. I have provided good work and good results for the camp. I am obligated to do only that, and as long as I do so, Isaac keeps me here.

"There have been times when my work is complete, and I let the new hides dry by themselves. They do not need me to watch them. I have traveled to the Jordan River, to let my body float on its waves. I have even traveled to the land of the Tarshish, and my eyes have seen the regal peacocks and jumping monkeys for themselves. I have not been to Haran, but I am certain it would be a great adventure—and a great joy to bring you there," he said.

I wanted to hear of the peacocks and monkeys, but there was something I wanted even more. "And Rebekah? Will you bring her with me?" I asked.

"Certainly," he said.

I ran back to tell her immediately, and a great deal of activity began at once. Food was prepared, carts were packed with rugs and cushions for the journey. Orry selected three young men to accompany us, and Isaac gave us his blessing. Rebekah said he had agreed immediately for her to go; it was only he who should not leave. He trusted all of his servants and knew we would be safe. "Kiss my son when you see him," were his parting words when we left within a month of hearing from Jacob.

I had never guessed that I would return to Haran, but the journey was a great blessing. It was the first and only time that I was able to share my life with Rebekah and Orry at the same time. Our practice of celebrating the moon together had continued, but, of course, then I was with Rebekah only. When it was not moon time, I was with Orry. The two of them were never together, as they lived in different worlds, though only a short walk apart.

I had once wondered aloud to Orry whether Isaac was like the pharaoh. This had made him laugh. I did love it when he laughed! But I had not intended it as a funny question. The pharaoh had a city of workers. My father and brothers had grown his grain. Orry had carved his stones. Others had cooked his food and scribed his words, built his dwellings and his ships. The more time I spent with Orry, the more I saw that such a world existed for Isaac—and Rebekah and me.

Although Isaac looked after his sheep and instructed his men regarding the flocks and the crops, he did not do all the work. Likewise, Rebekah and I cooked meals and wove rugs and belts, but most of our tunics were made by others, just like our food, our cushions, our tents, our carts, our lamps, our pots, and so much more.

"Isaac is not the pharaoh here," Orry said. "Isaac works in service of his god, Yah, and has been blessed manyfold to have workers who help him. I have seen camps greater than his, cities, even, with more products and more power. Isaac is a wealthy man, but he is no king. Pharaoh serves nobody; he is the god, so others serve him. It is not the same."

This was the truth. It was not the same. Still, there was a separation in our camp between the members of our family and the other members of the tribe. On the trip to Haran, that separation did not exist. I slept under the stars with Orry on one side of me and Rebekah on the other. Orry entertained us with the stories of monkeys and peacocks and other wonders from Tarshish. I did not need to retell these stories to Rebekah, for we both heard them. Rebekah and I talked of our sons across the hills and valleys, while Orry listened, adding to the conversation only occasionally. But he was there. We were all there together. What a gift it was for me.

We separated only as we came to an end of our journey to Haran. It was then we decided it would be the wisest for Orry to approach Lavan alone first and then come back for us when he knew it was safe. This was a good choice, for when Lavan heard that Orry was there with a message from Rebekah, he spit on him when hearing his sister's name!

"'Certainly she has grown old and ugly,'" Orry reported Lavan as saying. "'And she thinks my daughters would be like her. But they are not. My daughters are strong, good workers, and already Leah is with child. My sister was foolish and disrespectful to send her son here with nothing to give me for these women. I long to spit on her myself, but I trust you to do so for me.'"

Lavan did not extend any hospitality to Orry and left as soon as his message was delivered. When we heard that Lavan felt this way, Rebekah decided it was best for her not to see him. She had no desire to see him, other than, perhaps, to inquire about her parents. But she had long ago thought Betuel and Metuyeshet dead, so knowing when and how they had died was less important. Especially as she was far more eager to see Jacob.

We decided that Orry would seek him out in the fields and bring him to us. We kept our distance and put up our tent beside a small stream. Orry was gone for a day and a night and most of the next day, but when he returned, he had Jacob with him. Oh, what a joy to see his face again! As soon as he came into view, Rebekah and I both started crying. By the time we were close enough to embrace, my tears had stopped, and Rebekah's had increased.

Jacob approached and joined her in tearflow. The two held each other for a long time, until they were both calm. Then Rebekah took him by the face, his dark beard in her hands, and held him still so she could look him in the eyes. Finally, she released him so that I might have a turn to reunite. Our hug was brief, but just as meaningful. I thought of this as a moment when I could feel jealous of Rebekah, could feel that Jacob was not my son. I had the opportunity to feel those things, but they were not genuine. I knew his joy in seeing me was sincere.

"Mother," Jacob said. "Auntie. Welcome. What a surprise and a blessing when this kind man found me and told me of your arrival! If I had known you were coming, I would have had a feast prepared. Orry told me of his meeting with Lavan, though. That is no surprise. He is not a kind man, nor fair, nor interested in my well-being—nor in that of his daughters. And what daughters he has! My wives! Mother, Auntie, you will be pleased with my wives."

When he said that, I heard the little boy in his voice. He had grown into a strong, muscular man, as large and hairy as his brother. I did not dare tell him about his brother and the way he came to the camp with his sons and his meat, though I wished I could. I wished he would find it joyful, but in case he would not, I kept quiet. It was a better choice, for it allowed us all to hear of his life in Haran.

"Lavan's flocks have grown under my care," he said. "I believe there are two reasons for this. One is that he is lazy, and anybody who is not lazy would have more success with his sheep than he does. Another reason is that I have been talking with Yah every evening. In fact, I have discovered that it is the evening that is the gateway to the morning, and not the other way around. The rest of the night prepares us for when the sun rises again. It is also the time of dreams. So that is when I walk with my god, and pray, and talk, and listen."

Jacob paused his story and looked to me for approval. My pride was deep. I had taught him this. Not I, alone, of course, but I had helped him find the words, helped him find the practice, and it was serving him well. But there was more.

"When I left you," he said, "I was scared. I did not wish to show you how scared I was, for I did not want you to worry for my safety. But I was not used to traveling alone. I secretly admired Esau for the days he spent searching for his hunt, but I never had a desire to do the same. I appreciated my time by the tents. And so, to go so far, alone, and always with the possibility of a great hunter being on my trail, gave me great fear.

"The first night after my departure, I was nearly shaking with dread that I would be found in the darkness. I stayed on the outskirts of Luz, the first city I had seen. I did not enter the city but went off the road and behind bushes, lest my brother look for me within the walls. There was a large rock there, flat, like a stone that could be used for sacrifice. I remembered the story of my father being bound to such a rock and being saved. I told myself that I could be blessed with safety if I would just lie there, too, and trust in Yah."

I was thankful that Rebekah had not known of Jacob's fear until so many years later. Her imagination had kept her busy worrying, but I had been able to soothe her, reminding her of Jacob's skills. Now, I could see her body tensing with worry even though this had happened so long ago. Thankfully, Jacob eased her concern as he told her of what happened next.

"So I began breathing *Yhhhh, Whhhh*. In and out, I brought my god to me, and myself to my god, just as I had learned. I had no instrument with me, but my chest pounded like a drum. It took me a long time to calm down, but finally I did. That night, I had visions of a ladder that reached from my very resting place, directly up, up, up, beyond where I could see, and even beyond that. On the ladder, there were angels, some going up, others coming down. And so I knew I had found a place that was connected to Yah, and I was safe.

"Indeed, I heard Yah's voice come down the ladder. *I am YhWh, the god of your father, Abraham, the god of your father, Isaac. The ground that you lie upon, I shall give to you and your seed*. And then, Yah gave me the blessing of my fathers, that my descendants will be as numerous as the dust of the earth and spread west, east, north, and south. Tears bathed my face. First my father had blessed me, and now Yah. I swelled with pride.

"And almost as immediately, I began to wonder. Could I truly be good enough to receive these blessings? Could I be worthy of having the people of the land be blessed through me? Was I wise enough, strong enough, good enough, was I even safe enough to live to receive these blessings?"

Had I been by Jacob's side as he traveled, I believe I would have praised him for this. He did not yet understand that it was this beautiful combination of pride and humility that was the sign that he was, indeed, worthy. But I was not there. Rebekah was not there. Isaac was not there. But he was not alone. His help came from Yah. He told us this with awe ringing in his voice.

"Yah knew my thoughts and spoke again, saying, *I am with you, I shall protect you wherever you go and shall bring you back to this land. I shall not leave you until I have done what I have promised you.*

"When I awoke in the morning, I rose from what might have been my sacrificial bed and stood it upright, to become a sacrificial pillar. I anointed it with oil and praised Yah and called the place Beit El, for I had slept not in Luz, not in the wilderness, but in the House of God that night. As I poured the oil, I entered into a covenant with Yah. I vowed that should this god, indeed, remain with me, giving me bread to eat and clothing to wear, until I have a safe return to my father's camp, then this will be my god. Thus far, I have been sustained, and though I am still in debt to Lavan, there will come a day when I shall return to the land that Yah has promised me, return to you, Mother, Auntie, and I trust that Yah will protect me."

Rebekah's shoulders relaxed, as did her brow. She became so relaxed, I almost worried she would fall. For more than seven years, her body had held a worry about her boy. That was falling away with each word he spoke. She said as much when he stopped. "Oh, Jacob, how grateful I am to hear these words! Yah spoke to me so many years ago, telling me that you would receive your father's blessing, and yet I worried if we had done the right thing—if I had done the right thing. I still do not know the answer. But I feel better seeing my young man grown into a wise man, and a married man. We must meet your wives! We have brought enough food to sustain us on our journey and celebrate with a feast. We shall begin our preparations today. Only promise that you will return when the sun begins to set tomorrow and bring Leah and Rachel with you."

"I promise," Jacob said. "With Elohim as my witness, I will bring my wives to meet my mothers." When we looked at him with questions in our eyes, he added, "I told you of my meeting with Elohim using the name Yah, for I know it is a name that has great meaning to you. As it does for me. But since the dream of which I spoke, I now call my god Elohim. This is the same One who is the god of my father Isaac and the god of my father Abraham, only by another name." With that he parted, and we began our preparations.

For the rest of the day and into the night we cooked and talked, cooked and talked. Finally Orry convinced us to sleep so that we could enjoy the celebration we were so anticipating. The next day, when the food was ready and the carpets laid out, we put on our celebration robes we had brought with us just for this occasion. The feast that followed was more than we could have dreamt of. For while we had been preparing, so had Leah and Rachel. They arrived in their finest clothes with stews and barley, figs and wine. In addition, they brought us gifts! A jar of honey for me and dried dates for Rebekah. We were pleased by their thoughtfulness. We, too, had brought gifts for the brides. A drum I had made for each of them, of course, and an oil lamp that Rebekah had painted for each. They looked pleased.

We ate and drank well into the night, watching the sky fill with stars. Once Jacob realized that Orry was not only his father's manservant but also my husband, I was pleased to see him begin a conversation. He inquired about news from home and listened to Orry's stories of our journey. The two men talked of sheep and goats, weather, and hills, and more that I could not hear, for most of my attention was focused on our own conversations.

Leah and Rachel were two strong women. We learned of their struggles growing up with Lavan. Their mother had died when they were young, and his next wife died shortly after they wed. When his third wife grew sickly, he became even angrier, they said, and lazier. They did their best to keep their distance from him. It was not hard, for they tended the sheep and carried water, cooked, and wove, and had no reason to seek out their father, and he had little reason to go to them.

Lavan fathered six children. Leah and Rachel were the only daughters and were inseparable in childhood. They shared everything, confided in each other, consoled each other, and knew the other's deepest hopes and loudest laughs. And they had devised a way to stay together, even after marriage. With the younger of the two about to wed, the sisters knew that Lavan would keep the older in his tent to serve him, trapping her in her father's tribe forever. But if Leah were to marry Jacob first, she would be saved that fate.

Rachel told us she knew that it would be hard to identify the bride in the low light of the early night. With the veil covering Leah's face, and Rachel staying hidden in the tent, nobody would know it was Leah until it was too late. Their father, for one, would be too drunk from the festivities to know his own hand in front of his eyes. And Jacob was such a kind man, they hoped he would not be angered. The fact that Jacob was not angered, but pleasantly surprised, did bother Rachel sometimes. But she openly spoke of being the favored wife, and of not wanting to part with Leah, nor leave her, unmarriable, to grow old with Lavan. This was something Rebekah and I knew well.

"Did you have nursemaids?" I asked. They both did, of course. We learned that Leah's nursemaid was named Zilpah, and Rachel's, Bilhah. I requested that they both join us, with Leah and Rachel, of course, for another feast the next night. Oh, how I wished the moon would be full! I knew Rebekah wished the same. But it did not prevent us from having a night of song and dance, music and stories. And when the six of us women joined hands and danced in a circle, it was not important that the moon was hardly more than a sliver. We were completely full.

In the morning, we woke with smiles still on our faces, then bade each other tearful goodbyes. We knew it would be a short visit, for the journey took several days each way, and Orry could leave his duties for only so long. Parting was difficult but made easier with the knowledge that in less than seven years, Jacob and these four wonderful women would return to us. Leah shared that she was, for the first time, with child. "I hope I shall bring this baby with us," she said. I put my fingers together and prayed. Yes! She would bring this child. Two? Three? Four? More? Yes!

Joseph, I have seen your older brothers remind you that you are younger than they are. You know well that Leah is the mother of many. But on that day, she held only the first one inside her, and even for the one, we were grateful.

On the walk back to Be'er Sheva, Rebekah and I relived every moment of the visit several times. We told each other of the colors of the women's finely woven tunics and reminded each other of the flavors in the stews. We noted that Rachel, though younger than her sister, was slightly taller, and that Zilpah had a long scratch on her right arm. Bilhah was quiet most of the time but, we agreed, had a warm and open smile. And Jacob. Jacob was truly a strong man, a hard worker, trusting in Yah, and growing a family!

Poor Orry. He said he needed to walk ahead of us several times so that his ears could have some quiet. But I saw the happiness he felt for me and the pride on his part in making this wonderful reunion happen.

"He is a good man, and I am confident he will deal well with all he inherits from Isaac when the time comes," Orry said. "I look forward to meeting with him again when he returns in seven years."

But sadly, it was not to be. Jacob neither returned after seven years, nor did Orry ever meet him again. Ten summers after Orry gave me the leather bracelets, he began to sleep past the sunrise. He could no longer lift the wet skins to hang them to dry, and his leather carvings became less and less detailed. For a year I watched him struggle more and more; for a month I brought him broths and coaxed him to take small sips. And for three days and nights, I held his head in my lap as he slept. I traced the lines on his face with my fingers. I whispered words of gratitude, praise, and love that I was not sure he could hear. When his breath stopped, I held him just a little longer.

"Hallelu Yah," I whispered. You might think it difficult for me to utter words of praise when the man I loved would never say another word to me, would never give me another kiss or another gift. We would never again go on an adventure or to the market, would never again enjoy treats under the trees or nights in our tent. But I praised Yah for Orry's life, and for the ten years that was our life. I praised Yah for the meals we ate together, the birdsong we heard together, the flowers we smelled together, for the time we spent side by side, and for the time in each other's arms. I even praised Yah for the day when I had tripped and fallen on him while he was carving, and his blade cut his arm from his wrist to his elbow. Orry cried out in pain, but not in anger. And when the cut healed, we whispered to each other that he had a carving of the Nile on his arm. I thanked Yah for those memories, and so much more. And I cried. I cried so very much.

Katib was a good son. He honored his father with a fine funeral. Orry's two oldest grandsons carried his body, wrapped in a linen shroud woven by Katib's wife with a depiction of the

Nile and a border of leather that Orry had made himself. The words he carved told the story of his life: his boyhood in Egypt, his first wife and their son, his work for the pharaoh in the temples, his travels north with Katib, and then, finally, me. Katib read the story loudly and proudly in front of me and Rebekah and all the manservants and maidservants who had gathered to bid Orry farewell.

A hole had already been dug in the hard, cracked dirt. I had requested that Orry lie beneath the tree where we had often enjoyed sweets together, and Katib had obliged. He had already placed Orry's carving tools in the hole, and now there was room for only the body. But it looked so small. How would my husband with his strong arms, with muscles that flexed with the strokes of the leatherwork by day and held me close at night, fit into such a hole? But he did fit, and there was even room for the dirt to cover him.

This is how I remember the funeral. I do not remember all of it. It felt like a dream to me. Like I was at once walking and sleeping, that what I was seeing was not real, though the absence of Orry by my side made it too real. I shed many tears in the tent I returned to with Rebekah. I could not bring myself to stay in the tent I had shared with Orry without him. What would I do? Making drums was something we had done together. We had made hundreds. It was enough. The men and women there accepted me when I was with Orry, but alone?

"I am glad to have you back," Rebekah said. "Though I am truly sorry for the reason. You know that?"

I did know that. Rebekah's love for me is true. Her desire to be with me, and mine to be with her, does not weigh more than our desire for the other to be happy. I was able to find my happiness again and my rhythm of sharing a life with Rebekah. I held my memories of Orry tight, and many nights felt him holding *me* tight, even though I knew it was my imagination.

I was disappointed that he did not get to meet with Jacob again but more disappointed that Jacob's return was so many years after we had expected. Once he completed his debt to Lavan, he took on yet another, this time so that he would be able to leave Haran with more than he had arrived with. In the seven years since his weddings, he had become the father of many children but had no flock of his own, only Lavan's. And so he would stay yet another seven years in exchange for the speckled and spotted animals. To wait another seven years felt unbearable to me and Rebekah, and even Isaac was disappointed when we received word of Jacob's new delay, yet somehow, we managed. One day was like the one before, full of work and walking as we had done during all the other years he had already been gone. Our daily patterns were interrupted only by Esau's visits and our dances under the moon. We savored both of these.

Finally, we were greatly pleased and surprised when a messenger arrived telling us that Jacob was on his way back after only six extra years instead of seven! "Hallelu Yah!" Rebekah exclaimed when the message arrived. "Hallelu Yah!" That very day, Rebekah made it her business to walk the length and breadth of the camp, inspecting every clay vessel, every basket of food, every plant in the garden, every wheel on every cart, every tent and rug and cushion. Jacob was already on the way, and though he could not arrive soon enough to satisfy her, she also wanted the time to make sure everything was in order.

I sent a messenger to Esau, not sharing the news that Jacob would soon return to the camp but requesting that Esau do so. I wished to speak to him before his reunion with his brother. He came quickly and sought me out as soon as he arrived at the camp. "What is it, Auntie? I was alarmed to receive your message. You look well, I hope that you are."

I hugged him. "All is well," I assured him. "I did not intend to worry you. Please, walk with me." We walked together, away from the camp. He shortened his stride to match mine. Only the birds spoke as we walked. Esau's tolerance impressed me. My memory of him as impatient needed to be left in the past. He was a grown man with a camp of his own, many wives and children, manservants and maidservants, tents and riches. He was blessed. We stopped in the shade of date trees, and I told him this.

"Esau, you are blessed. Your father has blessed you, Yah has blessed you. You live the prosperous life of a rich man." I paused for a moment. "I am proud of you, Esau." His coloring always revealed his blushes quickly. He could not prevent the joy this brought him from showing on his face.

"Thank you, Auntie," he said.

I knew he was curious to learn why I had requested he come. I did not make him wait any longer. "Esau, Jacob is returning," I said.

"But you said he would be gone another seven years after the first fourteen," he said. "Only six have passed. He should be gone another year." Esau clenched his teeth and his fists. His face became red again, this time with anger. He allowed me to gently open his fingers and place my hand on top of his, but I did not feel it calming him.

"Tell me, Esau, why does this anger you? Has your father not blessed you also? Has Yah not provided for you manyfold?" We sat in silence for a long time. I could feel the anger seething through his body. "Esau," I said, "when Rananyah died, I was sad and I was angry. Why would Yah let me hold this beautiful baby boy, only to take him away from me? And . . . and the blessing of the firstborn, that was yours only because Rananyah died. You were not the firstborn son, Esau. That blessing belonged to Rananyah. And yet he never lived to receive it."

Now it was Esau's hand that was on top of mine. I did not mention Rananyah for his sympathy, though that had been his unchanging reaction since he was hardly more than a toddler. "Esau, I remind you of this not so you can feel sad for me. I hope to show you an example of turning sadness away from anger and into joy. For had I remained angry, I could not have fed you Rananyah's milk. Did I not give you the very life from my bosom? If I had allowed my anger to put a stop to life, the very breath you take now would be moving through the sheep and the goats, the trees and the hills, not your body."

I took a deep breath in. *Yhhhh*. Esau followed my lead automatically, *Yhhhh*, just as he had done when he was younger. I wondered if he did this in his own camp now, with his children. But I did not ask. I continued. *Whhhh*. As did he. *Whhhh*. We laid down in the dust of the earth and breathed Yah into us, and ourselves into Yah while the sun moved across the sky. When we sat up again, his body was relaxed, and underneath the forest of red hair that covered his face, I saw my little boy.

"Listen, Esau," I said, "Yah is our god. Yours, mine, your father's, Jacob's. Yah is One. You cannot interfere with Yah's wishes or plans. I hope your anger has subsided enough so that you can let your brother live. To take his life is to take the life of an entire world, his children, his children's children, and their children. If you spare his life, you save an entire world. Through you, Yah's plan can move forward. Yah has put that in your hands. Yah trusts you, relies on you. As do I."

"I shall visit my father," he said. "I shall spend the night in his tent, then return to my camp and prepare to meet Jacob." He rose and helped me to my feet. On the way back, he again matched my stride. Since he did not tell me of his plans for meeting Jacob, I chose to believe that not bolting away from me was a good sign. I closed my fingers and prayed that he would not harm his brother, and I received no answer from Yah that day, neither yes nor no.

THE TWENTY-FIRST PARCHMENT

Jacob had been gone for twenty years. Of all that time, it seemed as if waiting the last month before his arrival was the most difficult. Thirteen summers had passed since Rebekah and Orry and I had laid our eyes on him. Thirteen summers since I had embraced him, heard his voice, sat with him. Twenty since he had seen his father. He would come back to this promised land as a father himself and a wealthy man, and we knew he would bring wives and children, and the waiting was nearly unbearable.

"Perhaps we should go look for him," Rebekah said. It had been fourteen days since we had heard of his leaving Haran. We did not know what Esau would do, if anything. And even if the harm did not come from Esau, there were other dangers. I was as eager as she was, but less worried. Still, she persisted. "It does not take this long to travel from Haran," she said. "We have done it twice, each time in a matter of days."

"Each time it was just us," I reminded her. Our first arrival from Haran had been with Eliezer, when we moved our lives here. He had told us we needed nothing, so we left nearly everything behind. The second time was with Orry, and even though we took a longer route in order to enjoy some time by the river, it still took only a few days to return from Haran. "We had no animals," I said, "other than beasts to lighten our burdens. We had no children, no flocks."

"Pray, Deborah," she pleaded.

"What shall I ask?"

"Ask if Jacob is well."

I took a deep breath, in, out. "*Yhhhh. Whhhh.* Is Jacob well?" She saw me press gently against my thumb and chirped with joy and relief. "Now you pray," I said.

"Blessed are you, Yah," she said, "who watches over my son and keeps him safe to return him to me well and whole."

We both felt better after that day, though no more patient. We kept busy all day, doing anything we could to make the camp look better, though it always looked like what it was: an area of work and wealth. Finally, a month after receiving word that Jacob was on his way, we saw him and his family approaching from the distance. Jacob walked with a limp, but otherwise our prayers had been answered; he looked strong and well.

Now, Joseph, I shall begin to tell of a time that you know well. The time when you and your father, your mothers and brothers and sisters finally came to our camp. Soon I shall share stories of your yearly visits here. I shall tell of things that you remember, but I may tell it differently. For these are my scrolls, my memories. Even if yours are different, you will continue to write my words exactly as I speak them.

And write this down as well: I have offered you some lines of your own in this section of the scroll. As a gift. You have been a great scribe for me. In six years, you have written as many scrolls. Your listening is patient and attentive. Your writing is careful and beautiful. I am proud of you. Katib is proud of you. Jacob, your father, is proud of you. But you have declined my offer of some lines in this scroll, telling me that you do not want lines of your own, but scrolls of your own. You told me that your story will be worth telling someday, and that when that day comes, you will do so without hesitation or limitation, as I have always done. And now, I shall continue to do so.

Oh, what a sight it was to see your father! Our son with four women and sixteen children! I nearly ran off to meet them, but it was in that moment that Rebekah found her patience and insisted that we wait longer.

"He will want to honor his father with the news of his return. We shall wait in our tent."

So we did. We kept our excited hands busy with spinning while we waited for him to arrive at Isaac's tent, give him gifts, and introduce his family. When Rebekah's legs no longer agreed to sit idly, she stood and left our tent, watching as Jacob approached. It was not a long watch, for as soon as he left his father's tent and saw his mother, he began to run. Even with his limp he was able to move quickly. I saw this from where I waited, just under the last shade of the tent.

The two held each other in an embrace for a long while. The younger children began to shift their weight from one leg to the other. They were hot and ready for the next thing to happen, but finely dressed for their important moment of presentation, they dared not move and get dusty. When Rebekah and Jacob could finally release each other, Rebekah went to each of the women—Jacob's wives, whom we had met all those years ago, now the mothers of his children. Each one kissed Rebekah's hand and was met with Rebekah pulling her close. When she had greeted all four, she said, "Finally, I shall have women around me!" I thought this was the perfect time for me to step forward.

"And what about me?" I asked. "Am I not a woman?" Now it was my turn to be wrapped in Jacob's arms. He had grown older, with a few white hairs decorating his dark beard, but his arms were just as strong as they had been when we saw him in Haran. Being a shepherd required more physical work than learning to read and write did, and even without seeing his flocks, I knew he was a good one.

"Jacob," I asked. "Have you seen your brother?"

"Yes, Auntie," he said. "He accepted my gifts and offered to escort me here. All is well."

Joseph, certainly you must remember meeting Esau. I imagine you saw him for the first time as looking similar to your father but covered in red hair instead of black. They do look so much alike if you do not look too closely at their colors. Or perhaps you thought him an older version of your red brother, Levi. What you might also not have looked closely enough to see was that Esau had thoughts of killing your father, so strong was his jealousy. I was overjoyed to see Jacob again, but even happier to know that the brothers had made amends. With that relief, I could welcome the women.

I, too, received kisses from each of the women. Leah, Rachel, Zilpah, and Bilhah. I remembered their names, as did Rebekah. We had spoken of them nearly every day since our first meeting, dreaming of their lives with Jacob and the children they would give him. Despite his limp, Jacob stood tall and proud as he introduced his family. It was not easy to look at these young ones for the first time and remember so many names as well. But we would learn them soon. And Rebekah, who had done all the waiting she was willing to do, made sure that soon would begin right away.

"We shall have a feast!" she said. "Jacob, take your sons to the flocks and choose the finest kids. Deborah and I shall get to know your wives and daughters."

And just like that, we saw Jacob limping away with his sons, and Rebekah and I were wrapped in embraces again by his wives. For many moments, we all simply stared at each other in wonder and joy. Finally, Rebekah turned to the oldest girl and spoke.

"What is your name, girl?"

"Ahuvah," the girl said.

"I am the sister of your grandfather Lavan. We were born of the same father and mother in Haran, but that is the only way in which we are the same. And, of course, I am the mother of your father. You may call me Grandmother," Rebekah instructed her. "And you may call her Auntie," she said, referring to me. "It is the same for all of you," she said. "You should all call me Grandmother and call Deborah by the sweet name Auntie."

Rebekah turned back to Ahuvah. "Who is your mother?" she asked.

"I have four mothers," Ahuvah responded. This was not the answer Rebekah was expecting, and she was silent while she worked out what to ask next. Ahuvah thought the silence meant she could still speak. "I have one who birthed me," she said. "It is my mother Leah who gave me life and who teaches me to weave as beautifully as she does and in whose tent I dwell. It is my mother Zilpah who helped me keep my life when I was born with a hungry twin, Judah. Zilpah never let me be hungry then; she still will give me her last morsel of food. It is my mother Bilhah who sits with me and comforts me when needed, who strokes my cheek, lets me rest my head on her shoulder. It is my mother Rachel who sings with me as we work in the garden and delights with me at the wonders both inside and outside the garden. Although we have no garden now, for we have left our home."

"What are some of the wonders you saw on the way from Haran?" I asked.

"The river!" The river had clearly made an impression on her. She told us at length of first hearing it, then seeing it, and finally crossing it. "The hills are just as beautiful," she added, "though very different, of course. Even different from our hills at home."

"You mean, our hills in Haran," another girl corrected. We learned that this girl was Annah. She did not say more than that. Her cheeks still burned with shame from having spoken out of turn.

"The hills in Haran were so much greener," Ahuvah went on. "Here they are browner. But I love this brown. And it is not only brown. For there are flowers, sometimes tall flowers, sometimes little ones that you could miss if you did not look closely."

Rebekah turned to the next girl, who was clearly a few years younger than the two we had already met. "What is your name?" she asked.

"Deenah," she answered. "And I also have four mothers. The one who birthed me is Leah, and I also crossed the river and I also saw the brown hills and flowers, large and small. I am very good at noticing things. I saw many things in the city when we stopped there. And smelled them, too. A girl gave me cinnamon. She gave some to Joseph, too. We were the only ones who got it because we were the only ones who stopped, and so she gave us some. We were also the only ones who stopped to admire the sandals and bowls of the craftspeople in the city, but we did not get any of those. I notice that you have lovely things here, Grandmother and Auntie."

I smiled. Here was a girl who loved adventure as much as we did. I could hear it in her voice and see it on the cuts and bruises that come from running and climbing and taking small falls. That day, your sister Deenah reminded me of the day I met Rebekah. There was not enough room in her body to contain all her excitement, so it simply spilled out of her mouth in words. "And these are my little sisters," she added. "Tirzah and Emunah." The little girls each cuddled into women that I imagined Deenah would tell me were the mothers that birthed them. Of course, I had noticed Emunah right away. It was impossible not to. Her face looked like that of an angel . . . and like a smaller version of Isaac's before it was marked by sun and dirt and wrinkles.

"Now," Rebekah said, "let me hear from your mothers. I want to hear everything, but the first thing I must hear are the names of the wonderful children who have come to our camp, my grandchildren! I have committed to memory the names of my granddaughters according to their age: Ahuvah, Annah, Deenah, Tirzah, and Emunah. Now, each woman will tell me the names of all the children she birthed, boys and girls, in order. Who is first? It must be you, Leah."

"Yes," Leah said, then she listed the names of the first five children. "Reuben is the firstborn, Shimon and Levi, who are twins, and Ahuvah and Judah, also twins."

Bilhah spoke next. "Annah and Dan and Naftali," she said, "they are not twins. Naftali plays the flute."

"Gad and Asher," Zilpah said.

And then Leah spoke again. "Issachar, Zevulun, who we call Zevvy, and Deenah." I counted eight children for Leah, and Rachel had not yet named one. Finally, it was her turn to say one name. Yours, Joseph. Then it was back to Bilhah who added Tirzah, and Leah who named Emunah as her ninth child.

"Can you remember all of that, Rebekah?" I asked.

"Can you?" she asked me back. "Reuben, Shimon, Levi," she said.

"Ahuvah, Judah, Annah, Dan, Naftali," I said. We smiled. We were impressing our guests and enjoying it.

"Gad, Asher," Rebekah said.

"Issachar, Zevvy, and Deenah, who likes adventure," I said. Deenah enjoyed my addition.

"Joseph, Tirzah, and"—Rebekah gave a wide smile to Emunah and got one in return, and the two said her name together—"Emunah." The women and the girls clapped for us.

"Now," I said, "tell us about yourselves."

Leah went first. "I birthed my first twins, Shimon and Levi, less than one year after Reuben was born. Surely one or all three of them would have died had I not had the help of Zilpah. And when Judah and Ahuvah were born a year later, I thought it was I who would die. So many babies! All of them hungry, crying, and when they could move, crawling and running in different directions. Rachel and Bilhah helped, too, of course. There were just so many babies! Five babies before even the first was weaned!"

I could see how difficult this would be, even with four mothers. I also recognized the pain on Rachel's face as her sister spoke. I had seen it for years on Rebekah's. That pain was loss and death and desire that could not be replaced by her son Joseph, no matter how wonderful he was. She loved all the children, but she wanted to carry and birth and mother more of them.

"After that," Leah went on, "all the other children felt easy. The easiest ones were the ones that did not even need to pass through my body." Leah gave a little laugh. "But even Issachar and Zevvy hardly felt a bother since there were only two of them, and the girls, of course, are so helpful. Each one as sweet as honey." Leah paused and smiled at each daughter. I could feel her love and gratitude going toward them.

"Emunah," she said, "of course, we were worried about her. I cried and cried when she was born. I did not think she would live through the night. But Jacob, he said Yah was watching over her, and he was right. She struggled with suckling, but she managed. I thanked Yah every day that she had no twin, for it took her so long to get her nourishment that she was at my breast nearly all the time. When she could take food, she often choked, until after some time, she made her own way of chewing and swallowing that her tongue would allow. And she did everything later than all of her other brothers and sisters, but still, she did do everything."

Emunah reached out and took her mother's hand. She nearly shone with sweetness and the spirit of Yah. I remembered the first time I saw Isaac and that same spirit flowing through him. He was older and feeble now, but the spirit was no less noticeable. Seeing Emunah as a small child, I could understand Sarah's struggles to help and protect Isaac. She had done well, and Leah was doing well with Emunah. She went on to reveal a different struggle.

"Mother, Auntie," she said, "I have been blessed with the company and help of my sisters, but before this moment, I have not had the wisdom of women who came before me. I am grateful that I no longer have babies attached to my breast or eating dirt or falling down in it. But I am struggling with the older boys. Reuben, Shimon, Levi, and Judah grew like a little pack of wolves. Reuben and Judah are becoming responsible leaders, but Shimon always follows Levi, and Levi leads off the path."

When my eyes first landed on Levi, my feet had nearly jumped with the surprise. He looked so much like a young Esau. He was strong and wide, and though he was not yet old enough to grow a beard, his arms and legs were already covered with thick, red hair, as was his head. He had a scowl that could be seen as menacing, or as deep thought; I was not sure which one.

"Levi no longer listens to my pleadings. When he is the most trouble, Jacob will speak with him, and Levi will not speak disrespectfully to his father. He is not a bad boy. He is strong and will help with anything when asked. But he also uses his strength to scare the other boys, and even hurt them. 'They are not your enemy,' I told him. He agreed but has not stopped."

"He reminds me of Esau," Rebekah said. "And you remind me of me. When my twins were young, I favored Jacob. I did not know how to be a good mother for Esau. Thankfully, Deborah did."

My heart grew ten times to hear these words from her.

"Perhaps she will speak with Levi."

Leah looked at me hopefully, "Would you, Auntie?"

I agreed to do so. Leah relaxed, and the turn to speak went to Rachel.

"I cannot tell a story of motherhood as my sister does," Rachel said. "Mine is a story of loss and love. The love belongs to Jacob and Joseph. I did not love Jacob on the first day that I saw him, as he did me. But every day that I saw him after that, my love grew a little bit, because of all his love for me. He poured it on me like the water that flows through the river we crossed on our way here. It is never-ending and always fresh.

"I did love Joseph on the first day that I saw him. Even before. Too many times I buried my blood with little babies in it. Finally, finally, a living son! He was not just the fulfillment of my dreams but special even if he had been the eleventh son—which he is, for Jacob."

This is how your mother spoke of you, Joseph. She said, "Joseph has a connection with Yah that I do not understand, that he does not understand. He angers his brothers sometimes, but he does not mean to. He is just more special than they are, and he cannot help that." The other women shifted their weight slightly. I could see they were used to this story yet still bothered by it.

Joseph, Little Dreamer, Yah speaks to you and through you in powerful ways. I believe you will one day be recognized for all this just as strongly as I feel you will one day see the great land of Egypt. But I love your brothers and sisters no less than I love you. I know you are favored by your mother, and even your father. I saw the destruction that kind of love brought to my boys. And I see it happening again. I will tell you that as much as Leah and Zilpah and Bilhah love both you and your mother, they will never think their children are any less wonderful or important than you are. And they are not always patient with Rachel's claim of your superiority, even though on that day they were quiet as she told her story.

"Those are my loves," Rachel said. "My losses are, first, the loss of my mother, whom I do not remember. The loss of my brother, Mett, who died in my sixth summer, his seventh. I saw him fall into a cave when he was looking after the sheep. He did not see the hole in the ground. Nor did I, until I saw him fall in. I ran and called after him, but he did not respond. When I arrived at the hole, I laid on the ground with my head inside the darkness and called and called. Nothing. I threw a pebble down. I heard it land in water. I called again, 'Please, Mett, please!' When there was still no answer, I ran to my father, Lavan, but he did not go for my brother. He told me to go back and get the sheep before they fell in, too."

Leah and Rachel both cried. "He was kind," Leah said. "The only brother who was." Rachel nodded in agreement.

"My other losses," Rachel said, finishing her story, "were the babies. So many babies not born. I try to think more about the love than the losses, but sometimes, I am not able."

I silently asked Yah if Rachel would have more living children. Yes. Many? No. I prayed to know more, and then I told Rachel what Yah had told me through my fingers.

"Rachel," I said. "I have prayed, and Yah has told me that you will have another son. Not soon, but one more son who will live."

Rachel's whole body relaxed. She simply sat differently from one moment to the next, and again the tears flowed from her, and from the others as well. It was beautiful to see how much they all wanted that for her.

"Hallelu Yah!" Rebekah said.

"Hallelu Yah!" was shouted back by every one of us.

It seemed Rachel had finished, but we all sat in silence before moving on to the next story. In that silence, I prayed again. "Yah," I whispered under my breath, "will one of these girls learn to pray the way I do?" I had tried to teach Rebekah many times, but she did not understand the answers she received when she prayed with her fingers as I did. Esau and Jacob tried but did not learn either. Now I received a clear yes from Yah. I would teach one of these girls. My heart smiled. I listed their names in the order of their birth. It would be Emunah. *Yes!* Not yet, but she would learn.

Just as I was going to share this with the others, Rachel surprised us. Slowly, softly, she added to her story, "I have one more loss." She paused, unsure if she should continue, but she had our attention, and so she did. "It is Jacob," she said.

Rebekah gasped. Leah, however, nodded her head knowingly.

"What does this mean?" Rebekah asked. She could not hide her concern.

"Jacob was my love," Rachel went on. "But now he is a changed man."

"That is not so," Leah said. "Yes, he is changed in some ways, he is older, wiser, but he is still the same man."

"Yet he insists that we no longer call him by his name," Rachel said.

Now I was just as surprised as Rebekah.

"On our way here, we were separated. He was alone when he met with someone. My firstborn, Joseph, and Leah's firstborn, Reuben, went to look for him when the sun rose. They brought him back, safe and whole, but for his limp and his name. He said he had wrestled with Elohim and won, and that we should now call him by the name Israel instead of Jacob."

"Not call him Jacob?" Rebekah asked. "But that is his name!"

"That *was* his name," Leah said. "He said he wishes to carry on with the name Israel, which represents his triumph, not the name Jacob, which represents him holding his brother's heel as they fought to be first from the womb."

"But . . . ," Rebekah stammered, "they *did* fight to be first from the womb. He did come out holding his brother's heel. He is Jacob, my son."

"Jacob, my husband," Rachel echoed. "I do not know this man, Israel. I do not whisper this name under the stars. I do not smile at the sound of this name."

"Yet, this is the same man who protected and fed us," Leah argued. "Now, he has returned to his homeland, with us. He is not the boy who left; he has taken a new name to represent the man he is now."

"So, you say he *is* different," Rachel argued.

"I am called Leah," Leah continued, "because our mother was weary when I finally exited her womb after nearly three days of trying. I can imagine her weariness." It was clear in Leah's body that she could, indeed, imagine this weariness. "It saddens me to speak ill of my mother. I can feel her exhaustion, even now, when she is long gone."

"She has soft eyes," Annah said to us in Leah's defense. "They see beauty that others sometimes miss and hurt whenever they see pain in people."

Leah smiled gratefully at the girl and stroked her cheek before going on.

"Whenever my name is spoken, I am reminded of my mother's weariness and my own. Why could she not have named me Zipporah, recalling the beauty and possibilities contained in a bird, instead of her weariness? Sometimes, I have dreamt myself to be named Zipporah instead of Leah."

"Now I must call my husband, Jacob, by the name Israel, and my sister, Leah, by the name Zipporah?" Rachel exclaimed.

"I do not intend to change my name, I only say that sometimes I wish a different part of me had been the part that was named. I can understand Israel wanting to shed his baby name, his coming-in-second name, for a more triumphant one."

"Baby name!" Rebekah interjected.

"Rebekah," I said, "do you recall that my name has not always been Deborah?" I told the other women the story of the bee at the market and becoming the messenger between my mother and grandmother, and then later the messenger between my grandmother and her own father, and even now, a messenger between the generations that have passed and the ones just beginning. Then I reminded them that even Sarah and Abraham had once been called Sarai and Abram but got the addition of the *H* sound in their names when Yah made a pact to increase their descendants. Yah, the same One that Rachel just reminded us that Israel called Elohim—to no objection.

There was silence in the tent as each woman held to her idea about names. This was the first time that Rebekah and I saw them disagree about something, but not the last. Four strong women with more than a handful of children found many reasons to disagree. Sometimes their voices were loud, and sometimes they avoided each other in anger. But they always returned to each other in time. Time was what Zilpah was thinking about after Leah and Rachel had shared their stories.

"The moon is high in the sky," she said. "Perhaps I should not tell my story."

"There will be no work for us tomorrow," Rebekah said, moving back to the women before us. "We shall talk the whole night if that is how long it takes. I have waited too long to meet up with you again, and too long to be in this circle of women . . .

mothers, daughters, sisters, friends. Do not make me wait longer."

Zilpah smiled. "I remember little of my life before I was by Leah's side. But I know that it was not a happy one. I was not treated well. My scars remember the stories, but I do not. I think this is a blessing. I am told that I traveled far before I reached Lavan and was taken on as a helper for one of the cooks. My hands were small and unsteady. I was clumsy and often spilled her hard work. I tried not to soil the rugs when I tripped, at least that, and so the hot stews I carried often fell on me. The cook could not tolerate me one more day. I know because I remember hearing her say as much to Lavan. I am glad that she did because Leah heard her, too, and rushed to her father. 'Father,' she said, 'the cook is frustrated by the girl, but do not sell her. I am frustrated by my nursemaid. Let us exchange them.' I believe Leah saved me that day," Zilpah said.

"Why?" I asked. I did not know I was going to speak in the middle of her story.

"Had she not said anything," Zilpah said, "I would have been sold and made just as much of a mess of my next job, I am sure. And then the next, and the next, if I still lived."

"This is not the meaning of my question," I said. "I shall ask again. Why did she say something?"

"She pitied me, I suppose," Zilpah answered. "She could see that I would be sold again and again, or worse, and she took pity on me and saved me."

"Zilpah!" Leah said. "That is not what happened. I spoke to my father because I could see you were a mess, covered in stew."

I looked at Rebekah and happily found her smiling eyes looking at me. We continued to listen to Leah. "A girl who would have the hot stew fall on herself instead of the rugs is a girl who thinks fast and acts fast and is even willing to make a mess of herself or be hurt if that is what it takes. We were young at the time; I am certain I did not know the words I know now. I would not have said then that you are a wise problem solver, but I have told you that many times. It is true now, and it was true then."

Zilpah smiled. "I am always thinking," she said. "I enjoy solving problems. I did not know how to solve my spilling problem. But it has gone away. And I have solved other problems. Like when we had all the babies, I devised a way to sew clothes that could help us each carry two babies at once. And sewed sheep bladders and filled them with goat milk so Leah would not have to feed all the babies alone."

"That is wonderful!" Rebekah said when Zilpah had finished. "We have heard Leah's story of a mother of many, formerly exhausted, but no longer. We have heard Rachel's story of love and losses. And now we have heard the story of a problem solver. What is your story, Bilhah?"

"My story?" Bilhah asked. She was quiet for a moment. "I am just happy to be here," she said.

"This is true," Rachel said. "Bilhah does not say much, but she does always seem happy to be here."

Bilhah nodded her head in agreement. The night, in fact, had been a very long one. And wonderful! The girls had fallen asleep on the rugs much earlier, and now their mothers' bodies were drifting down toward them. We all decided to lie down, and when the sun rose, not one of us did. We were women of leisure all day, enjoying the shade in the tent, singing and telling stories as we braided each other's hair.

They especially loved hearing about their husband and father when he was a young boy, and of my life in Egypt when I was a young girl. They all shared of other things that had happened in Haran; even the little girls and Bilhah said a few things. It was wonderful to be leisurely together! We did not go out until the sun started setting and the sky started cooling. It was then that I sought out Levi.

He was easy to spot among the boys. His red hair set him apart. But it was not only that. He was a leader among his brothers, even if not always leading them in good directions.

"Levi," I said, "come and walk with me in the hills."

He was surprised but obliged. We walked away from the camp in silence. His gaze was fixed ahead of us, his stride measured, slightly faster than mine. Even when I moved faster, he did, too. It was clear that he did not wish to walk beside me. We stopped in the shade of an almond tree. The rains had stopped, but the blooms had not. I kept him there quietly wondering for a while before I spoke.

"Your mother tells me you are a leader."

He grunted.

"You may call me Auntie," I said.

"Yes, Auntie."

"What do you like to lead your brothers to do?"

"Anything," he said. I waited for him to say more, but he did not.

"You look like your uncle, Esau," I said.

Levi grunted again.

"You may call me Auntie," I reminded him.

"Yes, Auntie."

"Why do you think that Yah gave you a red face and red hair?" I asked.

"To mock me," he said. This surprised me.

"To mock you?"

"Yes," he said. "My father has scorned me since I was a young boy. Perhaps since I was a baby and I just do not remember. I never knew why until we came here. On the way we met his brother, the red one, and I saw that we were alike. My father fears his brother, so he has feared me. He is right in doing so. I am strong! He was cowardly when he met Esau. We are many. We could have defeated him."

"Did Esau attack?" I asked, nervous about what the answer would be.

"No," Levi said. "But he can do so any time. My father is a coward."

"So, you would rather attack him first?" I asked.

The boy nodded.

"Tell me, Levi, what are you good at? What do you like to do?"

"Those are the same things. I am good at preparing meat for feasts and festivals. I am good at having my brothers do my bidding."

"These are the things that serve you," I said. "Which of these serve your father? Which serve Yah?"

Levi was quiet for a long while. Then he shrugged his shoulders.

"You may call me Auntie," I said.

"I do not know, Auntie."

"I see that you are bothered," I said. "Breathe with me for a moment. Let us be with Yah. I trust you know how to do this." In fact, I was not certain. Had Jacob taught his sons? I relaxed when I heard Levi take a long inhale. *Yhhhh*. I breathed with him. *Whhhh*. His body did not relax; he did not give himself to Yah. We continued several more times, until I saw the shift in him, and then several more before I finally spoke again.

"What do you like about slaughtering the animals for the feasts?"

This time, Levi spoke easily. His words were quick and excited, his chest high and forward with pride. "My brothers turn their back on this duty, but I am not afraid. Yes, the blood and the sounds are unpleasant, but I am stronger than those things. And if it were not for me and my willingness to do this messy work, the festivals would not be the same. Our bellies would not be so full of food, our ears not so full of song, our eyes first wide with delight, and then soft with peaceful sleep."

"My brothers," he said, his voice deepening and his fists clenching, "they are weak. They will not do the work unless I tell them. And so, I can tell them to do anything. And they will do anything I tell them, because they know I am strong and brave and determined and can make them do it if they don't do so fast enough to my liking."

Joseph, write that you just interrupted me to complain about Levi not telling you to do tasks like he does with your brothers and that he has explained himself by calling you one of the girls.

We shall talk about this later. I remind you that this is my story. I am happy to answer your questions, but do not interrupt me again to ask them.

"Levi, you are a strong young man, a leader," I told him. "One day, you will inherit this land from your father. You will not be a young man, but a man. You will not need to serve your father then. But if you are going to show that you are truly wise, you must choose to do the things that serve Yah."

Levi grunted, but without reminder he then said, "Yes, Auntie," and we walked back to the camp together. I had done what I could. I often did not know what would come of my talks with Esau, but with time and patience, I found him to be kind and generous when he was not frustrated. I hoped the same would be true with Levi.

I felt I had more success when teaching Joseph. He was surprised to hear me call him a dreamer. He was surprised when we had the feast and I knew he had dreamt and asked him to share his dream with us, right then, around the fire. He shared that he dreamt of ten fish surrounding him on land. And that the meaning was that his brothers would follow him to the river. He was too young to understand what this meant, but I did. He would have been surprised a hundredfold if he knew what else I understood about him, and even more so if he understood what Yah had planned for him.

I could not claim to know the details of Yah's plans, only the importance of remaining ignorant of such matters. There are things that are so big, only Yah can hold them. When we dream, when we have visions and hearing and knowing, these are merely tastes, and even those are often too big for our little selves. But

Joseph was open to learning, and I wished to teach him. When we had feasted and eaten of the lambs that Levi had prepared, listened to Naftali's flute playing, and danced until Israel could no longer stay on his feet, he slept with his sons in his father's tent, and the women and girls returned with us to ours.

Quietly before we drifted off to sleep, Rebekah told me she could not tolerate the thought of them leaving quickly, for tomorrow would be the third day, and surely Jacob would take his family back to Sukkot where he had left his camp. "I shall ask Jacob to leave the women and girls here with us for longer," she said, "for we must all dance under the moon together. We must."

"Ask him to leave Joseph with us," I added. "The spirit of Yah is strong in the boy, and he does not know how to handle it. He needs more training."

Rebekah agreed as she drifted off to sleep, and in the morning, when she shared her wishes with the other women, they also immediately agreed. I wondered what might need to be done to have Israel take all the sons but not Joseph. I quickly learned this would not be a struggle. It took only Rachel's asking, and it was clear that singling Joseph out from the rest of the boys was not unusual.

It was not so hard to part from Israel this time, as we knew he would be back to retrieve the ones staying after the full moon. Until then, we women would have days and nights together to learn about each other and be with each other. Joseph spent the nights in Isaac's tent. This was also a good thing.

Rebekah went to Isaac's tent very infrequently. There were only a few nights a year that she slept there now. He required the help of Elioded not only in the fields but also for rising and walking. And at night, Isaac had begun to have nightmares. He would cry out, looking for the sheep for the sacrifice. His screams never woke or disturbed him, but though they were only once in a while, they disturbed and scared Rebekah when she was there. Joseph would have a place to sleep, Isaac would have company, and we would have our women time.

On the first day, I separated myself from the other women in order to walk with Joseph. As with Levi, I took him away from the camp, to the quiet and beauty around us. His legs were much shorter than mine, but he kept step with me. We stopped and viewed the emptiness ahead of us while the camp was behind us. For as far as our eyes could see, there was beauty.

"What do you see?" I asked him.

"I see land," he said.

"Whose land is it?" I asked him.

"My father says that one day, this land will be ours. My father says that Elohim has promised this land to him and his descendants. I am one of his descendants, so it will be mine."

"If it will one day be yours," I said, "whose is it now?"

"I suppose it belongs to my father now, or perhaps to my grandfather until his death," Joseph said.

The boy had only had seven summers. He had holes in his mouth where his milk teeth had left and his adult teeth had not yet grown. Even a dreamer such as he could not answer the question, and so I helped. "Joseph," I said, "you said Yah promised you this land, so we know that it belongs to Yah, for Yah promised to give it to you."

He nodded.

"You may call me Auntie," I said.

"Yes, Auntie," Joseph said.

"Is Yah not wonderful? To give you this beautiful land? To you and your descendants after you?"

"Yah is wonderful!" Joseph said.

"Your father talks to Yah every day, Joseph. And listens. Do you do that?"

"No, Auntie," he said. "I am not a man like my father. Reuben will be the first to be a man. He will be a good one. Judah, too. And I shall, also," he added. "Shimon and Levi scare me, but Reuben and Judah watch over me. When I am a man, I shall watch over myself, and I shall speak to Yah, like my father."

"You need not wait until you are a man," I said, "Nor should you. Joseph, Yah has blessed you with more than land. Yah has blessed you with dreams. But you are young. You cannot understand such things. If you wish to understand them when you are older, it will be possible only if you practice. You cannot wait until you are older and then expect to suddenly have the ability without practice."

"Yes, Auntie," he said.

"Your grandfather Abraham, he was the father of your grandfather Isaac. Abraham talked with Yah each morning. Your grandfather Isaac, the husband of your grandmother Rebekah, also talks with Yah each day, when the sun is beginning to set but is not yet down. And your father, Jacob, he talks with Yah each night. Now you will learn, too."

Joseph looked up at me with eagerness. He stroked his chin and stood a little taller.

"Say the words that I shall teach you now," I said. "Blessed are you, Yah, god of my father Jacob, god of my father Isaac, god of my father Abraham. *Yhhhh. Whhhh.*"

Joseph repeated after me exactly.

"Now," I said, "you will stay here, and talk with Yah, your god. And listen."

"But, Auntie," he said.

"I shall send someone to fetch you when it is time for your return. You will be back to eat and sleep. Talk. Listen."

I left him there. I felt a tinge of guilt, knowing that he was little and confused, but I also knew that he would figure it out, not that day, but with practice. We did this every day until our last. On that day, he was permitted to come back early and be with us for the celebration under the full moon. Rachel had become so filled with excitement in the anticipation—we all had—that she insisted that he be included.

Oh! To be celebrating with generations of women under the moon like in Egypt! My skin was covered in wrinkles from my eyelids to my toes, yet I felt like a girl again, surrounded by love. It was different people giving and receiving that love, but it was the same love. I went to the back of the tent where we had the piles of rugs and jugs and baskets, and where I had been storing a jug of blue lotus wine since buying it at the market with Orry long ago. Tonight, we would know Yah. I would be in Hallel's shoes, and these beautiful girls in mine, the four mothers taking the place of my mother and her sisters. In truth, I did not need to drink the blue lotus to know Yah. I was living the miracle that was my life, given to me by

Yah. That does not mean we did not have a ceremony. We did. We had a wonderful ceremony!

We made a small fire outside and gathered under the darkening sky. The moon was beautiful, rising gently and bringing us light and love. Rebekah told the story of Addah, and of her own request that we begin these celebrations. We had enough drums that each of us could take our pick of which one to use that night. I resolved in that moment that I would let each woman and girl—and Joseph—keep the one they chose.

Under the moon, we sang the song that Rebekah and I had sung alone together so many, many times. When we started, she was not yet a woman. We had not borne babies or had them at our breasts. Our skin was taut, and all our teeth still lived inside our mouths. We walked in comfort, sometimes ran with joy. And now, here we were, looking at the next women. Singing with the next women. And we would know YhWh with them, too.

My grandmother had given a silver cup to everyone, but I could not do that. Instead, I took a bowl and poured the liquid in. I let it sit in the bowl, under the moon, while we danced and sang. Sometimes we held hands, sometimes we danced separately. Sometimes one woman went in the circle, and we all poured our love and admiration on her as we danced. Often our arms were wide open to receiving the beauty of the night and each other. And before we were too tired, I invited everyone to sit. Then I took the bowl and approached each person in turn, beginning with Rebekah, of course.

"Do you know of Yah?" I asked her.

"Yes," she said.

"Tonight you will know YhWh," I said, and she drank.

"Do you know of Yah?" I asked Leah.

"Yes," she said.

"Tonight you will know YhWh," I said, and she drank.

I repeated this with each woman and then each child. When everyone had their turn to drink, I sat and looked at these women and girls around me, in the circle with me. Oh, the glory! "Each breath, the whole breath, will praise Yah!" I said.

I instructed them to lie down, and they did. And we breathed. *Yhhhh. Whhhh. Yhhhh. Whhhh.* I began to drum while they continued to breathe. *Yhhhh.* All the way in. Then *Whhhh*, quickly out, returning again to *Yhhhh.* I played the drum; they breathed. I could see them moving into their new understanding. My hands drummed on their own and, eventually, got tired on their own. Only then did I stop, drink, and lie down.

Oh, how comforting and comfortable to be embraced by the land. The land, which now welcomed Israel back, welcomed his sons to inherit it, his wives to grace it, and his daughters to bless it. With my back on the ground, I felt the vibrations of countless footsteps as they crossed the land and settled here. The children of these women, as numerous as the stars, but right here on the land. These children, not yet born, yet stepping on the land, these children and their footsteps were the crown on my head. The weight of this crown was immeasurable, yet not unbearable, actually comfortable. I fell asleep with my head gently stuck to the ground by the weight of the crown of the generations to come.

When I awoke, I knew Israel would return and take the women and children back with him. After he witnessed us have a teary goodbye with each one of them, it was no effort to show Israel how meaningful our time together had been.

"Jacob," Rebekah said, "please, bring your wives and daughters back at this time next year, that we may spend another month together."

"And Joseph," Rachel added. "For he must continue his studies."

So, for ten years the women and Joseph returned for one full month out of every year. Rebekah and I spent most of the other months awaiting their return. We still wove, she still painted, I still took long walks, but as the years passed, we spent more time lying under the trees. We ate simpler meals and sat together in silence more often. Many full moons came in which we danced to only one song, and then went to sleep.

Until the women came back.

What a delight it was to see the girls grow bigger each year! When they came one month with the news that Ahuvah would marry soon, we all anointed her. And then, realizing we would likely not be able to celebrate Annah, Deenah, Tirzah, and Emunah in the same way when their time came, Rebekah decided to do it then.

On one of Esau's many visits, we suggested he send his wives and daughters, but they still felt strongly about their gods, he said, and would not come. We did not wish to create trouble between him and his wives. We enjoyed his visits, and the visits from his sons, but they were brief and respectful, mostly there to honor their father and grandfather with their fresh hunt, though they always brought us some, too, and kissed our hands upon arrival and departure.

The one time that Israel's son Joseph and Esau's son Reuel were both here at once, Rebekah and I delighted to see our children's children together. The boys quite enjoyed each other, as far as we could tell. They shared meals and ran around together. I saw Joseph teaching Reuel how to write his name. Joseph had been studying with Katib for many years and took to reading and writing as easily and enthusiastically as his father had. And on every visit, he spent several days with me, writing these scrolls in his practiced hand.

Rebekah requested that Elioded take her to the market one day. There she bought a beautiful jar for me to keep the scrolls in. At the end of each visit, Rebekah and I admired Joseph's fine writing, and then she had me read it to her.

"I know you can read, Deborah," she said the first time she asked. "I saw you learning with Jacob. I see you checking what Joseph writes. I do not know why you have him scribe it instead of doing it yourself."

"It is not a secret that I can read," I said, though not many people realized. Katib knew. For years he had been sending me the same note, as he promised his father he would, at the beginning of each month. It was as reliable as the moonless nights that came before the morning of the deliveries. Although I knew the words without reading them, I enjoyed the feel of the papyrus he used, and I smiled every month to see my name so close to Orry's.

Deborah, beloved wife of my honored father, Orry.
Please send word if you need or want anything.
I shall do everything in my ability to get it or do it for you.

Blessings to you and all you love.
Katib

In all the years that he had been sending the note, I did not once write one to him. And only two times did I ask for things. Once was less than a year after Orry died. I requested that if Katib held any leather that Orry had carved, that he could part with, that he allow me to have it. Of course, I had many pieces. But I thought it would be a thrill and a comfort to hold something of his which I had never held, never seen. Katib obliged and sent me a cushion with a soft, worn leather covering, and I did enjoy it very much.

The second time was when we learned that Jacob would be gone another seven years. I considered asking Katib to take us to Haran, as Orry had, but felt it would be too much. Instead, I asked him to take us to the market. It was not the same, of course, but it was a distraction, nonetheless. I was surprised to see a drum there that I had made with my own hands. The man selling it was going to give me a fair price, he said, and did not understand why I laughed.

Katib still sent the notes, even though I got to see him when Joseph visited. It was brief, but he reported to me about Joseph's studies. Of course, he reported to Israel, too, but I think he enjoyed the excuse to see me. He always made sure one of his grandchildren was nearby to greet me with beer and fruit. And every time, I told him how proud his father would be of him. I did not say it for him to feel good, but because I knew it to be the truth.

"Rebekah," I said, "although I can read and write, I have Joseph scribe for me so that he has the writing practice, and so he might hear all the stories. I am an old woman. As are you, by the way, and some day, I shall not be here to tell these stories. Someday Ahuvah and Annah, Deenah, Tirzah, and Emunah will have stories of their own to tell, and they might not remember all of ours to tell their daughters. Perhaps some stories that we did not remember to tell them even lie in these scrolls. Now they will have it written, and they, too, will know of Rebekah and Deborah."

"Deborah and Rebekah," she said, her eyes locked on mine.

"Deborah and Rebekah," I said.

THE TWENTY-SECOND PARCHMENT

When Joseph arrived alone less than a year after our last gathering, our first reaction was worry. But when we heard that the reason for his visit was to announce that Rachel would soon give birth, we were overjoyed. Rebekah and I knew the pain of longing for a child. Even though she had Joseph, and for many years had had peace with his being the only live birth, she still longed. Joseph reported that he had come not only to deliver the news of the nearly completed pregnancy, but also to deliver his mother's request that Rebekah and I come to her.

"My mother said, say these words: 'Auntie, the baby you told me so long ago would come is coming. I wish for you and Mother to be by my side.'"

Rebekah would have leapt for joy if her old knees had let her. She was excited to have another opportunity for a journey. She began recounting some of her favorite moments of past travels—flowers she remembered, views that took her breath away, tasting new herbs, meeting other women along the way, and the river. Of course, the river.

"Rebekah," I said, "we are not young girls, or even young women. My bones are old and tired. They hold me up well in this familiar territory. My skin enjoys the sunshine here, my nose the flowers that grow here."

"But, Deborah," she said, her excitement undampened by complaints, "our daughters are there!" She clapped her hands together once and then raised them to the sky. "Hallelu Yah!" she shouted. And with that, she easily convinced me. In truth, our lives had been pleasant, though uneventful for some time. We looked forward to the women coming to us each year, but when they were gone, we worked hard to persuade each other to dance under the moon. Each month we danced less and less and lay under its brightness more and more. It was relaxing, familiar, lovely—and routine. It would be fun to do something new. It would be good to be with our tribe.

Joseph had brought a large gift for Isaac. Israel was a grown man, father of eleven sons himself, and still trying to win his own father over with gifts. My sadness was deep that he did not know that Isaac loved and admired him. The gift did not sway Isaac's feelings one way or another. But he did enjoy it. It was a large basket, and inside it was another basket. Inside that one, another, and another, and another. He enjoyed opening the baskets, laughing as lifting a lid revealed yet another, and another basket. There were twelve in total, and Isaac commented on how well they were woven. In the smallest basket there was a well-oiled rock, and a scroll. Isaac held the rock in his hands, rubbing his fingers over the smoothness. His eyes could no longer read, but Joseph's were expert, and he read loudly for his grandfather.

Honored Father. Please accept this rock. It comes from an altar I built for Yah, your god and mine, the god of our father, Abraham, and of my sons, as well. I built this altar in Beit El with my own hands, anointed it with oil I pressed from olives, and it is on the land where I have settled. I send you this rock, now, as a message to say that all that is mine is yours. I give you this small piece so that you may have it with you, but should you wish to return it to the altar, it, the oil, and the surrounding land will become yours.

"You read well," Isaac said to Joseph. Joseph took his grandfather's hand and kissed it. "Tell your father," Isaac continued, "that I accept his gift with gratitude. Tell him he has done well."

"But you will come, Grandfather. To tell him yourself."

"This is where I shall stay," Isaac said. "It is true, Eliođed does most of the work, but my presence here is still important. And my son Esau comes to visit me here, or sends one of his sons. Joseph, your father has eleven sons and sends none to visit me. And though I am grateful that you share my tent when you come, I know you are here with the women. Deborah has taught you well, I am certain. But I shall not go live on another man's land, even though he makes a ceremony of giving it to me. I shall stay here."

Joseph kissed Isaac's hand again. He took a mat from the tent and brought it outdoors, too disappointed, or perhaps rejected, to sleep in his grandfather's tent. He made himself a place to sleep beside the camels. Before he slept, I asked him to do one more thing.

"Joseph, go to Katib, please. Tell him there is something I need. Ask him to come right away."

"Yes, Auntie."

It was not long before the two returned, a concerned look on Katib's face. I realized then that I might have saved him some worry by sending a longer message. It was too late for him, but not too late for Esau. I paused and prayed to know whether Esau was in his camp and received the answer that he was.

"Katib, thank you for coming," I said. "Soon I shall be departing for Shechem with Joseph. Please go with him now, leave immediately, and ask Esau to come here. I do not wish to worry him the way I worried you. Please, tell him that all is well, but that I shall be leaving shortly and I wish to see him."

Katib thanked me for giving him the opportunity to help me, and he and Joseph did leave at once. I knew the three of them would return the next day. When I saw Esau's face, it was not covered in worry, but did show sorrow. He came to kiss my hand.

"Auntie," he said softly, "Katib tells me you are going to Israel."

"I am going to Rachel," I said. "Israel will be there. I shall be glad to see him, as I am glad to see you, Esau. You have brought me joy, challenge, honor, and love since the moment you came into my arms. I thank Yah for placing you there."

"Auntie," he said, pausing to choke back tears, "I shall remember all that you have taught me, in words and in deeds. You have nourished me in more than milk. It began there but will never end, even though we are parting."

I took this big man into my little arms. He took me in his. It was the only time that he held on longer than I did.

The camels were packed with sufficient provisions for the three of us to make the short journey to Rachel, and we would want for nothing when we arrived. My bones, as old as they were, did not think they would ever return to this place. While Rebekah prepared her possessions for the journey—gifts for everyone, comforts, and necessities—I said I would take only my small satchel, the one that used to belong to my mother, the one I had brought from Egypt. And these scrolls.

I put the pillow made from my mother's dress in the satchel, along with the smooth rock from Isaac, and the wooden bee that had long since lost its string, but never its beauty. The tiny drum I had made so long ago in Egypt fit, too. The only other possessions I took were the beautiful bracelets from Orry, which I still wore on my wrist. Thus, I was prepared to go. And so I spent my time slowly walking the hills and sitting on the rocks, quietly saying goodbye to them and receiving their blessings for the last time.

Rebekah went to inform Isaac that we would be gone for a few months, three, perhaps four. Whether Rebekah will return or not, I do not know. But I shall not. The thought of being apart from her saddens me deeply. My whole body wants to lie down from the weight of it. But I cannot change it.

I went to bid Isaac farewell, for we, too, would be apart. I took a lamp and walked to his tent. It was difficult to see in the light of the small flame, but the surroundings were familiar. I was grateful that Joseph slept outside so that we might have a private moment for parting.

"Isaac," I called from the edge of the rugs.

"Deborah," he acknowledged me. "You are welcome." Isaac's voice was soft, even though mine was loud so that it could be heard by his struggling ears. He was lying on his sleeping cushion but still awake. He turned his head to me and reached out his hand. I took it in mine, held it there for a moment. The roughness it held when he had worked with the sheep had already turned to the softness of an old man's skin. Yet I knew in the sunlight I would have been able to see dirt under his nails as old as his children. Older. This land that Yah had promised to him would always be a part of him. I kissed his hand.

"I wish to thank you, Isaac," I said. "You have been kind to me. For all these years, you have been kind. I have been safe, protected, provided for, included, loved. Thank you."

After allowing me time with my feelings, Isaac spoke. "I wish for you to stay here tonight."

Did he want me to be his wife again? I laughed. "I am an old woman, Isaac."

"And I am an old man, Deborah. You think me feeble. My own sons thought me a fool many years ago already. But I am neither. I have done my work for Yah. I have done my work for my flock, my servants, and my land. I have done my work for my sons and my wives—my wife and my sister." Isaac paused. It was long enough for me to once again fill with gratitude that he had allowed me to become Orry's wife.

"You are leaving," he continued. "Rebekah is leaving. I shall remain here alone and oversee the camp. When the hunt is good, I shall enjoy my son and my grandson and their tasty morsels until Yah says it is time to gather my bones in the Cave of Makhpelah with my father and mother. Before that happens, I wish to share my bed with another once more. I wish for you to stay the night. Sister, I ask you to."

I blew out the oil lamp and lay beside him, putting my head on his shoulder, my hand in his. How full of generosity, of love, of surprises my life at Isaac's camp—our camp—had been. I thought of my grandmother and the stories she had told me. They never included her brother Isaac. She had not known about him, so neither had I. Later he became my husband, even if I did not know we were married. I did not know of this husband. I did not know of this brother. Only now, as I have grown old, do I feel an understanding of all Isaac and I have been to and for one another. I cannot help but wonder what more I do not know about myself. It is a question I will never be able to answer, but I drifted off to sleep while trying to do so. When the sun announced it would soon rise, I slipped out of Isaac's tent with a silent goodbye.

Joseph was feeding the camels and attaching Rebekah's sacks to one of them with a cord. I went into our tent for the last time. Rebekah was still lying on our mat, though she was beginning to stir, and I could see that while part of her slept, another part was waking. I lay beside her, and she brought her body close. In the dim light, I whispered goodbye to the cushions, the jars of oils, the baskets of wool, the rugs, the roof, the familiar scent, the way the breeze blew through.

"We shall not be gone long," Rebekah said.

I heard the wistfulness in her voice. I met it in silence.

"Should we stay here, Deborah?" she asked.

"No," I said. "We shall go." I rose and gathered these scrolls from the earthen jar where they lived between Joseph's visits. The bee that Rebekah had painted on the jar, using dye from the forsythias that exploded with yellow after a rainy season so long ago, and the last of the kohl she had bought when we left for Gerar, was so faded that it was recognizable only to those who knew it was there. Rebekah helped me gently unroll the scrolls so I could see their distance. Soon, they would receive my final words, then take a journey with me to be with the younger women. There, they will carry on without me. Beyond me. But first, it was wonderful to see that from end to end they are even longer than our tent.

This is my life in parchment and ink. The life of Deborah, daughter of Daganyah, daughter of Hallel, daughter of Sarah, beloved friend of Rebekah, wife of Orry and of Isaac, mother of Zacharyah, Auntie of Esau and Jacob and of multitudes. I am the girl who listened to her mother's stories, and carried messages and sweetness to places beyond my imagination. I carry Yah within me, and am carried within Yah. I am a sister, mother, daughter, and friend. I have lived a life worth living. I have sung my song, and told my story. Hallelu Yah!

THE SEVENTH SCROLL

THE TWENTY-THIRD PARCHMENT

My Auntie is dead. She died in the morning light, and we buried her among the trees and cried for the remainder of the day. The sun set long ago, yet I cannot stop crying. And though my tears are falling on the parchment and I must be extra careful with the ink, I shall finish these scrolls of her life as I know she wants me to. I have lit all the oil lamps I could gather so that it is as light in this area of the tent as it was once in Hallel's home. I shall write all night, if necessary. Then I shall give this parchment to My Grandmother. She will know what to do with it.

I am Joseph.
Son of Jacob.
Son of Isaac.
Son of Abraham.

I am the scribe of the Scrolls of Deborah, and I shall finish My Auntie's story.

I brought Grandmother and Auntie here only a number of days ago. My Mother wished for them both to be here when she delivers My Brother, but it will not be so. The journey was difficult for My Grandmother in her old age, and even more so for My Auntie, who had always claimed to be even older. They agreed to ride on camels, not letting their pride insist that they travel on foot. I gave them water to cool their necks and guided the camels as smoothly as possible. But a camel's feet go where they want, and the women were often jostled.

When we arrived in the last light, they were overjoyed to be reunited with the other women. Leah had begun walking in our direction, so eager was she to see them again. Of course, My Mother could not make that trek, for she is too large with child. Deenah, Tirzah, and Emunah, the only sisters who are not married and still at the camp, stayed to prepare food and accommodations for the honored guests. Never had they come to our camp, and everyone wanted it to be lovely when they arrived.

And lovely it was. My Auntie said so as soon as she alighted from the camel. She had asked for my hand in descending, so she would not fall. She said as much to Grandmother. "Let us take care, Rebekah," she said, "so as not to fall from the camels." And the two of them laughed together. Leah escorted them to the tent where they would stay with her and My Mother and the other women. They had waited all this time to be together. From this moment forward, they would not be apart.

I, however, was sent on my way. I was not truly saddened. In two nights' time, the moon would be full, and I would dance under it as we always did when we were together. At least, I hoped that would be so. We had always been in My Grandfather's camp for these celebrations, never our own. Would I still be included here? What would My Brothers think?

I was, indeed, included. And My Brothers did not care about what the women were doing. They might not have even noticed if it had not been for Leah inviting their wives to join at My Auntie's insistence. "We shall have the grandest of dances tonight," she said, "and I wish to be surrounded by all the wonder and joy." And so it was, just as she wished. The women brought drums and sang and danced under the moon. My Mother could move her body only from side to side, but she experienced no smaller measure of gladness. And though My Brothers' wives were surprised by my presence, they did not say anything. They danced and played their drums and quickly learned the song that Auntie had created so long ago.

Sister, Mother, Daughter, and Friend
You shine with love from beginning to end
We give you our hopes, our dreams, and our pain
You keep them safe, until we meet again.

Over and over we sang the moon song. At some time in the night, Grandmother and Auntie asked me to bring them cushions and their red and gold pillows. It was then that I noticed they had not been dancing with us, but watching, smiling. I put them in the center of the circle, and they sat while the other women and I continued to dance and sing around them, under the light of the full moon. We would have continued on like this all night long had Auntie not clapped her hands to get everyone to stop so she could speak.

"Sit," she said. We all did. "Let us thank Rebekah," she said. There was a long pause before she continued. I noticed then that she was waiting to get enough breath to speak again. It seemed as if she had been dancing for too long, though she had not been dancing at all. "It was Rebekah's desire, and her courage to speak it, that created these moon circles."

"Thank you, Rebekah," Leah started. "Oh, how we have loved the moon circles!"

"Thank you, Rebekah," My Mother echoed. "To sing and dance with you under the moon has been one of the greatest joys of my life. Second only to being the mother of Joseph, and soon, another child."

At once Bilhah and Zilpah, Deenah, Tirzah, and Emunah and I thanked My Grandmother. And then she spoke.

"Yes," she said. "I was brave. I have always been braver since I met you, my dear Deborah." Then she turned to My Brothers' wives. She thanked them for celebrating this full moon with her and sent them back to their tents. When they left the circle, she continued. "Deborah, I have been braver since you came into my life. I have been more of everything because you are here with me." My Grandmother choked back tears but then put a smile on her face. "Now," she said, "Let us all tell Deborah a way in which she has made our lives better. Leah . . ."

Leah walked to the cushions and took My Auntie's hand in hers. "Beloved Auntie," she said. "If you never said a word to me, I would still have learned from you how to love Yah, for the spirit of Yah beams from you and through you always." Leah kissed her hand and stepped aside, and My Mother waddled over. I helped her lower to sit on the cushion. Then she let go of my hand and took My Auntie's hand.

"Auntie," she said, "beautiful Deborah. You are radiant. I have always been called the beauty, but I did not truly know what beauty was until I met you. If I have even half your beauty, I am very blessed." My Mother kissed her hand and held it a while. Then I helped her rise from the cushion so that Zilpah could have a turn.

"Honored Auntie," she said. "You have taught me to dance. Until we met, I was dedicated to Leah and the children, but never to myself. You taught me to smile, to step lightly, and to enjoy. I did not have these things before I met you. Thank you." Zilpah kissed My Auntie's hand, and they smiled at each other. Zilpah rose, and Bilhah sat on the cushion in her place.

"Dearest Auntie," she said, "I mourned my station in life until I met you. You showed me that a woman can be of a lower class without being a lesser person. I have sought and found my own happiness because of you. I stand straight and proud because of you." Indeed, My Auntie always walked and sat straight and proud, even as tired as she was in that moment under the moon receiving her praises, she sat straight and proud.

As Ahuvah and Annah were already living elsewhere with their husbands, Deenah was the next oldest. It would soon be my turn, but I could not think of words, I could only watch Deenah. As children, we had laughed and played and been each other's closest confidants. Our love grew even stronger as I became a man and she a woman. But for many months, ever since My Brothers brought her back from her brief marriage to the prince, she had stayed in her mother's tent and I had not seen her until this day. Now, she approached My Auntie crying, and if she said anything, it was too soft for me to hear.

"Deenah," Auntie said to her, "You think I do not know, but I do. You carry a song inside you, as beautiful as that of a bluebird. It is one that will uplift the tribe of Israel to higher abundance. Do not fret." Deenah nodded her head and kissed Auntie's hand, which she then placed on her own stomach for a long while before passing it to me.

"Auntie," I said, "you have taught me how to be a scribe like My Father. And you have taught me to learn from my dreams. You taught me how to speak to My God, and how to listen. Thank you for being my teacher." I wish I had said more. I kissed Auntie's hand, and she ran it over my chin, feeling the beard that had finally begun to grow there and giving me a smile.

"Auntie." Tirzah came and kissed her hand. "One day soon I shall marry and go to a new life. You went from one life in Egypt to another life in Haran and another life here. All the while, you survived and thrived. I shall be like you in that way. I shall not be afraid of what new lives will come next."

Finally, Emunah approached. She took Auntie's hand in hers. After a long silence during which they looked into each other's eyes, Emunah simply said, "Thank you for being you," and kissed Auntie's hand before returning to her place in the outer circle.

"You are loved," My Grandmother said. "You are loved. Hallelu Yah."

I saw My Auntie's mouth form the words *Hallelu Yah*.

"And you are tired," Grandmother said. She turned to the rest of us. "My dear Deborah and I shall sleep on these cushions, under the light of the moon. You are free to do as you wish." My Grandmother cradled Auntie's head in her arm as they lay on the cushions, and the other women gathered around them, lying on the dirt, surrounding them like a litter of kittens all curled up on each other. I walked back to my tent and slept on my soft pallet.

Oh, how I wish I had stayed! If only I had known it would be her final night. But it cannot be changed now. I am grateful that I was sent for in the morning. When I arrived by the cushions I had set out the night before, I understood that she was dying. She was surrounded by her tribe of women. I knew she was happy. Even in all the tears that flowed, I could feel the peace in her body.

My Father, who had also been summoned, approached her. None of the women moved aside from where they were, but there was room enough for him to kiss her hand and then lay his forehead upon it. I saw his mouth form the word *Auntie*, though his throat could not make the sound come out. He stayed that way for a long time, until Grandmother gently told him it was time to go.

I followed My Father's example and knelt by her side, taking her hand in mine. When had her hand become so little? I kissed it gently, then put my forehead down on it, feeling her skin against mine as I bowed at her side. Before Grandmother could send me away, I raised my head to look into her eyes. "I shall finish your scrolls," I said. "I shall finish your scrolls." She did not utter a word, but moved her fingers slightly, and I knew that she heard me. I kissed her hand again, before stepping aside. My Father had gone, probably to talk to Elohim, but I stayed only steps away.

The women began humming the full-moon song. On and on they hummed. I saw Auntie looking at each one of them, until her eyes landed on My Grandmother.

"Deborah," Grandmother said, her voice quiet but strong, her tears flowing, but not stopping her words. "Deborah, I love your eyes. The eyes that have looked at me with love, every time." My Grandmother gently touched each eye, one at a time. "I love your nose," she said, moving a finger down it. "Your nose has told us what is safe to eat and what is not, and when to tease me for burning the bread." I could hear a smile in her voice.

"Oh, how I love your lips," she said, "the lips that have told me stories for nearly my whole life, and your throat," she said, bringing her fingers lower, "your throat that brought the voice to those stories and that carried the laughter that often continued until we were doubled over on the floor."

Auntie's lips moved into a smile, and her eyes closed. Her chest still rose and fell, slowly, and more slowly each time.

"I love your neck," Grandmother continued. "I love every wrinkle. I smile when I see them, knowing that we have gotten to spend so long together that we have grown wrinkles on our necks."

"I love your breasts. They nourished Esau into a strong boy and brought comfort to him and Jacob many times.

"I love your arms. I love the countless embraces of your arms, in sorrow, in joy, in dance, in celebration, in comfort, in life . . . in all of life. I love your hands, which have plaited my hair, decorated me with kohl, anointed me with oil, mixed herbs, picked fruits, and held mine.

"I love your womb, which carried Rananyah and brought us our first child.

"I love your knees, which took you to the hills to talk with Yah and teach Jacob and Joseph to do the same.

"I love your feet, which brought you all the way from Egypt to me, so that we could spend our lives together.

"Deborah, there are no words that can explain how I shall miss you. And that I shall have to do this difficult thing without you! You have always been by my side. There will not be a moment in the rest of my life, however long Yah determines that I must live without you, that I shall not remember you. I know I shall talk to you. And I shall hear your voice in my ears always. And though you cannot speak to say so, I know that your love for me is the same as mine for you. And that is the most beautiful part of all of it, is it not?"

She was correct. Auntie could not speak. As I listened to these parting words, my eyes remained on Auntie's chest. It was still rising and falling, though each breath seemed more shallow than the last. My Grandmother wiped tears from her face and neck. She looked at the women and then at me.

"It is time for you to go," she said to all of us. And so we did. Each walking slowly in our own directions. I went to talk with My God.

"My God," I said, remembering the first time Auntie had instructed me, "YhWh, God of My Father Jacob, God of My Father Isaac, God of My Father Abraham." I said aloud the words I had repeated three times a day for so many years. Then I paused and added, "God of My Auntie Deborah." I paused again. I wished to ask My God for something, but I did not know for what to ask. So I just listened. For a long time, I stood still, looking at the pastures and the hills, the tents and the sky, and I breathed. *Yhhhh. Whhhh.*

And then I heard a scream. It did not sound like the scream of a frail old woman; it sounded like an animal being ripped to pieces by a beast. But it was not. It was My Grandmother. And the scream did not stop. And I knew that My Auntie, Deborah, had died.

The whole camp came and gathered around My Grandmother. The women wailed along with her long past when the sun was high in the sky. Before it sank too low, My Grandmother beckoned for My Father.

"Under a tree," she said, and he nodded. He quietly collected me and My Brothers, and we found a beautiful blooming almond tree. My Auntie would have remarked at the white flowers and the bees that were attracted to their sweetness.

Together we dug a grave for her under that tree while the women removed her cloak and wrapped her body in the most beautiful blanket we had. It was red, with gold threads running through it, like her mother's palace cloak, and had blue trim—like the river—all around the edges. One purple hollyhock was stitched into the center. My Auntie would have been pleased.

My Father and I carried her and gently placed her inside the grave. I could not persuade my arms to cover her body with dirt, but My Brothers did so with kindness. When they were finished, we all stood together in tearful silence as the sun finished its descent. Just before it slid behind the hills, My Grandmother shouted, "Hallelu Yah!" And we all returned the call:

Hallelu Yah!

AUTHOR'S NOTE

The book of Genesis provided fertile ground for my imagination, and I am grateful for the open questions and holes it offered. *The Scrolls of Deborah* contains some possible backstories that have emerged from my hours spent with the stories in the Bible.

In this novel, numerous references to God are presented with the word "god" written in lowercase letters, which may seem unusual to many readers. The decision to adopt this style was intentional, as it aims to convey the perspectives of Deborah and her contemporaries. In their worldview, the term "god" was not necessarily used as a proper name but rather as a synonym for "deity," hence the absence of capitalization.

The modern convention of capitalizing "God" emerged because it has become a specific name for the One whom Deborah identified as Yah (capital Y). This distinction in capitalization reflects the transformation of language and beliefs over time.

Names in the Bible have always fascinated me. Many characters in the novel come directly from the Biblical text, such as

Abraham and Sarah, whose names also hold profound meanings—Abraham, signifying "father of many," and Sarah, meaning "princess."

The character Hallel, their daughter, is a creation of mine inspired by Genesis 12:5, where "Abram took his wife Sarai, his nephew Lot, and all the property they had accumulated, and the *nefesh* they had made in Haran, and they went to the land of Canaan . . ." One translation of *nefesh* is "soul," which I used to bring Hallel to life.

In addition to biblical names, I also had fun inventing other names for characters, like Amitza, meaning "brave," who assisted in delivering Keturah's baby, and Ro'ee, whose name denotes "shepherd." Hebrew speakers may understand the meanings of the names at first glance, and readers from all backgrounds can revel in the wonder that every name—whether newly crafted by me or rooted in the Biblical text—reflects something significant about each person. Together, I believe the previously known and invented characters make quite a remarkable tribe.

THE TRANSFORMATION OF these stories into scrolls and then into a book has been a tribal effort. Many thanks to everyone who has been a part of this project.

To Rebekah Borucki, thank you for believing in this story and bringing it to life. Your belief, insight, and masterful direction have helped turn my daydreams and downloads into a book for countless readers. You are an inspiration, and I am honored to be a part of Row House, where so many have helped this dream become a reality.

A special thank you to Kristen McGuinness and Janet Collier, the first two editors of *Scrolls*, for helping me refine my writing and shape this story into a book. Thank you also to my friend Julie, who frequently and generously responded to my intermittent grammar questions at all hours, and to Hope, who, when I asked if she'd like to talk about a question at the intersection of grammar and God, was on the phone thinking it through with me within the hour.

I am incredibly grateful to the highly skilled editor Gina Frangello, whose careful reading, insights, questions, and support elevated this book to new heights. It would not be what it is without your expertise. I can't wait to celebrate with you over a bowl of hearty lentil stew—my treat!

Thank you to Rabbi Gordon Fuller, who, long ago, gave a *d'var Torah* (sermon) that presented the intriguing and imagination-grabbing theory that maybe Isaac had Down syndrome. Isaac was a late-in-life baby, the child of half-siblings, and had diminishing eyesight, among other things. I liked the thought-provoking and inclusive idea of having someone with physical and intellectual differences in the group of matriarchs and patriarchs, and so I ran with it.

I want to thank Kara Cooney, a favorite Egyptologist whose wonderful nonfiction books provided a captivating backdrop for my imaginings of ancient Egypt during Deborah's time. While this novel is a work of fiction, it is informed by deep research.

To Phil Levine, aka Phil the Guide, former high school friend turned expert tour guide, I offer my thanks for sharing the fun fact about the eye of the needle and many other fascinating details during our journeys through the streets and rooftops of the Old City of Jerusalem. My feet and heart were with you in that setting that so beautifully let my imagination wander the past.

So much love and gratitude go out to my first two readers, Netta and Shira. It's been almost agonizing having to wait to share this book with the world. Thank you for letting me share it with you in thoughts, pieces, and early drafts. Your ongoing interest and cheerleading have been invaluable. Shira, thank you for bringing song to these pages. Netta, every leaf—and frond—in this book is dedicated to you.

I deeply appreciate my small group of early readers who were willing to read the not-yet-final version of *Scrolls*. Anat, Debbie, Jan, Judy, Maggie, Nurit, Rowena, Shira L., Wendy, and Yael. Your thoughts and feedback were instrumental in shaping the final version. To the early readers of the final version, thank you for sharing *Scrolls* through reviews, social media, and personal recommendations to your sisters, mothers, daughters, and friends. Your support helped bring this book to a wider audience.

A heartfelt thank you to *all* the readers of this book. Whether you're a drummer or a dancer, a dreamer or a doer; whether you're a singer or a scribe or someone who has fought over stew; whether you know Yah or not; whatever your combination of those qualities and others, your presence is important. It really does take a tribe. I'm glad you're in this one. Bring your friends. Bring your family.

Thank you to my amazing children. You endured my never-ending quest for your thoughts and opinions about Torah stories and ancient Egypt. You brought fascinating and valuable insights and plenty of accolades for me and for *Scrolls* in every phase of this journey. Of course, your amazingness goes far beyond your contributions to this book. I can sum it up by saying: you're the best.

I extend my gratitude to Sydney Pollack for your profound impact on this book with your words, "Maybe they had a daughter." Your gift has enriched the lives of countless readers.

Finally, thank you to Deborah and Rebekah, Rebekah and Deborah, for allowing me to get to know and love you. It has been an honor to scribe your scrolls.

ABOUT THE AUTHOR

Esther Goldenberg, a Chicago native now residing in Israel, is an author, educator, and mother to two children. Though once a reluctant reader, Esther's innate fondness for captivating narratives led her to discover a deep passion for writing. Alongside her writing endeavors, Esther remains committed to teaching individuals and groups of all ages, sharing her knowledge and creative insights. In her free time, she cherishes adventures with her children, enjoys communal chanting sessions with her neighbors, and revels in the serenity of nature through leisurely walks. *The Scrolls of Deborah* is Esther's debut novel and the first installment in the Desert Songs Trilogy.